FRESH AIR
AND FOUL
PLAY

ALSO BY SG BRYANT

Boss
Taken In
Death in Black and White

 Simon Bryant grew up on a farm, a soldier settler block in the south-east of South Australia. After graduating with an English literature degree from the University of Adelaide, he has pursued a number of paths, including farming, managing a radio station, working in tourism, and, most recently, an extended spell in the public service in Canberra.

Now retired, he is dedicating his time to a lifelong interest in creative writing, and, in particular, to writing Australian historical fiction.

S G BRYANT

FRESH AIR AND FOUL PLAY

BORDER BOOKS

First published in 2024 by Border Books
Canberra ACT 2611

Cover and text design by Sandy Cull, www.sandycull.com
Typesetting by Shaun Jury
Cover images: pier © Silas Manhood / Trevillion Images, and birds © Chandra Ramsurrun / Alamy Stock Photo

Author portrait by Andrea Bryant Photography

Printed and bound in Australia by Ingram Spark and Lightning Source Australia

ISBN 978-0-6480375-6-9

A catalogue record for this book is available from the National Library of Australia

FOR ANDREA

For believing in me, and pushing me to follow my dream.

1

A DELIGHTFUL SUMMER'S DAY was in the offing, as Inspector Harry Holloway leaned on the stern rail of the *Ozone*, watching the two lines of churning foam running away from him towards Melbourne's distant shore.

Beyond the pleasant expanse of Port Phillip Bay, Harry fancied he could just make out the city's outline. Though what he saw was probably just the smoky heat haze, the grimy fog that seemed to permanently envelop the city in this mid-summer weather. But here, on the open water, the air was clear and the sun invigorating.

Perhaps Harry's enjoyment of the morning had more to do with the two weeks of seaside holiday that stretched before him, two glorious weeks in Sorrento, free from the daily grind in Melbourne's Criminal Investigation Branch. And even more welcome was the two weeks of freedom from the frustrations of dealing with his boss, the overbearing Chief Inspector Winston Marks.

Behind him, Harry could hear the excited chatter of the ship's passengers, mainly family groups, crowding at the paddle steamer's bow and eagerly scanning the rapidly approaching Sorrento pier. Among them were Harry's own family, his wife Effie and their children, Alfie and baby Daisy. In tow also were Harry's parents, Clem and Millie, slightly overawed by this grand holiday excursion, so far removed from their normal stamping ground in working-class Brunswick.

Harry smiled quietly to himself, imagining young Alfie's innocent delight in this great adventure. And he was also pleased that he had persuaded his reluctant parents to join them, at his expense of course. They needed the holiday and besides, it would provide more-than-willing babysitters for the two children, while Effie enjoyed some well-earned time off from her teaching position at Merton Hall.

Less than a mile from the pier now and Harry straightened, preparing to rejoin his family for disembarkation. As he turned, his attention was briefly caught by the South Channel Fort, standing out in the water to his right, some five hundred yards away. It loomed large and foreboding, a man-made, monolithic island, bristling with weaponry across its entire rocky surface.

In Harry's mind, this fortification was completely unnecessary and a testament to the Victorian Government's long-held paranoia about foreign invasion. There was precious little evidence that Harry could see for such an invasion happening, but who was he to argue with the wisdom of his betters? If they, and their British masters, wanted to waste their citizens' money on building extensive Port Phillip Bay defences at South Channel, Fort Nepean, Fort Franklin, and Fort Queenscliff, so be it.

They were now approaching the pier and Harry made his way towards the bow to join the family.

As the ship slid up against the pier, Harry expected the crowd at its bow to disperse and move towards the disembarkation point on the side of the ship. But the throng of passengers did not disperse. Instead they stayed clustered around the bow, and their excited clamour increased. And Harry now detected shouts of alarm amidst the noisy babble.

Before he could reach the bow rail to find out what was going on, he saw Effie hurrying towards him, baby Daisy clasped tightly to her, with Millie close behind, her hand in Alfie's.

'Quick, Harry!' Effie cried, before Harry had a chance to speak. 'Get over there! Someone's overboard!'

Harry dashed to the bow rail, pushing through the crowding passengers. 'Stand aside, I'm a police officer!' he shouted.

He reached the bow rail and looked down. Some ten feet below him, almost wedged between the *Ozone* and the pier, floated a man's body, fully-clothed, face down and arms outstretched. And one look at the man's swollen grey hands was enough for Harry to know this man had not just fallen off the *Ozone*. He had been in the water a lot longer than that.

Harry turned to the passengers, still craning forward, and sternly instructed them to stand back. The crowd shrank away, no-one of a mind to challenge his authority. Turning back, Harry noticed a young worker standing on the pier, mooring rope in hand, staring at the body in the water.

'Hey mate, see if you can find a hook to fish that poor devil out! I'll come ashore and give you a hand. And get someone to fetch the police. As quick as you can now.'

Harry stood on the pier and looked down at the dead body, floating in the water below. Behind him, clustered a little way off, stood a number of gawkers, resisting the efforts of the *Ozone*'s crew to clear the pier, but not daring to come within Harry's immediate ambit. Further down the pier, almost out of viewing range, Effie had shepherded the family into a small, shaded shelter, and was endeavouring to distract Alfie from the gruesome task she knew Harry was facing.

Harry braced himself against one of the pier's mooring bollards, reached down with the gaff hook and managed to thread it through the dead man's trousers. He gave a firm yank and the hook end appeared through the clothing. So far, so good. Now to get the poor bugger out.

Leaning against the bollard for support, Harry heaved on the gaff hook. But the weight of the water soaking the man's clothing was too much, even for someone of Harry's exceptional strength. He turned to the young pier worker, who had identified himself as Jamie and was standing diffidently a little way off.

'Righto, young fella,' Harry instructed him. 'No sign of the constabulary yet, so it's you and me, I'm afraid. Stand here next to me, and I'll tell you when to pull.'

Jamie was looking rather pale, but he took a deep breath and joined Harry at the pier's edge. On Harry's command, they heaved in unison, and the sodden body emerged from the water. They held on until most of the water had drained from the corpse, then Harry called for another effort from his helper. This time the body rose quite easily and was soon deposited on the pier. Jamie turned away, gasping for breath, distressed as much by the sight before him as by his physical exhaustion.

Harry patted the young fellow on the back and thanked him for his help. He then carefully turned the body over, but not before noting a large gash at the back of the man's head. A gash made with the application of considerable force, Harry thought, judging by the deep indentation in the skull.

With the body on its back, Harry studied the man's features. It was a fairly nondescript face – regular features, thick black hair and beard, matted and dirty now, a prominent nose – and a small scar running down the right side of his face, below one eye. The clothing told him nothing much either: a grey, Gansey sweater and woollen worsted pants were all that were visible, along with a pair of old boots on his feet. A fisherman, perhaps, Harry thought.

'You know this bloke, Jamie?' he asked.

Jamie glanced at the body on the ground, then quickly turned away again, shaking his head emphatically.

'You've never seen him before?' Harry persisted.

'Nup. Never seen him.'

'You haven't seen anyone fishing from this spot this morning?' Harry continued. 'It's ten o'clock now, so it would have been fairly early he went in, I would think.'

'Nup,' Jamie promptly repeated. 'I been here since six this morning, and there's been no-one here. Anyways, they're not allowed to fish here, it's where the boats come in. They gotta go over there.' Pointing to the landward end of the pier.

'Hmm, fair enough,' Harry replied, noting that it wouldn't take long for a body to wash down to this spot from any part of the pier. Or from further out in the harbour, for that matter.

'Sorry, Sir,' Jamie offered, somewhat disconsolately. 'Sorry I can't help you.'

'Never mind, mate. Don't worry, you've been very helpful. Anyway, perhaps this bloke can help,' Harry suggested, gesturing towards a young police constable who could be seen hot-footing it down the pier towards them.

'What's going on here, mate?' the young constable exclaimed as he arrived, breathing heavily and staring at the bedraggled corpse spreadeagled on the ground. 'We were told someone's gone into the bay.'

'You were told right,' Harry replied. 'We've just fished him out.'

'And who might you be?' the constable exclaimed, eying Harry sternly. 'This is police business.'

'Inspector Holloway, Melbourne CIB,' Harry responded. 'Sorry to intrude on your patch, mate, but it was an emergency.'

The young constable's demeanour changed instantly. 'Sorry, sir,' he said, touching his hat and coming to attention. 'I didn't know. And sorry to put you to this trouble. I came as quick as I could, once I heard.'

'Don't worry, mate,' Harry replied. 'There's nothing we could do for this bloke anyway. Now, I've told you my name, what's yours?'

'Constable Walter Morris, sir.'

'Good. Well, Walter ... Wally, do you recognise this poor bloke by any chance?'

Morris peered carefully at the body, its dead eyes staring expressionless into the sky. 'Well, I'm not too sure, sir. His face sort of looks familiar, I reckon, but I can't place him for the moment. What happened to him, anyway?'

'We found him floating in the water down there,' Harry replied, pointing to the pier's edge. 'So I assume drowning is the likely cause of death. Though he got a hell of a whack to the back of the head, and that wouldn't have helped either. Probably died early this morning, or even last night, judging by the colour of him.'

Morris shook his head slowly. 'Maybe it was an accident, sir. Maybe he had too much to drink at the Sailors Arms last night.' And he pointed to a low-slung building, some one hundred yards away, not too far from the end of the pier.

'Maybe, and maybe not. That's what you blokes will need to investigate. Look, I've got my family waiting for me over there, so I'm going to have to go, I'm afraid, Wally. Could you organise for this body to be taken to the police station? Who's your boss here in Sorrento? He'll need to be alerted pronto.'

'That'll be Sergeant Newgate, sir,' Morris replied. 'And Constable Staples is my other colleague. Although, actually, I don't think they're in the station at the moment.'

'Well, track them down as quick as you can. Your sergeant will need to make a decision about a post-mortem and police inquiry.'

Harry looked at the young constable, standing there, staring uncertainly at the body on the ground. He was obviously at a loss.

'Wally, I'd suggest this as a course of action. Leave young Jamie here to keep an eye on the body, and you get back to the station and track down your boss. If you can't find him, I suggest you find a horse and cart from somewhere, bring it back here and get the body back to the station quick smart. Making sure you interfere with it as little as possible. Okay?'

Morris nodded, though still uncertainly. I've done all I can, Harry thought, and strode off down the pier to join his family, now standing next to a horse-drawn carriage, emblazoned on its side with the words, *Welcome to the Back Beach Palace,* and with a liveried driver lounging aboard.

'All fixed?' Effie asked, as they clambered aboard and took their seats. But her anxious expression said a lot more. Don't get involved, it said, we're on holidays.

'I hope so,' Harry replied. 'Not sure about the local plod though. That young bloke's a bit wet behind the ears. And I'm not sure the other locals are up to the mark either. This kind of death would be a rare occurrence around these parts, I'd say.'

As their horse trotted off on what must have been a well-worn route to their accommodation, Harry sat ruminating on what had just happened. He was satisfied that he had at least got the dead man out of the water and handed over to the local constabulary with appropriate instructions. The problem was, judging from the young constable's reticence, Harry had some doubt that his instructions would be adequately followed, and that the man's death would be properly investigated.

He glanced across at Effie and gave a half-smile. She didn't smile back and her worried expression betrayed her fear that their holiday was about to be ruined.

'Don't worry, dear,' he reassured her. 'I'm sure that their sergeant will do the right thing. I won't need to be involved.'

Effie pronounced herself satisfied that the Back Beach Palace met its advertised standard of *'comfortable family accommodation'.* The Holloway clan's two rooms on the third floor were spacious and clean, and from their balcony they were afforded a spectacular view towards the rocky back beach and the open ocean beyond.

And now, in the boarding house's spacious dining room, well away from the heat outside, the Holloways were being treated to an enjoyable luncheon of local steamed fish and vegetables. And once their hostess, Mrs Meriwether, discovered she had under her roof Inspector Holloway of the CIB, she lavished her very best service upon them, instructing her maids to see to their every need.

Both Effie and Harry were slightly embarrassed by all this attention, while Harry's parents, Clem and Millie, seemed simply overwhelmed. But it was still to be enjoyed, Effie thought, especially after the stress of that upsetting business on the pier. She glanced at Harry who, while tucking into his food with his usual gusto, still seemed pre-occupied and not his usual jovial self.

'You're not still thinking about that poor chap who drowned?' she asked.

'Sorry, Effie,' he responded apologetically. 'I'm probably not good company, I'm afraid. I'll try to put it out of my mind.'

'Yes, please. We're all on holidays, remember, trying to forget about your work, and mine, for a couple of weeks. Why don't you leave it to the local police to deal with, eh?'

Harry nodded reflectively. 'I should, I know. But I can't help having doubts about how they'll handle it, judging on what I saw this morning. And I'm struggling to get the image of that poor fellow out of my mind.'

Alfie looked up from nudging his fish around his plate. 'What happened to the poor fellow, Dada? Did he go for a swim?'

'Not exactly, sonny boy,' Harry replied. 'How about you just worry about eating your lunch, eh?'

'Yes, darling,' Grandma Millie added quickly. 'Eat your food up now, if you want to grow up to be a big strong man, like Dada.'

Alfie grinned at his grandmother and made a big show of attacking his lunch with his knife and fork.

The door to the kitchen opened and Mrs Meriwether entered the dining room, smiling welcomingly at her new guests.

'Is everything to your satisfaction, Inspector Holloway?' she enquired solicitously.

'Top notch, thanks, Mrs Meriwether.' Harry leaned back in his chair and fixed her with his best smile. Mrs Meriwether positively glowed and Effie smiled to herself. Harry's boyish charm seemed to work on everyone, even fifty-something, respectable matrons.

'Now, I know you've just arrived,' Mrs Meriwether continued, a touch breathlessly. 'But once you've settled in, you may wish to avail yourselves of some of the delights our beautiful town has to offer.'

'We certainly will,' Effie replied. 'What would you suggest, Mrs Meriwether?'

'Oh well, let me see, I hardly know where to start. There's so much to do. First though, I would recommend you catch the steam train. It goes past here, both ways, on a regular basis. To the front beach, where there's a beautiful promenade, a lovely tea room, and for the more adventurous, perhaps a dip in the sea baths.'

'Goodness me,' Effie said. 'That sounds lovely. I'm sure that's something Lydia would be interested in too.'

'Really?' Mrs Meriwether eyed Millie rather doubtfully.

Effie smiled. 'I'm not talking about my mother-in-law, Mrs Meriwether. My friend, Lydia Brown, Dr Brown's wife, is staying here in Sorrento at the moment. At their beach house. I'm looking forward to her showing us all the pleasures you speak of.'

'Oh, I see.' Mrs Meriwether seemed even more impressed by this reference. 'How wonderful for you. I'm sure Mrs Brown will be an excellent guide. But do make sure she takes you down to the back beach, won't you. It's very beautiful, and there are many fascinating walks to be had. Very romantic.'

'Sounds like just the thing for you and me, Eff,' Harry grinned. 'A romantic walk while Mum and Dad keep an eye on the kids here.'

'Might I suggest one more thing,' Mrs Meriwether enthused. 'Because perhaps Mrs Brown may not be aware. But Mr Coppin is currently at his residence, at the Anchorage, and is putting on a special performance. At the Athenaeum, I believe. You've heard of Mr Coppin, have you not?'

'We have indeed,' Harry replied. 'Or at least, Effie and I have. Not so sure about Mum and Dad though?' With an enquiring glance in Clem and Millie's direction.

'Can't say I know of the bloke,' Clem responded. 'Some sort of actor, is he?'

'More than that, Dad, much more than that,' Harry said. 'Actor, parliamentarian, entrepreneur, there's not much that George Coppin hasn't done. He was even President of my Blues at one time.'

'Your Blues?' Mrs Meriwether eyed Harry blankly. 'Who are the Blues, might I ask, Inspector? Some sort of theatrical troupe?'

Harry chuckled. 'Not exactly. The Carlton Blues, greatest footy team in Victoria. But that's not Coppin's biggest claim to fame around these parts. He's been the driving force behind the growth of Sorrento, they tell me.'

'Oh yes,' Mrs Meriwether exclaimed. 'A truly great man! He's done so much for Sorrento. The steam railway, the ferries, and many of the magnificent buildings in the town. They're all thanks to Mr Coppin.'

'As a matter of fact, Mr Coppin is well known to my friend, Lydia,' Effie chimed in. 'They're great chums. A shared love of the theatre. I'm rather hoping to meet him while we're here.'

'Oh my goodness, how wonderful!' their hostess exclaimed. Lydia had now clearly risen even further in Mrs Meriwether's esteem. 'I've heard he is the most delightful company. But I'm terribly sorry, I've taken up too much of your time. Do excuse me.'

'Before you go, Mrs Meriwether,' Effie said. 'You told us Mr Coppin was putting on a show. Is it one of his comedy performances?'

'Oh no, he's not performing himself. No, I understand he's bringing a dancing troupe to Sorrento. We are to have the premiere performance before it opens in Melbourne. Cossack folk dancers, I believe, all the way from Russia.'

'My goodness!' Effie exclaimed. 'How exotic! We must be sure not to miss that.'

'Indeed you must not, Mrs Holloway,' Mrs Meriwether agreed. 'Now, do excuse me, I must go. There's always so much to do.'

'I'm sure there is,' Harry replied cheerily, as Mrs Meriwether bustled away. But no sooner had she left than Harry relapsed into a more thoughtful mood, reflectively stroking his chin as he studied his now empty plate.

'I know that look, Harry Holloway,' Effie said, and again her voice was tinged with suspicion. 'You're still thinking about that fellow, aren't you?'

'Sorry, Effie, afraid I am. It's just that we may have a murder on our hands, and it needs to be properly investigated.'

'He can't help it, Effie,' Millie interjected. 'He's a good policeman, and he feels it's his duty to look into these things.'

'I know, I know,' Effie conceded ruefully. 'I do understand and I'm not blaming you, Harry. It's just that I was so looking forward to this holiday and having you all to myself for a change. But I'll tell you what, I have a suggestion that might keep us both happy.'

'Suggest away,' Harry replied. 'I'm all ears.'

'Well, how about this? Why don't you head down to the police station and see for yourself? If everything's under control and they're looking into the death properly, that's wonderful, you can relax and enjoy your holiday. If they're as incompetent as you suspect, then give the Chief Inspector a telephone call back in Melbourne and get him to send one or more of your team down here to investigate. And again, you won't miss out on your holiday. You'll be able to join me on that romantic walk Mrs Meriwether was talking about.'

'Great idea, Eff,' Harry said, brightening visibly. 'Why don't I come up with these clever solutions?'

'Because the female brain is clearly superior, my darling, that's why. Now, here comes our pudding, so let's eat up. The sooner you get off to the station and sort things out, the sooner we can begin our holiday in earnest.'

※

The Sorrento police station, at 12 Hotham Road, adjacent to the seafront, was an attractive building, constructed recently from red brick and the region's creamy limestone. It had been built for the dual purpose of police administration as well as housing the local sergeant. The front of the premises, overlooking the beach, was the domestic part of the dwelling, while the rear portion consisted of two rooms, a public access area and an interview-cum-meeting room. Behind the station a small two-room cell block had been built.

The station was functional but not extensive, and one thing it did not have was any facility to house a dead body, even on a temporary basis. So, for want of any alternative, the body had been stored in one of the cells, and in the growing heat of the late morning, the atmosphere in there was already beginning to grow uncomfortable.

Apparently, Sergeant Newgate had considered storing the corpse in his laundry, but Mrs Newgate had threatened to flee the premises, never to return, if he dared to try that option.

Now, on Harry's instruction, the dead man had been carried inside and was laid out on the table in the interview room, where at least they could all examine it properly.

The more Harry studied the large indented gash at the back of the man's head, the more he was convinced that the fellow had met with foul play.

But his opinion was clearly not shared by Sergeant Newgate, who expressed a strong view that this was death by accident, rather than malicious intent.

'It's obvious, Inspector. This bloke's some sort of down-and-out who's had a skinful and then come to grief. We get lots of his kind at the Sailors Arms, I can tell you.'

His offsider, Constable Staples, nodded in agreement with this conclusion. 'Reckon you're right, Sarge. Banged his head on the way down into the drink, I'd say.'

Harry was not altogether surprised by Newgate's view. Death by accidental drowning was the easiest way to deal with this incident. And Harry had quickly formed the impression that the easy way out was going to be Newgate's preferred approach.

Even a brief period in his company had given Harry a strong insight into Newgate's character. He seemed to be the epitome of the comfortable country copper, leading an easy life in this low-crime seaside haven, and more than happy to see out his remaining years to retirement doing as little as possible.

It was also clear that Constable Staples was of a similar ilk, his florid complexion and large girth signalling his addiction to the good life.

The third member of the team, Constable Walter Morris, was, it seemed to Harry, a different kettle of fish; a young policeman, newly posted to Sorrento within the past year, and obviously keen to get ahead in the force. But inexperienced, and way out of his depth investigating a suspicious death.

Harry quizzed all three policemen as to whether they recognised the dead man. Again, Morris was unable to identify him, and Newgate and Staples were both similarly vague.

'Can't say I've come across him before, Inspector,' Newgate stated. 'Don't reckon he's a local. I reckon I know everyone by name who lives around here.'

Harry persevered. 'So that makes him a visitor to the town then? Or perhaps a seasonal worker?'

'Well, he aint no tourist,' Newgate suggested, pointing at the body. 'Not judging by the cut of his clothes, anyway.'

'Yeh, I see what you mean,' Harry replied, noting the rough clothing. 'So, a seasonal worker then? Do you get many of them here?'

'We do,' Newgate asserted. 'As you can see, it gets pretty busy in the town over summer. So, a lot of the businesses take on extra workers to help with the tourist trade.'

'Hmm,' Harry pondered. 'I wouldn't have thought this bloke would have been on the frontline dealing with tourists. He's dressed more like a manual worker, I'd say. Perhaps a fisherman? Is that likely?'

'Possibly,' Newgate responded. 'He's not a regular fisherman, though. Like I said, I know them all. But sometimes they take on extra hands. Particularly at this busy time of year.'

'What about the lime kilns?' Morris suggested. 'They're always looking for workers. Maybe he was working at one of them.'

'Maybe,' Newgate conceded, but the shrug of his shoulders indicated his doubt about that possibility.

'I don't know much about that industry,' Harry said. 'Are there many lime kilns around these parts?'

Newgate paused for a moment or two. 'Maybe about a dozen or so, I'd reckon, up and down the coast. Bit of a dying industry around here though. It used to be real big, but most of the lime for Melbourne comes from Geelong these days. The business downturn a few years ago didn't help either. The building trade fell in a hole and if you're not building, you don't want lime.'

'Fair enough, Sarge,' Harry said. 'That's useful information. Okay, then. Let's have a closer look at him, shall we? Could you blokes give me a hand to get his gear off? Carefully now.'

Both Newgate and Staples seemed reluctant to get involved in this grim task, but Morris came forward promptly and assisted Harry in removing the man's clothing. It wasn't a pretty sight, with the pallid grey corpse stretched out on the makeshift table, the dead eyes staring blindly at the ceiling. Harry leaned forward unflinchingly and methodically examined the body.

He straightened. 'Have a look at that!' And he pointed to the man's torso, where a large purple welt ran at an angle across the left-hand side, with bruising spreading widely around it.

The others looked on silently, apparently struggling to see the significance.

'Can't really see how that could happen as a result of a fall,' Harry added. 'Particularly given he's also got a hell of a whack on the back of the head.'

'Oh, I see,' Newgate said. 'So you reckon he was involved in a blue, Inspector? Some sort of drunken brawl?'

'Maybe,' Harry replied. 'But whatever happened, it needs investigating. Now then, what do we make of this?'

Harry leaned forward again, pointing to a small tattoo on the dead man's upper arm. It was faded but still quite legible. He examined the image, which looked to be some sort of writing, but in a strange script that Harry had never seen before.

Harry took out his notebook and carefully copied the image, as best he could.

'*Я люблю Наталью*' was how it looked.

'What the hell is that, I wonder?' Harry mused, a rhetorical question but Newgate answered anyway.

'Dunno, Inspector, looks foreign, doesn't it?'

'It certainly does,' Harry agreed. 'But what nationality it is, I've got no idea.'

He paused in thought for a moment. 'Do you have many foreign workers around here?' he asked the room at large.

'A few,' Newgate responded. 'From time to time. Tell you what, we've had a few runaways in the past, from the Quarantine Station down the coast. Maybe he came from there.'

Harry was intrigued. 'What do you mean, runaways?'

'Well, sometimes ships are quarantined there for a fair while. If it's an outbreak of something serious, like malaria or typhoid. And some of the crew might get tired of being holed up and decide to nick off. Especially if they were planning to overstay their welcome anyway. If you get my drift.'

'Right,' Harry said. 'I see. And they'd come through here on their way to Melbourne?'

'Yeh, that's right,' Newgate replied. 'But sometimes, if they're looking for work in the fishing game, they've been known to stop here. The fishing boats are often looking for workers.'

Harry stared again at the body. He was nowhere near identifying the fellow, apart from the tattoo marking him as probably foreign. While it was early days, no-one had come forward yet to report him missing. So he'd need to organise a photograph and run it round the fishermen and all the local places of residence. Surely someone would recognise him.

From what he'd seen on the man's body, there was a strong suspicion of foul play. It certainly warranted a post-mortem examination. And that meant contacting his boss, Winston Marks, to organise for the police pathologist, Dr Crawford Mollison, to head down from Melbourne. And to get Marks' approval for one or more of Harry's team to head down here to investigate, so he could resume his holiday.

'Righto,' he announced. 'We're going to have to get the police pathologist to examine this bloke. I'll get onto it straight away. Then I'll organise a team to carry out the investigation.'

'Bloody hell,' Newgate exclaimed. 'How long will that take? This bloke's really gonna be on the nose pretty soon in this weather. What's my missus gonna say? It'll stink up the whole house.'

'Sorry about that,' Harry replied, undeterred. 'But here's a suggestion. Why don't you find the coldest place you can to store him until Dr Mollison arrives? There's a few pubs around the town, aren't there? Surely one would have a cool room with enough space to store him for a day or two. I'll count on you blokes to sort all that out while I get on the blower to my boss in town.'

And Harry strode from the room, leaving the three policemen pondering the challenging task of finding temporary cold storage for their unwelcome guest.

*

Harry had no trouble persuading Mrs Meriwether to provide him the use of her private facilities for his important telephone call to Melbourne. Flushed with the importance of the role entrusted to her, she ushered the inspector into her small office and settled him behind her desk.

'There you are, Inspector. Please be assured you'll have your required privacy here. I'll make sure you're not disturbed.'

After some initial difficulty getting a connection, Harry managed to be put through to the Russell Street police headquarters, and then to Chief Inspector Winston Marks. He explained the situation and his growing suspicions to the Chief Inspector.

Marks' initial reaction was predictable. 'Good god, Holloway, you can't be bothering me whenever some hobo gets killed in a drunken brawl. Why not leave it to the locals?'

'Well frankly, sir, I'm not sure the locals are up to it. And I'd point out also that this was a very public incident. The body was seen by a whole boatload of passengers, some of whom were undoubtedly well-known people. And you know how people talk, sir. It wouldn't be good for rumours to be getting around about this incident, and for a perception to arise that the police were doing nothing about it.'

There was a significant pause on the line. Harry could hear Marks' heavy breathing as he pondered Harry's words.

Then a begrudging response. 'I suppose you're right, Holloway. I suppose there are bound to be some pretty important chaps down there at the moment.'

'Yes, sir. Matter of fact, I reckon I noticed Mr James Service on the boat coming over,' Harry lied, recalling that the former Premier had a summer residence in the town. 'And from what I hear, there's plenty of other bigwigs here as well.'

'Hmm,' Marks muttered. 'All right, we'd better get onto it as quick as we can. An early arrest will be a shot in the arm for the CIB. Might get us a bit more funding from the Treasurer in the next budget. He's not there too, by any chance, is he?'

Harry was tempted, but resisted lying about the Treasurer's presence. 'Not that I'm aware, sir. But you never know.'

'Yes, yes, Holloway, you've made your case. Just get on with it, and sort it out quick smart, eh?'

'I will, sir. I'll get a couple of my team down here pronto, to work with the locals on a full investigation.'

'What are you talking about, Holloway?' Marks exclaimed. 'You're quite capable of dealing with it by yourself. With the help of the local fellows, of course.'

Harry stiffened, as he realised where the conversation was heading. 'Well, as you know, sir, I'm on holidays. Been planned for quite a while. I've got the whole family here, actually. But of course, I'm more than happy to brief my blokes on what's happened to date.'

'Nonsense, Holloway,' came the immediate stern reply. 'I can't afford to send men down there, while you laze around having a good time. No, you'll just have to put your holiday on hold, while you track down the killer. Should only take a couple of days, I would think. Then you can get back to whatever you're doing with the family.'

'But sir ...'

'No 'buts' about it, Holloway. That's final, you'll have to put off your holiday until you make an arrest.'

'All right, sir,' Harry responded resignedly. Then he had a thought. 'But I'll certainly need some backup. Could I get Sergeant Milton down here to give me a hand? He's just back from his honeymoon, and I know he's not busy on anything. That would help me a lot. In clearing it up quickly, I mean.'

Another breathy pause on the line. 'I suppose so,' came the begrudging reply. 'If you must.'

'Good, thank you, sir.' Harry was relieved that at least he would have his best man to help him. 'I'll organise to get him here as soon as possible. And I'll need to get our pathologist, Doctor Mollison, down here quickly as well.'

'Yes, yes, man. Just get on with it. And make sure you make an arrest just as quick, eh? And keep it under wraps until that happens. I'm counting on you, Holloway, don't let me down.' And a click as the line went silent.

Harry was unperturbed by his superior's hectoring tone. He was well used to it. Of far greater concern was Effie's inevitable reaction when he informed her that their romantic seaside holiday had been summarily postponed, at least for him. Then he remembered that Effie's best friend Lydia and her husband Ed Brown were in town. He'd have to rely on them to provide the diversions necessary to soften her disappointment.

With a sigh, he rose from Mrs Meriwether's desk and made his way back to their quarters to face the music.

2

THURSDAY 8 JANUARY 1898

EFFIE AND LYDIA MADE THEIR WAY down the stone path from Lydia's cottage, high on the hill in Bowen Road. Before them was laid out the sweeping vista of the Sorrento front beach, already alive with colour and light on this sunny January morning. To their right stretched the calm waters of Port Phillip Bay, and as they neared the Esplanade, with its throng of promenading holiday-makers, Effie could not help but notice on their left a grand villa, perched high on its own hill, with a commanding outlook over all below.

'That's the Anchorage,' Lydia observed. 'George Coppin's little hideaway. Impressive, isn't it?'

'Very,' Effie agreed. 'Majestic is how I'd describe it.'

'It certainly is,' Lydia agreed, as she adroitly side-stepped a largish pile of horse droppings on the road. 'But majestic is not how I'd describe George. Far from it.'

'Really?' Effie exclaimed. 'You mean to say you have reservations about him? How *would* you describe him then?'

Lydia laughed. 'No, I don't mean any criticism of George, I can assure you, darling. All I mean is that he is the most down-to-earth, lovely fellow. Wealth has not affected him in the slightest. He's the most charming company, and always terribly amusing. Anyway, you'll have the chance to find out for yourself this very evening.'

'Oh, how exciting! What's the occasion?'

'A small intimate dinner party at my place. Ed and I have invited George and his wife, Lucy, to dinner and it would be wonderful if you and Harry could join us. That's assuming Harry can come, of course, at such short notice. You were saying he's been sidetracked by this murder investigation.'

'Yes, it's all very inconvenient,' Effie replied, frowning slightly. 'Though I can't blame the poor dear. He's tried to get out of it, but his pompous fool of a boss has put his foot down. So there's nothing he can really do to avoid it. It's put a dampener on our holiday, I'm afraid.'

'What a shame.'

'Not that I'll show Harry any sympathy, mind you,' Effie added. 'I need to keep him on his toes, just so he doesn't neglect me completely.' And she gave Lydia a sideways grin.

'A sound strategy,' Lydia agreed, smiling back. 'Which means you must dragoon him into coming to our little dinner party.'

'I'll do my very best,' Effie replied. 'I'm sure he'll be keen to meet Mr Coppin, and hopefully his investigation won't start in earnest till Willie Milton arrives tomorrow.'

By this time the two friends had joined the crowd on the Esplanade, all taking the morning air and intent on being seen promenading in fashionable Sorrento. Most of the gentlemen, Effie observed, were ill-dressed for the warm morning, being clad in dark suits, almost as if they had just come from business meetings. Those more daring were sporting light linen suits and boat hats, and very occasionally some young blade could be seen coatless and with an open-neck shirt.

For their part, the ladies were also mostly uniformly and conservatively dressed, in full-length, cotton summer dresses, and carrying dark umbrellas, held aloft against the already burning summer sun.

Among them, Lydia seemed like some gorgeous tropical flower, with her flowing cream dress, lined at the hem and sleeves with a brick-red band, and with a sailor-style squared collar in the same colour. Her outfit was topped off with a red boat hat, set at a jaunty angle, and an elegant cream parasol. No chance of losing her in the crowd, Effie thought, smiling to herself.

'You look wonderful, dear,' she complimented. 'I feel so dowdy in comparison.'

'Nonsense, darling,' Lydia replied. 'You look as beautiful as ever.'

And she was right. Tall and slender, Effie moved with an eye-catching natural grace. And her abundant auburn locks, overflowing beneath her wide-brimmed hat, were highlighted by her simple white dress. In short, she looked, as always, stunning.

'Where shall we go?' Effie asked, looking around at the uniformed throng. 'I don't think I want to spend my day among this lot. We could just as easily be in Collins Street.'

'You're right,' Lydia concurred. 'What say we take some tea?' And she pointed to a small building on the foreshore, standing at the beginning of another long narrow pier.

'Lovely. I'm already parched in this heat. An iced tea would be very welcome. But what is that place? And that little pier?'

'The sea baths tearoom,' Lydia said. 'Otherwise known as the Rustic Retreat. And the baths themselves are at the end of that little jetty. Very popular at this time of year. Another of the activities I've planned for this week, to take your mind off your absentee husband.'

'I'll look forward to it,' Effie replied, but this time a little doubtfully.

'Don't worry,' Lydia said gaily. 'You'll love it, it's great fun. Now, let's pop in here for a cuppa.'

'Won't it be rather busy?' Effie suggested. 'With all these people around, I mean.'

'Probably not,' Lydia replied. 'This lot are too busy being noticed to worry about refreshments.'

But Lydia was proved wrong. When they entered the small building, all twenty or so tables in the room seemed to be occupied. Apparently, the warm morning was just a little too much for some of the promenaders.

'What a nuisance,' Lydia muttered, tapping her foot in exasperation as she surveyed the room. Then her eyes lit up as she noticed a table with only one occupant; a broad-shouldered young man in an open-neck white shirt, sitting with his back to them.

'Look over there, dear. That young chap seems all alone. Perhaps he wouldn't mind the company of a couple of presentable matrons for a half hour or so.'

'I suppose so,' Effie replied hesitantly. Then, looking more closely, she exclaimed, 'Wait, I think I know that chap!'

Hearing her raised voice, the young man put down his cup and turned towards them.

'Michael!' Effie exclaimed again. 'It's Michael!'

And indeed it was Michael; Michael Standish, Effie's teacher colleague and a dear friend to both the women.

After heartfelt hugs and greetings, Michael motioned for them to join him at his table.

'What a coincidence bumping into you here,' Effie said, patting him on the hand affectionately. 'I had no idea you were holidaying in Sorrento. Is James here too?'

'Well, yes and no. He's the reason I'm here alone, actually.'

'How mysterious,' Lydia said. 'Do go on.'

'Effie, remember how I told you James had been invited to an artists' camp?'

'Oh yes,' Effie recalled. 'So that's happening down here at the moment, is it?'

'Yes,' Michael said, pausing to sample a jam tart from the tray in front of them. 'It's run by a woman by the name of Jane Sutherland. You may have heard of her. A very well-known artist. Very good too, I might add. Vastly underrated.'

'Indeed I have heard of her,' Lydia said. 'So that's where he is now, off creating masterpieces with his fellow artists? Tell me, where are you two staying?'

Michael smiled and leaned back against his chair. 'Not together, actually. An artists' camp is exactly how it sounds. He's off in the sand hills somewhere, roughing it in a tent. I'm only seeing him when he gets the occasional half day off.'

'Poor James,' Effie chuckled. 'He seems far too refined for that sort of lifestyle. And what about you, dear, where have you pitched your tent?'

Michael grinned, a touch shamefacedly. 'Somewhat upmarket from that, I have to admit. I'm camping up at the Continental.'

Lydia chuckled, 'Oh dear, lucky you! And poor James, battling the flies and mosquitoes, while you recline in luxury.'

'So the Continental is rather grand, I take it?' Effie inquired.

'You could say that,' Lydia replied. 'It's that huge building on the hill. You can see it from here if you look out the window. Another of George Coppin's creations.'

'My goodness,' Effie exclaimed. 'Is there anything that Mr Coppin hasn't built in this town?'

'Very little,' Lydia laughed. 'And speaking of George, Ed and I are having him and his wife for dinner this evening at our seaside cottage. If you're on your own, Michael, why don't you come too?'

'That would be marvellous!' Michael replied enthusiastically. 'But are you sure? I don't want to intrude, if it's a private occasion.' And he gave a glance in Effie's direction.

'Don't worry,' Lydia chuckled. 'The more the merrier. Effie and Harry are coming too. If we can drag Harry away from his murder investigation, that is. No, you must come. I know how much you love the theatre, and George is the Australian theatre personified. But I do have one stipulation.'

'Certainly, whatever you wish. Name it.'

Lydia eyed him conspiratorially. 'You're forbidden to mention the dinner to James. On top of you staying at the Continental, it would be more than he could stand.'

Michael laughed heartily. 'Very well, it'll be our secret. But I must inform you, James has surprised me, the way he's taken to the outdoor life. He's become quite the nature-loving rustic these past few days.'

'Well, make sure he takes time off from communing with nature to say hello to us,' Effie insisted. 'I'm desperate for company now that Harry's been waylaid.'

'I'll do my best,' Michael reassured her. 'By the way, how are the children? I assume they're with you.'

'At the Back Beach Palace, being extremely well cared for by Grandma and Pop. So this holiday is my chance for a little break from them too. Though I must say, after an hour away I miss them already.'

'I'll bet you do,' Michael replied. 'They're so delightful. And what a shame poor Harry has been called into this murder business. So disappointing for you, with your holiday spoiled.'

'It is annoying, I must say, but it can't be avoided,' Effie replied.

'This mysterious death, it's all quite shocking, isn't it?' Michael continued. 'Everyone's talking about it. Actually, people here are quite nervous, it seems, with a killer on the loose.'

'I suppose so,' Effie replied. 'But they needn't worry, Harry will track him down soon, I'm sure. And he'll have Willie Milton down here to help him. Harry doesn't think much of the local constabulary, I can tell you.'

'Not up to scratch?' Michael raised an eyebrow.

'Sound asleep, is how Harry described them. For the most part anyway. He said there's one young fellow who seems quite keen, but the others are seat-warmers, doing as little as possible till they retire.'

Michael chuckled. 'A week or two with Harry and they'll be knocked into shape, I'll wager.'

'Maybe,' Effie replied. 'Anyway, I'm pleased Willie's coming down. He's a married man now, you know, and his new bride, Rachel, is the sweetest person you could ever meet.'

'I remember her,' Michael said, his tone serious now. 'Her brother was that poor fellow, the Collingwood footballer, who was murdered. Another case solved by Inspector Holloway. Anyway, I'm so glad she's found happiness now.'

'Yes,' Effie agreed. 'And I shall make it my business to make sure she enjoys her stay here. While her new husband is also dragged away too, investigating this awful murder.'

🍂

The Sorrento Hotel was an imposing building, a two-storeyed edifice adjacent to the pier. At its front a cast iron balcony stretched out into the street like an elaborate apron, and behind that rose a large square turret, like some oversized chimney.

Though clearly overshadowed by the magnificent Continental Hotel, standing some half a mile behind it in the upper part of town, the Sorrento nevertheless attracted its fair share of well-heeled customers, keen to be accommodated close to the Esplanade, where all who mattered could be seen promenading.

And keen too, even at eleven o'clock in the morning, to be sampling the refreshment the hotel had to offer. Indeed, the front bar was crammed with customers, exclusively male of course, enjoying a cooling draught before venturing forth to join the womenfolk in the heat of the day.

Mind you, their enjoyment might have been sobered if they had witnessed the scene taking place beneath their feet in the hotel's capacious cellar. Here, surrounded by beer kegs and walls stacked with wine and liquor bottles, a greying corpse was spread out on a makeshift table, consisting of a trestle supported by two large beer barrels.

Harry had chosen the Sorrento as his temporary morgue because of its immediate vicinity to the police station. Under his instruction, the dead body, wrapped in an old sheet and carried on a stretcher, had been surreptitiously relocated in the early morning, when most good citizens were at rest.

Now Harry stood in the gloomy cellar, together with Sergeant Newgate and Melbourne's most eminent pathologist, Dr Crawford Mollison, surveying the dead man. As much lantern power as could be mustered was focused on the body, so that it glowed brightly in the shadowy room. The scene almost resembled a Caravaggio chiaroscuro painting.

Dr Mollison was a small, dapper fellow, sporting a cream linen suit and bright floral waistcoat. He stood now, his thumbs stuck into the pockets of that waistcoat, and contemplated Harry confidently.

'Well, Molly, what's the verdict then?' Harry asked.

Mollison removed one hand from the waistcoat and stroked his immaculately groomed hair. He paused, seemingly for dramatic effect, before answering.

'Murdered, I'd say, Harry. Without a shadow of doubt.'

Harry whistled softly. 'Are you quite sure?'

Mollison eyed Harry, a touch scornfully. 'Of course, I'm sure. I wouldn't say so if I wasn't.'

'Blimey!' Newgate exclaimed. 'There's a turn-up.'

'C'mon, Mollie, spill the beans. Dazzle me with your brilliance. Explain your reasoning.' Harry knew how to get the best out of Crawford Mollison.

Mollison beamed and expounded carefully. He could have been addressing a gathering of his medical students.

'Well, first things first. This fellow was dead before he entered the water. How do we know? Simple. He had no water in his lungs. So, given that irrefutable fact, we now examine the two major obvious injuries, the very significant wound on the back of the head, there, and that blow to the torso, there.'

'Fair enough, Doc,' Newgate cut in. 'But maybe those wounds were the result of some drunken brawl? Could it have been a fight gone wrong?'

'Hmm,' Mollison reflected. 'A fair question, Sergeant. I examined the level of alcohol in the blood, and while it is certainly true that our victim had been imbibing to a considerable degree, my view is that he was probably not in a completely drunken state. And those two wounds were the only signs of physical trauma. No other bruises on the body, no marks on the hands at all, defensive or otherwise. So no, I don't think this fellow was brawling.'

'So, some sort of attack then,' Harry suggested. 'Perhaps he was caught unawares. By the look of him, this bloke'd put up a good fight, given the chance. So, what was the likely scenario, d'you reckon?'

Mollison stroked his chin thoughtfully. 'My assessment is that the blow to the torso came first. Why? Because that very significant indentation in the back of his head would have felled him straight away. Likely killed him, then and there, I would suggest. So, in that case, no need to apply any further blows to the stomach area. No, that strike to the torso came first, and while he was no doubt doubled up, then came the killer blow to the back of the head.'

'Very good, Molly,' Harry said. 'What do you reckon, one attacker or two?'

'Impossible to tell, Harry. Could have been either. Here, let me demonstrate, Sergeant.' And he approached Newgate, bending the reluctant sergeant from the waist to a doubled up position. He pointed to the back of Newgate's head, now in plain sight.

'See, a single assailant would be presented with this sight, once he had delivered the first blow. From here, a blow to the back of the head would be the obvious next move. And entirely consistent with the shape of the wound. Equally, an accomplice could very well have stepped in to deliver the coup de grâce. Your guess is as good as mine.'

'All good, Molly, you've been very helpful. Give us your report and I'll declare this a murder inquiry, and away we go. By the way, there's one other thing. You probably can't help, but I'll raise it anyway. It's that funny writing on the fellow's upper arm.' And he pointed to the tattoo, with its inscription, *Я люблю Наталью.*

Mollison slapped his thigh in annoyance. 'My apologies, Harry, very remiss of me. I was going to raise that with you.'

'Yeh, bit of a mystery, isn't it?'

'No mystery at all,' Mollison replied, smiling broadly. 'You see, I fancy myself as something of a polyglot.'

'What the hell's that?'

'Languages, old chap. I love to learn new languages. A real hobby of mine. Very stimulating, I can assure you. And it takes my mind off the rigours of my profession.'

'Do I take it you know what those words mean?' Harry asked, his hopes rising.

'I certainly do. It's Russian Cyrillic script, if I'm not mistaken. And I never am. I suppose you'd like to know what it means?'

'Of course.'

'It says, *I love Natalya.* Obviously a reference to this chap's wife. Or lady friend.'

'Great work, Molly, you're a genius. So, it's reasonable to assume this fellow's Russian?'

'Can't think of any other reason for him to have a Russian inscription on his arm.'

'Indeed. Well, that's that then. Very helpful. By the way, have you organised for a photographer to capture a likeness of our man here, as I requested? It's important, given that we've got nowhere to put him on display, for identification purposes.'

'Already done, Harry. I'll have the photographs to you within a couple of days. Might bring them down myself, as a matter of fact. Quite an enjoyable little spot, Sorrento, isn't it?'

'Excellent work, Molly, as always. Okay, Sarge, you can make arrangements for this fellow to be disposed of now. An unmarked grave, I suppose. And let your wife know. No doubt she'll be greatly relieved he's not returning to the station.'

In Effie's view, Ed and Lydia's seaside residence, at the top end of Bowen Road, could hardly be called a cottage. Sitting in the spacious dining room, with commanding views down the hill to the Esplanade, and with a housekeeper waiting on them, Effie was reminded that her friend, independently wealthy and now married to one of Melbourne's preeminent doctors, was definitely a member of the society elite holidaying here at Sorrento.

Not that Lydia blatantly flaunted her wealth. On the contrary, she was at ease in any company and got on with everyone. It's what Effie loved about Lydia most – her enthusiasm for life and her willingness to involve herself in all manner of interests and causes. Tonight, it was one of Lydia's great loves, the theatre, and the company of their special guest, George Coppin.

Like Lydia, Effie too marvelled at Mr Coppin. She gazed admiringly at the short, rotund, balding figure at the head of the table. George Coppin was pushing eighty but was still the life of the party tonight, regaling them with tales of the theatre and his entrepreneurial efforts over the years, particularly in Sorrento.

All the other guests were similarly in thrall to the great man's words. It was the first time that Effie had witnessed Lydia being overshadowed; usually, it was she who dominated the conversation.

Effie glanced across at Harry who was listening politely but not really engaging in the theatrical discussion. She knew what was on his mind. The dinner guests had raised yesterday's sensational death with him early in the evening; apparently, it was already the talk of the town. But Harry had made it clear that was a subject on which he was not at liberty to speak.

However, Harry did get involved when the conversation turned to sport, and George Coppin's tenure as President of the Carlton Football Club.

'Well done, George,' Harry piped up, his interest aroused. 'You chose the right team to support there.'

Coppin chuckled. 'Ah, you're a Carlton man, I take it, Harry. But, you know, I do like to spread myself around. I was also President of the Richmond Cricket Club at one point.'

Harry smiled. 'I don't know how you've found the time and the energy for all your achievements. The Old Colonists Association too, I understand.'

Coppin nodded and sat for a moment in silence, contemplating his life's work. 'But I think my proudest achievement is this place,' he then observed to the table at large. 'It's not everyone who can say they've built a town. Particularly one with all the attractions of Sorrento: the Mechanics' Institute, the development of the back beach, the steamships, the sea baths, the steam train. Though I think perhaps the Continental is the crowning glory of my achievements. But forgive an old man; I'm indulging myself, I'm afraid.'

'No, no, George,' Ed Brown responded immediately. 'You've every right to be proud. And I imagine all those investments have been quite profitable for you too.'

A slight frown now creased Coppin's ruddy features. 'For the most part, Ed, I suppose. Certainly, during times like we're enjoying at the moment.

But that recession a few years back made life tough, I can tell you. Almost sent me under. Wouldn't be for the first time, either. The story of my life, I'm afraid. Up one minute, down the next.'

'I'm sorry to hear that, Mr Coppin,' Effie commiserated.

'Please, call me George, my dear. We're all friends here.'

Effie smiled sheepishly. 'Of course, George it is.'

'Anyway,' Coppin continued, 'it's meant I need to keep working in my decrepit old age. A good thing really, I wouldn't know what to do with myself if I didn't have my work.'

Lydia reached over and patted Coppin on the arm. 'What we need, George, is for you to revive some of your comic characters. What about an evening with Paul Pry? Or even better, Billy Barlow.'

Coppin leaned back in his chair and surveyed Lydia benignly. 'Alas, dear lady, those two gentlemen only make fleeting appearances these days. My gout impedes me a little, I'm afraid. No, I'm more of an impresario these days. Equally rewarding, I might add. Indeed, I'm putting on an international performance of high renown, next Saturday evening, right here in Sorrento, at the Athenaeum.'

'Yes, our landlady told us about it,' Effie said. 'A Russian dance troupe, she said.'

'That's correct,' Coppin continued. 'Of course, I'll also put them on in Melbourne, at the Royal of course, but Sorrento will see the Australian premiere. So you all must come.'

'We certainly will,' Effie promised.

'You might have noticed the posters around town,' Coppin added. 'I've been promoting it quite heavily. It's been in the offing for some months. Takes a bit of organising, a show of this scale.'

And with the conversation returning to Coppin's theatrical achievements, the great man was off and running again, with tales of Nellie Melba's rendition of 'The Angel at the Window' at the Athenaeum in 1885, his long-term collaboration with J C Williamson and Charles Keen, and any number of other fascinating recollections. All helped along by a liberal dash of Ed and Lydia's best port, despite his gout and wife Lucy's admonishments.

Eventually, the evening came to an end, fond farewells were exchanged and Harry, Effie and Michael prepared themselves for the walk back to their respective lodgings. But Coppin had his carriage waiting in the driveway and insisted on chauffeuring them home, despite Harry's protestations that the walk would do them good. In this case, Harry was quite happy to be overruled; the day had been long and tomorrow would likely be equally taxing.

As they trotted down the hill towards the Back Beach Palace, with Effie snuggled beside him in the backseat of George Coppin's phaeton coach, Harry gazed out at the peaceful scene before him, the lights of Sorrento's dwellings twinkling, and the rhythmic lapping of waves in the bay beyond.

It'd be nice to be on holiday, he reflected wearily. Oh well, at least Willie will be here in the morning. And you never know, we might be able to wrap this thing up quickly. He resolved to hope for the best as he extended an arm around Effie, drawing her tightly to him.

3

FRIDAY 9 JANUARY 1898

HARRY AND EFFIE STOOD on the Sorrento pier watching the approaching *Ozone*. At their side stood an excited Alfie, who had been promised he could meet Uncle Willie if he in turn promised to be good for Grandma the rest of the day.

It had seemed a good idea to bring the little fellow along to welcome Sergeant Milton and his new bride, Rachel. That is, until he looked up at his mother and inquired, 'Will we see the man in the water again, Mama?'

'No, son, don't worry about that,' Harry hastily reassured him. 'Look, there's the big boat coming in. Now tell us, what are you going to say when you see Uncle Willie and Aunt Rachel?'

'G'day Sarge!' Alfie exclaimed and grinned cheekily, looking up at his father for approval. Despite Effie's stern look, Harry couldn't resist grinning back.

'He's a chip off the old block, eh?' Harry suggested to Effie.

'Unfortunately,' she shot back, but still couldn't resist a smile.

As the *Ozone* approached, slicing noisily through the placid waters of the bay, Harry noted the usual cluster of passengers at the bow. And among them, he also spied the fair curly hair and burly figure of Willie Milton, leaning against the bow, one arm wrapped protectively around his new wife's shoulders. Harry was never more pleased to see his trusted offsider.

'You're sure you don't mind looking after Rachel, while Willie and I sort out this business?' Harry asked, turning to Effie.

'Of course not,' Effie replied. 'You know I love Rachel, she's like a younger sister.' She gave Harry a playful punch on the shoulder. 'Anyway, how dare you suggest that Rachel needs looking after? She's a married woman now, not the innocent girl we knew last year. I'm sure she's more than capable of looking after herself.'

'Fair cop,' Harry replied, smiling. 'You're right, as always.'

'Mind you,' he added, serious now, 'you can take a fair bit of credit for her progress, dear. She's blossomed since you helped her kick off her teaching career at Merton Hall.'

'Thank you, darling,' Effie smiled. 'Recognition duly appreciated.' And she waved to Willie and Rachel, who in turn spotted them and waved back.

The Miltons were soon disembarked and being welcomed by the Holloways. Willie was forced to relinquish his hold on Rachel while he scooped a delighted Alfie into the air.

'More, Sarge, more!' Alfie cried, as he was lifted aloft.

'How was the honeymoon, mate?' Harry asked, though from the appearance of both of them, he knew the answer to the question.

'Terrific, boss, terrific!' Willie replied enthusiastically, while Rachel's happy smile signified her agreement.

'Did you get any time to see the sights?' Harry continued, innocently enough. 'They say Lorne has quite a lot to offer.'

Willie grinned and Rachel blushed. Harry felt a sharp elbow to the ribs and detected a stern sideways glance from Effie.

'Anyway,' he continued, unabashed. 'Here you are, from one seaside resort to another. It'll be just like a second honeymoon.'

'Except that the groom will be absent from the scene,' Effie interjected. 'Leaving his poor new wife all alone.' And she gave Rachel a sympathetic and conspiratorial smile.

'I don't mind,' Rachel responded happily. 'I understand it's an important case, and after all, we'll be together in the evenings, won't we?'

'I don't think so,' Harry replied promptly, his expression deadpan. 'I'm likely to have him on the job till all hours of the night, I would think.'

'Oh, really?' Rachel's smile disappeared, until she noticed the broad grin spreading across Harry's face.

'Take no notice of him, darling,' Effie suggested. 'He's just a dreadful tease. Don't worry, I'll make sure Mr Smarty-pants here doesn't monopolise your Willie in the evenings.'

'Is that our transport?' Willie cut in, pointing to the Back Beach Palace carriage standing a little way off. 'Let's get going, shall we? Sounds like we've got a tricky case on our hands, and the sooner we get going, the sooner we get it sorted, I suppose.'

❦

It was one in the afternoon, and Harry and Willie were ensconced in the front bar of the Sailors Arms, each with a large tankard of the pub's finest foaming brew in front of them. And Willie with a clear conscience about deserting his new bride. Because both he and Harry had been summarily dismissed by Effie, who had informed them their company was no longer required. She and Rachel were proposing to spend the day taking in the local sights with Lydia, and they'd be back at dinner time.

The Sailors Arms was doing a decent trade, even at this hour of the day. Glancing around, Harry could see that this was most definitely the working man's pub, judging by the dress and demeanour of most of the clientele. The atmosphere of the place had the beer-soaked, rowdy ambience that Harry knew so well. He could have been in the bar of his local, the Caledonian, in

North Melbourne. The only thing missing, as far as he could tell, was an SP bookie plying his trade in a corner of the room.

'Seems a tricky one from what you say, boss,' Willie mused, sipping appreciatively on his beer. 'No idea who the victim is, apart from the fact he's Russian. No murder weapon, no witnesses. It's gonna be a tough one to crack.'

'And not much support from the local wallopers either, mate. Gonna make it even harder. But I'll pull you up on one thing.'

'What's that?'

'You're a bit pessimistic on the witness side of things. I know we haven't had anyone come forward to make a statement yet, but there are some potential witnesses we might be able to dig up.'

'Not sure I follow. Where are you suggesting they might be?'

'Right here, mate, right here. We know from Molly that our bloke had been drinking that night, and there's only two pubs within close vicinity of the pier; the Sorrento and this one. The Sailors Arms is a bit further away from the pier, I know, but still close enough, and judging by our bloke's clothing, this would have been his pub of choice. I can't imagine him drinking with the nobs over at the Sorrento.'

'Fair call,' Willie replied. 'Not a bad assumption.'

'I know it's just that, an assumption,' Harry conceded. 'But at least it's a start.'

'So, we run the dead bloke's photograph round the bar?' Willie suggested. 'Once we get it from Mollie.'

'Got it already,' Harry replied. 'Turns out Mollie brought down twenty prints on this morning's ferry. He must have been on the *Ozone* with you and Rachel.'

'Didn't see him aboard,' Willie said. 'Not surprising, I suppose. He would've been in the first-class lounge.'

Harry chuckled. 'Mollie likes the good life, that's for sure. He's down here for a few days, he tells me. Got himself ensconced at the Continental for a little holiday.'

'Anyway, good on him,' Willie commented. 'He must have been up late last night developing those photographs. So, we should show them to the patrons in here, I suppose. No time like the present.'

Harry paused while he flicked away a small insect that had settled in the froth of his beer. 'Maybe not right now,' he mused. 'Our bloke would've been drinking in the evening, and that'd be the after-work crowd. Fishermen, dock workers, lime-burners, those sorts of blokes. Some of them here now, no doubt, but better chance of scoring a hit tonight, I'd reckon. Sorry about that, mate, I'll be keeping you from your lovely wife.'

Willie shrugged. 'Don't worry, boss, we've got a lifetime together. Anyway, Rachel understands how important all this is.'

Harry eyed his Sergeant. 'You've got a ripper there, mate, you know. Hope you realise that.'

Willie's reply was heartfelt. 'Don't worry, I count my blessings every night.'

Harry swivelled in his seat again, spotting a tall, shirt-sleeved fellow standing behind the bar, in conversation with one of the bartenders. 'Tell you what though, Willie, we might introduce ourselves to that fellow over there. He looks like management material. Let's see if he's mine host and can fill us in on who was on the job here Tuesday night.'

Downing their beers, the two sauntered over to the bar. Something in their bearing, or perhaps their relatively clean attire, must have given them away as officials of some sort, because the tall fellow spotted them and, abruptly concluding his conversation, walked over to them.

'Good afternoon, gentlemen. Another beer? Or is there something else I can help you with?'

'We're not that obvious, are we?' Harry quipped, producing his badge. 'Inspector Harry Holloway and Sergeant Willie Milton, Melbourne CIB.'

'Arthur Chester, hotel manager,' came the reply. 'A pleasure to meet you, gentlemen. And a relief, I might add. Thought you might be from the Licensing Board.' This comment accompanied by a thin smile.

'Really,' Harry replied, smiling in return. 'You've got nothing to worry about with the Licensing Board, have you?'

'Heavens, no,' Chester replied hastily. 'Just my idea of a little joke, really. Though the inspectors are a bit of a nuisance, mind you. Fussing around and wasting our time. But never mind, just part of running a business, I suppose.'

'Well, hopefully we won't waste too much of your time, Mr Chester,' Harry continued. 'But it might be best if we continued this chat in a more private spot, eh?' And he glanced around the bar to indicate the crowd of drinkers around them.

'Of course, Inspector,' Chester replied. 'Nothing wrong, is there?' he added nervously.

'Not necessarily,' Harry replied calmly. 'But we're on a sensitive investigation that's best not discussed in a public setting like this. Got a private room?'

'Well yes, I do, as a matter of fact.' And Chester swung open the hinged bar divider, joined them on the public side of the bar and shepherded them through the crowd, then through a door at the end of the room. They entered a small space which obviously served as both office and storeroom, judging by the sundry cases and boxes piled up against the walls. Chester gestured toward a table in the centre of the room and took a seat at one end.

Harry and Willie took their seats on either side, and Harry began. 'Fact is, Mr Chester, we're keen to understand whether you or any of your staff noticed a certain person in the hotel last Tuesday evening.'

'Certainly, Inspector, I'll do my best. Do you have a description?'

'Better than that, I have a photograph.' And Harry produced Mollison's photograph of the corpse from his coat pocket. He placed it on the table in front of Chester.

Chester extracted a pair of spectacles from his waistcoat, perched them on his nose and peered at the photograph. He gave a start and drew back. He looked up at Harry, his complexion wan. 'My goodness, Inspector, this poor fellow's dead!'

Harry looked at him evenly. 'That's right, Mr Chester. We're investigating his death. We fished him out of the bay on Wednesday morning.'

'Oh yes, of course. I should have realised. I heard about that. Terrible business, everyone's talking about it.' Chester's eyes darted nervously between the two policemen.

'I thought you might have recognised him,' Harry said evenly. 'Judging by your reaction.'

'No, no,' Chester replied immediately. 'No, I can't say I've seen him before. I was just ... um, startled to see a dead man. Not expecting it, you understand. When did you say he might have been in here?'

'Last Tuesday, the sixth. Three nights ago,' Willie informed him. 'In the evening.'

Chester sat in thought for a few moments, absently fiddling with his spectacles. 'I was in from time to time that evening. Coming and going, as it were. But as I said, I don't recognise the fellow.'

'Well, which staff did you have on that evening?' Harry queried.

'Oh, quite a few, undoubtedly,' Chester responded vaguely. 'It's a very busy time of year. I normally put on a number of temporary staff to cater for the increased demand.'

Harry was beginning to find Chester's prevarication frustrating. He leaned forward, gave Chester his best interrogative stare and said, slowly and deliberately, 'Mr Chester, I would like to speak to a regular member of your staff who was behind the bar on the evening of the sixth. Someone who would most likely know this man if he was a regular drinker at your hotel.'

Chester recoiled slightly in his chair. 'Of course, Inspector. I think perhaps Mildred might be the best person to speak to. And Gloria too. They were both on that evening, I would imagine.'

'And they're both available to speak to today?'

'Not at the moment, I'm afraid. They're on evening shift, you see. But if you come back tonight, they'll both be here.'

'Sounds good,' Harry said. 'We'll have to come back and force down another drop of your excellent beer. Tell me, which of those two ladies you mentioned would be most likely to know our man?'

Chester shrugged. 'Not sure. Mildred's been here much longer, so she should know more of our customers. But she's rather quiet, just goes about her business and doesn't fraternise much. Gloria, on the other hand, she loves a good chat. I sometimes have to speak to her about focusing more on serving the customers rather than talking to them. And Gloria has ... er, certain other attractions that appeal to the blokes as well. So she's very popular.'

'Good.' Harry made a mental note that Gloria would be the one worth investing some time into. He glanced at Willie, rose and picked up his hat. He extended a hand to Chester. 'That's all we need for the moment. Thanks for your cooperation. We'll pop back this evening to talk to the two ladies you mentioned.'

As they made their way from the cool confines of the bar into the afternoon sun, Harry paused briefly in the shade of the front verandah. 'Gloria sounds like a promising witness,' he suggested to Willie. 'We'll give her a try tonight.'

'Sure thing,' Willie replied, but Harry detected a slight hesitation in his voice.

'Sorry, mate, let's make that an 'I' rather than a 'we',' Harry said. 'On second thoughts, I need to come back alone tonight. I'll be in serious trouble with Effie if I drag you away from Rachel too much after hours.'

'Thanks, boss. Though Rachel wouldn't have minded if I was gone for an hour or two,' Willie assured him. But Harry detected a definite note of relief.

◆

Effie and Rachel sat on the Palace's balcony and contemplated the scene before them. They were looking south, in the direction of the back beach, only some five hundred yards away From here the beach was not completely visible, partly hidden by low sand dunes, largely covered with dense coastal ti-tree. The Ocean Beach Road wound through the dunes, recently built as part of George Coppin's dream to link the front and back beaches. Under the early afternoon sun, brilliant white sand blazed from an occasional break in the ti-tree.

Similarly brilliant was the limestone-paved road, with its two sets of narrow train tracks running along it. Over these tracks, Mr Coppin's steam train chugged on a regular basis, taking day-trippers to view the wild beauty of the back beach.

It was the arrival of the steam train that Effie was now anticipating, and with it their friend, Lydia. The plan was for Lydia to meet them at the Palace, and then for the three women to take an easy downhill stroll to the back beach. From there they planned to wander as far as their inclination and the warmth of the day would allow.

Effie closed her eyes, leaned back and enjoyed the gently cooling southerly breeze. Behind her, through the glass doors in the upstairs lounge, came the babble of Alfie's excited chatter, as he and Pop worked their way through his favourite storybook. Effie smiled to herself as she heard Alfie explaining the oh-so familiar plot to Clem.

Effie briefly opened her eyes and gave a sideways glance at Rachel, who caught her look and smiled back.

'Shouldn't be long now,' Effie said. 'Lydia told me the train comes through every hour.'

'Actually, I think I can hear it,' Rachel replied.

As she spoke, Effie too detected the faint puff and rattle of the approaching steam engine. The sound grew gradually louder, until it appeared from behind their building and came to a complaining halt at the makeshift stop adjacent to the Palace. A couple of solidly built matrons climbed aboard one carriage, while Lydia alighted from another.

'Wear something comfortable,' she had instructed them. 'Particularly on your feet, we've got a bit of walking to do.' And she was true to her word; clad in a loose-fitting white shirt and ankle length culottes, together with pink-and-white-striped plimsolls on her feet, and a matching striped, broad-brimmed hat. She looked a bit like a giant lollipop, Effie thought, but as always Lydia carried it off and somehow managed to look fashionably exquisite. Effie glanced down at her own long pleated skirt and sturdy walking boots and felt decidedly dowdy.

She and Rachel stepped back inside, bade farewell to Clem, Millie and the children, and hurried down to meet their friend. After the requisite hugs and kisses, the three women set off down the limestone road toward the back beach. It really was a perfect summer's afternoon. The sky was a brilliant blue, and a gentle breeze blowing off the Southern Ocean ahead of them was enough to take the discomfort out of the sun.

As they walked through the cutting, the full sweep of the back beach came into view. The bay curved gently on either side, the wide sandy beach dotted here and there with rocky outcrops and today, with the tide low, occasional rocky ledges and rock pools extended out into the water. In front of the three women stood the back beach rotunda and kiosk, nestled in front of the dunes where the steam train tracks terminated, and sitting safely above the high-water mark. Lydia explained that these were another innovation of the redoubtable George Coppin.

'I'd suggest a cup of tea and scones,' she added. 'But I don't think we've earned it yet. A decent walk along the beach is called for. Now, which way should we go, left or right?'

'Either way looks equally beautiful,' Effie replied. 'We'll leave it up to you. You're the local among us.'

'In that case, we're going that way,' Lydia decided, pointing to their right. She indicated the broad sweep of the secluded bay before them. 'Once we get out of this natural amphitheatre, the coastline becomes much more rugged and spectacular.'

And so they set off down the beach, on one side the green-blue ocean, flecked with white where the breeze whipped up lines of small breakers; and on the other the towering, scrub-covered dunes, seabirds soaring and calling above them.

Lydia was right; once they had passed the headland of the bay, the scenery became more imposing, with jagged cliffs looming in front of the dunes and a number of low rocky outcrops running down to the water. At the bottom of the cliffs they saw occasional recesses, perhaps small caves, no doubt where the cliff face had been eaten out by eons of crashing waves.

For the most part, they were able to navigate their way through the rock outcrops by carefully picking their way around them, and in doing so came across a number of rock pools. They paused by one of these and Lydia flipped over a small flat stone at its edge. A small crab scuttled away into the water, and Rachel couldn't help but jump back in alarm. The others laughed at her momentary discomfort.

Eventually, after a mile or so, they encountered a rocky barrier ahead that stretched tall above them and appeared to run from the cliff face some twenty or thirty yards out to sea. Its jagged edges jutted from the waterline like the teeth of some giant, prehistoric reptile.

'This will have to do us, ladies,' Lydia suggested. 'I don't fancy us scaling that ridge.'

'I think we've come far enough. We've earned our afternoon tea,' Effie replied. She looked around at the scene, the high dunes, the sharp crags jutting into the sky. It seemed a long way from the gentle seaside idyll at the Sorrento front beach.

'It's certainly a rugged stretch of coastline,' she said. 'I can imagine it would be rather dangerous in stormy weather.'

'It is,' Lydia agreed. 'And it gets even wilder the further round you go, towards the Heads. It's no wonder a number of ships have been wrecked on these rocks.'

'Really?' Rachel was intrigued. 'I would have thought they'd try to keep well away from the shore in stormy weather.'

'They would,' Lydia agreed. 'But apparently the problem happens when ships are entering Port Phillip Bay through the Heads. A combination of a westerly blow and dangerous currents often forces ships off-course. And onto the rocks, in a number of unfortunate cases.'

'How terrible!' Rachel exclaimed. 'Have many people lost their lives as a result?'

'Afraid so,' Lydia replied. 'Only last year the *Sierra Nevada* went down round there during a dreadful storm one night. Only a few miles around from here, near the Heads, at a place called London Bridge. Twenty-three men were lost, a terrible tragedy. Still, it would've been a lot worse if she'd been a passenger ship.'

'So they were all sailors who died?' Rachel asked.

'Yes, most of the crew in fact. She was a cargo ship bringing in all sorts of things to Melbourne. Including a large number of cases of whiskey. Of course, once the word went around, every man and his dog were over the sand dunes and down at the shore looking to pilfer a bottle or two. The police had to mount a guard to keep them away. Not that it helped, precious little was retrieved.'

Effie shook her head, 'How awful. You'd think there'd be a little more respect for those poor dead sailors.'

The three women stood silently for a while, staring out to sea; all no doubt imagining the sheer terror of those sailors as their ship crashed against the rocks, the sea raging, the wind howling.

They turned and began to make their way back around the shore, to the relative tranquility of the back beach. As they began their walk back, Effie caught a glimpse of something out of the corner of her eye, up on the summit of one of the dunes. At first, she thought it was a sea bird, wheeling above the sand. But then, as she focused, she made out the clear figure of a man, walking along the top of the dune, his figure silhouetted against the sky.

'Look!' she cried to her friends, pointing upward. 'There's someone up there.'

'So there is!' Lydia exclaimed. And as they watched, the man halted and stood motionless, facing them.

'I think he's spotted us too.' Effie waved vigorously in the fellow's direction.

But the man didn't wave back. Instead he turned abruptly and walked away, quickly disappearing beyond the lip of the hill.

'Not very friendly,' Lydia suggested. 'Three lovely ladies, I would have thought we'd be worth a wave.'

'What do think he's doing up there?' Rachel asked.

'Who knows,' Lydia replied. 'A bird fancier, perhaps.' Then, turning to Effie, she added, 'Perhaps he's one of James' artistic colleagues, looking for a classic seascape scene to paint.'

'Perhaps,' Effie replied. 'Anyway, enough of him, let's get going. This sea air has given me a ravenous appetite. I can't wait to tuck into a couple of scones.'

The evening crowd in the Sailors Arms was slightly different from the one Harry had encountered that afternoon. Gone were the smattering of day-trippers and beachgoers, the clientele now wholly the working men of Sorrento. And judging by the rancid smell in the place, made up mainly of fishermen and their ilk.

Harry pushed his way through the noisy, grimy pack to the bar, and looked down its length to see who was about. There were two women behind the bar, and Harry had no difficulty establishing which one was Gloria. She had to be the younger one, blonde, rosy-cheeked and a bit on the plump side, but pretty with it, and chatting animatedly to a couple of blokes while she poured their beers. Her compatriot, Mildred, an older, more austere woman, was serving further down the bar.

Harry leaned his large frame over the bar and endeavoured to catch Gloria's eye, quite a challenge, given the number of thirsty customers also seeking to attract her attention. After a few minutes, however, she spotted Harry, waved cheerily and made her way to him.

'G'day, ducks, you look like you're desperate for a drink,' she ventured. 'What'll it be?'

'A pint of your finest, since you ask,' Harry replied, then showed her his badge, adding, 'And a minute or two of your time, Gloria, if you can manage it. I can see you're busy, but you might be able to help me.'

Gloria looked him up and down, and apparently liked what she saw. 'Sure thing, ducks, these blokes can wait another minute or two.' She examined Harry's badge, still held out in front of her. 'Well, it's Inspector, is it? You look too young to be a big shot.'

Harry grinned. 'I'll take that as a compliment. But a bit less of the 'Inspector'; 'Harry' will do.'

'All right, Harry,' she smiled back. 'How can I help the law tonight?'

Serious now, Harry produced the photograph from his coat pocket and placed it on the bar in front of Gloria.

'This is the bloke who was killed the other night, not far from here. We think he might have been a regular in here. I reckon if anyone would know him, it'd be you.'

Gloria stared at the photograph for a few seconds, then pushed it back to Harry and looked up at him. Her rosy cheeks had paled. 'I do know him,' she said quietly, and Harry had to lean forward to hear her over the hubbub around them. 'That's Sam. You're right, he was fairly regular in here.'

Harry nodded his acknowledgement. 'Thanks, my dear, that's very useful. We think he might have been Russian. Is that likely?'

'Well, he was certainly a foreign fella,' Gloria agreed. 'Judging by his accent, anyway. He didn't have a lot of English. And his real name wasn't Sam.'

'How do you know that?' Harry asked.

'Because I asked his mate, Dave. They were together in here all the time. He was foreign too. I asked him once what Sam's real name was, and he let slip that it was Sergei. I don't think he meant to tell me, but he'd had a few drinks and I think he was trying to impress me. I asked him why they changed their names, and he said it was because they wanted to be real Aussies. But I'm not sure that was the actual reason. Anyway, he told me not to let on to Sam that I knew his real name. So I said I wouldn't.'

Harry took a long swig on his beer. It was cold and wet, just the way he liked it. And with a fair bit of flavour to boot. He could appreciate why the pub was so popular.

'That's terrific information, Gloria,' he said. 'And it'd be even better if you could tell me where this fellow, Sergei, worked. And his mate, for that matter.'

Gloria's pretty features wrinkled in thought. 'Well, to tell the truth, both of them never talked much about their work,' she replied eventually. 'But I reckon Sam...Sergei, was a fisherman. He had that smell about him.'

'Good. And Dave?'

'Not sure. Not fishing, I don't reckon. But he would come in here looking pretty dirty from time to time. I reckon he was a labourer of some sort. Maybe he worked in one of the lime kilns, quite a few blokes in here do. They come in after they finish loading the bags onto the boats.'

'And have you noticed Dave in here the last couple of days?'

Again Gloria paused while she considered his question. 'I don't think so. But that doesn't mean he hasn't been in. As you can see, it gets a bit hectic here and I'm always fairly busy. I might've missed him.'

'One other thing, Gloria,' Harry continued. 'Did you ever see Sam get into a blue with anyone in here? Or Dave, for that matter? I imagine you must see a few fights from time to time.'

Gloria shook her head firmly. 'No Harry, I'm happy to say we don't get too much aggravation here. If anyone wanted to step out of line, they'd need to deal with Bruno over there.' And she pointed to the far end of the bar where a gigantic, bald-headed fellow stood, casually surveying the room with a baleful eye.

Harry made some scribbles into his notebook, then slipped it into his coat pocket. 'Thank you, Gloria, you've been a tremendous help. I'll let you get back to work now, a lot of these blokes are starting to give me the evil eye. Don't want them to die of thirst, do we?'

Gloria chuckled and flashed Harry a warm smile. 'That's all right, Harry, they'll survive. Anyway, I'd be happy to get waylaid by the coppers any day, if they were all like you.'

She turned to attend to her parched customers, then had an afterthought. 'There's one other thing, Harry. I don't know whether it's useful.'

'All offerings gratefully accepted,' Harry replied. 'What is it?'

'Well, I told you that Dave was always trying to impress me. I reckon he might have been a bit sweet on me, sometimes the blokes in here go on a bit like that.'

'Perfectly understandable,' Harry suggested, winking at her. 'I wouldn't blame them.'

Gloria laughed. 'I can see you're a bit of a charmer, Harry. I bet your wife keeps a close eye on you.' And she glanced at the ring on Harry's finger.

Harry smiled back. 'Just being a gentleman, Gloria, nothing wrong with making the occasional compliment to a lovely lady. But I've interrupted you.'

Gloria leaned confidentially over the bar. 'The thing was, Sam never tried to make any passes. Quite the opposite, in fact. He would sometimes tell me about his girl back home. After he'd had a few and was getting ... sentimental, if you know what I mean. I could see he was missing her quite a bit.'

Harry studied Gloria contemplatively and took a sip on his beer. 'And I reckon her name would have been Natalya,' he suggested.

'It was!' Gloria stared at him in surprise. 'How did you know that?'

Harry shrugged. 'Let's just say he was wearing his heart on his sleeve.' And with that cryptic comment, Harry quaffed the remainder of his beer, picked up his hat off the bar, and bade Gloria a grateful good night.

4

⚜

SATURDAY MORNING AT THE Sorrento Police Station, and five policemen were crowded around the small table in the interview room. At its head sat Harry, perched precariously on a rickety chair and surveying his colleagues contemplatively. He had just recounted his investigations of the previous evening.

'So that's it,' he announced. 'I think we can call that a positive identification of our victim. He was Sergei, going by the name of Sam, likely a fisherman, and his mate's name is Dave. Though that's probably an assumed name as well. And chances are, both these fellows are Russian. Agreed?'

Nods from around the room.

'So, with the sort of info Gloria gave us, it shouldn't be too hard to track down where this bloke Sam worked, and who he might've associated with. We should start by finding his mate, Dave, I guess. Given he seems to have gone to ground, he's probably our prime suspect at this point in time.'

Sergeant Newgate nodded. 'I'd reckon you're right on the money there, boss. We need to track down this Dave fella, quick smart.'

'Isn't that what I just said, Sarge?' Harry retorted, mild irritation in his voice. 'But let's also find out where Sam worked and what his story is. By the way, I take it two foreigners called Sam and Dave, regulars at the Sailors Arms, aren't familiar to you blokes?'

The three policemen glanced at each other, before there were head shakes all round.

'There haven't been reports of any foreigners causing trouble at the Sailors Arms?'

Again a chorus of head shakes, before Wally Morris spoke up. 'I never heard of any trouble from anyone called Sam and Dave. Nor seen it either. We drink at the Sailors Arms sometimes after work, and there's never much trouble at all, really. Well, maybe a couple of blues from time to time, but their bouncer sorts those out pretty quickly.'

'I didn't realise the Sailors Arms was your local,' Harry remarked.

'Well, it's right next to the station here,' Newgate explained. 'So it makes sense to drink there. But we don't fraternise with the other customers much. Not a good look, if you know what I mean.'

'I do, Sarge, I do,' Harry replied. 'Very commendable. I take it you weren't there Tuesday night, though?'

Newgate scratched his head in thought. 'Well, actually, me and Arthur did pop in there after work, I reckon. Now that I remember. Just for a short while though, I think.'

'Might have been useful to mention that before,' Harry remarked, his irritation growing.

Newgate simply shrugged. 'Didn't think it was relevant. We weren't there late, as I recall.'

Harry was becoming more and more annoyed at Newgate's slackness. But he suppressed his anger. 'Anyway, you didn't see anything untoward?' he continued, as calmly as he could manage.

Newgate shook his head. 'Nah, all under control, as far as I remember.'

Harry paused and thought for a moment, before turning to Morris. 'I want to pick up on something you raised, Wally. The bouncer, Bruno. Is he there most nights?'

'Pretty much,' Morris responded. 'You can't miss him. Real big bloke.'

'Yeh, I know, I saw him,' Harry replied. 'Gloria agrees with you, she reckons he keeps pretty effective control over the place, as far as any ruckus goes. I might pop in again tonight and have a chat to him. Willie, can you contact Chester and set up a meeting?'

'Will do, boss,' Willie replied.

Harry turned to the others. 'And you blokes have an urgent job too. I want you to interview every fisherman in town about whether this fellow, Sam, worked on their boat. If that doesn't hit the jackpot, extend your enquiries to Rye and Portsea. And then to anyone who might be handling fish – buyers and so forth. I want you reporting back to me within forty-eight hours.'

There were murmurs of assent round the table, but there didn't seem to be a lot of enthusiasm for the task at hand, Harry observed. He could see that he would have to ride these blokes pretty hard. He made a mental note to brief Willie on the required approach.

'By the way,' Newgate said, 'I forgot to mention, your boss called on the telephone this morning. Wants an update from you on how the investigation's going. Seemed like he had a bit of a bee in his bonnet.' And his lips curled into the faintest hint of a smirk.

'Thanks, Sarge,' Harry replied evenly, overlooking the smirk. 'I'd better do that then.'

Newgate chuckled. 'Reckon he makes your life a bit hard, that bloke. Rather you than me.'

Harry ignored the comment. 'Right then, I'll give him a ring now. And you blokes get to it, pronto. There's a lot to do, so we need to get busy.'

'What's going on down there, Holloway? Have you sorted it out yet? Got yourself a suspect?'

Harry took a couple of deep breaths and told himself to stay calm. 'I wouldn't say that, sir. It's early days, after all, but we've made some strides in identifying the victim. Things are under control.'

A muffled snort on the end of the line. 'That's not what I'm hearing, Holloway. They tell me there's panic around the town. People scared of some killer on the loose, when you and I know it's probably the result of some drunken brawl between a couple of no-hopers. And the sooner you prove that and clear it all up, the sooner certain people down there will get off my back.'

Harry paused before replying. Should he go along with Marks' assertion of a drunken brawl for the moment, while he got on with his investigation? The prospect of no Marks browbeating him for a few days was enticing, but on the other hand, Harry knew the truth was likely to be different and he would eventually have to correct his boss's false assumptions. So he settled on honesty as the best policy.

'Well actually, sir, we don't think this killing was the result of some random brawl. It looks like it was a premeditated attack. A deliberate act of murder. Which is not to say that it will be repeated, of course. In my view, it's unlikely that anyone in the town has anything to fear from another attack.'

'Seems to me you're splitting hairs, Holloway,' Marks replied. 'I don't really care whether it was premeditated or not. Just find out who's behind it and reassure the public they're not in danger. Is that too much to ask?'

'Well, as I said, sir, we've made some real progress already in identifying the victim, as well as one of his close associates. Who might, in fact, be the prime suspect.'

A pause on the end of the line. 'Well, who is this bloke? What have you found out?'

'We've identified him as Russian, sir. And his associate as well. We think the victim might have been working as a fisherman.'

A longer pause, and some heavy breathing. 'Hang on, Holloway, did you say Russian?'

'That's right, sir.'

'And there's more than one of them?'

'Well, yes,' Harry replied, somewhat mystified by Marks' line of questioning. 'We think his associate was probably Russian as well. Judging by reliable evidence provided by one of our witnesses.'

'What the hell are a couple of Russians doing, sneaking around Sorrento?'

Harry remained mystified. 'I'm not sure, sir. Working as fishermen, it seems.'

Marks' tone suddenly became low and conspiratorial. 'Holloway, this is very troubling. And sensitive too, I might add.'

'What do you mean, sir? I can't really see what his nationality's got to do with it.'

'Are you being deliberately obtuse, Holloway? Let me make it clear to you. Some Russian mystery man gets murdered at the entry point to Melbourne. How do you think that will look to the public? The man could be a spy, for all we know. And his fellow Russian's still on the loose!'

'Sir, I hardly think ...'

'Holloway, why do you think our government's spent a damn fortune on all those fortifications down there? At Portsea, Queenscliff, and god knows where else. It's because of the Russians and their damned imperialistic ambitions.'

It was now becoming increasingly clear to Harry the direction this conversation was heading. He should have realised Marks would go straight to the assumption that the dead Russian was some sort of spy. Harry thought that scenario highly unlikely, even if not beyond the realms of possibility.

'You're right, sir, it's an angle that must be explored ...'

'Damn right I'm right! Now, listen carefully, Holloway, there's two things that are going to happen.'

'I'm listening, sir.'

'First, you and your men are not going to breath a word to anyone about these two Russians. We can't alarm the public.'

'But surely that'll make it difficult to conduct our enquiries, sir? I mean, their nationalities might well be relevant to what happened.'

'Rubbish, Holloway! You can call them whatever you like. Foreigners, continentals, expatriates, whatever you like. Just not Russians! Get me?'

'Yes, sir.'

'And secondly, Holloway, this has suddenly become highly sensitive. I need to alert the appropriate authorities.'

'Really, sir?'

'Yes, I need to brief Commander Jackson, as a matter of urgency.'

'Commander Jackson?'

'Yes, Commander Jackson, head of the Victorian Military Forces. He'll want to put his artillery forces at the Heads on high alert.'

'Yes, of course,' Harry replied, though he thought this was an over-reaction to what he considered an unlikely possibility.

Marks was not yet finished. 'And I can tell you, Holloway, given the sensitivity of this issue, Commander Jackson will want to take direct control of managing this threat. And since he'll no doubt want to attend down there in person, I'll need to be there too, to represent the interests of the department. Expect us down there as a matter of priority. Possibly today, in fact. If I can organise a police launch in time.'

Now Harry was beginning to fully appreciate the difficulties ahead. 'Is that really necessary, sir? I mean ...'

'Enough, Holloway, I'll brook no dissension. Just get on with your enquiries and leave the important stuff to me. I'll expect to be briefed tonight on your progress. In person.'

And a click, as the line went dead.

〰

The steam train came to a noisy halt at the back beach terminus, and Effie stepped down from the second carriage. She walked to the rotunda deck and looked about for Michael.

She was feeling rather on top of the world, wearing a newly purchased pair of plimsolls and ankle-length culottes, an image stolen unashamedly from Lydia. It just seemed sensible to follow the lead of her friend, who was indisputably a fashion icon. And after inspecting herself in the bedroom mirror, she had pronounced herself pleased with the result. She looked smart, but with a hint of bohemian. Just the right outfit for a visit to the artists' camp.

The prospect of the alternative types they would meet at the artists' camp had been perhaps a little too much for Rachel, who had declined the invitation. Effie suspected Rachel's reticence might also have been driven by the alternative prospect of spending the afternoon with the children. She was already enchanted by baby Daisy and had jumped at the invitation to join Harry's parents on child-minding duty at the beach.

Effie found Michael in the kiosk, enjoying a coffee. 'Would you like one before we go?' he asked. 'It's just billy tea up at the camp, I'm afraid.'

Effie declined and suggested they start their journey. 'I imagine it's quite a trek through the sand hills.'

'Not really,' Michael replied. 'Only about ten minutes walk past Coppin's lookout. I think the artists didn't want to be too far from the pub. James tells me there's a post-dinner pilgrimage to the Sorrento every second night or so.'

They set off along a crushed limestone path, winding gently upward into the sand hills on the western side of the amphitheatre. They soon came to the summit of the first ridge of sand hills, where a seat and small monument had been installed to mark the spot as Coppin's lookout. And very well chosen, Effie thought as she gazed at the panoramic view; the long gentle sweep of the natural amphitheatre on her left, the wilder coastline of jagged rocks and low cliffs to her right, and ahead the grand vista of the Southern Ocean, its white-flecked lines of breakers stretching out as far as the eye could see. A southerly breeze was wafting into their faces, pleasantly brisk enough to dry the small beads of perspiration that had already gathered on her face during the walk.

'It's lovely,' Effie murmured, as much to herself as to Michael.

'Yes, it is,' he concurred. 'You can see why Jane Sutherland chose this area for her artists' camp. If this view didn't inspire one to paint, nothing would.'

'Indeed,' Effie smiled, then glanced around. 'Where do we go from here? Back into the hills, I suppose.'

Michael nodded and pointed to an unsurfaced track that ran off through a gap in the low ti-tree scrub behind them. They set off, Michael leading the way, the going much more difficult now along the soft, sandy path winding through the low hills.

They trekked on for a good quarter of an hour, the soft sand proving to be hard going underfoot. So Effie was relieved when they eventually came upon an open circular clearing, in which were erected a motley collection of a dozen or so tents and canvas shelters. In the centre of the clearing a ring of stones had been built, containing the still smouldering ashes of last night's fire. A few canvas chairs surrounded this hearth, interspersed with other more rudimentary seating, consisting of a selection of small boulders and timber logs.

'Hullo!' Michael called. 'Anyone about?' The camp seemed deserted.

There was an immediate rustling from one of the tents and James' handsome features materialised. He smiled broadly and welcomed them both with a warm embrace.

'Welcome to our rustic paradise, Effie dear. What do you think?'

'It's charming, James, quite charming. Are you getting some painting done?'

'Absolutely. I'm making good progress on a rather promising piece. Now, first things first, how about a cup of tea?'

'That would be delightful. But where is everyone? Where are all your colleagues?'

'They're off painting. In various locations. It's all so beautiful, everywhere around here.'

'I'm sorry to interrupt you then, dear,' Effie exclaimed. 'We must be taking you away from your work.'

'No, no,' James replied without hesitation. 'There's plenty of time for that.'

James wandered over and examined the smouldering campfire. 'Hmm, I think we can revive that,' he observed, but his tone was far from confident. 'I'm afraid I'm not much good at the art of camping. Jane is the one who looks after all that stuff.'

'Don't worry,' Michael smiled, 'I think we can muddle through between us.' And he gathered a small pile of twigs that someone had place by the hearth, and settled them on the smouldering ashes. 'I think you blow on it, somehow.' He proceeded to blow gently on the smouldering twigs, which dutifully sprang into flame.

Effie was suitably impressed. 'Goodness, Michael, you're quite the bushman! I had no idea.'

'Just another of my hidden talents,' Michael smiled, as he piled some larger sticks onto the fire. James filled the billy with water from a large drum nearby, spooned in some tea leaves, and before long the brew was bubbling away.

Tea was poured into pannikins and soon they were all convivially seated around the fire.

'I was hoping to meet Miss Sutherland,' Effie said, sipping on her tea.

'She's much admired among my circle of friends. For her commitment to the suffragette movement, as much as for her painting.'

'I hope you will,' James replied. 'I mentioned you and Michael were visiting, and she indicated she hoped to return in time to meet you. With her friend, Clara Southern, who's here as well.'

'Wonderful!' Michael enthused. 'Two champions of the *plein air* movement. And two great suffragettes to boot. What a treat!'

James smiled. 'Indeed, they're two wonderful women, and brilliant artists as well. There are many who consider them in the same breath as Streeton and Roberts, but maintain they're less popular only because of their sex.'

'I'm sure that's the case,' Effie commented, frowning slightly. 'I'm not surprised at all.'

James smiled. 'Good on you, Effie. Let them know: it'll be music to their ears.'

He paused for a moment, then continued. 'Actually Effie, here's another thing guaranteed to raise your hackles. The only reason Clara's here this week is to chaperone Jane.'

'What do you mean?' Effie was perplexed. 'Why does Jane Sutherland require chaperoning?'

'Apparently the prospect of a woman sharing a campsite alone with a number of men was too much, even for our enlightened male artistic brethren. She would have been required to stay in Sorrento and trek out here every day. It was only with some reluctance that they accepted two ladies in the camp. Keeping an eye on each other, as it were.'

'Unbelievable!' Effie cried. 'It just shows how little progress we've made.'

'Ridiculous, isn't it?' James agreed. 'Though I don't think either woman minds. They're great friends, and they're both doing some great work out here.'

As they spoke, the sound of women's voices became apparent in the distance, growing steadily louder. Shortly, the two women artists appeared on one of the sandy tracks. As James introduced them, Effie observed the two with interest.

Jane Sutherland was short and slight, clad in a plain, practical calico smock over pants and boots. She had fair hair, tied back in a bun, and lively, expressive features. Clara Southern, on the other hand, was much taller, more elegantly attired in a stylish blouse and long skirt, with striking red hair and classical good looks.

'Oh my goodness, Clara!' Sutherland exclaimed as she shook hands with Effie. 'Effie here could be your twin.'

Southern laughed gaily and Effie smiled, slightly embarrassed.

'James cut in, smiling broadly, 'That's a tremendous compliment, Effie. To be compared to the beauteous Clara Southern is a feather in your cap, my dear.'

Southern came forward and shook Effie's hand enthusiastically. 'Delighted to meet you, Effie. Always a pleasure to meet another redhead. We must stick together, you know.'

With the ice broken, two more pannikins of tea were procured, and Sutherland and Southern joined them around the campfire. The conversation explored mutual interests in the suffragette movement, and mutual friends as well.

Both the artists were well acquainted with Lydia, and Effie again marvelled at her friend's wide circle of friends. Both women also displayed a lively interest in Effie's and Michael's experience teaching at the all-girls school, Merton Hall. Inevitably, the subject of the artists' camp also came up, and Effie asked which well-known artists were in attendance.

'Charles is here,' Sutherland replied. 'Charles Condor. But you probably wouldn't have heard of many of the others. There are a number of younger artists, mostly unknown at this stage of their careers. We're trying to promote new work, trying to be inclusive in our approach. Actually, one example of an outstanding new talent is sitting right here. Wouldn't you agree, Michael?'

'I would indeed, Jane,' Michael responded, smiling and placing a loving arm around James' shoulders. 'He's too modest about his ability, he needs a complimentary word or two.'

'You're far too kind,' James demurred, though Effie could see from his smile that he was chuffed by their praise. 'I think the work you're doing, Jane, and the approach you're taking, is tremendously valuable,' he added, serious now.

'Thank you, James dear,' Sutherland replied. 'We do our best.'

James hesitated for a moment, then continued. 'As you say, you seek to be inclusive, but perhaps, could I suggest, to a fault at times?'

'Really?' Sutherland asked. 'What do you mean?'

James hesitated again. 'Well, I probably shouldn't say this, but I think perhaps one or two of the unknown artists here may be exploiting your generosity. Well, one in particular, actually.'

'I'm perplexed, James. Who do you mean?'

'Well, I don't wish to denigrate my fellow artists, but that fellow, Petrenko. The red-headed chap. I'm not sure he's worthy of your support. He doesn't seem to paint much, and from what I've seen, what he does produce doesn't have much artistic merit.'

Michael glanced at James with a slightly concerned expression. 'I'm not sure that such criticism is warranted, James. I'm sure this Mr Petrenko is doing his best.'

'Oh no,' Sutherland responded promptly, 'I don't mind some critical analysis. In fact, we encourage it. As far as Vladimir Petrenko goes, I appreciate that his style is not to everyone's taste. But we see something in him, a certain primitive expressionism. Something to be encouraged. And after all, he's another redhead, so Clara is naturally sympathetic.' And she smiled archly at Effie.

James looked shame-faced. 'I'm sorry, I shouldn't have said anything. It was remiss of me.' And he lapsed into silence.

'Don't be hard on yourself,' Michael said, patting his knee. 'You're entitled to your opinion.'

'Of course he is,' Sutherland agreed. 'As I said, we encourage different opinions.'

Michael rose from his seat. 'Actually, Effie and I must think of getting back and leaving you artists to get on with your work.'

And so, with thanks and best wishes all round, the two friends made their departure, back through the sand hills toward the back beach.

'What was that with James back there?' Effie asked, once they were out of earshot. 'That wasn't like him at all, to be so critical of a colleague.'

'You're right,' Michael mused, 'he does have a bit of a bee in his bonnet about it, I must say. He raised this fellow Petrenko with me last time I visited. He told me he had a bit of a feeling about him. That he didn't seem genuine or something.'

'Oh well, Miss Sutherland ... Jane, I mean, obviously supports the fellow. So perhaps James will be put at ease now.'

'Let's hope so,' Michael agreed. 'If not at ease, perhaps he'll at least put it out of his mind.'

Willie sat in the backroom of the Sailors Arms, deputising for Harry, who had been summoned to the Continental by Chief Inspector Marks. Across the bare wooden table from him sat Arthur Chester and Bruno the bouncer. Chester had insisted he too be present when Willie had requested a brief chat with his security man. The raucous din of the bar next door was only slightly diminished by the thin wall separating them.

At first, Willie couldn't quite tell whether Bruno was going to prove a helpful witness or not. The big man sat bolt upright on his chair, his huge arms crossed, fixing Willie with a blank stare.

'Thank you for making the time to meet with me,' Willie began. 'We appreciate your cooperation.'

The blank stare didn't alter, but Willie fancied he saw the faintest inkling of an acknowledging nod.

Willie pushed on, producing the photograph of Sergei and sliding it across the table towards Bruno. 'I'm wondering if you were familiar with this person as a customer here? He went by the name of Sam.'

Bruno gave the merest glance at the photograph in front of him, before replying gruffly. 'You mean that foreigner bloke? What they found in the harbour? Yeh, I seen him in here.'

'Was he a regular?'

'Yeh. Him and his mate. In here most nights. 'Cept when they were working. Or whatever it was they got up to.'

'What do you mean by that?' Willie asked, leaning forward.

Bruno shrugged his enormous shoulders. 'I dunno. You hear things sometimes. You know, goings on.'

'You mean, illegal goings on?'

But that was the extent of Bruno's candour. He shrugged again and resumed his silent stare.

'Is that the extent of your questions, Sergeant?' Chester interceded, getting to his feet.

'Not quite,' Willie replied and turned back to Bruno. 'I wonder if you saw Sam in the pub last Tuesday night?'

Without hesitation, Bruno replied. 'Yeh, I did.'

'You seem very sure?'

'Course I'm sure. I heard on Wednesday someone got tossed in the harbour, see. Then I heard Gloria say it was one of them two foreign blokes, and I remembered I saw him in here Tuesday night. Sitting by himself, he was.'

'So he didn't have his mate with him?'

'Nah, he didn't.'

'How did he seem? According to our pathologist, he'd had a fair bit to drink.'

'He wasn't causing trouble, if that's what you mean. Most blokes in here have a fair bit to drink. That's why they come in here. Long as they don't cause trouble, that's all right with me. If he was causing trouble, he'd be out on his ear.'

'So he didn't get into a blue?' Willie asked. 'You didn't see him arguing with anybody?'

Bruno glanced briefly at Chester before returning his gaze to Willie. 'I told you he wasn't causing trouble,' he repeated testily. 'I dunno if he was arguing with anybody. I don't call that causing trouble. That's all I look out for; blokes causing trouble.'

Realising that this was going to be the limit of Bruno's contribution, Willie closed his notebook, stood and offered his hand. 'Thank you, sir, you've been very helpful. And thank you too, Mr Chester, for making your time available. I'll see myself out.'

And he turned and made for the door. Bruno followed close behind, returning to his regular station at the end of the bar. Arthur Chester stayed seated at the table, watching Willie's exit with studied indifference.

Harry strode up the wide sandstone steps leading to the Continental Hotel's foyer. He paused on the terrace before entering, turning to survey the scene from this elevated outlook. It was indeed spectacular – the sun setting golden over the sand dunes to the west, bathing the beach stretching below him in a softening light. Harry saw that the promenaders on the esplanade had not diminished in number. Indeed, the crowd seemed to have grown, taking advantage of the pleasant early evening breeze.

Harry felt slightly envious of the carefree holiday-makers below; and a twinge of guilt too that he was not with his family, enjoying the sights of Sorrento on this beautiful evening. Never mind, duty was duty and must be endured.

And besides, he knew that Effie fully appreciated his difficulty with Chief Inspector Marks and would make the best of the situation. She wasn't one to mope about, fretting in his absence. Anyway, Effie wasn't due to return to teaching at Merton Hall for another three weeks; there would still be time for a holiday together, once he had sorted out this case. He needed to make sure that Marks would stand by his word to let him stay on for a while.

Making a mental resolution to stay firm on that score, Harry turned from the tranquil scene before him and strode to the hotel's entrance door. To be met by a liveried flunky, who eyed Harry's slightly unkempt attire with a degree of disdain, but nevertheless swung open the heavy glass door to allow him entry. Once inside, another uniformed attendant approached, showing a more polite demeanour and saying pleasantly: 'Good evening, sir, how can I help? Will you be dining with us this evening?'

As a rule, Harry didn't like pulling rank, but on this occasion he couldn't be bothered going through the required pleasantries. Pulling his badge from his waistcoat fob, he flashed it before the startled fellow's eyes. 'Inspector Holloway to see Chief Inspector Marks. He's expecting me.'

'Certainly, sir,' came the instant reply. 'The Chief Inspector is in one of our private lounges, I believe. This way, please.' And he scampered off down a wide, richly carpeted passage, into the bowels of the grand building, with Harry striding behind. Several passageways later, they arrived at the aforementioned private lounge and the attendant knocked on the oak door. A muffled response came from within, and opening the door, the attendant proclaimed: 'Inspector Holloway to see you, Chief Inspector.'

Harry entered, to find Winston Marks reclining in an oversized arm-chair, cigar in hand. Also in the room were two other men. One was clearly Commander Jackson, judging by his ridiculously over-embroidered dark navy jacket, with red collar and numerous elaborate rows of gold chord running across its front. It gave the wearer something of the appearance of a golden skeleton. This incongruous impression was enhanced by Jackson's small rotund physique, pink, balding features and large handlebar moustache. The second man was also unknown to Harry, a well-dressed fellow of slim build, with slicked-down dark hair and a pencil moustache.

Marks said nothing, just curtly motioning Harry to an empty chair. Harry took up the invitation, but not before extending a hand to both the strangers and introducing himself. Jackson muttered a brief how-do, but the other fellow, who introduced himself as Oliver Ridgeway, was more cordial. 'Welcome to my hotel, Inspector. A great pleasure to have you with us.'

'Good to be here,' Harry reciprocated amiably. 'You're the proprietor, I take it.'

'Manager, actually,' Ridgeway replied, leaning back in his armchair. 'For Mr Bensilum.'

'Of course.' Harry had heard of Isaac Bensilum, right up there with George Coppin as an entrepreneur and major player in the development of Sorrento.

'Mind you, he leaves everything to me here. I have a pretty free hand running this place.' And Ridgeway fixed Harry with a self-satisfied smirk.

Harry smiled back but said nothing, not sure whether he should proceed to business with this stranger in the room. So he resorted to small talk. 'Looks like a good holiday season, Mr Ridgeway. Business good?'

'Call me Oliver, Inspector. And yes, it has been a good start to the season. Though this Russian fellow getting murdered is a bit of a worry. Winston here has been telling us all about it.'

Harry raised an eyebrow and said nothing. Marks cut in hastily.

'I provided only the bare details, you understand, Holloway. I'm hoping you've got more to add?'

'Possibly, sir, but perhaps in confidence?'

Marks cleared his throat. 'Yes, of course. The Commander needs to be briefed on the military implications, but, Oliver, would you mind?'

Ridgeway leaned forward and extinguished his half-smoked cigar. 'Of course, Winston, I completely understand. I've got business to attend to, in any event. Please excuse me, gentlemen.' And he rose, shook hands cordially all round, and made his exit.

As the door closed behind him, Marks spoke in conspiratorial tones. 'Now, Holloway, I want you to brief Commander Jackson here on the latest developments.'

Harry relayed the facts of the case so far. Commander Jackson leaned forward in his chair, listening intently to Harry's account. When Harry had finished, Jackson turned to Marks.

'Alarming Winston, most alarming.'

Marks nodded grimly. 'Couldn't agree more, Charles. It's damned alarming.'

'Well, yes,' Harry said, alarmed for other reasons by the Commander's reaction. He attempted to bring Jackson back to the reality of the case. 'We do find it concerning in cases like this, Commander, where there's very little information about the man's identity, and the circumstances of his death. Makes it difficult to get to the bottom of.'

Jackson fixed Harry with a grim expression. 'Inspector, the circumstances you've related are of great concern to me from a security perspective. In short, these events have all the hallmarks of foreign interference in the affairs of this state. Russian interference, to be more precise.'

Harry knew where the discussion was heading, and again made an attempt to return to the facts of the case. 'I realise that such a possibility must be explored, but at this stage it's just one of a number of scenarios. All of which we must investigate.'

Jackson spoke calmly and slowly to Harry, as if explaining some simple concept to a child. 'Inspector, I understand what you are saying, and I agree with you. But let me explain my perspective, and my priorities. The Victorian Government, and therefore my Victorian Military Forces, have for some time been preparing for a foreign incursion. We live in a dangerous world, Inspector, and we believe that certain foreign expansionist powers ...'

'By which you mean Russia,' Harry interrupted.

Jackson nodded sagely. 'Precisely, Inspector. Russia has long-held imperialist ambitions, and we believe that they have also long had their eye on the riches that our fair state generates. The gold from Ballarat, the wool from our rich pastures, the great mercantile capacity that marvellous Melbourne has generated. So, this state, as you probably know, has invested heavily in fortifying the city of Melbourne, and particularly the naval entrance, against any foreign attack.'

Harry endeavoured a diplomatic nod and some carefully chosen words. 'I understand all of that, Commander. A prudent approach, for sure. But still, there may not be ...'

Jackson cut him short. 'I know what you're going to say, Inspector, that this murder may not be related to Russian interference. But believe me, when a Russian is found floating in the Sorrento harbour, and no-one can identify who he is and what he was up to, then it is our absolute duty to investigate and to place our forces on high alert.'

Again, Harry sought to calm the waters. 'Of course, sir, but we must also keep our minds open to other possibilities. It's entirely possible this fellow's death has nothing to do with an imminent invasion.'

Winston Marks gave an irritated snort. 'Good god, Holloway, don't be so obtuse. There's a very good chance the man was a Russian spy, scouting out the fortifications at the Heads.'

'Even so,' Harry persevered, 'it's difficult to see in that case why he was killed.'

Marks snorted again, more loudly this time. 'Use your brain, Holloway, for heaven's sake. This Sergei chap could have been threatening to go over to our side. In which case there are obviously other undercover spies operating in this area, ruthless men who would stop at nothing. His death only increases the priority to ready ourselves.'

Harry briefly considered challenging this highly speculative stretch of logic from Marks, then thought better of it. In any event he was saved by Jackson's intervention.

'Come now, Winston, let's not be too critical of Inspector Holloway. He is perfectly entitled to consider other possibilities in his investigations. That's his job as the good detective we know him to be. As long as he also recognises and investigates the possible security implications I've raised. And it'll be important, Inspector Holloway, to stay in close communications with my people at the Heads as you undertake your investigation.'

Marks said nothing, just continued to eye Harry with a critical look.

'Absolutely, Commander,' Harry responded, glad to get the conversation onto a slightly more sensible track. 'We'll certainly explore the possibilities you've raised. And we'll do what's needed to keep your people in the loop.'

'Excellent, Inspector, excellent.' Jackson leaned back in his armchair and smiled benevolently at Harry. 'And to that end, I have alerted the artillery officer in charge at Fort Nepean that you will be meeting with him tomorrow at the fort, to establish communications and to compare notes, about this case and all things Russian.'

'Certainly,' Harry responded, privately considering that such a meeting could do no harm. 'And who would the commanding officer be, sir?'

'Lieutenant Matthew Windsor, one of our brightest young officers. He may well be able to assist you, Inspector. He ensures his squadron keeps a very close eye on the fortifications at the Heads, and on their immediate environs. As well as on all the other strategic locations in the bay, for that matter.'

'Good,' Harry replied promptly. 'I'll look forward to meeting Lieutenant Windsor and briefing him on our progress so far. Thank you, Commander. If that's all, I'll take my leave.'

Harry stood and moved forward to shake Jackson's hand. 'Good to meet you, Commander. No doubt you'll be heading back to Melbourne in the morning?'

Jackson shook Harry's hand firmly. 'No, Inspector, given the possible implications of this incident, I intend to remain here in Sorrento for the time being. I shall expect ongoing reports from you as you make progress. Both via Winston here, and in person, as I see fit.'

Harry winced internally as he visualised the amount of wasted time ahead. 'Certainly, sir, I'll make sure you're kept informed of developments,' he responded, before wishing both men a pleasant evening and making his escape.

God help us, he thought as he made his way down the hill towards the Back Beach Palace. Now I've got two pompous fools getting in my way. He just hoped that Lieutenant Windsor would be a tad more reasonable.

5

SUNDAY 11 JANUARY 1898

THE HOLLOWAY CLAN was seated at breakfast in the dining room of the Back Beach Palace. Their table was positively groaning under the weight of the fare Mrs Meriwether had assembled – fruit, toast, eggs, bacon, kippers, lamb's fry, black pudding ... a feast fit for a king. Or at least for a hungry Inspector Holloway, who was doing an approving Mrs Meriwether proud, devouring his second well-stacked plate.

'And what investigations do you have in mind for today, my darling?' Effie inquired, as she hopefully waved a spoonful of porridge in front of a defiant Daisy's face.

Harry glanced up from the gastronomic business at hand. 'Military today, Eff, military. And that's all I can say, actually, all a bit hush-hush.'

'Really?' Effie was intrigued. She turned her attention to Willie and Rachel, who had joined them for breakfast. 'What about you, Willie? If Mr Secret Spy here won't tell me anything, perhaps you can enlighten us? Are we about to be invaded? Should we fear for our lives?'

Willie simply grinned and tapped his nose with a forefinger. 'Sorry, Effie.'

Harry leaned back and smiled fondly at his wife. 'Oh well, on further consideration, I don't suppose I'd be giving away state secrets if I said I'm off to visit Fort Nepean. But that's about all I can say about my movements.

Willie's going to spend the day nosing around the scene of the crime here in Sorrento, looking for witnesses.'

'Fort Nepean! How intriguing!' Effie exclaimed. 'Though I don't think you've satisfied our fears about an imminent invasion, darling.' Her teasing smile flagged her lack of concern that such an event was likely.

'What about you folk?' Harry asked, turning to his parents. 'A day on the beach, perhaps? What have you got in mind?'

'I think we'll walk down to the beach for a little while, dear,' Millie replied. 'Alfie wants to build sandcastles, don't you, darling?' And she patted young Alfie on the head, as he looked up at her, nodding enthusiastically.

'But we won't stay too long,' she added. 'The sun was very hot yesterday, and Alfie had quite a bit of colour last night.'

'What about you, Dad?' Harry asked, turning to Clem. 'A quiet day for you too?'

'Reckon so,' Clem nodded. 'Maybe not today, but some time I wouldn't mind doing a spot of fishing down at the pier. It'll remind me of when I was a kid, we used to go fishing down at the docks fairly regular. You never know, I might catch a Russian or two.' And he grinned and winked at Harry.

'Be quiet, Clem!' Millie admonished. 'Not in front of the children. That's not funny.'

'Sorry, dear,' Clem replied, but a continuing grin indicated his lack of repentance.

'And what about you, Eff?' Harry asked fondly. 'What have you and Rachel got planned?'

'Harry Holloway, I do wish you'd listen to your wife,' Effie chided him teasingly. 'I told you last night, but you obviously had your mind on other things. We're off to the Mechanics' Institute with Lydia and Michael. Jane Sutherland is putting on an exhibition of all the achievements from the artists' camp.'

'Really?' Harry was intrigued. 'I thought the camp was meant to go for another week or two. I'm surprised that they've finished their work already.'

'Oh no, they're not all finished, not by any means. There'll be some finished works, but most of it will be works in progress. Jane is keen for people to understand and appreciate the creative process, and the progress of a painting, from initial sketches to finished works. And the Institute Committee has very kindly made the hall available for the artists' displays.'

'Great idea,' Harry commented. 'Should be very interesting.'

'Yes,' Effie replied. 'Apparently there's a lot of interest around the town in what they're doing. And among the tourists from Melbourne too, I would think.'

'Actually,' she added after a pause, 'there's one artist in particular I'm keen to look at. It's a chap by the name of Petrenko.' And she went on to describe James' views on the mysterious Mr Petrenko, and his perceived lack of any artistic talent.

As she related the story, Harry listened with increasing attention. 'That's interesting,' he commented when she had finished. 'And this fellow seems to be foreign, you say? Not Russian, by any chance?'

'James didn't say what his nationality was.' Effie replied. 'I'm not sure he knows. I must say, Petrenko does sound Russian though, doesn't it?'

'It does,' Harry agreed. 'I'll be interested to hear from you tonight about his artistic ability, Eff. See if he's the real deal.'

At that moment, their conversation was interrupted by Mrs Meriwether, sweeping dramatically into the room, waving a sealed note in the air. 'Do excuse me, Inspector,' she exclaimed, slightly out of breath. 'I have an important note for you. From Mr Coppin, no less.'

She thrust the note into Harry's outstretched hand and stood there expectantly. 'Shall I wait?' she queried. 'In case you have an urgent reply. It may relate to your investigation.'

Harry smiled at her. 'Don't worry, Mrs M, I'll find you if I need to reply. You're not going anywhere, are you?' And he fixed her with a mock, interrogating stare.

'No, no, of course not,' Mrs Meriwether replied, taking a flustered step backward. 'I'll be in my office if you need me.' And she hurried from the room.

Harry tore open the note and perused its contents. He whistled quietly to himself.

'What is it, boss?' Willie asked. 'Coppin got some relevant information?'

'Not exactly,' Harry replied, glancing at the note again. 'He wants to meet with me tonight. Privately, for dinner at the Continental. Together with some bloke called Nikolai Matyunin. Just the three of us.'

'Mr Matyunin definitely sounds Russian,' Effie commented. 'This town seems to be positively teeming with them. I wonder what it's about. And what he wants.'

'Or what he can tell us,' Harry added. 'Mrs M may be right, I reckon. It may well be relevant to the investigation. So I'd better go. Willie, get a note back to Mr Coppin saying I'll look forward to meeting him for dinner.'

Harry was again traversing the calm waters of Port Phillip Bay, but this time aboard a police launch, the same one that had carried Chief Inspector Marks and Commander Jackson to Sorrento. It was piloted by one Constable Jones, a cheerful young fellow who was only too glad to be enjoying his time away from Melbourne for a few days. They were bound for Fort Nepean, at the tip of the peninsula. Rugged cliffs and billowing sand dunes prevented any ready land access to the fort, so by sea they must go.

As they made their way along the coast in a westerly direction, they passed several fishermen's huts with their rickety piers jutting out into the water. Then they spotted the tiny village of Portsea; just a few cottages really, clustered around a small shop. And after a few more minutes they also passed the Quarantine Station, where a large vessel lay anchored at the pier. Ahead and to their right, Harry again noted in the distance the monolithic stone hulk that was the South Channel Fort, standing guard against any intruders who might have breached the initial defences at the Heads.

Another ten minutes further on and they came to a small pier, jutting out from the base of the dunes. Beyond it, a row of small huts hugged the shoreline, and above, sitting atop a steeply rising hill, Harry could make out a rounded construction of some kind, presumably one of the four gun emplacements that constituted the fort's artillery capacity.

Constable Jones eased the launch up against the pier and made fast. As they alighted, a soldier appeared from one of the buildings, clad in the khaki uniform and red lapels of the Victorian Artillery, and came forward to greet them. Introducing himself to Harry as Sergeant Will Thomas, he apologised on behalf of the fort's commander, Lieutenant Windsor, indicating that the Lieutenant was just finishing up drills at the moment, and would be pleased to meet him in the officers' mess.

Harry thanked Thomas and asked which of the adjacent buildings was the mess. Perhaps the one on the end, built separately from its neighbours and constructed of red brick rather than weatherboard?

'Oh no, sir, that's the engine room,' Thomas replied. 'All of the officers' facilities are on the embankment. Up there.' And he pointed skyward, up the face of the cliff's steep rise.

'Up those steps is the way,' he added, pointing to their left, where steep stone steps wound through the undergrowth.

Harry whistled. 'I bet that keeps your men fit, hiking up there every day. Once'll be enough for me.'

Thomas grinned and led the way up the steps. Harry fancied himself reasonably fit, but he was puffing and sweating freely by the time they reached the top. They came out onto a large rectangular quadrangle, one side of which accommodated a series of cannons pointing westward towards the Heads, the other side featuring a number of red-brick buildings set into the hill face. It was to one of these that Sergeant Thomas led Harry.

The officer who came to the door was surprisingly young, perhaps no more than thirty, tall and angular like Harry, fair-haired and with a clean-shaven ruddy complexion. He introduced himself as Lieutenant Matthew Windsor and invited Harry to come in and take a seat.

'How can I help you, Inspector?' he asked amiably. 'I understand you've had a murder over at Sorrento, and my bosses tell me you suspect a Russian connection. Apparently, the powers-that-be think there may be state security implications.'

Harry smiled and gave a slightly embarrassed laugh. 'Well, I don't know about that. Frankly, we don't know much at all about the victim yet. Or who was responsible for his death. But it seems there's a good deal of sensitivity about the Russians at the moment, particularly in your part of the world.'

Matthew Windsor's lips curled slightly in a suppressed smile. 'You're right there. A very good deal, I'd say. Not sure there's a great chance of a Russian invasion any time soon, mind you. Or of some Russian pirate ship raiding our city's gold supplies, which is apparently their main concern. But we do our job and keep a sharp lookout.'

'From what you say, my next question might be pointless,' Harry continued. 'I take it you haven't seen any suspicious-looking strangers wandering about near the fort. Or any suspicious boats, for that matter.'

Windsor shook his head. 'We certainly take the issue of unidentified boats very seriously, Inspector. And we have a first-class view of the Heads, the bay and the open ocean from our various gun placements. There's nothing untoward to report on that front.

As far as land-based incursion goes, the same applies, really. We can see the shoreline and the sand dunes back towards Sorrento beach very clearly from our lookout points. We do see the odd hiker or beachcomber from time to time, wandering through the sand hills or along the beach front. Particularly on the bay side. Most recently we've noticed a number of those artists from the camp wandering through the dunes or doing their sketching. Nothing to worry about there, I wouldn't think.'

'I wouldn't think so either,' Harry replied reflectively. 'Though let me know if you notice any of them showing more interest in you blokes, rather than the scenery. I'm staying at the Back Beach Palace.' And he handed the Lieutenant his visiting card.

'Thank you,' Windsor replied, glancing briefly at Harry's inscription. 'Tell you what, if we're going to be in contact a bit, why don't we ditch the formality? I like to, when I can. It's Matt for me.' And he stretched out a large hand to Harry.

'Why not?' Harry replied readily. 'I'm of the same mind. Harry's my moniker.' And he shook the Lieutenant's hand heartily.

'Well, that's about all I need for the moment, Matt,' Harry continued, picking up his hat and rising to his feet. 'I'll bid you good day.'

Windsor rose as well. 'Look, while you're here, Harry, why don't I show you around? At least to the gun placements. It'll give you a good understanding of our defence capacity, and the extent of our surveillance ability. Do you have time?'

'Sure do,' Harry agreed readily. 'That'd be very useful.'

Windsor escorted Harry from the room, not back out to the quadrangle, but through a door set in the far wall. This led into a gloomy brick-lined tunnel which stretched ahead of them a good distance. They walked down this passageway, turning at a number of junctions, climbed a steep flight of steps towards a day-lit exit, and came out onto a paved circular space, rimmed with low, thick stone walls. In the centre of this space stood a large artillery gun, sitting atop a circular metal platform. The barrel of the large cannon was pointing westward, directly at the stone wall in front of it.

'Blimey!' Harry exclaimed. 'That looks a bit dodgy. Wouldn't that blow the wall out if it went off?'

Windsor laughed heartily. 'That, my friend, is our famous disappearing gun. When it fires, that mechanism it sits on lifts it up above the wall into its firing position. And then drops it down again after it's fired. Meant to make it indestructible.'

'Bloody marvellous,' Harry commented, genuinely impressed.

Windsor smiled again. 'Only problem is, it's not that reliable. If it's not cleaned out properly between firings, it can discharge before it gets to full height. We actually blew one of our walls apart at one of the other placements.'

Harry whistled. 'Wouldn't like to be there when that happened.'

'No,' Windsor replied. 'So the inventors have gone back to the drawing board, and we're expecting something to replace it soon. Anyway, enough of that. Come up onto this viewing platform and have a look around. This is the Eagle's Nest, the highest point lookout.'

He led Harry up a flight of steps on one side of the enclosure and onto a small platform. Harry marvelled at the view on all sides. The wild Bass Strait on the seaward side, on the other a calmer Port Phillip Bay with Melbourne in the distance, then to the west was the other side of the Heads, with Fort Queenscliff prominent. Finally, Harry turned and looked down the narrow line of sand hills of the Nepean peninsula, with the buildings of Sorrento clearly visible in the distance.

Close by, Harry noted the lines of buildings that constituted the Quarantine Station, running along the bay side of the peninsula, at two or so miles distant. And he also noted again the large ship, tied up at its pier.

'Looks like the quarantine mob have got a customer,' he suggested, pointing at the ship. 'Know anything about it?'

Windsor nodded. 'Yeh, we get briefed on all the arrivals there. Good to know who our neighbours are. It's German, they tell me. Smallpox outbreak.'

'Been there long?'

'About a week,' Windsor replied. 'Apparently there's a reasonable number of immigrants on board.'

As they made their way back down from the lookout platform Harry said, 'Must be a bit frustrating for the healthy ones among the crew and passengers, stuck there for weeks. I suppose some might be tempted to clear out. What security do they have there?'

Windsor eyed Harry and snorted. 'Very little, mate, I can tell you. Only four policemen stationed there, as I understand, a sergeant and three constables. And there's no proper fences or anything. If people want to nick off in the middle of the night, a few coppers aren't going to stop them. There's been quite a few runaways over the years.'

'And where do they go?' Harry enquired. 'Not this way, I wouldn't think.'

'You're right, they head to Sorrento and Rye.'

'On their way to Melbourne?'

'Mostly, off to Melbourne and then the goldfields. Though sometimes they go to ground locally. Get into the fishing business. Or lime burning. Generally speaking, the police can't be bothered chasing them down. And we don't care, as long as they're not coming in this direction. We make sure of that.'

Harry stood in thought for a moment. 'Thanks, Matt, you've been very useful,' he said. 'I'll get going. But I might make an unscheduled call at the Quarantine Station on the way back. I take it any sick passengers are well isolated?'

'Yeh, they are,' Windsor replied. 'You should be right if you just pull up at the pier. I imagine one of the coppers on duty will meet you. Part of their job's to keep away unwanted strangers.'

'Thanks,' Harry said. 'I'll do that. It might be a good opportunity to get a handle on their security arrangements too.'

Matt Windsor was right. As the police launch glided up to the Quarantine Station pier, a uniformed policeman strode purposefully out of a small adjacent hut.

Apparently, the constable was unfamiliar with the police launch, because he waved his arms about angrily and exclaimed: 'Hey mate, don't you know this is a restricted area. Bugger off.'

Harry smiled, leaping from the launch to the pier as the boat hove to. 'Well done, Constable,' he replied, waving his badge at the policeman. 'Inspector Harry Holloway of the CIB.'

The constable peered at the badge, then promptly transformed his gesticulations into a belated salute.

'I'm terribly sorry, Inspector,' he stammered. 'I wasn't expecting you.'

Harry examined the name badge on the fellow's chest. 'Don't worry, Constable Andrews, you were doing the right thing. I was on my way back from Fort Nepean, and thought I'd just pop in to speak to whoever's in charge here. Who would that be, might I ask?'

Constable Andrews considered Harry's question briefly. 'Well Inspector, Doctor Johnston is the resident doctor here. Doctor Couper Johnston. But I would suggest you speak to his wife, Mrs Johnston. She runs the administration side of things, and just about everything else too, for that matter. She'd be the one, if you're interested in anything non-medical.'

'Good,' Harry replied. 'The other person I wanted to talk to is the captain of the ship. Is he available?'

'You should be able to speak to him,' Andrews replied. 'I know he's not ill. If you could wait in there, Inspector, I'll head up and find Mrs Johnston. And the captain.'

He gestured to the hut, but Harry waved him away, indicating he would be happy to wait on the wharf. While Andrews was away, Harry wandered down the pier to where the ship was tied up. She was sizeable, close to a thousand tons in Harry's estimation. The gangplank was down, and he could hear the sound of voices on board. No doubt the ship was being scrubbed, from stern to bow.

'Excuse me, Inspector!'

Harry wheeled around to see a grey-haired, rather stout woman standing with Andrews at the head of the pier. Behind them was a short, dark fellow, with a full black beard and clad in a calico shirt and black britches.

Harry strode back towards the group. 'You must be Mrs Johnston.'

'I am she,' the lady replied sternly. 'I understand you to be Inspector Holloway. What is your business here, sir?'

'You may not be aware, Mrs Johnston, but I'm investigating a murder over at Sorrento. As part of our inquiries we are talking to a range of people and organisations around the district. Just routine, you understand.'

'Very well, Inspector, I am at your disposal.'

'I was also hoping to speak to the captain of that vessel,' Harry ventured, pointing to the ship behind them.

'Indeed, I was informed of your wish. This is he, Captain Romanov, the captain of that ship, *The Queen of Hamburg*.' And she indicated the fellow standing behind her with a dismissive gesture.

'Very good,' Harry replied. 'Thank you for meeting with me, Captain.'

Romanov said nothing, responding only with a surly nod of acknowledgement.

'I must say, it is rather warm today,' Mrs Johnston observed. 'Do excuse me, Inspector Holloway.' And she unfurled a large white parasol she was carrying and held it aloft.

'No, please excuse me, Mrs Johnston,' Harry replied. 'For calling on you unannounced and interrupting your day. You must be very busy, dealing with this latest arrival to your station. Smallpox outbreak, I'm told.'

'We certainly are busy,' Mrs Johnston replied grimly. 'Two hundred and eighty Silesian immigrants and twenty-five crew. And you are correctly informed, smallpox is rife amongst them. Poor devils, fleeing religious persecution back home and then encountering this awful situation. They must think there is no justice in the world.'

'Yes, it's very unfortunate,' Harry sympathised, then added, 'I notice that work has commenced to disinfect the ship.' And he glanced at the captain who nodded his affirmation. But Mrs Johnston had more to say.

'And not before time, Inspector. We found the conditions on board to be quite appalling. The passenger quarters were filthy in the extreme. No wonder there was an outbreak of disease.' She pursed her lips and gave a stern sideways frown at the captain.

Harry turned his attention to Captain Romanov too. 'A difficult situation for you, Captain. It'll no doubt mean your schedule will be interrupted?'

Romanov shrugged and extended his arms in a gesture of futility. 'What can I do, Inspector? I must obey the laws of your state. But it is a damn nuisance.'

'A question or two, if I may, Captain. Won't take long.'

Romanov shrugged again. 'Whatever you want, Inspector. I have nowhere to go.'

Harry smiled. 'I suppose not. Well, first up, I'm wondering if all your crew are still with you? I'm informed that it's not uncommon for sailors to jump ship in Melbourne. Perhaps to seek their fortune in the goldfields. Maybe a few have taken the opportunity to leave your crew already, from this location?'

'I believe two of my crew have gone missing,' Romanov replied off-handedly. 'I recall my purser informing me yesterday of that fact.'

'You seem quite unconcerned about it, Captain?'

Romanov shrugged. 'It happens frequently, Inspector. What can I do? As you say, the lure of your gold is strong. And your authorities do very little to pursue runaways.'

Harry ignored the captain's barb and continued. 'I'd also be interested to know whether those two blokes who've gone missing are Russian.'

Romanov eyed Harry curiously. 'How would I know that, Inspector? I do not ask my men where they come from. As long as they can speak some German and sign their name, that is enough for me.'

'Well, perhaps your purser can help with that,' Harry continued patiently. 'Surely he would notice if his men were conversing in a foreign language. It'd be useful to us to establish whether they're Russian or not. That might possibly be helpful to us in our current inquiry.'

Romanov eyed Harry intently, then shrugged again, a gesture that was beginning to annoy Harry. 'Perhaps they were Russian, Inspector. I will ask him.'

'Thank you,' Harry replied. 'And a question for you, Mrs Johnston. I assume you're responsible for the passengers in quarantine?'

'We are indeed, Inspector,' Mrs Johnston replied immediately. 'And no doubt you are about to ask whether any of them have gone missing. The answer is no, we do a head count every second day, and all the passengers are accounted for.'

'Thank you for that, Mrs Johnston, that's helpful,' Harry replied. 'I think that's enough for now. I'll send someone back in a day or two to get the answer to that question, Captain. About the nationality of the two runaways, I mean. I suppose you'll still be here?'

'They will, Inspector,' Mrs Johnston stated firmly. 'This ship won't be released until I'm satisfied the outbreak has been cleared up and all persons are no longer infectious. Otherwise we would be in severe trouble with the health authorities in Williamstown.' And she gave another stern glance at the captain.

Bidding them farewell, Harry headed back towards the police launch, accompanied by Constable Andrews. Harry quizzed him as they walked. 'I've been told, Constable, that there's been quite a few escapes from the

Quarantine Station in the past. By passengers who got tired of waiting. Or perhaps by crew who were always intending to jump ship once they got to Melbourne, anyway. Have you blokes had much experience of that?'

Andrews eyed Harry uncertainly. 'There's been a few, Inspector. But it's not really our fault, y'know. This place isn't very well secured. And we're always understaffed.'

'So, you didn't spot the two runaways that Captain Romanov was talking about?"

'We didn't, I'm afraid,' Andrews acknowledged, looking rather embarrassed.

'I'm not blaming you, mate,' Harry reassured him. 'I'm sure you do your best. But from what you say, it's obvious that if someone wanted to abscond from here, it wouldn't be too hard.'

'No, I suppose not,' came the reluctant admission.

'Good, that's all I wanted to know.' Harry patted the crestfallen constable on the shoulder, before climbing into the police launch. 'I'll see you in a couple of days then. And hopefully we'll get an answer to that question I asked the captain.'

Effie and Rachel made the short journey from the Back Beach Palace along the Ocean Beach Road to the Mechanics' Institute on foot. They were both well-protected from the midday sun, with wide-brimmed hats and parasols, but Effie still felt uncomfortably warm by the time they had completed the half-mile journey.

Lydia met them at the Institute's sandstone-fronted entrance, looking cool, elegant and quite beautiful in a flowing white skirt with puff sleeves, set off with a striking mauve hat worn at a jaunty angle.

'Hello, darlings,' Lydia exclaimed, embracing them both. 'Goodness, you both look a little pink. Let's go inside and cool down.'

They entered through the small gabled portico into the main hall of the Institute. The thick sandstone walls ensured a comfortable temperature, offering the women welcome relief from the heat of the day outside. Lydia explained that they would be Michael-less today. She had invited him to join them, but apparently he was off somewhere with James, enjoying some shared time together on one of the camp's few days off.

'Goodness me, this is quite impressive,' Effie commented, looking about. The Institute walls were adorned with canvasses, in various stages of completion, while down the centre of the hall easels had been set up, and sketches on paper pinned to them. All the works had the artist's name identified on an adjacent card. A reasonable number of attendees, mainly well-dressed matrons, were wandering around the exhibition, taking in their dose of culture. Effie guessed that the few men present were probably the artists themselves, judging by their raffish attire and studied air of ennui.

As they stood there admiring the works, they spied Jane Sutherland approaching, still clad in her plain calico smock and boots. Clearly her art took priority over any concession to fashion. She greeted Lydia as an old friend, then, turning to Effie, expressed pleasure at meeting her again and thanked her for her interest in the artists' work. Effie introduced Rachel, who was also greeted warmly.

'I'm so glad you've all come to see what our artists have achieved,' Sutherland declared. 'Let me show you around. I can perhaps provide some context to what you see.'

'Gladly, my dear,' Lydia responded. 'Very kind of you.'

And so they wandered around the hall viewing the exhibits, with Sutherland occasionally commenting on the strengths of certain artists, the extent of development of particular works, or the locations that the scenes portrayed.

There was certainly a wide variety of subjects. Some were sweeping panoramas of the Sorrento township, others were clearly views over Bass

Strait and its rocky shoreline. Others ignored the lure of the seascapes, focusing instead on capturing the shimmering beauty of the sand dunes themselves. Clearly, Jane Sutherland's artists had been roaming far and wide to capture their artistic opportunities.

One painting in particular caught Effie's attention. It was a simple morning scene of the sun rising over the dunes. It was still unfinished, but the artist's bold brushstrokes had already brilliantly captured the play of golden light and shadow on the dune undulations, contrasted with the dark green of the fringing scrub. Effie was not surprised to read the name, *James Mathieson*, inscribed neatly on the small card beside the painting.

'One of our most promising artists,' Sutherland observed, noticing Effie's interest. 'James is a rising star in this state's arts firmament.'

'We think he is too,' Effie responded, feeling a sudden swelling of pride in her friend.

'Reminds me of some early Streeton works,' Sutherland continued. 'Not surprising, James sees Arthur as one of his key influences.'

They wandered on, examining the works-in-progress. Some were promising, other less so, perhaps bound eventually to be discarded. Effie found the sketches pinned to the easels down the centre of the room to be particularly interesting. While some were entirely rudimentary, others were more developed and one could see within them the artist's vision for the finished painting.

One of the latter sketches was a dramatic view of the wild Bass Strait shoreline. In the drawing, two lonely figures were perched on a jagged rocky outcrop, their bodies standing out against a storm-stricken skyline. The artist's vision was wildly romantic, perhaps overly so, but one could not help but be impressed by the violent power of the scene and the technical quality of the pencil work.

'My goodness, that will be an impressive work,' Effie exclaimed, pointing to the drawing. 'What do you think, Rachel?'

'Oh, it's very beautiful, but also quite frightening,' Rachel replied. 'Those poor people on that rock. And it looks like a shipwreck. Aren't those pieces of debris in the water?'

'I think you're right, dear,' Lydia said, as she gazed at the sketch. 'How clever of you.'

Effie read the sketch's card: *Dimitri Petrenko*. She recognised the name.

'My goodness!' she exclaimed. 'Isn't that the fellow that James mentioned to us, Jane? You know, the one he thought had very little talent.'

Sutherland gave a half-smile. 'Now that you mention it, Effie, I do believe it is.'

'Well, this certainly belies James' opinion,' Effie observed, her brow knitting slightly in perplexity. 'I'd say Mr Petrenko has a good deal of talent, if this is an example of his work.'

'This particular work is certainly rather promising,' Sutherland responded off-handedly. 'Shall we move on?'

'Yes, let's,' Effie agreed, but she lingered, still confused. 'It's odd though, that James should consider him talentless. He is always such a good judge of artistic merit. And always generous to his colleagues.'

And she remained staring at the sketch, trying to reconcile the strength of this drawing with the opinion James had so firmly expressed.

'Oh well, we can't always agree, can we?' Sutherland suggested, rather airily. 'It would be a funny old world if we did. Now, can I offer you ladies a cup of tea? We have an urn set up, together with some delicious cakes and pastries from Sullivans bakery.'

'A splendid suggestion,' Lydia agreed. 'By the way, is it possible to meet the mysterious Mr Petrenko today? I notice that a number of your artists seem to be here.'

'I'm afraid not,' Sutherland replied abruptly. 'Mr Petrenko is a reclusive kind of fellow. He's back at the camp working on another piece.'

And she shepherded the friends towards the end of the hall where a large trestle had been set up, laden with an urn, a row of teacups and an inviting array of sweet delicacies.

☙

Harry reckoned he must be becoming a familiar sight at the Continental, judging by the now deferential air of the previously imperious doorman. Harry fancied the fellow might even have bowed slightly, together with the merest trace of a welcoming smile, before summoning another attendant to escort Harry to Mr Coppin's private dining room.

Again, Harry walked down several wide, red-carpeted corridors, before reaching the said dining room. Again, the knock on the door and the muffled invitation to enter, into what was a small but opulently furnished room, featuring a round dining setting at its centre.

George Coppin rose from his chair at the table and greeted Harry warmly. 'Thank you, Harry, for making the time to meet with us. I know you must be terribly busy dealing with this nasty business that's cropped up.'

'My pleasure, George, happy to oblige. It sounded important.' And Harry glanced briefly at Coppin's other guest, a dapper fellow, immaculately dressed, with wavy dark hair pushed back and a neatly trimmed beard. Probably in his late thirties, in Harry's estimation. He was introduced as Mr Nikolai Matyunin.

'Pleased to me you, Mr Matyunin,' Harry said, firmly shaking that gentleman's offered hand.

'Please, Inspector, call me Nikolai,' Matyunin replied. 'We are all friends here.'

'Nikolai has been appointed the Russian consul to Victoria,' Coppin explained. 'He's taking the place of Mr Von Sternberg, and before him Mr Putyata. The Russian Government views the consul's role as very important in improving relations with Australia. After some rather unfortunate misunderstandings in recent years.'

Harry smiled ruefully. 'There certainly have been.'

Matyunin eyed Harry intently. 'You know, Inspector, our two countries have much to offer each other. And already, I believe, we are beginning to seize the opportunities for mutual benefit.'

'Fair enough,' Harry responded. 'Good luck to you.'

'Now then,' Coppin declared, re-installing his portly frame into his chair. 'What'll it be first, business or pleasure? We have a rather pleasant dinner to consume, if you're peckish. Or would you rather talk first?'

'Let's get your business out of the way first, shall we?' Harry suggested. 'Then we can relax and enjoy our tucker.'

'Splendid idea,' Coppin agreed. 'In that case, I'll hand over to Nikolai here. He's more than capable of explaining his concerns.'

'Thank you, my friend,' Matyunin said, turning to Coppin and bowing his head slightly. He then turned back to Harry. 'Thank you too, for agreeing to meet me, Inspector. Or should I call you Harry? If we are to be friends.'

'If you wish.' Harry was beginning to think Matyunin a trifle overly friendly.

'Thank you, Harry. Well, as George said, it's my honour to represent my great country here in Australia. I have been here now for almost a year.'

'I see,' Harry said. 'And what does your role cover? Representing your countryfolk who've settled here, I assume.'

'In part,' Matyunin replied. 'There are approximately one thousand Russian immigrants in Victorian, and three thousand across the country. Though obviously, it is extremely difficult to deal with each individual's issues. I am only one man, after all.'

'Of course, I understand fully.'

'But you're right, I am here to assist Russian emigrants who are facing significant problems. And I also endeavour to represent the best interests of my countrymen at a general level,' Matyunin continued.

'As well as the more general interests of the Russian Government, for that matter. Principally, matters of trade and other commercial issues. As I said before, to develop opportunities of mutual benefit.'

'I see.'

'And that is really what I wish to talk to you about.' Matyunin's expression took on a slightly worried air.

'Go on.'

'Well, as you may be aware, Harry, over recent years there has been a good deal of commentary, both in your press and by certain public figures here in Australia, about the intentions of my government. More specifically, what are alleged to be hostile intentions.'

'I've heard some commentary to that effect,' Harry replied. 'But I'd hope that's pretty much over and done with.'

Matyunin smiled briefly, and leaned forward as he spoke. 'I would hope so too. But unfortunately there remains a degree of suspicion in some quarters. I can assure you though, it is all misplaced. My government has nothing but peaceful intentions. No, more than that, amicable intentions. That is in fact why they sent me, and my predecessors, to Australia, to reinforce our good will towards your country.'

Harry nodded. 'I accept what you say, Mr Matyunin. But I'm sure you understand I can't speak on behalf of our government. Or talk about matters that might be seen as national or state security.'

'Of course, Harry, of course,' Matyunin replied hastily. 'I would not expect you to. But I would raise a matter that is within your jurisdiction.'

Harry suspected he knew where the conversation was going. 'I take it you're referring to our current investigation?'

Matyunin nodded earnestly. 'Indeed I am. The tragic death of a person who, it appears, was one of my countrymen.'

Harry straightened in his chair. 'You understand, Mr Matyunin, that I'm not in a position to reveal any particulars about that case. To you, or to any other person.'

'Naturally, Harry, I understand that. But already there is a good deal of speculation and rumour about this poor fellow's death. Including that it may be connected somehow to some Russian plot, or malicious activity against the Australian people. That speculation is my concern. That is the scuttlebutt I want to prevent. It can only exacerbate any existing, residual tensions.'

Harry drew in a deep breath and considered Matyunin's words. Then he spoke deliberately. 'Look, Mr Matyunin ... Nikolai. There is not much I can do to stop people rumour-mongering. As you point out, the Russian conspiracy genie is already well and truly out of the bottle, and has been for a long time. As I said, I'm in no position to give you any guarantees about any residual tensions that might exist.

But I can give you this assurance. We in the police force will not be indulging in any speculation about this case, of the kind that concerns you. We'll maintain a completely objective and open mind, and we'll act on the evidence as it comes to hand. That is the only assurance I can give you.'

Matyunin sat back in his chair. 'Thank you, Harry, that is greatly appreciated. We must do all we can to prevent further public hysteria. For that is what it is.'

George Coppin had been sitting silently throughout this exchange, but now he turned to Harry. 'There's one other thing I would mention, Harry, in relation to what Nikolai has been saying.'

'Happy to hear it, George.'

Coppin paused a moment, considering his words carefully. 'As I mentioned to you the other evening, a group of Nikolai's countryfolk are due to arrive in Australia in the very near future. And to Sorrento initially. I'm referring to the Cossack troupe which will be performing here on Saturday evening.'

'Yes, I remember you mentioning them.'

'I have some concerns that in the current less-than-rational climate there may be some risk to those folk. Risk of violence, I mean.'

Harry looked hard at Coppin, eyebrows raised. 'Surely not, George. I mean, anything's possible, but it seems very unlikely.'

'Unlikely perhaps, but still a risk, I think. And it would be disastrous for our government's relations with Russia should such violence be perpetrated. I would ask for extra police protection to prevent such an occurrence.'

Harry paused, considering Coppin's request. 'We'll do what we can, George, but our resources are limited,' he replied, in a slightly apologetic tone. 'We're all flat out on this investigation, really. Anyway, what sort of protection did you have in mind?'

'Well, it's really the night of the performance that concerns me. The troupe will be accommodated here in the Continental during their stay, and I'm confident no harm will come to them here. As you can see, the hotel is well-staffed and well-secured. But on the night, at the Athenaeum, with a large crowd in attendance, that's when some troublemaker could cause mischief.'

'We can certainly help you on the night,' Harry replied, inwardly relieved that this was the extent of Coppin's request. 'We can get all hands on deck to keep a close eye on things. Both front of house and backstage, so that there's no chance of any skulduggery. Don't worry, Sergeant Milton and I are experienced in dealing with large crowds.'

'Excellent!' Coppin exclaimed. 'That sounds first-class. A weight off my mind.'

'No problem, happy to oblige. Now, if that's all, gentlemen, I reckon you mentioned something about dinner, George. So let's not hold that up, eh?'

'Let's not indeed,' Coppin replied enthusiastically, glancing at Matyunin, who smiled and nodded too. Coppin reached over and picked up a small brass bell from the tabletop, rang it vigorously, then nodded at the waiter who immediately appeared in the doorway. Within minutes the first of four generous courses appeared before them.

Harry tucked in with relish, it had been a long day and he suddenly realised he was famished. The conversation flowed as readily as the fine wine, and it soon became apparent that Nikolai Matyunin was no staid government bureaucrat. His knowledge of the arts, society and business affairs was as comprehensive as Coppin's, and his enjoyment of that man's company was very apparent.

Harry found himself taking a shine to the fellow, somewhat to his surprise. Also to his surprise, Harry found himself able to express an opinion on many of the various artistic topics raised by the other two. Must be Effie's civilising influence, he thought to himself, as he took another sip of wine.

Several glasses of wine later, and with a good dinner disposed of, Harry made his farewell, leaving Matyunin and Coppin to their port and cigars.

He mused about the meeting as he walked back down Ocean Beach Road to the Back Beach Palace. Was Matyunin really concerned about promoting friendly government relations? Or was there an ulterior motive for his desire to get Harry's investigation away from the possibility of a Russian conspiracy? Unlikely, Harry thought, but you never know.

One thing Harry was sure of: the man was no fool. On the contrary, Matyunin seemed a clever and well-practised diplomat, who had been sent to Victoria by his government with a specific agenda. Harry resolved to keep an open mind as to what that agenda might actually be.

Letting himself into the Palace with the key provided by Mrs Meriwether, Harry was about to head upstairs to their bedroom when Willie Milton appeared from the direction of the lounge.

'Not in bed yet, Willie? We've got a big day tomorrow.'

'I would be, boss, but I needed to catch you.'

'Why? Something up?'

'I'd say so. Looks like we might have another murder on our hands.'

6

⚜

THE POLICE TRAP JOGGED along the coastal road, heading east from Sorrento. At this early hour, the sun was still low in front of them, just peeking over the dunes, and the cool ocean breeze made for a pleasant morning. It was enough to put a man in a good mood; except that Harry and Willie had another death to deal with, and from the sound of it, a highly suspicious one.

'Tell me again, Arthur,' Harry said, 'Everything we know.'

'Not much to tell really, boss,' Constable Staples replied, peering into the rising sun as he guided the pony along the rutted track. 'One of the workers at Sullivan's lime kiln, just up the road here, found a human skull among the lime at the drawhole. Late yesterday arvo, we were told. Gave him a hell of a fright, apparently.'

'And we've secured the site? Nothing touched?'

'Not since the lime worker shovelled it out of the hole. He left it on the ground, and it's still there. The Sarge sent young Wally Morris down there to guard it. He's been there all night, poor bugger.'

'Good,' Harry said approvingly. 'Good police work.'

'This is the way,' Staples pointed out, as they came around a bend and spotted a rough track heading off to the left towards the shoreline.

He turned the pony's head, and they jolted their way down the track for a hundred yards or so before coming out at a clearing in the scrub. Harry could see that it ran up to the cliff's edge, and he assumed that beyond it was the beach below. Several large piles of limestone stood by the cliff edge, adjacent to a large brick-lined hole. Piles of brushwood were also stacked nearby.

As they entered the clearing, a tall weather-beaten fellow with wild silver locks and a flowing beard came forward to meet them.

Harry jumped from the trap and extended his hand. 'Morning to you, mate. I'm Inspector Holloway. You the manager of this kiln?'

'Yeh, Tom Wilkes,' was the reply, and he seized Harry's hand in a steely grip.

'But you're not the one who found the skull, I understand?'

'Nah. Young Sam Georgenson, one of the workers here. He was a bit shaken up last night, I can tell you. Not something you see every day.'

'Is he here now?'

'Nah. Should be here soon though. That's if he's got his bottle back. He wasn't real flash when he went home last night.'

Harry glanced around. 'Right then, while we're waiting for him, let's go have a look, shall we?'

'All right then. This way.' And Wilkes pointed to a rough path on one side of the clearing that led down the side of the cliff to the beach, some forty feet below. They stepped carefully down the steep path in single file and came out onto the beach. From here Harry had a better view of the brick-lined kiln, rising up against the cliff face. A smallish opening at its bottom was obviously the drawhole, where the burnt lime was collected. A rickety-looking, small pier ran some thirty yards or so from the beach out into the water.

A weary-looking Constable Wally Morris was leaning against the kiln wall, but he leapt to attention when he spotted Harry.

'At ease, Wally,' Harry said. 'You've done a good job here, mate.'

'Nothing to report, sir,' Morris replied. 'Quiet all night.'

Looking around, Harry immediately spotted Georgenson's grisly find. The skull sat atop a small pile of lime near the drawhole. Around it, Harry also noted a scattering of burnt bones, undoubtedly also part of the human remains. There was no other evidence that Harry could see, no burnt flesh or clothing.

Harry turned to Wilkes. 'I suppose it gets pretty hot in there, Mr Wilkes? When it's fired up?' he inquired, pointing to the kiln.

'Needs to,' was the gruff reply.

Harry walked over to the skull and, leaning over, studied it carefully. It was lying on its side, more or less intact, except for a chunk that was missing on the rear right-hand side. Harry stood upright, his expression grim.

'Any idea who this poor fellow might be?' he inquired of Wilkes. 'The obvious question is, are any of your workers missing?'

Wilkes eyed Harry hesitantly for a few seconds. 'Not sure,' he replied eventually.

'What's that mean? Either someone's missing or they're not. Do you have any workers who aren't here when they're meant to be here?' Harry was beginning to get exasperated with this fellow's curtness.

Wilkes hesitated again, then appeared to come to a decision. 'Well, Dave Simpson went missing last week. But I thought he'd just walked off the job. It happens sometimes.'

Harry looked intently at Wilkes. 'And why would you assume he'd just walked off the job? Why would he do that?'

Wilkes ran a gnarled hand through his unruly locks and again appeared to be thinking deeply. 'I don't think it was his proper name,' he volunteered eventually. 'He was foreign, not sure where from. Probably not too reliable, I reckon. He's done it before. Buggered off, I mean. For a while. Now and again.'

Harry eyed Wilkes closely. 'I'm guessing he wasn't too legal either,' he suggested. 'Someone off a boat, perhaps?'

'Maybe,' was the surly response. 'I didn't ask him for his life story.'

'Could he have been Russian? From his accent, I mean?'

'How the hell would I know?' Wilkes replied, folding his arms in a defiant pose. 'As long as he could do a good day's work, that's all I needed.'

Harry eyed the length of the brick chimney. 'If a bloke went in the top of that kiln, how long do you reckon it'd take for his skull to come out the bottom?'

'Dunno,' Wilkes replied shortly. 'Maybe a couple of days, maybe more.'

'So there's a fair bit of stuff in there when you're burning? Timber and stone. Piled up pretty high in the kiln, I mean?'

'Yeh, of course, pretty high. That's fairly obvious, aint it? Look, are you done here? Time's money, we need to start working the kiln again.'

'Not quite, mate. I need to have a word with your workman, and if I'm not mistaken, that's him coming down the path.' Harry pointed to where a fresh-faced young fellow was making his way down the path through the low brush.

Wilkes scowled at the sight of his man and barked out, 'Get over here, Sam. This copper wants to ask you a coupla questions.'

Young Georgenson approached nervously, removing his hat in deference to Harry.

'Relax, Sam,' Harry reassured him. 'The boss here's told me a bit, but you might be able to add something.'

'Yes, sir,' Georgenson replied, replacing his hat and shuffling nervously. 'If I can, sir.'

'What I really want to know is, when was the last time you saw Mr Simpson? Your workmate.'

Georgenson stood in thought a moment or two, clutching his hat. 'It would've been last Tuesday, I reckon. In the afternoon. I knocked off a bit early, and he was still here then. Cutting some timber, ready for the next day.'

'And you haven't seen him since?'

'No, sir. I wasn't here last Wednesday, y'see. I had a day off 'cause I worked through the weekend before. And Dave wasn't here on the Thursday when I come in, even though he was meant to be. I thought he'd nicked off for a few days. He's done it before.' Georgenson looked up and stared at Harry, as a realisation slowly dawned on him.

'D'you reckon that might be him?' he stammered, pointing at the skull. 'D'you reckon he fell in?'

'Maybe,' Harry replied slowly. 'That's what we need to find out. Though I can't see why he'd fall in if he was just cutting timber.'

'Are you finished yet?' Wilkes interrupted. 'Like I said, we're busy.'

'Not quite,' 'Harry replied. 'I'd be interested to know, Mr Wilkes, whether you were in last Wednesday, and whether Mr Simpson was here with you?'

Wilkes paused and examined his dirty finger nails, before looking up at Harry. 'As a matter of fact, I wasn't. Off on other business. Dave was meant to be cutting timber here all day. Now are we done?'

'Patience, my friend,' Harry replied calmly. 'I do appreciate that Mr Sullivan would want you to get the kiln going again but we're just about done.'

'It's not Mr Sullivan,' Wilkes responded abruptly. 'Mr Coppin owns this kiln now. Bought Sullivan out. And he leaves it to me to run the show. Which is what I'm trying to do. If I'm allowed to.'

Harry ignored him, but not before noting that here was yet another pie that George Coppin had a finger in. 'Wally and Arthur,' he instructed, turning to the two constables. 'I want you to carefully bag up this skull, plus any bones you can identify in this lot.' He pointed to the pile of lime ash, strewn on the ground.

'Have a poke around in that drawhole too,' he added. 'There might be more bones and stuff in there. And it might be a good idea to bag the lime on the ground here as well. You never know, we might find something else.'

'Righto, sir, we're onto it,' Morris replied.

'Willie and I'll go upstairs and have a good hunt around that clearing. It's unlikely, but there might be some useful evidence up there. Then, and only then, you can have your site back, Mr Wilkes.'

Wilkes scowled at him. 'Bugger me, how's a man meant to earn a living? You might as well knock off for the day, Sam. These blokes'll be here all day. And it looks like I might have to find a new workman.'

Leaving Morris and Staples to their task, Harry and Willie climbed the path to the top and began to carefully walk the perimeter of the clearing.

'Don't know what we're looking for, really,' Harry muttered as they poked about the low coastal scrub at the edge of the clearing. 'But best to be thorough.'

There was nothing to be found in the verge of the bush, so at Harry's suggestion, the two men systematically began walking around the entire clearing, in diminishing circles.

'Keep a close eye out for any trace of dried blood,' he instructed Willie. 'If there's been funny business here, it'd probably have been somewhere in this clearing, near the kiln mouth.'

They continued their search without any immediate success. But then Willie stopped in his tracks.

'Hang on, boss, have a look at this.' And he pointed to the ground in front of him.

Harry saw what had piqued his interest. A patch of vegetation and topsoil in front of Willie had been spaded away to a depth of an inch or so. A rudimentary attempt had been made to smooth over the scraping, but the interference to the soil was obvious.

'Hullo, hullo,' Harry exclaimed, bending over and examining the bare patch. 'That's interesting. Consistent with removing something incriminating. Like blood on the ground. Can't think of too many other reasons for scraping off that grass.'

He straightened and looked around the clearing. He pointed in the direction of the large mound of limestone rubble adjacent to the kiln mouth. An old shovel was leaning against it.

'Mate, I reckon if someone's done the dirty on someone, and then disposed of the evidence on the ground there, there's a fair chance they would have used that shovel over there. I can see it's got a steel handle. May be a chance of fingerprints. Can you take that into your custody, and I don't need to tell you to keep your mitts off the handle. Keep it with you until we can hand it over to Molly for testing. I don't want it anywhere near the local coppers either. I wouldn't trust our country cousins not to put their big paws on it. I'm not sure they have the slightest idea about fingerprinting.'

'No problem, boss,' Willie replied. 'I'm sure Mrs Meriwether has a safe spot where it can be stored for a day or two.' But he made no immediate move toward the shovel. 'Do you reckon it's our dead man's mate down there?' he said instead. 'You know, the one that barmaid was talking about.'

'I'd bet good money on it,' Harry replied, pausing for a moment in thought. 'It's too much of a coincidence, two foreign blokes called Dave going missing in the one week. And then we find a skull here, where one of the Daves was working.'

'Murdered, you reckon?'

'Dunno. Though I find it hard to imagine how he could have fallen in. And I'm very interested in the missing piece at the back of that skull down there. Anyway, Molly will have something to say on that, I'd wager.'

Effie, Rachel and Lydia were ensconced in the Rustic Retreat, the small tearoom at the head of the sea baths pier.

Lydia had cajoled the other two into visiting the sea baths. It would be a tremendously therapeutic experience, she had assured them, though Effie and Rachel were less certain of the health benefits of immersing oneself in the ocean. Rachel, in particular, was decidedly nervous, but some gentle encouragement from Willie and a promise from Effie that she would remain by her side, had combined to persuade her to take the plunge.

But when they arrived at the change rooms, it seemed they had got their times wrong. Apparently, the gentlemen's session was still underway, with the red flag in place at the front of the building, to indicate 'men only'.

The rather stern-looking proprietor, Mr Erlandsen, explained to a slightly peeved Lydia that it would be at least a full half hour before the gentlemen would be finished and the ladies' white flag erected.

And so a retreat to the Retreat was undertaken, not an unwelcome move in the now stifling afternoon heat. Inevitably the conversation turned to the subject dominating Sorrento gossip.

'I must say, the town is full of rumour and wild theories about that dead Russian fellow,' Lydia said. 'Most of it centred around spies and all sorts of other Russian machinations.'

'Harry's worried about that too,' Effie confided. 'He's afraid all the rumours could get out of hand.'

'It's already out of hand, if you ask me,' Lydia exclaimed. 'All this nonsense about a Russian invasion. Ed thinks it's a load of codswallop, and I wholeheartedly agree.'

Effie leaned across the table confidentially. 'Harry said that Mr Matyunin, the Russian consul, is worried about the direction things are taking. And Mr Coppin too, I believe.'

'Yes, poor George is worried about his Cossack show on Saturday. That there may be trouble there. Though there is an upside for him. All this rumour will ensure a full house.'

Rachel reached over and touched Lydia's sleeve. 'I think that lady's waving at us,' she said, pointing towards the door, where a woman could be seen waving her hand to attract their attention.

'Oh, it's Mrs Erlandsen,' Lydia observed. 'The other half of the baths management.'

Like her husband, Mrs Erlandsen was obviously of Nordic extraction. Tall and lithe, with grey-blonde hair swept back into a tight bun, she was the very epitome of the good health that her establishment promoted.

And, as if to emphasise the health benefits of the sea baths, Greta Erlandsen was dressed in what appeared to be a nurse's uniform, complete with cap perched on top of her immaculate coiffure.

Lydia waved back, and Mrs Erlandsen made her way across the room to them. 'Ah, Mrs Brown, so good to see you again. And how is Doctor Brown? Well, I trust. He is not with you today?'

'Sadly no, the poor dear is not a great fan of taking the waters,' Lydia smiled back. 'He's at home, ensconced in a book.'

Mrs Erlandsen's handsome features creased in a smile too. 'Ah yes, the good doctor prefers his own company. But you, my dear Mrs Brown, you understand the therapeutic benefits of our baths, yes?'

Lydia chuckled. 'Well, it's certainly a good way to keep cool in this heat. I know that at least. But let me introduce my two friends. This is Mrs Milton and Mrs Holloway.'

'Ah, you must be the wife of Inspector Holloway,' Mrs Erlandsen exclaimed. 'We are so fortunate to have such a renowned man in our midst to solve this terrible murder.'

'Oh, I don't know about that,' Effie responded, a little embarrassed, but proud at the same time. 'But hopefully, he can find the culprit soon.'

'Such a terrible thing for the town,' Mrs Erlandsen added. 'Coming on top of that dreadful business last year. It has been most difficult for us all.'

'Oh, what business was that?' Effie asked.

'Why, the *Sierra Nevada* of course. With all that loss of life. So tragic.'

'Oh yes, that's right. Lydia mentioned it the other day. Over near the Heads.'

'That is correct. The sea can be such a dangerous place at times, can it not? But not, I am pleased to say, where our sea baths are concerned. Here the sea is always a welcoming friend. Which is why I am here, ladies, to welcome you all as distinguished guests to our establishment, and to personally attend to you in the baths.'

'That is most kind of you,' Lydia responded. 'I take it that the white flag is now up?'

'That's right, follow me, ladies, if you please, to the dressing rooms.' And Mrs Erlandsen turned and strode from the room, with the three friends in pursuit.

'What does she mean by *attend to*?' Effie whispered to Lydia as they hurried out, past the small booth that served as a ticket office for the ferry, and along the narrow timber jetty leading to the baths.

'You'll see,' Lydia responded, grinning. 'An essential part of the experience.'

Mrs Erlandsen ushered the three women into the dressing shed, but not before providing Effie and Rachel with voluminous, white calico bathing dresses and lace-up, canvas shoes. Lydia had brought her own, it transpired, a smart two-piece tunic, in a red and blue design with white braiding.

All three appeared in due course at the sea bath steps, and were shepherded into the water by Mrs Erlandsen, who had also changed into a smart white tunic which, Effie suspected, displayed more of her shapely athletic legs than was strictly appropriate.

Both Effie and Rachel entered the waist-deep water with some degree of caution. But not so Lydia, who immediately submerged herself to the neck and began to swim the twenty yards or so to the picketed edge of the enclosure with effortless elegance.

'Come on, girls, last one in's a rotten egg,' she cried, and splashed some water in their direction.

Effie and Rachel continued to look on doubtfully, so Mrs Erlandsen intervened. 'Ah, Mrs Brown, she is the expert, as you can see. Perhaps you cannot emulate her, but you know, it is important that the body receives the full restorative effect of the sea water. So, allow me.'

And without further ado, she waded up to Effie and Rachel, seized each firmly by the shoulders, and immediately dunked each of them in turn, up to the neck in the water. Effie gasped at the sudden cold impact, but bravely stayed down, and very soon began to feel a comforting cooling tingle over her whole body.

'Gosh, this is actually rather pleasant,' she confessed. 'Now that I'm under. And you're right, Mrs Erlandsen, the cooling effect is very welcome.'

She looked across at Rachel, who also remained immersed, and who looked similarly pleased. She and Rachel even managed a splash or two, in imitation of Lydia, though it wasn't long before the pleasant cooling effect turned to a slightly chilling one.

Lydia, noticing their growing discomfort, suggested they call it a day. 'First time in for you both,' she said. 'Best not to overdo it.'

With Mrs Erlandsen closely supervising, they climbed back up the wooden steps and returned to the dressing shed.

'Well, that was certainly a different experience,' Effie commented as, fully dressed again, they walked down the small pier towards the Esplanade.

'And what about you, Rachel dear?' Lydia asked. 'Did you enjoy it too?'

Rachel smiled shyly. 'Yes, it was nice. Once I got used to it.'

Effie looked at her. Whether it was the effect of the cooling dip, or the warm summer sun, Rachel's already pretty features were suffused with a glow in the late afternoon light.

She's such a lovely girl, Effie thought to herself, and she affectionately slipped her arm through Rachel's. At Rachel's other side, Lydia did the same, and the three friends strolled, arm-in-arm, up the Esplanade towards the Back Beach Road and the Palace, where a promised cup of tea and refreshments were awaiting them.

☙

Harry Holloway and Willie Milton sat alone, on opposite sides of the table in the cramped interview room of the Sorrento police station. Harry was staring reflectively into space, while Willie was fixing his boss with a contemplative eye.

'What do you reckon?' Willie inquired eventually. 'What's our next move?'

'Not sure, mate,' Harry replied, a little gloomily. 'Apart from organising Molly to have a look at the burnt remains, that is. You've done that, haven't you?'

'Yep. He's here first thing in the morning.'

Harry nodded and resumed his thinking. He was feeling a little despondent and frustrated. Firstly, because he was missing out on the vacation he had been pleasantly anticipating for quite some time. He knew Effie would make the most of things without him, but he felt guilty nevertheless about letting her down.

And to make matters worse, this case was becoming increasingly complex and difficult. When the first body was discovered, he had expected it would all be resolved speedily, which of course it wasn't. And now there was this other death, highly suspicious, possibly another Russian. So soon after the first, it must be more than coincidence. In Harry's mind it pointed clearly to a level of premeditation and planning associated with some sort of criminal activity. But as to the nature of that criminal activity, Harry had no leads.

One possibility he had considered was some sort of xenophobic reaction against all things Russian, and that the two Russian men were the innocent victims of racist aggression. But, on reflection, that seemed highly unlikely, even given the current level of community paranoia about hostile Russian intentions.

Another speculative theory was that these two dead Russians were in fact part of a plot against the Victorian state. That was clearly where Winston Marks was already heading, but Harry thought that was similarly unlikely.

If such a scenario was correct, why were the two men killed? Perhaps because they were about to spill the beans and inform the authorities? But inform them about what? There was no evidence that any hostile Russian activity was afoot, in Melbourne or anywhere else.

No, it all seemed quite improbable. The explanation must lie elsewhere, and Harry and his team must keep methodically pushing forward until the explanation, supported by the evidence, became clear.

All very well, thought Harry, but he wasn't quite sure what pushing forward entailed, and in what direction he should extend their inquiries. At the moment, all he had to go on with his two dead bodies were the Russian connection, a possible connection to the Sorrento fishing trade, and a possible lime kiln connection. And that was a very broad basis for extending their inquiries.

Harry's brooding was suddenly interrupted by a loud rapping on the station's front door. Harry looked across at Willie.

'Blimey! Who's that?'

'I'll see,' Willie said, springing to his feet and heading out of the room. He returned within seconds, closely followed by a man in uniform. Harry immediately recognised the khaki and red colours of the Victorian Artillery.

'Private Lyons reporting, sir!' the fresh-faced young soldier barked out, standing to attention and saluting. 'With an urgent message from Lieutenant Windsor, sir!'

'No need to stand on ceremony, Private,' Harry replied. 'What's the news?'

In response, the private delved into his pocket and retrieved an envelope, which he handed to Harry. Harry ripped it open and read.

Harry
We've sighted an unidentified ship at the Heads and I have reported it to
my superiors. They are attending immediately. Would appreciate you getting
here too as soon as possible to assist, given current Russian concerns.
Matt

Harry had no trouble reading between the lines. 'Superiors' meant Colonel Jackson, and 'Colonel Jackson attending' meant Chief Inspector Winston Marks also attending. That volatile combination meant the distinct possibility of the situation getting out of hand. Matt Windsor was obviously looking for some support to manage the situation down a sensible path.

'Come on, Willie,' he said. 'We're needed at the Fort. You've got a boat, Lyons?'

'I do, sir. Tied up at the pier.'

'Good. Then let's go.'

Private Lyons escorted Harry and Willie the short distance to the pier where the squadron's gunboat, the *SS Mars*, was moored. In no time at all they were tying up at the Fort Nepean jetty.

Lyons led the way at a rapid pace up the stone steps, through a number of underground passages and out onto the main observation area, the large quadrangle with its ramparts and gun turrets pointing towards the Heads. Harry noticed that a number of these guns were now manned.

In the centre of the space stood Matthew Windsor, Winston Marks and Commander Jackson, the latter looking through a telescope he was holding to his eye. Harry followed the direction of the commander's gaze and immediately spotted what appeared to be quite a large vessel in the distance, making its way through the mouth of the Heads.

'Holloway! What are you doing here?' Marks exclaimed.

Harry performed some rapid mental gymnastics but could think of no convincing reason for his presence. He wasn't about to tell his superior that Matt Windsor wanted him there as the voice of reason.

Eventually, he replied, rather lamely: 'I heard a foreign ship has been sighted, sir. I thought it might have something to do with our murder inquiry.'

Marks stared hard at him, but then, to Harry's surprise, said, 'Well done, Holloway, you might actually be right. From what we can make out, it's Russian, and it's got no damn business being here. This might be what that dead spy of yours was plotting.'

'It's certainly flying the Russian flag,' Jackson observed, lowering his telescope. 'And I reckon that's Russian lettering on the bow. What do you say, Windsor?' And he handed over the telescope to the lieutenant.

Windsor looked in turn, and replied: 'Well, you're right, sir, it certainly is flying the Russian flag, but I can't make out the name on the bow.'

'Could it be a naval vessel, Windsor?' Jackson asked.

'Possibly. About two-fifty feet, I'd reckon, triple-masted, steam-powered. Can't see any guns, but they might be concealed if it's a naval vessel.'

'And you're quite sure there's no Russian vessel on the shipping register that's due for disembarkation?' Jackson continued.

'Quite sure, sir. I've checked. We keep an up-to-date list of ships that are due to dock in Melbourne. No Russians due now, nor in the immediate future.'

Jackson stared out to sea. 'Well, in that case, we must assume it has hostile intent.'

'Well, not necessarily, sir. We do have occasional unforeseen arrivals. Due to emergencies or administrative errors, and so forth.'

'Hang on, Charles,' Marks exclaimed. 'We can't afford to let a Russian invader through our defences, just on the off-chance there's been a bureaucratic stuff-up!'

'Wait, sir,' Harry interposed. 'Even if it is Russian, how do we know it's hostile? I mean, think about it. Why would they be flying the Russian flag if they were going to attack? They'd be flying a false flag, surely?'

Jackson turned to Harry for a moment or two, considering this point. 'That might be a logical assumption, Inspector,' he responded. 'But you may not appreciate that military affairs are not always governed by logic. The Russians are a damned arrogant lot, they might think they can waltz into our port without bothering to conceal themselves. A shot across their bow will test their intentions. And it might send them a salutary message into the bargain.'

Lieutenant Windsor gave Harry an alarmed glance, then spoke up. 'May I offer an alternative suggestion, sir?' he proposed. 'The gunboat is moored and ready to go. I can very quickly get an armed crew aboard and intercept them before they get past South Channel Fort. And if it turns out they do have aggressive intent, we can deploy our guns from there.'

Jackson eyed him doubtfully. 'I don't know, Lieutenant. That may well endanger you and your crew.'

'I don't think so, sir. I'm sure we have the speed to evade them, if necessary. But we must do our best to avoid an international incident.'

'And we must do our best to avoid Melbourne being put under attack,' Jackson rejoined, somewhat sourly. 'But I suppose it can do no harm. As long as you intercept them before they clear our defences.'

'Absolutely, sir. Do you wish to be on board too, sir?'

Jackson hesitated briefly. 'No, I don't think so. I'll stay here, to take command of the situation once I get your signal. Now, Windsor, get your crew together and out onto the water. Quickly now, there's not a moment to lose!'

Harry stood with Commander Jackson and Chief Inspector Marks and watched the gunboat ploughing through the waves toward the Russian ship. Windsor was making excellent time and Harry assessed that he would come alongside the Russian ship well before it got anywhere near the South Channel Fort, lying some two or so miles offshore to their right.

Harry could see that the Russian ship appeared to be making no attempt to avoid the gunboat. In fact, after passing through the Heads, they were now steering hard to starboard, entering the South Channel which would take them quite close to the watchers at Fort Nepean.

'Damned odd,' muttered Jackson, peering through his telescope. 'They're not taking evasive action. What's their game, I wonder?'

Harry had been provided with a telescope too, and he now got an increasingly clear view of the ship as it approached adjacent to them. He could see no sign of any activity on the deck, except for a few seamen leaning over the side and waving at the approaching gunboat.

'Steady, Windsor, steady,' Jackson cautioned, as the gunboat drew alongside the ship. 'It may be a trap.'

Suddenly they could see a burst of activity on the ship's deck, and a large number of men appeared, dressed in red, white and blue uniforms. They lined up in formation on the deck, in full view of the gunboat.

'My god!' Marks cried. 'You're right, Charles, it is a trap!'

But then Harry observed something very odd indeed. The men were joined by a number of young women, also dressed in red, white and blue outfits, and who began to whirl and pirouette around the deck. At the same time, their male companions also broke into vigorous dancing, jumping up and down on the spot while waving to the men on the gunboat.

'What's going on?' Jackson exclaimed. 'Who are those people?'

Harry suddenly realised what was happening. 'It's the Cossacks!' he cried. 'It's George Coppin's Cossacks! They're putting on a welcome for Matt and his crew.'

'Well, I'll be damned,' Jackson exclaimed, putting down his telescope. 'George Coppin's dancers! What idiot forgot to notify us about them?'

And what idiots almost blew them out of the water, Harry thought. At the same time, he gave thanks for Matt Windsor and his cautious, commonsense approach. He had quite possibly averted a nasty international incident. Not to mention putting an abrupt and premature end to George Coppin's Cossack show.

Harry picked up his telescope again and observed the scene out on the water. Matt Windsor was still alongside the Russian ship, now waving enthusiastically to the pretty girls leaning over the side, who in turn seemed to be blowing kisses in his direction. Harry smiled to himself, and inwardly congratulated the lieutenant on his efforts to promote friendly Russian–Australian relations.

7

.⸎⸎.

MID-MORNING IN SORRENTO, the sun already with a real bite, and the interview room at the Sorrento police station was certainly not the ideal location in which to stay cool. In fact, it was stifling, with Harry, Willie Milton, Sergeant Newgate and the pathologist, Dr Crawford Mollison, all crammed in together, and the morning sun pouring through the eastern window.

They were gathered around a table in the centre of the room, upon which were the skull and a pile of bones, carefully extracted from the lime kiln. On another small table in the corner was the shovel seized from the kiln site, its steel handle jutting over the table edge to ensure that any fingerprints were not contaminated.

Harry stood morosely, surveying the skull and bones spread out on the table in front of him. The oppressive warmth was not helping his frustration at the investigation's lack of progress.

Mollison however was in his usual jovial form. 'I hear there was a bit of a scare yesterday, Harry,' he chuckled. 'Almost blew George Coppin's dancers out of the water.'

Harry gave a wry smile. 'Yeh, bit of an administrative stuff-up, I'm afraid. Someone forgot to tell the garrison that a Russian ship was due.

Fortunately, we managed to sort it out before any damage was done.'

'All the talk in the bar at the Continental last night, I can tell you.'

Again Harry smiled. 'I'll bet it was. Gee, word gets around fast in this town, doesn't it? Still, no harm done, hopefully. Now, back to business, Molly. What do you make of this lot?'

Mollison turned his attention to the pile of bones. 'Well barbecued, wasn't he? Hasn't left much for us to work on.'

'I suspected as much,' Harry said. 'But you reckon it's a 'he', not a 'she'?'

'Undoubtedly. We have two femurs here in this pile, as you can see. And they're clearly of male origin. The femoral head shape here is quite rounded, as you will note. If it were female it'd be much flatter. And without going into too much technical detail, the trochanter shape and size is consistent with the masculine norm.'

'All over my head,' Harry replied. 'But I'll take your word for it. And it fits with our current thinking about who this pile of bones belongs to. We suspect it's probably the worker at the kiln, a bloke called Simpson, who's now gone missing.'

'Well, that's for you to work out, Harry, I suppose. I can't help you any further with who he was, but perhaps I can with what happened to him.'

'That's the ticket, Molly. I hope you're referring to that missing bit on the back of the skull?'

'Spot on, Harry. No reason for it to be missing, except as a result of a heavy blow to the back of the head.'

'Are you sure, doc?' Newgate asked. 'Maybe it was an accident. Tripped and fell into the kiln.'

Mollison smiled and shook his head. 'I don't think so, Sergeant. For a start to hit his head in that manner, he would need to have overbalanced backwards into the kiln. And even then, there would be nothing in the kiln to cause that sort of serious fracture. The contents were soft stone rubble and light timber brush, I'm led to believe.'

'That's right,' Harry said. 'And we also found evidence to suggest that there may have been an attempt to hide the location of the attack. There's a patch near the kiln that seems to have been cleared of grass and topsoil. Which is why we grabbed that shovel over there from the site for fingerprinting.'

'Aha, so that's why it's here,' Mollison grinned. 'I was thinking perhaps Sergeant Newgate had been doing a spot of gardening.' And he reached out for the shovel, taking care to hold it by the wooden shaft.

'No one's touched this handle since it was seized, I take it?' he inquired, looking around the room.

'Absolutely not,' Willie responded. 'I can vouch for that.'

'Good work, Sergeant.' Mollison examined the steel handle and blade carefully. 'It's possible we might find a print on that handle. Of course, we would need to discount anyone who might have used it since the incident.'

'That would only be Sam Georgenson, the other worker at the kiln,' Harry explained. 'He probably handled it quite a bit in the days after Simpson went missing. May have wiped out the possibility of any other prints being found. But I'll get Willie here to take Sam's prints and provide them to you. You never know.'

'Indeed,' Mollison agreed. 'We can but try. This fingerprinting is the way of the future, you know. We're limited now because we don't have many prints on file to compare with, but that will change over time. And it can provide compelling evidence in the event you do find a suspect.'

'I'm afraid finding a suspect might be a bit challenging,' Harry observed ruefully. 'We've got precious little to go on. Either with this bloke or the other one. We need to get a bit lucky, I reckon.'

Mollison gave Harry an encouraging pat on the shoulder. 'Luck won't come into it, my friend. With your deductive skills and my scientific support, I'm sure we'll get to the bottom of it.'

Harry smiled, realising how much he appreciated Mollison's boundless confidence. 'Thanks, Molly. I hope you're right.'

Effie and Rachel strolled down Ocean Beach Road toward the front beach. Alfie trotted along happily at their side, one hand in Effie's, the other with a resolute grip on his bucket and spade. Baby Daisy had been left at the boarding house, in the vigilant care of Grandma Holloway.

They reached the Esplanade and turned left towards the pier. The beach in front of them was at its widest, a broad stretch of bleached white sand, and crowded with beachgoers on this warm afternoon. All were well protected from the sun, with parasols abounding for the ladies and many of the men sporting white straw boaters. The air was filled with the cries of excited children, dashing to and fro, splashing in the shallows, or, as Alfie intended, engaged in the construction of sandcastles.

Effie and Rachel made their way through the throng to a small patch of vacant sand where, with Alfie's approval, they spread their rug and arranged themselves close to the water's edge. Alfie immediately began to put his spade and bucket to good use.

'Would you like to go in the water, darling?' Effie suggested, pointing to the shallows where numerous youngsters were happily splashing. 'It'll be nice and cool.'

Alfie eyed his mother suspiciously, shook his head firmly, and resumed his excavations.

'Oh well, maybe he'll have a splash once he tires of his sandcastles,' Effie said. 'We should take off our shoes and have a wade too.'

'I suppose it would be nice,' Rachel replied, a little hesitantly. 'But it's lovely here too. Just being near the water seems to make you feel cooler.'

'It is rather pleasant,' Effie agreed. Glancing around the crowded beach, her attention was immediately drawn to a group of around twenty young men and women, cavorting in the shallows directly in front of them.

They all seemed incredibly lithe and athletic, the young men in particular leaping about, some performing cartwheels and other gymnastic manoeuvres, much to the delight of their female companions. Their loud chatter as they skipped about, was clearly in some foreign tongue.

'I wonder who those people are over there,' she murmured to Rachel. 'Don't they look incredibly fit?'

Rachel followed her gaze. 'They do. Like circus performers.'

The two women continued to watch the carefree cavorting before Effie had a sudden thought. 'I know who they are. George Coppin's Cossack dancers! The ones who were on the ship yesterday.'

'Oh yes, perhaps it is.'

'The poor things, what a welcome to Melbourne. Fancy! Almost getting shot at.' Effie eyed the group again and came to a decision. 'You know, Rachel, I think we should apologise to them. Extend the hand of friendship and show them that we Australians really are a friendly and welcoming people.'

'Do you think so?' Rachel replied doubtfully. 'They won't be able to understand us though, will they?'

'Nonsense!' Effie retorted. 'The language of friendship knows no borders. A smile is universal. You stay here with Alfie, I'll go talk to them.' And she stood and made her way to the water's edge.

'Hello!' she cried waving pleasantly to the first young man she came across.

The man stopped in his tracks, and recognising her friendly intent, smiled and waved back.

'Russian?' she queried. 'Are you Russian?'

The young man looked puzzled for a moment before the penny dropped. 'Russkiy!' he replied cheerfully. 'Da, Russkiy.'

'Do you speak English?' Effie pursued. 'English?' And she spread her hands in a quizzical gesture.

The young fellow seemed to get her gist again because he raised his hands in front of him and exclaimed, 'Nyet! Ne Angliysky.' Then he turned and pointed to one of his female companions, a dark-haired young beauty standing nearby, and added, 'Da, da. Angliysky.'

Effie, delighted that their conversation appeared to be traversing national boundaries, pointed to the young woman and asked, 'You're saying she speaks English?'

'Da. Da. Angliysky.'

'Wonderful!' Effie beamed, approaching the young lady in question. 'Hello. Do you speak English?'

The young woman, petite, slim and startlingly beautiful, smiled back at Effie from beneath a large straw hat. 'Yes, speak English a little.'

'Lovely,' Effie replied. 'I just want to say welcome to Melbourne. We are very happy to see you.'

The young lady smiled back. 'Yes, we are happy here. Very happy.'

Effie pushed on. 'And I want to say how sorry we are for what happened yesterday.' Noticing the girl's now puzzled expression, Effie added, 'At the boat. Very sorry.'

The puzzled expression remained. 'No, we are happy. Happy at boat. Very nice welcome by your boat. We are very proud to be here.'

Suddenly realising that the Russians must be in blissful ignorance of the true mission of the gunboat, Effie did a rapid about-face. 'Of course. It is a great honour to have you here. Welcome to Sorrento. And to Victoria.'

Again, the young lady beamed with delight, emphasising her happiness with a small bow, a gesture which Effie found quite charming. The two continued to stand, smiling at each other, before Effie added, feeling a touch awkward, 'Well, I'll say goodbye then. I hope to see you again at your performance. My name is Effie, by the way.'

'Yes, I look forward to see you ... Effie. My name is Natalya.' And with a final smile, the young lady turned to rejoin her companions.

Effie walked back to Rachel and Alfie, but not before making a mental note to mention her meeting with the young woman to Harry. In particular, the rather odd coincidence of the Russian name Natalya cropping up twice in the one week. I wonder how common that name is in Russia, she pondered.

❦

Harry had been informed that George Coppin made a regular habit of holding court in the saloon bar of the Continental in the late afternoon, pontificating on matters theatrical to anyone prepared to listen. So Harry was taking the chance to encounter the great man, and to pull him aside to discuss some important matters.

While decidedly less formal than Harry's previous experience of the hotel, the saloon bar was still clearly the domain of the more exclusive residents of Sorrento. And among them Harry spied Coppin, perched on a bar stool, a large cocktail at hand, engaged in animated conversation with two well-dressed fellows. Harry immediately recognised Nikolai Matyunin, the Russian consul, who was looking as dapper as ever. The other man was unknown to him.

Spotting Harry, Coppin waved for him to join them, then introduced him to his companions. 'You know Nikolai here, of course, Harry, but let me introduce Archie to you as well. Archie Smythe, he manages the Wellness Clinic here at the Continental. Another of my innovations, if I may be so vain as to mention it.'

Harry shook hands with both men and inquired of Smythe exactly what the Wellness Clinic entailed.

'Certainly, Inspector, allow me to enlighten you. We provide a superior service to our clients, enhancing the already beneficial health effects of Sorrento's wonderful sea air. And it's healing salt water. You may well have heard of our internationally renowned, heated salt water baths, set up right here in the hotel.'

'Can't say I have, actually,' Harry confessed, beginning to regret his initial polite question, and fearing much more was to come. It was.

'Oh yes, the medical benefits are well established. The warmed salt water, pumped fresh from the sea and containing, as it does, all the other natural healing elements of the ocean, is demonstrably beneficial for sufferers of gout and rheumatism. And for a range of other maladies as well. It is just the thing for those patients of a more advanced age, who may not have the fortitude to withstand a plunge in Mr Erlandsen's sea baths. Perhaps not so much for a gentleman of your obvious vitality and health, Inspector.'

'Perhaps not,' Harry replied, one eyebrow arching upward.

'But if you have relatives or friends who you feel may benefit from our service, I can thoroughly recommend it.'

'Didn't you say the other day that your parents are holidaying here with you?' Coppin asked.

'Well yes, but I'm not sure ...'

'Splendid, Inspector,' Smythe interrupted. 'Please issue an invitation for your parents to attend our clinic. Absolutely gratis, I might add. They will be our honoured guests.'

'Well, I'll raise it with them,' Harry replied. 'Though I'm not sure ...'

'That's settled then,' Smythe insisted. 'I shall look forward to Mr and Mrs Holloway's presence within the next day or two.'

'Good show,' Coppin exclaimed. 'Now, Harry, I know you're a busy man. You're not here, like the rest of us, to enjoy the convivial pleasures of the Continental. How can we help you?'

'I was hoping to have a private chat with you, George. Though before that, I should take the opportunity, while Nikolai is here, to convey my apologies for what happened yesterday. Out in the bay. A regrettable mistake.'

Matyunin reached over and patted Harry's arm. 'Think no more about it, Harry. These administrative mistakes occur from time to time. And from what my sources tell me, you were not the man issuing the orders to intercept my country's ship. In fact, I am sure you would have been a moderating influence on that decision.'

Harry noted that Matyunin seemed to be very well informed about what had gone on at the garrison. He wondered how much of the consul's understanding was factual and how much was supposition.

'In any event, Harry, apparently my countrymen remain unaware, and therefore unconcerned, about the true nature of events on the water yesterday. And thus they will remain, in blissful ignorance. We do not wish to disturb their artistic equilibrium before the big show on Saturday.' And he winked conspiratorially at Harry.

With that, Matyunin bade Harry farewell, and taking Smythe by the arm, escorted him off to a far part of the bar, leaving Harry alone with Coppin.

'A decent fellow, Nikolai,' Coppin commented, watching the consul depart. 'And a great help to me, I might add, in organising this Cossack show.'

'And a great help to all of us,' Harry added. 'In dealing with that stuff-up yesterday. Could have been very embarrassing.'

'We certainly have some over-enthusiastic firebrands among our leaders,' Coppin said. 'Personally, I can't see what this panic about the Russians is all about. It's part of my reason for bringing the Cossacks out here, actually. To show people they're friendly folk, just like us.'

'Good on you, George,' Harry said, at the same time leaning over the bar to attract the bartender's attention. 'I fancy a beer after a tough day. Can I get you another of those concoctions?'

'Why not? Thank you, old chap. Now, what is it you want to talk to me about? The security arrangements for the show, I hope. Very important.'

'Don't worry about that,' Harry replied, as he ordered their drinks. 'As I said, we'll make sure we have our people watching at the doors, and in the theatre. All under control. No, actually I wanted to talk with you about the incident at your lime kiln. The one you bought from Sullivan.'

'Oh really?' Coppin paused in the act of downing the last of his cocktail. 'What's happened out there?' he asked, surprise in his voice.

'Haven't you heard?' Harry was equally surprised.

'No. What are you talking about?'

'Human remains were found at the bottom of the kiln. By your worker over there. Young Sam Georgenson.'

Coppin's ruddy features blanched noticeably and he gaped at Harry. 'Good god! What happened? Was there a dreadful accident?'

'I'm afraid it looks like murder. We found a human skull with the back of it caved in. We think it might be the other worker there, the one they call Dave. Though we think his real name might be something else. Russian extraction, perhaps.'

George Coppin briefly surveyed the floor, before looking directly at Harry, his expression distraught. 'I'm sorry, Harry, this is a terrible shock. You know I'd like to help you with your inquiries, but I'm afraid I can't. I don't have much at all to do with that kiln business. I rely entirely on that Wilkes fellow to keep the show going. I don't even know any of the workers, apart from him, as a matter of fact.'

'Understandable, George,' Harry reassured him. 'I know you're a very busy man, with all your theatrical activities.'

'Not just that, Harry,' Coppin replied, still looking rather shaken. 'I've got a number of other business ventures to deal with. Real estate, the steam train, and so on. It all takes up my time. As it turns out, the lime kiln investment was a bad idea. Very poor returns so far.'

Harry nodded. 'I've heard things aren't going that well for the kilns around this area. Running out of limestone, apparently, and prices not too good either.'

'That's true, and there's a couple of other factors as well,' Coppin replied. 'The building industry's been in decline these past few years, and they're opening up kiln production over Lara way, in direct competition to us. But I'm no fool, Harry, I took all that into account with the price I offered the Sullivans. Thought I'd got a bargain. But even so, the production has been way down on my discounted expectations. Very disappointing. Maybe I've spread myself a bit thin with that investment.'

Maybe you have, Harry thought. But he couldn't help but admire George Coppin, a man pushing eighty years of age but still full of enterprise and enthusiasm for life. He was about to offer some further consoling words to Coppin but was distracted by the sight of Constable Wally Morris appearing at the bar door and hurrying toward them.

'Excuse me, George,' Harry said, getting to his feet. 'I'd say this is police business heading my way.'

'Glad I caught you, Inspector,' Morris said, a little breathlessly, as he and Harry drew aside, out of Coppin's earshot.

'What's happened, Wally?' Harry asked, hoping that this might be news of a breakthrough in the case. 'Has someone come forward about our dead Russians?'

'No such luck, sir. No, this is a separate matter. There's a gentleman at the station, needs to see you urgently. Says it can't wait.'

'Who is it, Wally? And what's it about?'

'A Mr Simon Kozminsky. Says he's a jeweller from Melbourne. And he wants to report a jewel theft. A major jewel theft. Over at the Quarantine Station, sir. The Sarge told me to go get you, and Sergeant Milton said I might find you here.'

❦

Harry was well aware of who Simon Kozminsky was. With his brother, Isadore, he owned the most successful jewellery business in Melbourne, famed for the range of rare imported jewellery and *objets d'art* it offered its rich clientele. So he assumed that the theft being reported was likely to be significant indeed.

His expectation was heightened when he entered the police station to find a slight, dapperly dressed gentleman with an elegantly waxed moustache and neat beard. He was pacing the room in a state of high agitation. Clive Newgate was there too, leaning back in his chair at his desk, looking far more relaxed. He rose as Harry entered the room.

'This is Mr Kozminsky, boss. Reckons he's lost a shipment of jewels off that boat over at the Quarantine Station.'

'Not lost, Inspector. Stolen!' Kozminsky exclaimed, hurrying forward to shake Harry's hand. 'It is a disaster!'

'Now, Mr Kozminsky, first things first,' Harry said. 'Let's go back to the beginning.' And he indicated a chair for Kozminsky to take. But Kozminsky declined and continued his flustered pacing.

'This is the most precious jewellery we have ever imported, Inspector. A very rare collection of German art nouveau pieces. Of the Jugendstil style. Irreplaceable.'

'And I assume they were being carried on *The Queen of Hamburg*? The ship currently in quarantine?'

'That is correct, Inspector. The shipment was overdue, then I was informed the vessel was being quarantined. I began to be concerned about the security of my jewels, and no-one could, or would, give me any assurances that they were safe.

So I journeyed down in person to the Quarantine Station this afternoon, to satisfy myself. The captain assured me that the cargo was being guarded, but I insisted that he check my shipment. And that's when they were found to be missing. Gone! All of them, stolen!'

Blimey, Harry thought, this is the last thing I need. A bloody jewel theft on top of these murders. But he didn't let his frustration show.

'Before we talk more detail on your jewels, Mr Kozminsky, can I ask whether they were insured?'

'Yes, of course, Inspector. Do you take me for a fool? They were fully insured. We use Lloyds of London exclusively. But that is not the point, these pieces were unique, irreplaceable. I have some of my best clients here in Melbourne waiting with great expectation for this collection.' And Kozminsky continued his frenetic pacing, running his hand through his neatly styled hair.

Kozminsky's pacing was beginning to get on Harry's nerves. 'Please take a seat, Mr Kozminsky,' he urged, pointing again to the vacant chair. 'I need you to concentrate on my questions.'

Kozminsky gave Harry a harrowed glance, but obeyed his instruction, sitting himself down and leaning forward intently on the chair as he waited for Harry's questions.

'Thank you,' Harry said. 'Now tell me, where were the jewels kept on the ship, and what security arrangements were in place?'

'Certainly, Inspector. I made sure that my supplier in Germany required the most stringent security arrangements be put in place. The pieces were locked in a safe in a secure room, adjacent to the captain's cabin. When I arrived today, Captain Romanov assured me that they were safe and secure. But I insisted he check. I was not permitted to join him on board, the quarantine arrangements, you see. But he returned from his checking to inform me the safe had been picked, and my precious cargo gone. Stolen! And so I came straight to the police station.'

'Does the captain have any suspicion as to what has happened?' Harry asked.

'I regret to say he does,' Kozminsky replied forlornly. 'It transpires that two of his crew have gone missing. Russian sailors, apparently. And the captain informs me that these two fellows were rostered on at some stage to help clean the ship. So that is obviously what has occurred. The scoundrels have taken the opportunity to steal my jewellery while on board, and then made off with them. I fear they have fled to Melbourne already.'

'Perhaps,' Harry replied. 'Though if the jewels are as unique as you suggest, they may well have trouble fencing them. Most buyers would be reluctant to take on items that are easily traceable.'

'That's very true,' Kozminsky agreed, brightening a fraction. 'All the more reason to get on their trail immediately, don't you agree?'

'Of course,' Harry said. 'I'll alert my colleagues at Russell Street first thing in the morning. And I'll get my best man here, Sergeant Milton, off to the Quarantine Station first thing tomorrow too. I'd go myself, but as you might be aware, we're in the middle of a particularly difficult murder investigation here in Sorrento, so we're rather flat out at the moment.'

'I appreciate that, Inspector,' Kozminsky replied. 'Your sergeant here was informing me about the murders before you arrived. A dreadful business. The sergeant indicated that the victims were also of Russian heritage.'

Kozminsky leaned forward earnestly and added, 'Have you considered that these deaths might perhaps be related to the theft of my jewels? A quarrel among thieves perhaps.'

'Who knows,' Harry answered noncommittally. 'But if there is a link, Sergeant Milton will uncover it. He's an excellent detective, my most trusted man. I promise you, we'll do our very best to recover your jewels.'

'That is good,' Kozminsky concluded. 'I was told you are the best detective in Melbourne, so I am satisfied with your promise. I will bid you farewell. I intend to stay in Sorrento for a day or two, so you or Sergeant Milton can report back to me. And if you would be so kind as to instruct your colleagues in Melbourne to liaise with my brother, Isadore, that would be appreciated.'

And he rose, shook Harry's hand and departed, leaving Melbourne's best detective feeling somewhat overwhelmed by the mounting volume of issues to be resolved. He glanced across the room at Sergeant Newgate, still reclining casually in his chair, and felt a renewed gratitude that Willie Milton was down here to assist him.

8

A BRIGHT SUMMER'S MORNING, and Harry was treading a by now, well-worn path to the Continental Hotel, where the Russian dancers were ensconced. Harry had been summoned to a meeting with George Coppin and the troupe's manager.

It seemed Coppin was keen to impress his Russian guests with the finest accommodation in Sorrento. Or perhaps it was just that no other establishment had enough rooms available for the thirty or so members of the troupe. And serendipitously, the Continental was a mere fifty-yard walk to the Athenaeum across the road, where the Cossack performance was to be held.

This morning's meeting had two main agendas, according to the note sent to Harry. Firstly, Coppin was keen to introduce him to the manager, a Mr Ivan Borodin. Perhaps he wants me to go through the security arrangements for Saturday evening, Harry speculated.

The note from Coppin also indicated that Mr Borodin had now been made aware of the true purpose of the gunboat visit in the bay, and Coppin was hoping that Harry might pour some oil on what were perhaps troubled waters. Nikolai Matyunin had also been invited to the meeting, no doubt to add his soothing diplomatic charm to the calming process.

Harry considered that all those matters were quite straightforward and could be dealt with quickly. Indeed, he was a trifle irritated that the meeting was happening at all. It would take up his valuable time, when there was so much to do.

Except that there was another matter Harry considered well worth raising. He had been intrigued by Effie's revelation last night that there was a Natalya among the Cossack troupe. Probably a coincidence, he thought, but certainly worth asking the manager a few pertinent questions.

Harry was ushered into a sitting room where Coppin and Matyunin were enjoying a morning coffee. The third attendee at the meeting was a big bear of a fellow, with an empty shot glass and a bottle of vodka at hand. Coppin introduced him as Ivan Borodin and thanked Harry for meeting with them.

'I'm sorry you were called away yesterday, Harry,' he said. 'We could perhaps have dealt with security matters then and saved you this further meeting. Although it's perhaps an opportune time for you to meet Ivan and put his mind at ease. You know, to reassure him that we're a friendly lot and bear no ill will to our Russian friends. And that we're keen to further cultural exchanges between our two countries.'

Harry smiled politely at Borodin. 'I'm not sure I can add much to the reassurances that these two blokes have already no doubt given. Except to say that the naval interception on Monday was the result of a misunderstanding and a communication breakdown between our authorities. And I can assure you, Mr Borodin, that you can expect fair and welcoming treatment from the Victorian Police during your visit to our state. And we'll also ensure that your stay will be a safe one, I can promise you that too.'

Borodin beamed back at Harry. 'Excellent, Inspector, most excellent,' he replied. 'I would normally have no concerns about our safety, we have been welcomed most cordially wherever we have performed, in Europe and elsewhere. But I hear that two of my countrymen may have been murdered in recent days, right here in Sorrento. So it is best, perhaps, that we take precautions.'

Harry nodded, pleased at least that Borodin was not taking the incident in the bay any further. 'As for the specifics of securing your people, I am happy to outline our proposed approach,' he said.

'Don't worry about that,' Coppin interceded. 'I've told Ivan that you'll have men in the theatre and backstage, to make sure nothing untoward happens. He's very comfortable with that.' And he glanced at Borodin, who nodded his satisfaction with the proposed arrangements.

Good, thought Harry, now it's time for me to do a bit of exploring. 'Mr Borodin, I wonder if I might ask a question or two of you?'

'Of course, Inspector, perhaps you require more detail about our proposed movements on Saturday evening?'

'No, no, that's all in hand. No, my questions are about a member of your troupe. I take it you've got a good knowledge of all your performers?'

Borodin paused in the act of refilling his glass, looking at Harry in some surprise. 'Of course, Inspector, naturally. That is my job.'

'This might seem like an odd question, but I understand you have a young lady by the name of Natalya in your troupe?'

'Yes, indeed we do, Inspector.' Borodin eyed Harry quizzically. 'But you know this already, it seems?'

'I do. My wife had the pleasure of meeting her on the beach yesterday.'

'Ah yes, my girls and boys thoroughly enjoyed themselves on your beautiful seashore. The invigorating sea air, so restorative, is it not?'

'So they say,' Harry replied wryly. 'Though I've not had the chance to enjoy it myself yet. But I wanted to ask about Natalya, actually.'

'Yes, certainly, Inspector. A beautiful girl, and a very fine dancer.'

'First up, I'm wondering about her name. Is Natalya a common name in Russia?'

Again, Borodin's shaggy eyebrows rose in surprise. 'That is an odd question, Inspector. But since you ask, I would say, not so common. Quite unusual, in fact.'

'Thank you. I'm also wondering if you have information on her background. For example, how long has she been with you?'

Borodin tossed down the shot of vodka and stroked his beard in contemplation of Harry's question.

'Not so long, Inspector, now that you mention it. She came to me a month or so ago, seeking to join my troupe. I was happy to employ her for this tour, her dancing was superb. So full of grace and charm.'

'So, she has a background in the theatre? Or in dance, at least?' Harry asked.

Borodin shrugged. 'I couldn't tell you, Inspector. In fact, I asked about her situation, but she seemed unwilling to discuss it. It didn't matter, she was beautiful, she could dance, what more did I need to know?'

'Fair enough,' Harry replied, then paused a moment before continuing. 'Look, I hope it's not inconvenient, but would it be possible to talk with Natalya before the show on Saturday? With you present, of course.'

Borodin's craggy forehead now creased in a frown. 'I can't see why that is necessary, Inspector. I do not want my dancers being upset before the big performance. She is only a young girl, she may be frightened to be the subject of a police interrogation. And for what purpose?'

'No, no,' Harry reassured. 'It won't be an interrogation, I promise. Just a few simple questions on her background. It's just possible she may be able to assist on a case we're investigating. Probably not, but I would like to ask nevertheless.'

Borodin looked doubtful. 'Really, Inspector, I can't see how she could possibly help.'

Matyunin leaned forward and touched Borodin's sleeve. 'If it would help, Ivan, I could be present as well at such a meeting. To ensure that the girl is treated kindly.'

'Good idea,' Harry added. 'Nikolai's presence would certainly be welcome.'

Borodin sat back in his chair and shrugged again. 'Very well, if you must,' he conceded, rather testily. 'But at a time of my choosing, I must insist. I will not have any interference with our rehearsals.'

'Of course,' Harry replied. 'That goes without saying. I'll leave it with you, Nikolai, to sort out a time.'

'Good, that's settled then,' Coppin declared, smiling benevolently at Harry. 'I'll let you get back to your work, Harry. But before you do, I think I noticed Simon Kozminsky in the hotel last night. And he seemed quite upset. Carrying on about some jewels being stolen. Has he been to see you?'

Harry smiled back at Coppin. 'Police business, I'm afraid, George. Nothing more I can add.'

And he shook hands firmly with the three men, before striding purposefully from the room.

Willie Milton stood at the bow of the police launch and scanned the rapidly approaching pier of the Quarantine Station. The German ship was still anchored there, and Willie was pleased to see one of the station's police contingent standing on guard duty at the pier. Harry had insisted on such a guard, indeed had been surprised it wasn't implemented in the first place. He had suggested it might have saved Mr Kozminsky's jewels being lifted.

At his insistence, Simon Kozminsky was accompanying Willie, saying that he wanted to see first-hand what was going on. Fortunately, Willie had been spared Kozminsky's continuing expressions of outrage on the latter part of the trip. A rising southerly swell had turned him a delicate shade of grey, and he now sat crouched over a bucket by the helm, the loss of his jewels overtaken by a more pressing woe.

The launch was soon moored at the pier, directly behind *The Queen of Hamburg*, and again it was Mrs Johnston who appeared to greet them. Willie barely had the chance to introduce himself before Kozminsky, who by this time had regained his composure, went on the attack.

'Madam, our business is not with you. I demand to see the captain of this vessel immediately. He has much to answer for, and we will not leave until we know what has happened to my jewellery.'

Mrs Johnston's demeanour immediately changed from welcoming to cool disdain. 'I see your manners have not improved since yesterday. I'd thank you for a little more civility, sir. There is no need for that tone of voice. The captain has been summoned and is waiting for you in my office. My husband will meet us there too.' And with that, she turned on her heel and stalked back up the pier towards the station buildings.

Mrs Johnston led them through a gate and past three long, double-storey buildings, which she explained housed the ship's crew and second-class passengers. Willie noted that there was very little security to contain these detainees, just a low, easily scalable picket fence. He began to appreciate the challenge of preventing anyone from fleeing the premises. And he appreciated also the peril faced by any young woman unfortunate enough to be detained in this accommodation, at the mercy of being leered at or worse by the rough-looking sailors he could see lounging about in front of the buildings.

Further up the hill stood two more recently constructed buildings. One, a long brick building with a verandah and balcony above, had been built to afford more comfort to the first-class passengers. Willie could see a few of these folk reclining in armchairs on the balcony. Undoubtedly safer for the women, he thought, but doubtless no less tedious, when their pressing desire was to be in Melbourne, rather than cooped up here.

The second building, a large, rather stylish-looking villa, was the doctor's residence and administration headquarters, and it was into this building that Willie and Kozminsky were escorted. They were shown into a room on the left of the passageway, where Captain Romanov was waiting, together with a snowy-haired, avuncular fellow who Mrs Johnston introduced as her husband, Dr Couper Johnston.

Willie was about to introduce himself to the two men, but Kozminsky jumped in first. 'Captain Romanov, I demand to know what has happened to my jewellery! Do you have any idea how valuable they are? You have obviously been completely remiss in securing them.'

Romanov seemed completely unmoved by Kozminsky's strident approach. 'As I informed you yesterday, I have done everything possible to protect your property. It is not my fault that we have been forced to waste our time in this damned place. And we do not have the resources to protect property for an extended period in a place such as this. The security here is non-existent.' And he gave Dr Johnston a baleful glare.

Kozminsky turned to Johnston too, seizing upon another outlet for his ire. 'What do you have to say to that, Doctor? The captain is right. Your station is meant to be a place of containment, and you should have the capacity to ensure the security of valuable cargo that is also detained here. But there seems to be very little, if any, security provided.'

Johnston's avuncular demeanour left him immediately, and he glanced nervously at his wife before stammering a response.

'Well, I don't really know, Sir. I mean,... that is to say, my priority is the health of the residents here. And to ensure that the residents of Melbourne are protected from disease. As to the security matters you raise, well, I ... I mean ...'

'What my husband means, sir,' interposed Mrs Johnston, calmly stepping into the breach, 'is that our responsibilities extend only to the medical issues that we have been appointed to administer. Security issues are the responsibility of the police garrison stationed here. And frankly, I agree with you. That presence is inadequate. But that is a matter you must take up with the relevant authorities, rather than attacking my husband. Do I make myself clear?'

Kozminsky was scarcely mollified, but begrudgingly replied, 'I suppose so.' Then, turning to Willie, he added, 'I hope you will take this up with your superiors, Sergeant. It's clear that your police presence here is woefully inadequate.'

'I will convey your request, Mr Kozminsky,' Willie replied calmly. 'But I can't guarantee that any more resources will be made available. That's a matter for the government to decide. In the meantime, we'd best get on with investigating what's happened to your jewellery. That's what I'm here for.'

'Of course,' Kozminsky muttered. 'Though god knows where the jewels are now. Being hocked to some criminal enterprise in Melbourne, no doubt.'

'Possibly,' Willie replied. 'Though we need to keep an open mind on that. As previously indicated, we've notified our colleagues in the city to be on the lookout for any such attempts to sell your property. Given that they're apparently quite unique pieces, that should limit the capacity of thieves to fence them immediately. You've provided us with a detailed description of them, and we've passed that on to our colleagues as well.'

'Thank you, Sergeant,' Kozminsky replied, calming down slightly. 'I know you are doing your best.'

Willie nodded. 'Good. Perhaps we can start by asking you a few questions, Captain Romanov.'

'Certainly,' Romanov replied promptly.

'Well, for a start, could you give me the full details about how this robbery was discovered?'

'There's not much to tell, really. As you know, we had an inquiry yesterday from Mr Kozminsky about his jewels, and when we checked they were gone. That's it.'

Willie frowned. 'A bit more detail than that would be useful, Captain. For a start, where and how were they secured? Who had access to them?

And how were they stolen, if they were in secure storage? You understand what I'm asking?'

'Oh yes, of course. Well, the jewellery, and any other valuable cargo, were stored in the purser's storeroom. It's normally locked, and the jewels were kept in there in a locked safe. When we investigated yesterday, both the room and the safe were unlocked, and the jewels gone.'

'And no sign of forced entry?' Willie asked.

'No, none. It was clearly the work of practised thieves,' Romanov replied. 'It seems the lock had been picked. And the safe door closed shut again, so that no-one would immediately notice it had been broken into.'

Willie stroked his chin thoughtfully. 'Who among your crew would have the skill to do that? Pick a secure safe lock, I mean. It seems odd that you have, as you put it, practised thieves among your crew.'

Romanov shrugged. 'What can I say? We are always putting on new crew members before each voyage, and we do not have the capacity to fully check their background.'

Willie nodded. 'Well, what about the period between docking here at the station and yesterday, when the loss was discovered? Would any of your crew have had the opportunity to board the ship in that period of time? And break into the purser's storeroom?'

'Of course, thanks to these people,' Romanov replied, indicating the Johnstons with a dismissive wave of the arm. 'They required us to have men rostered on board, cleaning the ship, for days on end. So any of the crew would have had ample opportunity to carry out the theft.'

'Excuse me, Captain,' Mrs Johnston bristled. 'Your ship was in a disgusting state. Do not blame us for your own incompetence.'

Willie interceded, endeavouring to keep the discussion focused. 'Captain Romanov, when we met you on the weekend, we asked you to check the nationality of the men gone missing. What did you find?"

'I checked with my purser, Mr Schwartz,' Romanov replied promptly.

'His understanding is that those two fellows were of Eastern European extraction, in all probability Russian. And from what he said, they were of doubtful character. It's obvious to me that those two are the thieves. And they may well be connected with the case your Inspector is working on.'

'Really? It's a little soon to jump to that conclusion. Why does your purser say they're doubtful characters?'

Romanov shrugged. 'I'm not sure. But he has his reasons, I expect. They should be your suspects for the theft of this fellow's jewels. And for the other inquiry your Inspector was talking about, as I said.'

Willie ignored Romanov's speculations and asked instead, 'When did you notice the two Russian sailors missing?'

Romanov stared into the distance and thought. 'I'm not quite sure,' he replied vaguely. 'We don't do a head count every day.'

'Best guess then,' Willie persevered.

Again, Romanov paused in thought. 'Probably a few days after we were forced to put in here,' he replied eventually. 'So that would be perhaps four or five days ago.'

Willie scratched his head in slight puzzlement. 'If those two Russian sailors took the jewels, the safe would have been robbed before they absconded. Yet you only noticed the jewels missing following Mr Kozminsky's inquiry yesterday. Why did you not notice before then?'

Romanov shrugged. 'I had no reason to check. Nothing has happened in that period that would cause me to check. We have all just been marking time, stuck as we are in this hellhole.'

'I beg your pardon, Captain!' Mrs Johnston burst out, and the two exchanged angry glances.

Willie pulled out his notebook and checked his list of to-do entries. He looked up. 'I think that's about all for now, Captain. Except that I'll need to have a quick look at the purser's storeroom, and the safe that was picked. If you can lead me there, that would be appreciated.'

Romanov scowled slightly but reluctantly agreed to Willie's request. Bidding Mrs Johnston and her relieved husband farewell, they followed the captain out of the building and down to the pier.

'You wait here, sir, I won't be long,' Willie instructed Kozminsky, before following the captain up the gangway and onto the ship's main deck.

Romanov led the way to the aft of the ship, up a small flight of stairs to the officers' deck, then through a door and down a narrow passageway to the extreme rear of the ship. Here two doors stood side by side, one leading into the captain's quarters, the other into the purser's storeroom.

Willie examined the lock on the storeroom door as they went through. No obvious sign of tampering there. And when he examined the lock on the heavy safe, standing in a corner of the room, again there was no sign of any forced entry. Romanov was right, the locks must have been picked, which meant the theft was the work of professional thieves.

The safe now contained only a stack of papers, which Romanov explained were mainly items of mail for delivery to various addresses in Melbourne.

'Nothing else of value stolen?' Willie asked. 'The passengers didn't lodge any valuables with you?'

'Of course not,' Romanov scoffed. 'Most of them would have nothing of value to protect. They would have spent what little money they had on the fare to get here.'

'But I did notice a few first-class passengers on the balcony back there at the station,' Willie replied. 'I would've thought they might have some valuables to protect.'

'Oh yes, of course,' Romanov replied hastily. 'I forgot about those few. No, they kept their valuables to themselves in their cabins. The first-class cabins are quite secure.'

'I see,' Willie replied, then with one last look around, he added, 'We're finished with you for the moment, Captain. We'll let you know if we need you again.'

They rejoined Kozminsky on the pier, and soon Willie and the jeweller were back on the police launch. As they began to steam back towards Sorrento, Willie turned to Kozminsky.

'I know you've indicated to us that the missing jewellery is valuable, Mr Kozminsky, but can you give me an assessment of their actual value?'

'Well, that is somewhat difficult to answer, Sergeant,' Kozminsky replied.

'Why so?' Willie asked.

'You see, these were ... are unique pieces. Jugendstil jewellery is very rare, and greatly valued by those with exquisite taste in fine *objets d'art*. I was importing the pieces because some of my most valued clients here in Melbourne are willing to pay a handsome price for such treasures. I don't know, perhaps in total, the pieces would have sold for more than three thousand pounds. Even more, if they were offered back in Germany.'

Willie whistled. 'Blimey, that much! I didn't realise they were that valuable.'

'Why do you think I am so concerned?' Kozminsky exclaimed. 'They are irreplaceable.'

'But at least they're insured,' Willie consoled. 'So you said?'

'Yes,' Kozminsky replied gloomily. 'There is that, I suppose. Though I can expect a difficult argument with Lloyds as to their true worth.'

And with that, Kozminsky lapsed into sombre silence for the remainder of the journey, his only consolation a calming sea and a smooth passage back to Sorrento.

❦

Late afternoon at the Sorrento Police Station but very little heat had gone out of the day, and the five policemen crammed around the table in the small meeting room all looked hot and bothered.

Harry could see that the local blokes in particular were desperate to get out of there and head to their usual post-work watering hole at the Sailors

Arms. But damn it, if he and Willie had to catch up on what was going on, they could too. Though he knew their contribution to the investigation was unlikely to improve as a result.

'Okay,' he began. 'This is all starting to get a bit complicated, so I thought it'd be useful to work out where we're up to and establish our priorities for the next couple of days.'

'Fair enough,' Newgate replied. 'But can we make it quick? It's like a bloody oven in here.'

'I know, I know, it's the same for all of us. Don't worry, the beer won't run out over at the Sailors Arms.'

A snigger from Staples and a scowl from Newgate.

Harry continued. 'Right, let's deal with the two murders first, before Willie reports back on the jewellery theft over at the Quarantine Station. Where are we up to? What do we know? Clive, have you and your blokes found any connection between the first victim, Sam, real name Sergei, and any of the fishermen around the town?'

Newgate shook his head. 'Fraid not, boss. We've talked to most of the fishermen, but none of them seem to have had anything to do with him. Or at least, not that they're prepared to say.'

Harry frowned, wondering to himself just how rigorous Newgate's inquiries had been. 'Well then, lets extend our inquiries to the lime kilns. If Dave worked at one, it's possible his mate, Sam, did as well. I know that wasn't Gloria's impression, judging by the smell of him, but she might've been wrong. You never know. I'll leave that to you, Arthur, right?'

'I'm onto it, boss,' Staples affirmed. 'Straight away.'

Morris raised his hand tentatively. 'Excuse me, sir,' the young constable said.

'Yes, Wally, what's the problem?'

'I've had a thought, sir.'

'What is it, Wally? Don't keep us in suspense, mate.'

'Well, we reckon these two blokes knew each. And from what the barmaid said, they seemed to be pretty close. Like, they drank together all the time. I reckon there's a fair chance they were living in the same digs. So perhaps we should do a run around the boarding houses, and anywhere else they might have been shacked up. If we can find out where they lived, we might be able to find out more about them.'

'Good thinking, mate,' Harry replied. 'I had the same thought. Wally, we'll make that a job for you. Go round all the boarding houses here in Sorrento and up the way at Rye too. And extend your investigation to the fishing shacks as well. There's plenty of them up and down the coast, and some quite isolated. Useful for those two blokes to hide out, if they were up to no good. See how you go.'

'Yes, sir,' Morris replied eagerly, looking pleased to be given this important job. 'What about you, sir, anything we can do to help you?'

'No, no. I've been a bit sidetracked by this Cossack business, but it might have given us a lead.'

'Really?' Newgate asked. 'How so?'

'Well, one of the cast is a young lady by the name of Natalya. Same name as was tattooed on the drowned man's arm. Probably a coincidence, but I'm told it's not a very common name in Russia, so it's worth a chat with young Natalya. See if there's a connection with Sam.'

Newgate eyed Harry sceptically. 'Reckon you're grasping at straws there, boss. A long shot, at best.'

'You're probably right, but there's only one way to find out,' Harry replied calmly. 'Why don't you come with me when we talk to her? You'll be helping with security for the show on Saturday night, so it'd be handy for you to meet the manager.'

'All right, if you say so,' Newgate replied begrudgingly.

Harry ignored Newgate's insolence and continued. 'That brings us to you, Willie. How did you get on at the Quarantine Station? Any leads on the theft of that jewellery?'

'Not sure, boss. The ship's captain has identified two sailors who've shot through since the ship was quarantined. Most probably Russian, he reckons. They would seem to be the logical suspects, I suppose.'

'But you're not so sure?'

'I'm not. I mean, think about it. We need to believe these two runaways are expert safe-pickers and know how to fence some valuable and unique jewellery in a city they've never been in before. Not sure I buy it.'

'I see what you mean,' Harry agreed. 'Seems unlikely. Though somebody's taken them, and will undoubtedly try to get rid of them in Melbourne. So it might be wise for you to shoot down to Melbourne for a day, talk to the boys back in the office, and sniff around a bit through your usual contacts.'

'The Ferret?'

'The Ferret would be a good start,' Harry agreed, half-smiling. 'He might be helpful. Anyway, a trip to town'd be good to show the Chief Inspector we're taking the robbery seriously.'

'Speak of the devil,' Newgate grinned. 'Look who's coming.' And he pointed to the window, through which they could see Chief Inspector Marks striding purposefully down the road towards them from the direction of the Continental Hotel.

'Better show him in, Wally,' Harry suggested. 'Looks like we might need to calm him down.'

Harry was right. Marks burst into the room, accompanied by a waft of the Continental's finest whiskey, and glared accusingly around the room.

'What's going on with you lot? I've got everyone on my back about these murders,' he railed. 'Blokes getting chucked into the bay, others down lime kilns, and we don't seem to have made any progress. And now this Kozminsky fellow's at the Continental carrying on like a pork chop about some robbery over at the quarantine place. It looks like this town's having some sort of crime wave, and the police are powerless to do anything.'

Harry breathed deeply and reminded himself to stay calm and diplomatic. 'We understand your concern, sir, we really do. But these things happen sometimes, a little burst of crime. We'll get on top of it. At this stage we don't think the robbery at the Quarantine Station is related to these two murders.'

'That's not what I've heard,' Marks replied. 'Kozminsky reckons there's two Russian sailors shot through from there and holed up somewhere around these parts. Who knows what they might be up to? People tell me their womenfolk are living in fear. Too afraid to go out at night.'

'I don't really think there's any need for alarm, sir,' Harry soothed. 'Apparently detainees abscond from the station reasonably frequently. They're probably in Melbourne by now. Or on their way to the goldfields.'

'That's another thing, Holloway,' Marks continued, completely unmollified. 'There's meant to be a police presence over there, I'm told. All these runaways, it's embarrassing for the force.'

Harry briefly considered reminding Marks that an appropriate level of police resources might help that particular problem, but thought better of it. 'You're right, I'll get Sergeant Newgate here to meet with the sergeant over there and see what can be done to improve security.'

Harry glanced at Newgate, who was studiously examining the tabletop.

'Well, make sure that happens, Holloway,' Marks continued. 'And I want some progress on these other killings, all right? By the end of the week, no later.' And with that he turned on his heel and strode from the room, as abruptly as he had entered.

'Geez, he likes to give you a hard time,' Newgate sniggered. 'He's putting the pressure on. You'd better lift your game.' And Harry noted a surreptitious wink in Staples' direction.

Harry felt a prickle of annoyance, but kept his temper in check. 'I can look after myself,' he replied firmly. 'If I were you, Sergeant, I'd be worrying more about your performance than mine. If any game needs lifting around here, it's yours, I would suggest. You and your mate Arthur here, have had it comfy for too long. It's time you actually did a bit of police work.'

Newgate's sneer disappeared. 'Sorry, boss,' he replied, in a conciliatory tone. 'Just my idea of a joke. Didn't mean to offend. Come on, Arthur, Wally, we'd better get going. As the inspector says, there's lots to do.'

Harry watched as the three policemen left the building. Morris was heading off in one direction, towards Point Nepean Road, no doubt to begin his inquiries of the town's accommodation providers. Newgate and Staples were making a beeline for the Esplanade at the beachfront. In Harry's suspicious mind, their trajectory was in a direct line to the Sailors Arms.

'It's certainly a beautiful evening,' Effie sighed, as she gazed out from their first-floor balcony over the moonlit vista. Before them stretched the low sand hills, covered with ti-tree, and the white road winding through them on its way to the back beach. A gentle southerly breeze brought with it the faint salt tang of the ocean. Effie snuggled further into Harry's shoulder as they relaxed on the comfortable divan.

'You're right, Eff, it's a bottler of an evening,' Harry murmured, but Effie knew him well enough to know that he wasn't fully enjoying the scene that lay before them.

'Come on, darling, forget about the investigation for five minutes,' she admonished him. 'Tell him he has to relax, eh Willie?' and she glanced across the balcony to where Willie and Rachel were seated. No response from Willie, but Rachel answered in his stead.

'I think he's fallen asleep, Effie. 'Perhaps we might go to bed.'

'Good idea, darling. The poor dear needs his rest.'

Rachel gave Willie a gentle prod and whispered something in his ear.

He and Rachel rose and gave their goodnights. 'We'll try not to disturb the others,' Rachel murmured, as she opened the balcony door.

'Don't worry, Clem and Millie are well asleep. The kids too. This sea air is great for them. Sleep well, you two.'

'We will,' Willie replied. 'Night, Harry.'

'Goodnight mate, get a good sleep, you're off to town in the morning.'

'Now, Harry Holloway, it's time for you to relax,' Effie suggested when they were alone. 'Why don't we toddle off to bed too?' And she leaned into him and kissed him gently.

Harry returned the kiss warmly and replied, 'Soon, darling, but I'm still a bit wound up from today. Need to sit here a little while longer.'

'Is it the Chief Inspector giving you a hard time?' Effie asked. 'You shouldn't take any notice of him, you know.'

'I don't,' Harry replied firmly. 'No, it's not him, it's this damned case, we just don't seem to be getting anywhere. I can't quite understand why no-one's come forward about those two blokes. There seems to be some sort of web of secrecy about them. Very strange.'

'It is,' Effie agreed. 'A few strange things seem to be happening around here. All of them connected with Russians somehow.'

Harry turned towards her. 'What do you mean?'

'Well, your two murder victims seem to be Russian. And from what you say, the jewel thieves over at Quarantine Station are Russians too.'

'So it seems.'

'And I keep thinking about that odd painter, Petrenko, up in the sand hills with James and the other artists. James thinks he's probably Russian.'

'Maybe,' Harry said, but doubtfully. 'Though I'm not going to turn this into a Russian conspiracy, Eff. Just stick to the facts, eh? Anyway, I've briefed Newgate about your artistic mystery man, and told him to keep an ear to the ground about the fellow's movements.'

'Of course, darling,' Effie replied, putting her arm around his shoulder. 'I know you'll look at all the angles. And I know you'll get to the bottom of it all. Now, I've got a suggestion.'

'Always open to suggestions.'

'If you're not sleepy, why don't we go for a moonlight stroll? Down to the pier, perhaps. It's only nine o'clock, not too late. It'll be our little bit of romance for the day. It's such a lovely night.'

'Why not?' Harry agreed, rousing himself from the sofa. 'You're right. It is indeed a lovely night.'

So they made their way back into the boarding house, down the stairs, out onto Ocean Beach Road, and began the five hundred yard stroll down to the seafront, arm in arm. The evening was tranquil around them. The lights of the Continental Hotel shone brightly on their right as they passed, and they could hear the faint chatter of voices from within.

Further along, as they turned onto the Esplanade, they could see that the Sailors Arms on the corner was still doing a roaring trade, the sound of raucous carousing a jarring intrusion on the evening peace. Effie quickened her pace and they were soon at the start of the pier. Looking along its length, they could see no sign of activity.

'Why don't we take a stroll out to the end?' Effie suggested.

Harry agreed and so they set out along the pier. Soon they were at its end, the sound of human voices now undiscernible. Harry indicated a wrought iron seat, looking out to sea, and they set themselves down there, enjoying the gentle breeze, the distant mournful cries of shearwaters returning to their nests in the sand hills, and the rhythmic lapping of the gentle waves on the shore behind them.

'Look,' Effie suggested quietly. 'Isn't that Melbourne over there?' And she pointed ahead of them to a faint twinkle of lights in the distance.

'Yeh, I think it is,' Harry murmured. 'Home sweet home, eh?'

'Nice to be away from it sometimes, though.'

'Yeh. Mind you, it'd be nice to be away from work too.'

She smiled and squeezed his hand. Then pointed again, across the water to their left. Some two hundred yards offshore, they could make out the pale outline of a boat, moving across their line of sight, its billowing sails full as it captured the evening breeze.

'That's a couta boat, if I'm not mistaken,' Harry observed. 'Very popular among the fishermen around these parts, they tell me. Looks like it's heading down the South Channel.'

'Is it a fisherman, then?'

'It's going the wrong way if it is,' Harry replied. 'Should be coming back to land, I would've thought. To one of the fishing shacks along the coast here. That boat looks like it's heading towards Melbourne.'

And sure enough, as they watched, the vessel began to veer northward towards the open bay, clearly discernible now with its pale prow, heading in a direct line toward the distant lights.

'Oh well,' Harry observed. 'Maybe they're heading off for some night fishing. Though it's odd that it's going out so far. Maybe they know a good spot, eh?'

'It's getting a bit chilly,' Effie murmured, wrapping her shawl more tightly around her. 'Let's head back.'

She took Harry's arm and they began the stroll back to the Palace. The noise emanating from the Sailors Arms was still raucous as they passed. Glancing toward it, Harry couldn't help but think of the scene, only a week ago, when the Russian had been bashed and cast into the water. Had he come from that busy hotel? And who was with him to inflict the blow? And most puzzlingly, why had no-one come forward to report anything? Or even, apart from Gloria, to identify him, as a relative, a friend, or even just a workmate? Harry shook his head. It was puzzling, and Harry didn't enjoy being puzzled.

Effie must have felt his frustration, because she squeezed his arm and looked up at him. 'Did that walk relax you just a bit?' she murmured.

Harry smiled down at his wife. 'It was a lovely walk,' he replied. 'Great suggestion.'

'Don't worry, darling,' she consoled. 'You'll crack the case, and we'll still have time for a wonderful family holiday. Trust me.'

'I do,' he replied, and meant it. 'I always do.'

9

⁂

THURSDAY 15 JANUARY 1898

EFFIE HAD DESCRIBED NATALYA, the Russian Cossack dancer, as beautiful and effervescent when they met on the beach just two days ago.

Beautiful she certainly is, thought Harry. But the Natalya who sat opposite him in a meeting room at the Continental was far from effervescent. Face pale and tear-stained, eyes red-rimmed, she cast an entirely distraught and grief-stricken figure.

Nikolai Matyunin and Ivan Borodin sat close on either side of her, looking solicitous. Perhaps they had been trying to comfort her. At Harry's side sat Sergeant Newgate, under strict instructions to take notes and leave the talking to Harry.

'Miss Kuzmina is not well,' Matyunin began. 'She should be in bed, but we have persuaded her to take part in your interview. But I trust you will be brief, Inspector.'

'I'll try to be,' Harry replied gently. He could see that Natalya's distress was real, but he suspected it had nothing to do with physical illness. He needed to find out whether the dramatic change in her demeanour had anything to do with the death of Sergei, the murdered Russian. Had news of his death reached her?

But Harry also needed to be careful. He didn't want to distress the poor girl any further, and besides, looking at it from a practical perspective, if she became completely distraught, he would likely get no useful information from her.

'I understand from my wife that Miss Kuzmina speaks some English,' he began. 'Are you happy for me to question her directly?'

The two men exchanged glances, then Matyunin replied. 'You may, Inspector, but I urge you to be gentle with her. As you can see, she is in a delicate state.'

Harry turned to Natalya and offered her a sympathetic smile. 'Hello, Natalya, I'm sorry to see that you're unwell.'

Natalya didn't reply, merely raising her eyes briefly to his, then immediately looking down again.

'Let me first say, Natalya, that you have nothing to fear from the police. From either myself or from Sergeant Newgate here. You are not under suspicion of anything. Do you understand?'

Again, Natalya flashed him a timid glance, but she also gave a slight nod of the head. Good, Harry thought, let's push on.

'Natalya, we hope you might be able to help us with a tragic event that has recently occurred here in Sorrento. A young man was killed just over a week ago, and we think it is possible he may have been known to you. He went by the name of Sam, but we think his real name might have been Sergei.'

Harry's pronouncement of the dead man's name had a dramatic effect on Natalya. She gave a great wail and collapsed forward onto the table, her face buried in her hands. Her body heaved with uncontrolled sobs.

Matyunin put a concerned arm around her shoulders and murmured some consoling words in Russian, but the sobs continued. The young woman's reaction told Harry all he needed to know, but he had to hear it confirmed.

'I'm very sorry, Natalya, that I have to raise this matter. I understand then that you knew this man, yes? Was he a friend of yours?'

Natalya sat motionless for some moments, her head still in her hands. Again, Matyunin whispered something to her. Gradually the sobs subsided, and she looked up at Harry.

'Not know. Not know Sergei.'

'Are you sure?' Harry pressed, puzzled.

Natalya shook her head vehemently. 'Not know Sergei!' she repeated emphatically.

She looked desperately at Harry, imploringly. And in her eyes, Harry unmistakably saw panic. Panic and terror. And he knew then he would get no more from her at this meeting.

'I'm sorry to have caused you distress, Natalya,' he said gently. 'I understand the death of your countryman would be upsetting for you. I hope we can talk again. Perhaps when you are feeling better.'

Borodin looked at Harry sternly. 'I think Miss Kuzmina can add nothing further, Inspector. She must rest over the coming days and recuperate, so that she may take part in the performance on Saturday.'

Harry nodded his acknowledgement that the meeting was over, thanked Natalya and the two men for their cooperation, and took his leave.

'What do you reckon, Sarge?' he asked Newgate as they trekked back to the police station. 'I'd say she definitely knew our murder victim.'

'I'd say you're right,' Newgate agreed. 'Though I'm not sure you're going to get much out of her.'

'Maybe not,' Harry replied. 'But I'll give it a few days, and then we'll press her again. Perhaps a bit more firmly next time.'

Newgate nodded. 'Fair enough, boss. Not sure she can help much though, given she's just landed in the country. She's not going to be a witness to the murder, is she?'

Harry glanced at Newgate. The man's obtuseness was staggering. 'That girl knew our dead man,' he declared. 'She knew him well. And when she saw Effie on the beach the other day, she was obviously very happy to be in

Australia. Happy that she was going to be with him, I'd reckon. Now her demeanour is completely different. My assessment is she's dead scared. Of something, or someone. But who? That's what we need to find out.'

❦

Willie settled into his favourite booth at the Caledonian and surveyed the room. The lunchtime crowd here was a different kettle of fish to the post-work customers who Willie was used to mixing with. Less of the grime-covered brickworks workers, more a collection of touts and ne'er-do-wells, going about their dodgy, and probably illegal, activities.

But their goings-on were of no concern to Willie today, he was on the look-out for information. And information from a particular source, the Ferret, their usually reliable snitch, a man with no discernible moral compass and with a strong appreciation of the monetary value of providing information to the police.

Willie eyed, with some relish, the glistening lines of condensation running down the outside of his brimming beer glass. Melbourne was damn hot outside and a beer at lunchtime, strictly in the line of duty, was an unusual and most welcome pleasure.

The day so far had been less than productive. The morning ferry from Sorrento, a train to Flinders Street, and from there a long walk to the Kozminsky Studio on the corner of Bourke and Elizabeth Streets, for a meeting with Isadore Kozminsky, the other half of the Kozminsky jewellery business.

Like his brother, Isadore was in a state of considerable distress at the theft of the prized jewellery collection. Willie soon realised he wouldn't be able to add much about the circumstances of the theft. But Isadore was able to help in another important respect, by giving Willie a detailed description of the lost pieces, even going so far as to produce a few photographs of some of the most valuable objects.

Armed with these photographs, Willie had made the further hike up to Russell Street, to meet CIB colleagues and brief them on the Kozminsky brothers' lost jewels. It had turned out they had no word on the street that anything was being hawked around town, but at least they were now fully alerted to the details of the theft. And they had a good description of what they were looking for.

The CIB boys had a few good informants around the town, but no-one as reliable and as productive as the Ferret. He was an informant who had been of great assistance to Harry and Willie in the past, and was always on the look-out to make himself useful again. For a fee, of course.

So Willie took a decent swig of his beer, replaced the glass on the table and looked around the room in search of his target.

The room was only moderately crowded but Willie couldn't see the Ferret anywhere among the riffraff. That wasn't unusual; the Ferret had an uncanny knack, when he wanted to, of making himself inconspicuous to the point of invisibility. Except when he saw an opportunity for profitable trade, at which time he would appear out of nowhere, ready to please.

As he did now. Willie was just raising his glass for a second mouthful when the Ferret's sharp features, and accompanying odour, materialised in front of him. Well camouflaged under a tattered trilby and ill-fitting coat, the Ferret slid into the booth opposite Willie and eyed him expectantly.

'Fancy seeing you here, Sarge. I thought you was off on your honeymoon. What happened? The missus chucked you in already?' The Ferret gave a snigger and eyed Willie beadily with a lewd grin.

'No, all good at home, Ferret. Nice of you to enquire. But I'm back to work now,' Willie replied pleasantly. 'How's things with you? Had any good wins lately?'

The Ferret eyed Willie suspiciously. 'Yeh, I s'pose so. Enough to keep me going, anyways.'

'All legal, I hope.'

'Course.'

'We might have a job for you, Ferret. Chance to earn an honest quid.'

The Ferret's beady gaze sharpened and he stared at Willie hopefully. 'Bewdy. You know me, I'll get you the dirt on whatever you want.'

'Well, here's the thing, Ferret. This might be a long shot, so payment only on verified results. Five quid if you give us the good oil.'

The Ferret's glitter intensified as he contemplated this potential windfall. 'Righto, what you need to know, Sarge?'

'There's been a jewellery theft, Ferret. A big one, by all accounts. And we think those responsible might be being shopping the jewels around the town. They could be foreigners, so they mightn't be too discreet. They mightn't know who to go to, y'see.'

The Ferret nodded contemplatively. 'Jeez, that's a tricky one. I mean, I know most of the fences around the town, but not sure they'd be up for a big jewellery job. Particularly with blokes they didn't know.'

Willie had already guessed the Ferret's contacts would be small-time fences: he was probably one of their regular suppliers. But he reasoned that inexperienced Russian thieves might be trying to hock their merchandise in pubs, and that was definitely the Ferret's native habitat. It was worth a try.

'I realise that, mate,' Willie replied. 'Particularly since the gear is quite unusual. Might be hard to guess its value if you didn't know. But some of your blokes might have been approached all the same. Why don't you do the rounds, tell them you've got a buyer for some fancy jewellery, and see what happens?'

'Orright. You mean you'll pay up if I can put you onto a bloke what's been contacted, even if there's no deal and no jewels?' And the Ferret fixed Willie with a calculating eye.

'I suppose so,' Willie replied, realising that was his best hope of at least establishing that the thieves were in Melbourne.

'Goodo,' the Ferret exclaimed. 'When do you need the info?"

'Quick smart, so get onto it straightaway, eh? What say I pop in here in a few days' time and see what you've got for me?'

'You betcha!' the Ferret replied enthusiastically. 'Count on me, Sarge.'

And with a brief tip of his cap, he sidled off the bench seat and melted into the lunchtime throng.

Willie downed the last of his beer, donned his hat and prepared himself for the sweaty trudge back down to the Flinders Street railway station. He'd have to get a wriggle-on if he was to catch the afternoon ferry. He set off, visions of Rachel waiting for him in Sorrento lending extra strength to his tired legs.

❦

'Come on, Clem, do hurry up. We'll never get there at this rate.'

Clem Holloway continued his reluctant shuffle. 'Jeez, luv, do we have to go to this joint?' he responded rather forlornly to his wife. 'I'll feel like a flamin' idiot.'

Millie Holloway took Clem's arm in hers, and replied firmly, 'Effie says it'll be good for us. And anyway, it's free, so there's an end to it. We're going.' And she continued to drag a recalcitrant Clem down Ocean Beach Road in the direction of the Continental Hotel and its famed indoor baths.

By their side, Effie smiled to herself. She was surprised that Millie had so readily agreed to take up Mr Ridgeway's offer of a complimentary session at the health baths. And she was also not at all surprised by Clem's reluctance, and by his scepticism about the supposed health benefits of a dip in the Continental briny.

Lydia had explained to Effie that the baths were clean and healthy, with fresh seawater pumped in every day, and great attention paid by the staff to keeping the environs spotlessly clean. But all Effie's reassurances to Clem were in vain; for him, immersing oneself in water should be done infrequently, and then solely for the purpose of removing accumulated workplace grime.

Nevertheless, despite his grumblings, Clem allowed himself to be shepherded to the rear entrance of the Continental, where a large annex had been built to house the baths. They were greeted at the door by Mr Smythe himself, who had been advised by Effie of their arrival time, and of the possible requirement for some words of encouragement.

'A very great pleasure to meet you, sir and madam,' he gushed. 'I'm sure you'll find your visit to our establishment most beneficial. From both health and relaxation perspectives.'

And he ushered them into a large room which had been designed in the fashion of a Roman bath, with stone columns in the Doric style, surrounding a large rectangular pool, through which water was flowing at a depth of three or so feet. A few elderly women were sitting in the water on submerged stone benches around its edge. To Effie's eye, it looked very inviting on this very warm day.

'This looks quite lovely, Mr Smythe,' she enthused. 'Just the thing to cool us down on such a hot day.'

'Not just lovely, dear lady,' Mr Smythe replied. 'But of great health benefit as well. Bathing in this natural salt water, and indeed just breathing in the sea air, are remarkably conducive to an enhanced constitution. Particularly for those of ... mature years.' With the faintest glance in the direction of Clem and Millie, both of whom were looking, in varying degrees, nervous about the prospect.

'Jolly good,' Effie replied. 'Now, I've brought my bathing costume, but Mr and Mrs Holloway have nothing to wear. Are you able to supply them with a costume?'

'Think no more about it,' Smythe replied immediately, and with a snap of the fingers he summoned forward a uniformed, middle-aged, severe-looking woman who had been standing off to one side.

'Mrs Meadows, could you be so kind as to provide this gentleman and this lady with bathing costumes, and show them and Mrs Holloway to the changing rooms.' Turning to Millie, he added, 'As you can see from these ladies present, Madam, the costumes we provide are well-designed to both offer comfort and maintain modesty.' And indeed they were, being neck-to-ankle calico shifts through which no feature of the female anatomy could be discerned.

Mrs Meadows shepherded them through the Doric columns to a separate area, where a row of cubicles had been built to enable changing. Extracting two costumes from a cupboard, she handed them to the senior Holloways and ushered them towards the changing rooms.

'Hang on!' Clem protested, holding his costume up for examination. 'This is no good. They'll see my legs!'

'What are you talking about, man?' Millie exclaimed. 'Who'll see your legs?'

'Those women! Those women in there. This outfit has no proper legs!'

'Oh, for heaven's sake, Clem, what does it matter if they see some of your legs, anyway?'

'No,' Clem insisted defiantly. 'I'm not showing my legs in public. I'll look like a fool. That does it. I'm not going in!'

'Come on, Dad,' Effie cajoled. 'I know there's no men in there now, but they do come in, all the time. And you've seen them on the beach in these sorts of costumes, haven't you?'

'It might be all right for the young blokes, but not for me,' Clem maintained. 'No-one's seeing my legs, and that's an end to it.'

'Don't worry about him, Effie,' Millie interceded. 'Let's you and I get changed, and that old codger can do what he wants.' And she took Effie's hand and led her off towards the changing rooms.

'I'll be outside then, in the garden,' Clem said, and made a relieved exit, back through the Doric columns, and out through the entrance door.

The Continental had an impressive and substantial rear garden, with manicured lawns and hedges, mature shady trees and gravel paths, and it was to this sanctuary that Clem made his escape.

Clem enjoyed a good garden: his little plot in their Brunswick attached cottage was always carefully tended. Of course, this garden at the Continental was significantly grander in scale, and Clem looked about him with a gardener's appreciation of its beauty.

He set off down one of the gravel paths, bordered on either side by tall box hedges, with the intention of finding a shady secluded spot, where he could relax, free from the risk that Effie or Millie might have second thoughts and track him down.

Rounding a couple of corners and turning down another row leading to the centre of the garden, Clem spied a shaded garden seat that seemed to offer safety from any threat of female ambush. Seating himself and extracting his pipe and tobacco pouch from his coat pocket, he began to pack his pipe in anticipation of a relaxing smoke.

As he did so, Clem became aware of the approach of voices. His first fear, that this was Effie and Millie come to drag him back, evaporated as he realised that one of the approaching voices was male. Glancing both ways down the bordered path he saw no-one. Then he realised that the voices were on the other side of the tall border behind him, and that they had stopped when they became immediately adjacent to him.

Peering surreptitiously into the hedge, he could make out the outline of two seated figures, their backs to him. They were engaged in animated conversation, but for the life of him, he couldn't understand a word they were saying. It was some indecipherable foreign language, but even so, Clem could tell from the tone of their voices that the woman was upset and panicky, and that the man's soothing tone was an attempt to calm her down.

Despite the fact that he had no idea what they were talking about, Clem felt as if he was intruding on their privacy. He thought perhaps he should cough to indicate his presence on the other side of the hedge. But by the time that thought entered his head, he began to worry they might think he had been spying on them. So he just sat there silently, waiting for them to finish their conversation and leave his vicinity.

But the talking went on and on, the female voice becoming more and more agitated, and now punctuated by sobs and cries. Clem became even more uncomfortable, unavoidably listening in on what was obviously a private conversation. But, at the same time, he was also intrigued, wondering what language they were speaking and what was the cause of the woman's distress.

He sat silently, praying that they wouldn't notice him. But as he listened, he heard some rustling, then the sound of footsteps and the voices receding away from him in the direction of the hotel. From his vantage point he had a view of the hotel's rear verandah, and soon the couple appeared there. He could see that the man was bearded and smartly dressed and his companion young and attractive. They disappeared into the hotel without looking back. They hadn't noticed him.

Clem breathed a sigh of relief and sat for a moment in thought. Then he resumed packing his pipe, looking to get in a smoke before he returned to the women. At the same time, he ruminated on what he had just heard. Perhaps it was something that was worth raising with Harry.

He didn't quite know why, but some part of him sensed that his son might well be interested in that rather emotional conversation on the other side of the hedge.

'Good on you, son, for taking your old man for a drink. I know you must be busy.'

'No worries at all,' Harry replied, as he and Clem undertook the short walk down the hill to the Sailors Arms. 'You deserve a reward after your efforts today. Resisting Mum and Effie, I mean. And besides, I'm looking forward to a pint or two myself.'

'What do you reckon about those people I heard in the garden?' Clem asked. 'Was it useful to you?'

Harry smiled at his dad's eagerness to please. 'Could be, Dad, could be. From the brief squiz you got of them, it sounds like it could have been Matyunin and the girl, Natalya. Though we can't be sure, I suppose.

But if it was, it tells me that she knows a lot more than she's telling us. And probably Matyunin does too. I think I might ask Mr Matyunin what he was doing, having a long conversation with that girl in the garden, and we'll see what he says. Well done, old fella, we'll make a spy out of you yet.'

Clem grinned, chuffed that his unintended eavesdropping might turn out to be helpful to his son. The two walked on, an incongruous father-and-son pair; wiry, jockey-sized Clem, dwarfed alongside the broad-shouldered, lanky Harry.

Six o'clock on a summer's evening and the pub was doing a roaring trade. A few holiday-makers were present, but now outnumbered by the local workers, rehydrating after a hard day's toil. The mingling odours of tobacco, fish and sweat hung stale over the room. Except for the smell of the sea, we could be in the Callie on any working night, Harry thought.

Whether by good fortune or through the imposing presence of the law, the seas parted and Harry managed to find a free space at the crowded bar.

'Are you okay standing, Dad?' he asked solicitously. 'There's a few tables around, but they seem pretty full at the moment.'

'What're you talking about, son?' Clem replied, a trifle contemptuously. 'I'm on my pins all day at work, remember. They still hold me up all right.'

'Sorry,' Harry smiled. 'Now, how about that beer? Might need to wait a while though, it looks busy enough.'

But he needn't have worried. He had hardly leaned over the bar and scanned its length for a bartender, when the friendly features of Gloria appeared in front of him.

'My favourite copper, back again,' she beamed at him. 'What'll it be, Harry?'

'Beer thanks, Gloria, it's been a thirsty day.'

'Coming right up. And what about your handsome friend here?' With a wink in Clem's direction.

'Same thanks, love,' Clem replied, grinning.

'Never realised you're such a hit with the ladies,' Harry joked, as Gloria occupied herself at the beer tap.

A sly grin was Clem's only reply.

While Gloria was returning with their beers, Harry had a thought. He leaned conspiratorially over the bar as she placed the glasses in front of them. 'Glad we bumped into you, my dear,' he said to her in a low voice. 'It's about the murder victim we talked about the other day. You know, Sergei ... Sam.'

'Oh right,' Gloria replied, suddenly serious now. 'I thought I told you all I knew, Harry.'

'Yes, you did, and it was very helpful. But I was just wondering about his girl, Natalya. You know, the one he talked about a bit.'

Gloria nodded. 'Yeh, that's right.'

'Well, I'm wondering if he might have let slip that she was going to join him in Australia? Or even hinted at that possibility?'

'Not that I can remember,' Gloria replied, then looked down the length of the bar. 'Tell you what, they're lining up here, so I better get back to work. But I'll think about it and get back to you if anything comes to me. You'll be here for a while?'

'Maybe an hour,' Harry replied. 'Thanks, much appreciated.'

'We'll see if that bears any fruit,' Harry mused after Gloria had hurried off to her next customer. 'You never know.'

'She was a pretty lass,' Clem said. 'That girl in the garden, I mean. If she's the same one you're talking about, Natalya.'

'You're right, she is a looker,' Harry agreed, then thought some more. 'Anyway, I'll front Matyunin about it, and see what happens.' Harry sipped on his beer and surveyed his father. 'I'm sorry I've been waylaid over the last week, Dad. I was wanting this to be a real family holiday. Hope you and Mum aren't too disappointed.'

Clem reached over and patted his son's arm. 'Don't worry, Millie and I are enjoying ourselves. We're just liking putting our feet up and getting a bit of a spell. And looking after the little ones while Effie has a bit of time off too. She and Rachel seem to be enjoying themselves too, doing a few things with their mates.'

'That's good,' Harry replied. 'Hopefully, this investigation'll be over soon, and we can all do some things together.'

Clem didn't answer, and when Harry glanced at him, he saw his father staring across the room.

'I know that bloke,' Clem said quietly. 'I reckon that's Jim Cleaver.' And he pointed to a group of salty-looking fellows gathered at the end of the bar.

'One of your old mates?' Harry asked. 'Which one is he?'

'Eh, Jim!' Clem called, waving an arm furiously. But the din in the bar drowned out his cry.

'Just a sec, son, Think I'll go say g'day.' And Clem hurried off, making a beeline for the group of drinkers.

Harry watched as Clem grabbed the sleeve of one of the men, a grizzled, weather-beaten, round-faced old bloke, with a full white beard. Then ensued prolonged and enthusiastic handshaking and back-slapping, followed by handshakes all around, as Clem's old mate introduced him to the group.

Harry was pleased to see his dad reunited with an old friend. Must be from the brickworks, he thought, or perhaps one of his greyhound coursing pals. The latter proved to be the case, as Harry discovered when

Clem steered the old bloke back across the room and introduced him as an old mate from their greyhound days.

'G'day, Jim, pleased to meet you,' Harry greeted him, shaking the old bloke's hand. 'Let me get you a beer.'

'Good on you, son,' Cleaver replied immediately. 'Clem here reckons you're a big shot copper. Reckons you're onto that murder that everyone's talking about.'

'Yeh, that's right, Jim,' Harry replied, signalling to Gloria behind the bar for an additional beer. 'So, you used to muck around with the doggies with the old fella here?'

'Yeh, we used to have a few ding-dong goes,' Cleaver grinned, putting an arm around Clem's shoulders. 'We had some good dogs in our time, eh, Clem?'

'We did,' Clem agreed. 'And I've still got one. Black Bess, she's a beauty. What about you, mate? Still got any dogs?'

'Nah,' Cleaver replied. 'Not since I came down here. Too busy fishing.'

'That's right, I remember now you saying you were going fishing full-time.'

'Yeh, and I'm glad I did. We sold the cottage in Collingwood, got a little place down here, and had enough left over to get a boat. A couta, just the thing for fishing in the bay.'

'I reckon that's the same boat that one of my constables sails,' Harry commented. 'Arthur Staples, you know him?'

'Yeh, I know Arthur,' Cleaver replied, then paused to take a decent mouthful of beer before adding, 'Arthur's got a shack just up the coast from ours. He seems to spend more time fishing than he does being a copper, to tell the truth. But who wouldn't, if you had the chance?'

'Jim, you might be able to answer something for me,' Harry continued. 'I was down at the pier last night, about nine or so, and we saw what I reckon was a couta sailing up the South Channel towards the city. Seemed a bit odd to me at the time. Blokes don't normally go fishing at that time, do they?'

Cleaver shrugged. 'Nah, not usually. But could have been one of the lads taking some tourists out for a moonlight sail, I suppose. They love that sort of thing.'

'Yeh, I suppose they would,' Harry agreed.

'I mean it's not usual, but it also could've been someone doing some night fishing. The mulloway bite best at night.'

'Right.'

'Or it could have been someone doing a moonlight run to the city,' Cleaver added, with a grin and a wink to Harry.

'Oh, really?' Harry said slowly, an eyebrow cocked. 'Bit of that goes on, does it? Smuggling, I mean.'

'You'd be surprised,' Cleaver replied, and winked in turn at Clem.

'Dinkum? What sort of stuff?'

'Oh, I dunno,' Cleaver replied vaguely. 'Nothing in particular. But they tell me there's always a market in Melbourne. For all sorts of stuff. Y'know, this and that. That's what they say, anyway.'

'Right, I see.'

Harry considered Cleaver's words. Did his hints of smuggling reflect the reality of life down here on the coast? Or was it just pub talk?

'Tell me, Jim,' he continued, 'who down here owns a couta boat? Apart from you and Arthur Staples, I mean.'

'Every man and his dog's got one,' Cleaver replied immediately. 'Most of the fishermen down here would have one. Ideal for fishing in the bay. And on the other side too. They're damn good in the rip through the Heads.'

'Right.' Harry was disappointed. The mysterious sailing boat on the water last night could have been anyone, he realised. And it probably wasn't up to any nefarious purpose either. Probably just taking holiday-makers out for a romantic evening cruise.

Cleaver drained his glass, gave an appreciative belch, and extended his gnarled paw to Harry. 'Thanks for that, son, I'd better get back to my mates. Good to meet you, and good to see you again, Clem, after all these years.'

'Yeh, Jim, real good to see you too.'

Cleaver paused, then placed a hand on Clem's shoulder. 'Tell you what, mate, why don't I take you and the lad here out for a spot of mulloway fishing. The moon's bright enough, as I said, ideal time for the mulloway to bite.'

'Jeez, I'd like that,' Clem replied readily. 'What do you reckon, Harry, we got time for that?'

Harry grinned. 'Sure, Dad. If the ladies can have their beauty baths, we can have our spot of fishing. When did you have in mind, Jim?'

'No time like the present,' Cleaver replied. 'Like I said, the moon's just about full, so how about tomorrow night? Nine o'clock'd be a good time.'

'Terrific, we'll see you then,' Harry agreed. 'Where will we meet you?'

'I'll pick you up at the pier,' Cleaver replied. 'Eight o'clock, alright? I'll bring all the tackle.'

'You'll be in your couta boat?'

'Fair go, son,' Cleaver responded with a grin. 'Night sailing might be all right for the young, or for the reckless, but not for a half-blind old bloke like me. Besides, we're only going a hundred yards or so off the pier, so my little dinghy'll do the job. You can take the oars if you like, good bit of exercise for a big strong bloke like you.' And with a wink in Clem's direction, he rose and shook their hands in farewell.

After Cleaver had rejoined his mates, Harry downed his beer and motioned that Clem should to the same. But as he turned to go, he saw Gloria waving to him from further down the bar.

'Anything jog your memory?' he inquired as she joined them.

'Not really,' she replied. 'Not so far as that Natalya coming to Australia goes. But I do remember Sam and Dave one night. They'd had a few and Dave let slip that they were going to make their fortune. I asked what they meant. Sam sort of looked at Dave, gave him a bit of a stare, then said they were going off to the goldfields. To make their fortunes there, he said.

I thought they was just skiting. Pub talk, y'know, I didn't think anything of it at the time. Probably not much use to you, but I thought I'd mention it anyway.'

'Who knows, might be useful,' Harry replied. He thought Gloria was probably right: just pub talk. 'One other thing, if I could keep you from your customers for one more minute.'

'Sure, ducks, what d'you want to know?'

'Well, Jim Cleaver over there was talking about ships in the night. Kind of suggested there might be a bit of smuggling going on around here from time to time. I wonder if you've picked up any talk on the other side of the bar that would give weight to that.'

Gloria gave a slight chuckle. 'I don't know about that. You do hear some things, but it's probably just the drink talking, I reckon. I know it used to go on in the old days, from what I hear, but I don't know about now. Anyway, your local copper mates should be able to tell you better than I could. They're in here on a pretty regular basis.'

Harry raised an eyebrow. 'I wouldn't necessarily bet on that. Anyway, you're probably right. About the drink talking, I mean.'

Harry took up his hat, then had another thought.

'Tell you what, Gloria. I wouldn't mind you keeping an eye out in here over the next couple of days. An ear out too, I suppose. Any gossip, any strange faces in the pub. That sort of thing.'

'For you, Harry, anything,' Gloria smiled.

Harry grinned back. 'You're a good sport, Gloria. See you later, then.'

'See you, ducks. Good luck with your investigation. Hope you catch the bastard that did poor Sam in.'

'So do I,' Harry replied, grimacing. 'So do I.'

10

⁂

HARRY WAS BEGINNING TO TIRE of these meetings in the Sorrento police station. He was becoming weary of sitting here, trying to get some initiative from the local constabulary. But he was getting nothing, just blank faces around the table.

'Come on, are you telling me no-one knows where this Sam bloke worked? You've tried all the lime kilns, Arthur?'

'I have,' Staples confirmed. 'But no joy, I'm afraid. Sorry, boss.'

'Including Coppin's kiln? You checked with the manager, Wilkes? Sam might have done some work there with his mate, Dave.'

'Yeh, I checked with him, but he swears black and blue he never employed a bloke called Sam. And I showed him the photograph. Never seen him, he reckons. Seems like our bloke Sam kept to himself, with whatever he was doing.'

Harry paced over to the window and looked out. It was another beautiful summer's day in Sorrento, and he could see the tourists already on the Esplanade, enjoying the morning air and chatting with each other, seemingly without a care in the world.

Harry's mood was not so carefree. Things were not going well and he was starting to get desperate for a breakthrough.

He turned back to the room and directed his attention to Newgate. 'Perhaps he had a reason to keep his affairs private. Sarge, I've had a whisper or two that some boats might be used for a bit more than fishing. Have you had any reports or suspicions about night-time activities? Smuggling and the like?'

Newgate exchanged a surreptitious glance with his colleagues, then replied. 'Not really, boss. We've had a few run-ins with a couple of the fishermen. Allegations of nets being raided and the like. But nothing else really. Not sure what would be smuggled anyway.'

Harry eyed Newgate steadily. 'No reports of strange boats at night? Doing things they shouldn't be doing?'

Newgate looked puzzled. 'Certainly not on the ocean side. Too rocky and rough. I wouldn't fancy my chances unloading anything at night from there.'

'Fair enough. But what about on the bay side? Who are the fishermen you suspect have been doing the wrong thing? Raiding nets, like you said.'

Newgate shrugged. 'Oh, they're just allegations, really. No-one in particular. Can you think of anyone, Arthur?'

Staples shook his head firmly. 'No, no-one, Sarge.'

'What about that Madigan bloke?' Wally Morris suggested. 'Remember we had a complaint about him last year. Someone said he was raiding nets and flogging off other people's catches on the Melbourne market.'

'Oh, that's right, Tosh Madigan, I forgot about him,' Newgate said hastily. 'But there was nothing proven, as I remember. Probably just some bad blood, that's what we thought at the time. I mean, Madigan is a bit of a rogue, I suppose, but nothing proven so far.'

'Still,' Harry noted, 'that's useful information. Thanks, Wally, we might follow up on that. By the way, Clive, you did interview this Madigan bloke, I take it? Asked him if Sam worked for him at any point?'

'We sure did,' Newgate answered promptly. 'He said he hadn't. But you wouldn't believe too much of what Madigan says. He wouldn't lie straight in bed.'

Harry turned his attention to Wally Morris. 'What about you, Wally? You were going to check out all the lodgings and shacks around the place. Any luck?'

Morris gave a rueful shrug. 'Not really, Inspector. I've done a fair sweep of all the boarding houses along the peninsula, but no-one's heard of Sam. Same story with the fishing shacks. Though I did come across one empty one.'

Harry's ears pricked. 'Really? Any signs of recent habitation? You look inside?'

'Yeh, I did. It was unlocked, so I had a peek. Nothing much to report though. All empty, no sign of anyone living there. But the strange thing was, it was kind of clean and neat inside. No dust or signs of vermin, or anything like that. Like someone must've lived there recently, but has cleared out.'

'Hmm,' Harry mused. 'Or someone else has cleared the place out. Where is this shack, Wally? Close to any others who might have noticed any recent occupation?'

'Not really. It's kind of hidden from any others. Up a small inlet. But there are occupied shacks reasonably close by. Maybe I could go back and ask them that question. If they've seen anyone living there.'

'I've got a better idea, Wally. Why don't you, me and Willie here, get over to that shack this afternoon? It sounds like it's worth following up straight away. And Clive, organise for us to interview Madigan, as soon as possible. Let's see if a bit of pressure will jog his memory.'

'Righto,' Newgate replied, somewhat less than enthusiastically.

Harry gave the sergeant an irritated glance. His attitude was starting to get on Harry's nerves. Staples too, the pair of them were quite useless. At least young Morris seemed keen, and Harry made a mental note to give him a bit more responsibility, in preference to his slack workmates.

Harry had made a tactical decision to summon Nikolai Matyunin to the police station for an interview. If Matyunin did indeed have something to hide about his contact with Natalya, then a formal police interview might just help unsettle his urbane composure. But when Willie Milton showed the Russian diplomat into the cramped office, his manner was as unruffled as ever, cream trousers and blue blazer freshly pressed and spotless.

'Good afternoon, Harry. I understand from your sergeant here that you wish to see me. I am at your disposal. Is there anything I can do to assist your investigation?'

'Possibly,' Harry replied. 'I understand that you might have met yesterday with Miss Kuzmina?'

Matyunin looked puzzled. 'Of course, Harry. You and I both, as you may recall.'

'No, no. I mean after our meeting in the morning. In the afternoon, at the Continental.'

Matyunin glanced at Harry curiously. 'My goodness, Harry, you are certainly well-informed. I hope you're not spying on upright citizens going about their legitimate business.'

Harry felt a tinge of embarrassment at Matyunin's not-so-veiled criticism, but pushed on regardless. 'No matter how I found out, sir. I understand you had quite a detailed and animated discussion with the girl, and that she became upset and emotional as the meeting proceeded. I'm wondering whether you found out any further information that might be useful to our inquiry?'

Matyunin considered the question for a few moments, then calmly replied. 'Actually, Harry, I was planning to talk to you, but you have beaten me to the punch, as it were. Natalya did speak to me again, as you somehow seem to know, and she did reveal that she was indeed acquainted with the dead man you know as Sam. More than that, she was romantically involved with him. His name is Sergei Karpov.'

Harry nodded slowly. 'I rather suspected that there was a relationship there. That explains her obvious distress when she found out about his death. But it doesn't explain why she kept her relationship with Sergei hidden from us. Did she confide in you?'

Again, Matyunin eyed Harry speculatively. 'The thing is, Harry, the poor girl is afraid. As you undoubtedly noticed. It seems that Sergei was illegally in Australia, and I suspect that Natalya was planning to join him here. Now it seems, she is afraid that she too may be in trouble if she admits to their relationship and their proposed way forward. A foolish notion, and I certainly attempted to advise her to talk to you, but she could not be persuaded.'

Harry shrugged. 'I can understand that. A young, naive girl alone in a strange land. And her sweetheart murdered. It must be overwhelming for her. But she needs to understand that she's in no danger from the law here.'

'I tried to convince her of that very fact, but to no avail.'

Harry leaned forward in his chair. 'I respect that you didn't press the matter of Sergei's death with her. But did she, by any chance, inform you of Sergei's activities in Australia? Was he a fisherman, for example?'

Matyunin shook his head firmly. 'No, she didn't raise that subject, and I didn't pursue her about it. I was seeking to calm the girl down, not interrogate her further.'

Harry considered Matyunin's response. His explanation for the garden meeting seemed to make sense, and certainly fitted with Natalya's demeanour earlier in the day. A young, unworldly girl in a foreign land; maybe her panic and distress was based only on an irrational fear of the law, fear that she would be associated somehow with Sergei's illegal status and thrown in jail.

At any rate, there seemed to be nothing further he could glean from

Matyunin, so Harry rose, thanked the consul for his ready cooperation, and bid him good day.

The Russian's bland smile and firm handshake told Harry nothing, except that here was a man who was not easily rattled.

❧

Constable Wally Morris drove the police trap west along Point Nepean Road, reining in the horse when they came to a rough track on their right that led to the Port Phillip Bay shoreline. Morris was about to direct their horse down this track, but Harry stopped him.

'We'll tether the trap here, Wally, as long as you don't mind a little walk. I don't want to disturb the track, or the area around the shack when we get there.'

With the horse tethered to a sapling on the side of the road, Harry, Willie and Morris set off down the track.

Harry carefully studied the sandy ruts as they walked. He pointed to the ground. 'I reckon there's been a cart of some sort coming down this track. On more than one occasion, too. And look at those indentations, it's been carrying a fair load, I'd reckon.'

Harry surveyed the dense coastal tea-tree on either side of the path. 'And it's secluded enough here too. No one would notice a cart coming along this track.'

'Yeh, Inspector, it's like this all the way down to the shore,' Morris said. 'We could be in the middle of nowhere.'

They rounded a bend and came upon the old run-down wooden shack, nestled near the water's edge. Harry noted a small pier behind the shack, running some thirty-odd yards out into the bay.

When they prised open the rickety door and stepped inside, it was as Morris had described: surprisingly clean for a derelict building. There was certainly dust on the old pine floor, but the kitchen table was relatively dirt-free, and certainly bare of animal droppings. A few kitchen utensils stacked in a makeshift open dresser looked as though they had been in use in recent times.

'You're right,' Harry said, 'someone's been living here recently. Living fairly rough, maybe, but living here, for sure. Let's have a look in the bedroom.'

A glance into the bedroom told the same story: a single bed on either side of the room, each with a mattress and blanket, a couple of rough shelves, and that was it. No other signs of habitation.

Harry wandered over to one of the beds, lifted the mattress and looked underneath. Nothing. He repeated the inspection under the second bed and whistled softly as he pulled forth a large sheet of paper.

'Hullo! What have we got here?' One glance at the grimy sheet was enough. 'It's one of George Coppin's fliers. For the Cossack show.'

Morris examined the poster. 'These've been plastered around the town for months.'

'What do you reckon?' Willie asked. 'Our drowned Russian been shacked up here?'

Harry stood with his hands in pockets, taking in the view out through the small, dirt-stained window. 'A good chance, I'd say. Be pretty easy to keep a low profile living out here. No-one'd know you were here. Sure as hell explains why no-one else seems to know where he lived. And I'd reckon his mate, Dave, might have lived here as well. Anyway, let's have a look outside, see what we can find there.'

The exterior inspection was as straightforward as the interior. Nothing much to see, except the tangled bush encroaching on all sides. On one side of the dwelling though, the rough track continued on down to the small pier.

Harry knelt and closely examined the ground and the two ruts of the track. 'What do you reckon, Willie? This part of the track looks as though it's been in regular use too. Same sorts of indentations as we observed before, back up there.'

Willie nodded his agreement. 'Reckon you're right, boss. Those boys were carting something. Down to that pier, I'd say. Logical conclusion is they were shipping something somewhere.'

Harry nodded, then glancing around, pointed to the side of the house where an old steel drum stood. 'Reckon that's their rubbish bin. Always worth a peek, in my experience. A job for you, Wally, I'm afraid.'

Morris approached the bin and looked inside. Picking up a stick from the ground, he poked about. Harry came up and peered over his shoulder.

'Not much here that I can see, Inspector,' Morris suggested. 'Just a few old cans and some empty bottles.'

Harry reached in and extracted one of the bottles. 'Looks to be a few like this,' he said, examining the label. 'Hmm, Irish whiskey, Powers Gold Label, no less.'

'Not surprising,' Willie suggested. 'Not much else to do out here, I'd say.'

'I suppose,' Harry agreed. 'Though it doesn't look like the usual kind of rotgut you'd expect these fellows to be drinking. My understanding of Irish whiskey is limited, but it might be a good idea to check its price and availability, eh Wally? We know they frequented the Sailors Arms, so check with our friend Gloria, or her boss. What was his name? Chester, wasn't it?'

'I'm onto it, Inspector.'

'One more thing to examine,' Harry continued, pointing to the water's edge. 'Let's have a look at that little landing.'

They made their way down to the water and walked out onto the small pier. It was surprisingly more stable than it first looked. Harry walked its full length, inspecting the timber walkway as he went. He turned to Willie.

'This is solid enough. It's been kept in working order, I'd say. A few of these timbers have been recently replaced,' he added, leaning over to examine the structure more closely. 'They're not as weathered as the rest.'

'Spot on,' Willie agreed, performing a little leap on the spot and coming down hard on the landing. 'Solid as anything.'

At the end of the pier, Harry examined the timber pile that rose above the level of the walkway and served as a mooring bollard. Hard to tell, but it looked smooth and well-used. He leaned over and gazed into the water's depths.

'A reasonable draft here, Wally. Deep enough to accommodate a boat of reasonable size?'

Morris peered too, endeavouring to locate the bottom. 'Yeh, I'd say so, Inspector.'

'A couta boat, for example?'

Morris thought for a moment. 'I'd reckon so.'

Harry straightened and gazed silently out into the bay, deep in thought. 'Something was going on here,' he said eventually, to no-one in particular. 'And I reckon it involved our two Russians. But what it was, and who else it involved, that's what we need to find out. Find that out, and we're well along the way to finding their killer. Or killers.'

Though they could have walked, just for a lark, Effie, Lydia and Michael had caught the steam train from the Palace to the back beach. The little engine chugged steadily along, hauling its two carriages packed with tourists.

Notwithstanding the proximity of so many sweaty bodies, the three friends found their short journey enjoyable. Indeed, the open-air carriages, with their canvas rooves, offered welcome relief from the early afternoon sun.

Arriving at their destination, Effie and Lydia extended their parasols, ready for their walk along the beach. But Michael had other ideas.

'It's damned hot here in the sun,' he complained, removing his hat and wiping his brow with a silk handkerchief. 'What about a cooling drink at the kiosk before we tackle our walk?'

'A splendid idea!' Lydia agreed enthusiastically, executing a sharp left turn in the direction of the kiosk. 'Let's hope we can find a table.'

And find a table they did, but only just, with the room packed full of day-trippers sheltering from the summer sun. They settled in and ordered iced lemonades all round.

'This is the life,' Lydia declared, removing her hat. 'It's a pity Rachel didn't join us. I do hope she's not too put out, on her own and with Willie so busy with the investigation.'

'Don't worry about Rachel,' Effie smiled. 'She's having the time of her life with the children. I don't think we'll be waiting too long for her and Willie to start a family.'

'How's James enjoying his camp? Sick of the outdoor life yet?' Lydia asked Michael.

'Far from it,' Michael replied, smiling. 'He's says he's loving it. He doesn't seem to be missing me at all.'

'I'm sure he misses you, darling,' Lydia reassured him. 'He's roughing it for the sake of his art.'

'Speaking of the artist's camp, isn't that Clara Southern over there?' Effie said, indicating the far side of the room with a nod of her head, where a striking, red-haired woman could be seen in animated discussion with a male companion.

Lydia swivelled and stared, none too subtly. 'You're right, it is. And who's that with her?'

Michael looked too, then exclaimed in a low voice, 'By George, I think it's that Petrenko fellow. You know, the one James was talking about. The one who can't paint. James has pointed him out to me at the camp.'

They all watched as Clara Southern, unmistakeable now with her auburn hair and striking looks, chatted amiably to the mysterious Mr Petrenko, who seemed relaxed and at ease. He was a tallish fellow, pale and, like his companion, also with a mop of reddish hair. In addition, he sported a rather straggly red beard.

'What is it with that fellow?' Effie muttered. 'For someone who James says can't paint, he seems to command a lot of attention from Clara and Jane.'

'He does, doesn't he,' Lydia agreed. 'It's all a bit odd.'

'It's very odd,' Effie agreed. 'And James' view is odd too, given what we saw of Petrenko's work at the Institute the other day. I thought it was very promising.'

They continued to watch as Southern and her student chatted on. Then Petrenko leaned forward towards Southern, glancing around the room before saying something to her. Southern nodded as he spoke, her expression now much more serious.

'That all looks rather cosy,' Effie said. 'I'd love to know what they're talking about.'

'There's one way to find out,' Lydia replied, rising to her feet. 'Let's pay our respects.' And she set off across the room, the others in somewhat reluctant pursuit.

'Clara! What a wonderful surprise! Taking a spell from your artistic endeavours, I see. Good for you!'

Southern swivelled in her seat, her alarmed expression immediately replaced by a forced smile. 'Oh hello, Lydia. Nice to see you too.'

'And who is your companion here? One of your artistic proteges, no doubt,' Lydia continued, flashing a warm smile at Petrenko.

A quick glance was exchanged between Southern and her companion before she replied. 'Yes, this is Mr Vladimir Petrenko. He's one of our artists.'

'I thought so. You look every inch an artist, Mr Petrenko,' Lydia effused, extending an elegant hand, then making a great show of introducing Effie and Michael, standing behind her in embarrassed silence.

'Tell me, Mr Petrenko, all about your artistic experience,' Lydia continued.

'I haven't heard of you. You must be one of Clara's up-and-coming luminaries. Like Michael's friend, James Mathieson.'

Petrenko gave another brief glance towards Southern and shifted uneasily in his chair before replying in halting tones. 'My English not very good, madam. I am learning painting, but long way to go. Miss Sutherland very kind to allow me to attend her school.'

'Tell me, Mr Petrenko, who are your artistic heroes,' Effie interposed, beginning to get into the swing of Lydia's game. 'Who has influenced you the most?'

Petrenko stared at her blankly for a moment or two, then replied, hesitatingly, with a wave of the arm, 'Oh, all the great masters are my inspiration.'

'Of course,' Lydia beamed. 'But which masters in particular, would you say?'

Again, there was an embarrassed pause from Petrenko, before Clara Southern responded, 'You'll have to excuse Mr Petrenko. As he said, his English is not very good. And he is rather shy. But I can assure you, he is an artist of great promise. You saw some of his sketching at the institute, did you not?'

'We did,' Lydia replied. 'And you're right, very promising. Very assured, I thought. Surprisingly so, if you don't mind me saying.'

Southern looked at her oddly, glanced again at Petrenko, then pointing to the clock on the far wall, exclaimed, 'Goodness me! Is that the time? We really must be getting back to the camp. My students will be wondering where I am.' And she rose to her feet.

'Of course, my dear,' Lydia said pleasantly. 'We understand completely. So nice to see you again. And to meet you, Mr Petrenko. I shall look forward to observing your flourishing career.'

Southern murmured a farewell, Petrenko gave a hesitant bow, and the two scuttled off. Rather too hastily, Effie thought.

Lydia turned to her and Michael, grinning triumphantly. 'Well, that's as clear as daylight, I'd reckon. Mr Petrenko is no artist, wouldn't you say?'

'I'd say you're right,' Michael agreed. 'Most artists can't stop talking about themselves and their art. That fellow didn't have a word to say about his painting, and from what James has told me, he's not very keen on putting brush to canvas either.'

'I don't know about you, Lydia,' Effie mused, 'But I thought Mr Petrenko looked vaguely familiar. We haven't met him before, have we?'

Lydia paused a moment or two, tapping one elegant finger against her cheek, then said, 'I think you're right, darling, he *was* sort of familiar. And you know what it is? I reckon he was that fellow we saw up in the dunes. You know, when we walked on the beach. I remember now, I thought that fellow had red hair.'

'Are you sure?' Effie asked doubtfully. 'It was a long way away.'

'Absolutely, I'm sure!' Lydia asserted. 'That fellow up in the dunes seemed tall too. It was him, for sure. What was he doing up there, I wonder, sneaking about among the dunes?'

'I'd assume he was painting,' Michael suggested. 'After all, that's what they're up there for. That's hardly sneaking.'

'Nonsense!' Lydia retorted. 'That fellow had no painting equipment with him. And why did he dash off as soon as he saw us looking at him?'

Michael simply shrugged. 'I don't know. But surely it's not exactly suspicious.'

'Highly suspicious, in my opinion,' Lydia responded. Then, turning to Effie, she instructed, in conspiratorial tones, 'Make sure you tell Harry about today's meeting. And about our sighting of Petrenko in the sand hills. He needs to know.'

'I will,' Effie agreed readily. 'I'm not sure about highly suspicious either, but his behaviour is certainly very odd. And odd too that Clara Southern seems to be protecting him from any scrutiny.'

'Another Russian riddle, eh?' Lydia mused.

'Righto, time for our walk, I suppose,' Michael suggested, as they made their way outside. 'What do you think, ladies?'

'I think it's too dashed hot,' Effie replied, removing her hat and fanning herself with it.

'I agree,' Lydia concurred. 'The breeze has gone, I'm afraid. It's rather too stifling for exercise.'

'I was hoping you'd say that,' Michael replied. 'I have a better suggestion. What about my shout at the Continental? We can get our exercise walking back there.'

'Splendid, darling,' Lydia. 'Sounds perfect. And we'll still be able to feel virtuous, and proclaim to our husbands that we've taken our daily constitutional.'

Harry leaned into his work and soon the little skiff was fairly skimming over the water. Harry was not the most skilful of rowers, but what he lacked in technique, he more than made up for in strength. And he was enjoying the exercise, after the frustration of the past few days.

It was a calm night, with a spectacular moon sparkling the rippling water in their wake, as they made their way out into the bay from the Sorrento pier. Harry watched as the lights of the town dwindled into the distance.

'That's enough rowing, son,' Jim Cleaver instructed from the stern of the craft. 'At the rate you're going, you'll have us in Melbourne before we know it. I reckon we're about three hundred yards offshore now, so that'll do nicely.'

'No worries, Jim,' Harry replied, removing the oarlocks and placing the oars carefully on each side of the boat. 'That was good. I was working off a bit of steam.'

'I could see that, son,' Cleaver grinned. 'Now, I've brought rods for you and Clem here. That okay?'

'Don't worry about me, Jim. You and Dad do the fishing, I'll just sit here and relax. This sea air's doing me the power of good.'

'No worries. Pass over that bait bucket then, with those mullet in it, and Clem and me'll show you how it's done.'

While Cleaver and Clem busied themselves baiting their hooks and casting into the bay, Harry found himself ruminating as he gazed back at the town, its lights twinkling in the clear night.

He tried to take stock of where things were up to. What did he have as fact? Not a lot. Two dead Russians, mates and both the apparent victims of foul play. In Harry's mind, that clearly indicated a common killer. Or killers. And it seemed that both deaths were premeditated, to some extent at least. All of which, Harry's experience told him, pointed to the dead men being involved in some sort of criminal activity.

But what? Maybe it was connected with the theft of jewels from the quarantined ship. That seemed unlikely, though it was something they needed to follow up. Maybe his boss's wild imaginings of Russian invasions and spies abounding had some grain of truth to them. That seemed unlikely too, but he would need to keep it as a possibility.

And the final possibility to think about, as raised by Jim Cleaver, was some sort of organised smuggling racket. Though he had no evidence to point to that, apart from some apparent pub talk, and the interesting, but hardly conclusive, signs of activity detected at the empty shack. Still, it was probably his most promising lead to date.

And what of Natalya, the Russian dancer? It was clear that she was indeed Sergei Karpov's sweetheart, and that she had most probably joined the dance troupe with the express purpose of reuniting with him in Australia. But why was she so reluctant to reveal her intentions? Harry thought Matyunin's explanation that she was afraid she would be arrested as an illegal immigrant a possible cause of her distress, but perhaps not the only one.

Another scenario suggested itself to Harry. Perhaps Natalya was aware of what criminal enterprise her boyfriend was involved in, and was afraid of being arrested as an accomplice. Or even perhaps, her fear was that she might go the same way as Karpov if she told what she knew. Harry resolved to interview her again and try to extract the truth from her. Perhaps on Sunday, after the performance tomorrow evening.

Harry's ponderings were interrupted by a sudden jolt to the boat and a muttered exclamation from Clem. He looked up to see his father heaving on the straining line.

'Steady, Clem!' Cleaver urged. 'Pull him in steady now. Don't let him jerk off the line.'

Clem was getting on in years and was rather skinny and bent by Father Time. But he was still wiry and as tough as nails. Harry watched with quiet amusement as the old bloke gritted his teeth and did his best to follow his old mate's instructions. After ten minutes or so of pitched battle, Clem got the upper hand and steadily reeled in his catch. A large fish appeared out of the gloom, Clem leaned over with his gaff, and the boat rocked decidedly as a more-than-respectable mulloway joined them in the bowels of the boat.

'That's a beauty, mate!' exclaimed Cleaver. 'Thirty pound, if it's an ounce.'

Clem sat exhausted as the large fish thrashed about in the bottom of the boat.

Harry leaned over and patted his father's shoulder. 'Well done, Dad, but I don't know what we're going to do with it.'

'We're taking it back to the Palace, that's what,' Clem declared defiantly. 'There's a lot of good eating in that bloke.'

'Mrs Meriwether might have something to say about that,' Harry suggested. 'I doubt she'll want you lugging that monster into her kitchen.'

Cleaver gave a hearty chuckle. 'Don't you believe it, son! Agnes'll be tickled pink to get it. That bloke'll feed the whole guesthouse for free. Trust me, she'll welcome it with open arms.'

Harry eyed his dad, sitting triumphant next to his old mate. Triumphant and tired. The battle with the mulloway had fair done him in.

'Well, Dad, Jim, we're not going to do better than that tonight, I don't reckon. Time to head home?'

'Why not?' Cleaver responded. 'Get yourself on the oars again, son.'

Harry reached down to gather the oars and attach the rowlocks. But as he did so, his attention was caught by what appeared to be a white sail glinting in the moonlight, further out in the bay.

'That's a boat out there, isn't it, Jim?'

Cleaver swivelled around and gazed across the water. The moon shone down on them, giving sufficient light to discern a craft making its way across the horizon.

'You're right, son,' Cleaver agreed. 'It is a boat.'

'What's going on in this town?' Harry exclaimed. 'Effie and I saw a boat out there two nights ago. A couta boat, I thought.'

'That one's not a couta,' Cleaver explained. 'That's a square-rigger, a bigger boat. But I got no idea what he's doing at this time of night.'

Harry was intrigued. 'Really? What are the possibilities, do you think?'

Cleaver removed his battered old hat and scratched his bald head in contemplation. 'Dunno, really. Don't reckon they're fishing. Those bigger ketches are usually lime carriers. But not during the night, that's for sure.'

They watched in silence for a few seconds, then Cleaver added, 'It's heading eastward. I'd say it's in the South Channel, heading to Melbourne.'

They all sat silently, watching, as the white sails faded into the murk.

'What cargo could it possibly be carrying?' Harry persisted. 'What's moved from here to Melbourne on a regular basis.'

Cleaver shrugged. 'A few things, I suppose. The fish catch is taken up to the markets, but not at this hour. There'd be no-one around at the markets. Same with the lime cargo. There's regular runs of lime up to Melbourne too, but not in the middle of the night. They're always taken up in the mornings. Buggered if I know, son.'

'Never mind, Jim,' Harry consoled. 'We'll mark it down as a bit of a mystery. But it's a mystery I'm keen to solve.'

Then, as his mind went back to the morning's debrief, he added, 'The blokes at the station this morning mentioned a bloke called Tosh Madigan as someone who gets up to a bit of mischief. What do you reckon? Any truth in that assessment?'

Cleaver chuckled. 'Your blokes were spot on, I'd say. Madigan does a bit of fishing, a bit of lime carting, and the word is, a bit of all sorts of other stuff as well. Some of it sailing pretty close to the wind, by all accounts. And that ketch looked kind of similar to his. Hard to tell from this distance though.'

Harry paused from attaching the rowlocks. 'What do you mean, 'other stuff'? What sort of other stuff?'

Another shrug from Jim Cleaver. 'I dunno, it's just what you hear. Some say he deals in stuff that's not strictly his to deal with, if you get my drift.'

'That sounds rather suspicious,' Harry replied. 'Though, from what the boys at the station say, it seems like he's never been in any real trouble with the law. Still, I think we'll have a little chat with him. Ask him if he does any night voyages, eh? Now, let's get this boat back to shore. Never know, we might be in time for a quick beer at the pub, eh, Dad?'

Harry readied the boat and, with Jim Cleaver on the rudder, began a strong pace towards the pier and the twinkling lights of the Sailors Arms.

11

⚶

GEORGE COPPIN STOOD IN FRONT of the Athenaeum's spacious stage and eyed Harry morosely. 'I'm beginning to think this was one of my more foolish ideas,' he confided. 'I think perhaps I've misread the mood of the town.'

Harry, seated in the front row, looked up from his notepad and cocked a surprised eye. 'Not from what you told me the other day, George. You said you were expecting a full house.'

'Not what I mean,' Coppin continued, in the same downcast tone. 'Truth is, many will come simply because the dance troupe is Russian. The curiosity factor, you know, to see what all the fuss is about.

'But I suspect there'll also be a good number coming to demonstrate their antipathy to the presence of Russians here in Sorrento. No offence, Ivan, to you or your people,' he added to Borodin, the Cossack manager.

'None taken, George,' that gentleman replied calmly. 'But surely you are overestimating that kind of feeling in the community. I, for one, have not noticed any ill will towards us. Indeed, the hospitality shown to us has been most generous.'

'I hope you're right,' Coppin replied. 'But there's a good deal of anti-Russian feeling out there, I've no doubt about that. I've even detected it among the crowd I mingle with, the artistic community. And the mysterious deaths of those two Russians over the past week or so haven't helped. Rumours are flying thick and fast.'

'Don't worry, George,' Harry reassured. 'We'll have all hands on deck tonight to make sure there's no trouble.'

Harry's comforting words reflected his own views on the foolish paranoia that had gripped Australia in the seventies and eighties. Nothing had eventuated to justify the anti-Russian fears that had gripped the State. But, in truth, he was not convinced that such fears had fully abated.

The near encounter with the Russian ship only a few days previously, and the continuing xenophobia displayed by some civic leaders, such as his own boss, had demonstrated to Harry that anti-Russian sentiment had not fully dissipated. Not by any means.

But his security planning for this evening's event had less to do with that lingering negative sentiment, and more to do with the recent murders, and how they might relate to the visit of the Cossacks. And to the visit of Natalya Kuzmina, in particular.

'Let's worry about what we can control, eh, George? Let me take you and Mr Borodin through my plans for tonight.'

'Of course,' Coppin replied, nodding his agreement. 'Sorry for being such a doomsayer.' And he gave Harry his full attention.

'All right then,' Harry continued. 'As I said, we'll have all available men on duty tonight. That is, me and Sergeant Milton here, plus our local men, Sergeant Newgate and his two officers.

'Sergeant Milton and I will be in the body of the theatre. That's for a couple of reasons. Firstly, we'll be in plain clothes, so as not to alarm the audience, and secondly, to quickly get things under control if there's anyone in the audience wanting to cause a bit of trouble. Willie and I've had plenty of experience chucking troublemakers out of the MCG, so we can handle any rowdy or disruptive sort of behaviour here easily enough.'

'Excellent!' Coppin enthused. 'Just the ticket?'

'Now, I've checked out the situation backstage,' Harry went on. 'There's two dressing rooms – one for men, one for women – and a couple of storage rooms. More importantly, there are two external entry points backstage, a stage door on the right hand side, and a larger rear door, which I understand is used for the movement of backdrops and such like.'

'Yes, that's the layout as I understand it too,' Coppin agreed.

'We'll have a uniformed officer stationed outside each of those doors, to prevent any unauthorised entry. And finally, we'll have Sergeant Newgate here maintaining a careful watch backstage, just in case anyone manages to sneak back there somehow from the main part of the theatre.'

Coppin nodded his satisfaction. 'Very good, Harry, very good. I'm greatly reassured by that plan. Very discreet too. I like that.'

'Glad you're happy,' Harry replied. Then he turned to Borodin. 'There's one request I would make of you, if I may.'

'Certainly, Inspector, happy to oblige if I can.'

'It's about Miss Kuzmina, in your troupe. I know she's in rather a fragile state, following her discovery that the Russian chap we found in the harbour was her sweetheart. She now seems to be in great fear for some reason.

I think it would be in both our interests for you to reassure her of the importance we're placing on protecting her and her fellow dancers.'

Borodin nodded slowly. 'Of course, a wise suggestion, and one which I will undertake to fulfil.'

'Good,' Harry concluded. 'And now, if you'll excuse us, we're all rather busy with our investigation. We'll see you again this evening, eh?'

'I think I could get quite used to this,' Lydia ventured, as she bobbed up and down in the clear waters of Port Phillip Bay. Or more accurately, the clear waters of the Sorrento sea baths.

Today, Lydia had forsaken her colourful red and blue bathing outfit in favour of Mrs Erlandsen's calico uniform, explaining to Effie that she had no wish to stand out amongst the other ladies. Yet somehow, even half-hidden beneath a giant straw hat, Lydia managed to remain the most elegant woman of the twenty or so in the sea baths that morning.

'You're right,' Effie agreed, imitating Lydia's bob, but being careful not to wet her hair. 'It's surprisingly relaxing, I must say. And nice to know we're protected from any sea creatures that might be interested in having a nibble on us. Harry told me there are sharks about, and to be careful with Alfie down at the beach.'

'Sound advice,' Lydia agreed, smiling. Then she added, 'But you know, you're not guaranteed to be immune from marauding fish in here. There's a famous story that some young rascal threw a small shark over the picket fence and created mayhem among the ladies.'

'Really?' Effie replied, slightly alarmed. She glanced nervously around the perimeter of the baths.

'Don't worry,' Lydia laughed. 'I believe that was before the Erlandsen era. I don't think any larrikin would dare try that trick with those two in charge.'

'By the way,' she added, 'Where's our favourite inspector today? Making progress, I hope.'

'I'm not sure,' Effie replied. 'He's sounding a bit more positive about things when I ask him, but as usual he's not giving too much away. I know he's been a bit sidetracked by Mr Coppin's show tonight. You know, organising all the security.'

'Of course,' Lydia replied. 'I do hope it goes well for dear old George, I believe he's sunk quite a bit into it. I'm sure it'll be packed out tonight, all my friends tell me they're going. And George tells me the Melbourne bookings for next week are progressing well too. But I must say, he still seems quite nervous about tonight.'

'I do hope that young lady, Natalya, will be all right,' Effie mused. 'That's one thing Harry did tell me, that he's worried for her welfare. He said she seemed terribly upset when he met with her.'

'Really?' Lydia exclaimed. 'I remember you mentioned meeting her at the beach. But why is she upset? Does she have something to do with those murdered men?'

Effie inwardly admonished herself. 'Oh dear!' she blurted out. 'I don't think I was meant to tell you that. Harry'd be cross if he thought I was giving away confidences.'

'Nonsense, darling, you know you can trust me to keep a secret. My lips will be sealed. Come on, tell me all.' And she leaned forward in the water, conspiratorially.

Effie realised she might as well reveal what she knew, rather than face a continuing cross-examination from Lydia. Anyway, Harry had told her that the Russian consul knew of Natalya's attachment to the dead man, so perhaps it wasn't meant to be kept secret.

'Very well, but keep this to yourself.' And Effie told her about how the drowned Russian, Sam, was Natalya's sweetheart. 'Of course, she's devastated.'

'Really? How awful. The poor girl.' And Lydia lapsed into silence, for once at a loss for words.

'Anyway,' Effie continued, endeavouring to change the subject, 'All that's been keeping Harry busy. He told me he hasn't had a chance to investigate our mysterious Russian artist. So-called artist, I should say.'

'It's a mystery, all right. And I'm sure it's connected to the case. Oh my god!' And Lydia suddenly rose out of the water.

Effie looked at her friend in alarm, then stood up herself. 'What is it, dear? Is there something in the water?' And she peered into the sea around them.

'No, no, Effie! Look up there!' And Lydia pointed to the small booth attached to the tea rooms at the beginning of the pier. 'Speak of the devil! Isn't that Mr Petrenko up there, at the ticketing booth?'

Effie looked toward the booth, some fifty yards away, where a red-haired man could be seen talking to the attendant. They watched as he completed his transaction and turned to leave. As he did so, he faced them full-on and they could see that it was indeed Vladimir Petrenko, his red hair and patchy beard unmistakeable.

'Goodness, what's he up to?' gasped Lydia, *sotto voce*, though that was hardly necessary, at this considerable distance from the object of their interest.

'It looks like he's getting a ticket,' Effie replied. Then realising she was stating the bleeding obvious, she added, 'Back to Melbourne, I assume.'

'Yes, but why? Why's he leaving? According to James, the camp's got a week to go.'

Effie shrugged. 'I don't know. Maybe he's finally realised he can't paint, and he's giving up.'

'I'd say it's highly suspicious,' Lydia muttered, staring at the departing figure of Petrenko who was now heading at a good pace back up the promenade towards Ocean Beach Road. 'Your Harry needs to know about this.'

'You're right,' Effie agreed. 'I'll tell him tonight.'

'You'll do better than that,' Lydia declared. 'You'll give him all the detail about where that fellow's going. And when.'

Effie was perplexed. 'Sorry, dear, I don't follow you.'

'You will. I'll explain as we go.' And Lydia waded towards the wooden steps, calling over her shoulder, 'Come on.'

Ten minutes later, the two women emerged from the change rooms, fully clothed again, and hurried along the pier, Lydia in the lead. The ticketing booth was free when they arrived. The attendant, a pimply, bored-looking youth, was idly perusing a magazine on the counter in front of him.

'Excuse me, sir,' Lydia began briskly, 'you might be able to help me.'

The attendant looked up from his reading and stared off-handedly at Lydia. 'Right then. You want a ticket? What day? What ship?' he queried, in a bored tone.

'Actually, I don't want a ticket,' Lydia replied confidently. 'I'm Mrs Petrenko. I believe my husband was just here, purchasing a ticket back to Melbourne. Tall chap, red hair.'

The youth nodded. 'That's right. Just now. Got a ticket for Monday morning. First boat out. Didn't he tell you?' And he eyed Lydia with a slightly suspicious gaze.

Lydia smiled and replied, 'That's the thing. The poor dear's so absent-minded. Never tells me anything. Just that he's been called back to work and quite ruined our holiday. I'm trying to plan my week with friends in his absence. You know how it is.'

'Nah, I don't know how it is, actually,' the young fellow observed. 'Not for those of us who have to work. Be nice to get a holiday, wouldn't it?'

Lydia smiled brightly, ignoring this lament. 'You've been very helpful, young man. Thank you, and we'll bid you good day.'

The attendant said nothing, just looking Lydia up and down briefly, then returned to his magazine.

'Now you've got some really good information for Harry,' Lydia whispered, as they headed back toward the tea rooms. 'We've done well. In fact, I think we've earned ourselves some morning tea.'

❦

'George Coppin should be tickled pink,' Lydia whispered to Effie, looking around the Athenaeum from their front row seats. 'Standing room only, by the look of it.'

Effie, Rachel, Lydia and husband Ed were among George Coppin's special invitations. Harry, of course, was not with them, instead could be seen standing at the back of the theatre, slightly less dishevelled than usual in suit and tie, and keeping a close eye on the crowd. On the other side of the theatre stood Willie, equally alert and vigilant.

It certainly seemed that the Cossack performance was likely to be a roaring success. Lydia was right, all the seats were taken, and latecomers were standing three-deep at the back of the theatre. Some had tried to occupy space on the side aisles, but were sternly rebuffed by Harry and Willie, determined to keep some semblance of order and prevent any ready access to the side doors leading backstage.

Effie looked along their front row and noticed George Coppin in animated conversation with Nikolai Matyunin, the Russian consul. She saw that both were wearing broad smiles, no doubt delighted at the obvious popularity of the event. And judging from the glamorous attire of many of the seated patrons, the Cossack show had also attracted the celebrity element of Sorrento's holiday-makers.

'Isn't this exciting, dear?' Effie whispered to Rachel by her side, grasping her hand. 'What a treat!'

Rachel smiled back and nodded.

The large clock at the side of the theatre was now showing eight o'clock, and the buzz in the audience grew in expectation of the show's commencement. But instead of the curtain being drawn open to get things underway, it was George Coppin who now sprang to his feet, skipped nimbly up the steps on the side of the stage and, to thunderous applause, strode to the centre of the stage and bowed three times, to each part of the theatre in turn.

'Ladies and gentlemen, welcome to our Cossack extravaganza!' he proclaimed, his still powerful voice carrying easily to the patrons standing at the back.

'My friends, how wonderful to see you all here tonight, to experience the colour, the beauty, the grace of this outstanding troupe. They have come here to our little town all the way from mother Russia.' He paused as another wave of applause echoed around the building. 'Now, those of you who know me well are probably expecting a little something from me before the show starts. Perhaps a little ditty, or a turn from Paul Pry or Bob Acres ...'

At the mention of Coppin's famous comedic characters there was another burst of applause and a barrage of calls from the audience, encouraging him to perform. But Coppin smiled and raised his hands aloft, calling for quiet.

'Much as it would delight me to entertain you, my friends, I'm afraid that my role tonight is limited to an introductory one. To welcome this wonderful group of dancers, of course, but before that, it is my pleasure to acknowledge a special guest tonight, the Russian consul to Victoria, Mr Nikolai Matyunin!'

Matyunin rose, turned to face the audience and bowed, to applause that was distinctly more polite than enthusiastic.

Sensing the audience was becoming impatient for the main event, Coppin dramatically extended his arms again and exclaimed: 'Ladies and gentlemen, it is now with the greatest pleasure I present for your enjoyment ... The Moscow Cossack Extravaganza!'

And so the curtain was drawn and it began. Within seconds of the opening dance performance, an all-male sabre dance, the audience was enraptured. On the side of the stage a small band had been set up, consisting of two balalaika players, an accordionist, a fiddler and a drummer. They struck up a lively tune and a dozen or so lithe, handsome young men dashed onto the stage, each with a sabre in hand, and performed an extraordinary series of routines, flashing their swords around each other in intricate movements that, to Effie's eyes at least, seemed highly dangerous. The audience clearly thought so too, judging by the gasps and cries that arose with each spectacular movement.

Following this opening number, the Cossack manager, Mr Borodin, appeared on stage to welcome the audience and explain what they had just witnessed, its origins and its place in Russian culture. He then announced and explained to them the next group of dances.

The 'Barynya' featured three beautifully dressed couples in a boisterous dance, involving much foot-stamping and acrobatic leaping about, all accompanied by dramatic shouts from the band members.

Then came the 'Beryozka', which Effie found particularly enthralling. In this dance, the women in the troupe, clad in full-length, red bustle skirts, and each carrying a white silk scarf, glided serenely about the stage in time to the music. They danced without any movement of their upper bodies, and the effect was as if they were floating effortlessly across the ground.

The dancers smiled as they glided across the stage in time with the music, their only arm movements the waving of their silk scarves. Effie spotted Natalya amongst them and could immediately see that her smile was tremulous and forced. From her front-row vantage point, Effie fancied that the poor girl was holding back tears. But Natalya continued to perform her role as the dance continued, building to a finale in which the dancers formed two circles, one within the other, then somehow effortlessly unravelled into a straight line across the stage, bowing gracefully to the audience and waving their silk scarves in acknowledgement of the thunderous applause.

Natalya's smile had disappeared when she joined her fellow dancers in acknowledging the audience applause, and after the third round of bowing, as the dancers moved off-stage Effie could see that Natalya was the first to break away from the line, hurrying off ahead of the rest, her head bowed.

There was a pause before the troupe prepared for the next dance, and Effie fancied she heard the sound of raised voices from the side of the stage. But soon the band struck up again and the entire group danced onto the stage to take part in the 'Khozachok', which was to be the final performance before the intermission.

Except that Effie couldn't see Natalya among the dancers on the stage. She carefully studied the women dancers as they whirled about, but there was no sign of the girl. Effie concluded that Natalya's grief must have been too much for her, and that she could no longer perform. Effie glanced back at Harry, but he was standing impassively at the back of the theatre, his focus on the audience rather than the performers.

Effie resolved to seek out Harry at the interval and alert him to Natalya's stricken state. In the meantime, she allowed herself to be distracted by the dancers, who were performing the lively 'Khozachok', the elegance and grace of the women contrasting with the athletic vigour of the male dancers.

As the dance came to a rousing, dramatic finale and the final movement concluded, the audience rose to its feet as one and applauded wildly, whistling and shouting their appreciation. The shouting and whistling continued as the troupe lined up and bowed a number of times. Eventually Mr Borodin appeared from the wings and, beaming broadly, raised his arms, as a signal for the audience that their appreciation could conclude.

The clapping and whistling died away, but as it did, another sound could be distinctly heard. A police whistle, loud and shrill, coming from somewhere behind the stage. Quickly looking back, Effie could see that both Harry and Willie were already hurrying urgently from opposite aisles toward the stage doors, alarm written on their faces.

Harry and Willie were the first to arrive at the dressing-room door, where Clive Newgate stood, blowing frantically on his whistle. 'The girl!' he cried, 'I think she's been done in!'

Harry said nothing, pushing past Newgate to enter the room, Willie right behind him. Natalya lay on the floor, still in her dance costume. She was not moving. Harry leaned over and felt her pulse. Nothing. The girl was dead. And judging by her swollen features and the red marks and scratches on her neck, she had been strangled.

Harry looked up. Newgate had followed him into the room, and Morris and Staples too, racing in from outside in response to the whistle.

'I saw him, boss! I saw him!' Newgate exclaimed. 'He went out the window!' And he pointed to the room's window, which was wide open.

'Get after him!' Harry shouted back. 'For god's sake, man! Hurry! You blokes, too! Move!' he shouted at Staples and Morris, who had entered and were standing there aimlessly, staring at Natalya lying on the floor.

All three policemen made for the window, but Harry shouted again. 'Not that way, you idiots! You'll interfere with the crime scene. Out the rear door!'

As the three dashed off back down the passage towards the rear door, Harry knelt to check the girl's pulse again, hoping he had made a mistake. But there was no doubt about it.

He rose and turned to Willie. 'She's gone, mate. Damn it! I could kick myself! I thought everything was secure.'

'Should I get after those blokes? Give them a hand?' Willie exclaimed.

Before Harry could answer, Ivan Borodin burst into the room, recoiling in horror as he saw Natalya lying there. Close behind him, Harry could see other members of the cast hurrying down the passage. Quickly he ushered Borodin out of the room, indicating to Willie to shut the door and keep the room secure.

Harry addressed Borodin and his dancers in the passage way. 'Miss Kuzmina has been assaulted,' he announced solemnly. 'I'm afraid she's dead.'

There were cries and gasps from the dancers, who began crowding around him, trying to get in the door. Harry could see that he would need to take control. He held up his arms.

'I must ask you to return to the stage area,' he said in a loud voice. 'There is nothing you can do for your colleague. There is nothing to be gained from you being here. This area is now a crime scene, and we must protect it for any evidence. That applies to you too, Mr Borodin,' he added, stepping in front of the manager, who was about to try to re-enter the room.

Borodin nodded his agreement and began shepherding his dancers back down the passage. Harry re-entered the dressing-room and spoke to Willie. 'Mate, I need you to manage things in the theatre. Get these dancers back onto the stage, draw the curtain, go out front and tell the audience to disperse. In an orderly manner.'

'What shall I say?' Willie asked. 'About what's happened.'

'Just say there's been an incident and the performance is unable to proceed. That's all. I don't want panic.'

Willie hurried off after Borodin and the dancers. Harry looked again at Natalya and sighed. Turning to the window, he looked for signs of forced entry, but there were none. Clearly, the sash had been left unfastened and had been easily pushed up. Harry cursed himself again for not checking the security arrangements himself and relying on these incompetent local police to secure the building. He should have remembered how unremittingly slack they were.

He examined the brass window lifts for signs of fingerprints. He could see nothing but made a mental note that they were worth checking anyway.

He leaned out the window, which opened out to the left-hand rear side of the building. Peering out into the moonlight, Harry could dimly make out a large storage shed on his right behind the theatre, and ahead of him the dusty metal road that ran through to the Ocean Beach Road at the theatre's front. Beyond the theatre's storage shed, Harry noted a cluster of low trees in the vacant lot behind.

He straightened back into the room. He didn't hold out much hope of his men catching the assailant, who would have had enough time to disappear into the cover of night. His faint expectations were very soon realised with the reappearance of a crestfallen, red-faced Sergeant Newgate at the door, his two colleagues behind him.

'Sorry, Inspector,' Newgate said, his voice subdued and tinged with disappointment. 'He got away. No sign of him. We had no chance, really, he could have gone anywhere. And it's hopeless now. Too many people mingling around, coming out of the theatre.' And he relapsed into silence.

'Can't be helped,' Harry replied. 'But I need you to tell me exactly what happened while it's still fresh in your mind.'

Newgate scratched his head. 'Well,' he said carefully, 'I was keeping watch in the passage behind the stage when I saw the girl come past. I saw it was the Kuzmina girl, you know, the one who's connected to our investigation, so I took particular notice. But I could see she was real upset, all teary-like, so I let her go past into the dressing room. Out of respect, y'see.'

'Okay,' Harry said. 'And then?'

'I didn't think much more about it, but then I heard the sound of two people talking in there. Well, not really talking, more like arguing, I suppose. And I could hear one of them was a bloke. That went on for a bit, but I didn't think much of it. Thought it might be the manager, telling her to get back to the show. But then I heard a funny sound, not really a scream, more like a gurgling sound, and I pricked my ears up. Then it went quiet, and I started to get a bit worried, so I knocked on the door and asked if everything was all right. I heard someone moving about inside but no-one answered, so I opened the door and went in. Just in time to see some bloke disappearing out the window.'

'Did you get a look at him?' Harry asked. 'What did he look like?'

Newgate shook his head slowly. 'Sorry, Inspector, he was already half out the window and into the dark. All I saw was he was wearing a big hat, pulled down like, and a dark coat. He might have had a beard, but I can't be sure. Like I said, he was already almost gone.'

'So, you didn't see whether he lifted up the window to get out?'

Newgate stood for a while, staring at the ground as he considered Harry's question. 'I don't think so,' he responded hesitantly. 'As I said, he was half out the window when I saw him. So no, I wouldn't have seen that. And I suppose the window would have been open anyway, from when he came in.'

'That might be right,' Harry reflected. 'Though not necessarily so. We need to consider all possibilities.' He turned to the two constables. 'Which of you was on duty at the rear of the theatre? At the rear door?'

Staples raised a hand. 'Me, Inspector, it was me.'

'Did you see the killer come out the window?'

Staples glanced at Newgate before replying. 'The window is around the back corner, out of my eyesight. And when I heard the sergeant's whistle, I came straight in, through the rear door. So no, I didn't see nothing, nothing at all.'

'What about you, Wally?' Harry said. 'I suppose you saw nothing too?'

'That's right,' Morris replied promptly. 'I was on the other side of the building. At the stage door.'

Harry nodded. 'All right then. All of you, think hard between now and tomorrow, and see if you can remember any other details. Anything at all unusual might be useful.'

Newgate bowed his head and replied, 'I will, boss, I will. I'm just real sorry I didn't do anything earlier. Enter the room, I mean. I could have prevented it. But I thought it was nothing, it didn't seem suspicious.'

'No point in regrets,' Harry replied, though the set of his face did not indicate much sympathy for the hapless sergeant. 'But there's one other thing. How come that window was left unlatched? I gave instructions to check that the building was secure.'

Morris stepped forward shamefacedly. 'I'm sorry, Inspector, that was my fault. Sergeant Newgate told me to check the building perimeter, but I only did so from the outside. All the windows were definitely shut, but I must have missed seeing the latch on the inside of that window wasn't fastened.'

Newgate fixed his constable with a steely, accusatory stare, but Harry simply sighed. 'You should really have checked inside as well, Wally. Again, there's nothing we can do about past mistakes. But let's learn from them, eh? Now, here's what we need to do next. Wally and Arthur, I need you two to stand guard on this room till the morning. And make sure nobody, yourselves included, touches anything.'

Staples stared at him and pointed to the body on the floor. 'You mean, we leave her? You know, where she is?'

'That's exactly what I mean. Because there's one stroke of luck we do have. If you could call it that.'

'What's that?' Newgate asked, clearly puzzled about what could possibly be lucky about this fiasco.

'Molly's still in Sorrento, that's what,' Harry replied. 'He decided to take a few days off to enjoy the sea air. He might have been in the audience this evening, as a matter of fact. So I want him here first thing in the morning to examine this scene. In detail. With nothing disturbed. Do I make myself clear?'

'Absolutely, Inspector,' Newgate replied, promptly and respectfully. 'Leave it to me. These blokes will stand guard till the morning, I'll make sure of it.'

12

SUNDAY 18 JANUARY 1898

HARRY STOOD IN THE ATHENAEUM dressing room, watching Crawford Mollison kneeling over the lifeless body on the floor. Harry was feeling irritated. Irritated and frustrated with himself. Last night, Effie had revealed that she had spotted Natalya Kuzmina's distress and concluded she had retreated to the dressing room, and this revelation had only added to Harry's frustration. If only he had seen the girl leave the stage. If only he had headed backstage, he might have prevented the murder. Was he losing his touch, letting this murder happen right under his nose?

Then he thought of what Effie would say. What, in fact, she had said last night when he was down in the dumps. No point dwelling on the past, Harry, there's nothing you can do about that. Just focus on catching the villain that's doing these terrible things. And you *will* catch him, Harry, because no-one can outwit you. There's no better detective in the whole Victorian Police Force. So Harry resolved to get on the front foot and return his focus to the business at hand.

Mollison rose from his examination of the dead woman. He was not his usual cheerful self either, whether because three murders in a fortnight was a bit too much, even for him, or more likely, because the death of this innocent young woman was particularly distressing.

'Not hard to get the diagnosis right, Harry,' Mollison proclaimed grimly, looking down at Natalya's body, slumped on the ground. 'Strangled, all right. And with considerable force. She didn't have a chance.'

'Did you find anything on the body that might be useful? Or anything else that might give us a lead?' But Harry spoke more in hope than expectation.

'Not really,' Mollison replied. 'It was all rather sudden, I'm afraid. She didn't have the opportunity to fight back, by the looks of it. Only a slip of a thing, isn't she? Or wasn't she, I should say.'

'And not much hope of fingerprints on the window lifts either,' Harry suggested, rather forlornly. 'Looked pretty clean to me. He was probably wearing gloves.'

Mollison brightened as he replied, 'Ah well, Harry, you may be a top-shelf detective, but even you can be wrong sometimes. From my initial inspection, I think I might get a reasonable set of prints off those brass window lifts. I expect those prints might well belong to your murderer, if he lifted the window to escape. That's something, surely.'

'I suppose it is,' Harry responded, agreeably surprised by Mollison's revelation.

'Well, I think I'm done here,' Mollison declared. 'I'm heading back to Melbourne this morning. Let me know if you need any fingerprint matching against anything I've extracted from that window lift. Good luck, Harry, you need to catch the bastard who did this.'

'Couldn't agree more,' Harry muttered as he shook Mollison's hand. Mollison departed and Harry turned to Willie and Newgate.

'Righto, Clive,' he advised. 'We're about done with this poor girl, I'm afraid. Not much point taking her up to the morgue in Melbourne. I'm happy to authorise burial here in Sorrento. I'll leave it to you to sort out the paperwork.'

'Onto it, boss. I'll get it done right away.'

'Before you do though, Sarge, I'm wondering if you've had any more thoughts on last night. Can you remember anything about what you heard? And saw, when you entered the room?'

Newgate shook his head. 'Not really. I think I've told you all I know.'

'One thing that interests me,' Harry continued, 'is whether Natalya knew her attacker. You said you heard a conversation before she was attacked. I imagine if it was a stranger, she would have been immediately alarmed and her voice would have reflected that. Did it sound like the voice of a woman who had come across a stranger in her dressing room?'

Newgate stood silently, presumably trying to remember the detail of what he had heard. 'It's hard to tell,' he replied eventually. 'I mean, I think the voices were raised, that's why I heard them, I suppose. But whether that was because the bloke was a stranger, or whether she knew him and was arguing with him, I couldn't really say.'

'All right, fair enough,' Harry said. Then, pointing to the corpse on the floor, he added, 'I'll leave you to sort this out. Willie and I need to talk to the manager. There's a few issues we need to see to urgently.'

A private room at the Continental, with Harry and Willie seated opposite the Cossack manager. Borodin was bleary-eyed and grim-faced. He had what appeared to be a tumbler of vodka in front of him, despite that it was not yet lunchtime.

'Thank you for meeting with us,' Harry began. 'I know this must be a very difficult time for you. For all of you. But I do have a few questions.'

Borodin gave a curt nod, his hand resting on the glass.

'First of all,' Harry continued, 'can we be confident that the man who attacked Miss Kuzmina was not from your troupe?'

Borodin stared at him. 'Of course, Inspector,' he replied, a hint of anger in his voice. 'The entire troupe was on stage at the time of the attack. The dancers and the band members. Except for one male dancer, a fellow by the name of Federov, who was meant to be Natalya's partner in the dance. And he was by my side during the performance of the 'Khozachok'.

'And forgive my asking, but you yourself didn't go back to the dressing room at any stage during that dance?'

Borodin sat back in his chair. 'Excuse me, Inspector, are you implying that I could have attacked poor Natalya?'

'Not at all,' Harry responded wearily. 'We just need to be certain that none of the troupe were back there at that time. A process of elimination. We have to go through it.'

'As I explained to you, Inspector,' Borodin continued icily, 'I was with young Federov during the entire dance. You can check with him if you like. You see, I was concerned about how it would be performed, missing two of the dancers as we were.'

'No need to check,' Harry reassured him hastily. 'But what about others in your support staff? Would it have been possible for one of them to have gone missing during that time?'

'Certainly not,' Borodin replied after a short pause. 'We only have three such staff members, two men and a woman. And they are required to undertake a multitude of tasks during the performance. I'm certain they were present at the side of the stage at that time.'

Harry nodded. The answers were what he had expected. It was becoming clear to him that Natalya's murderer was a stranger to her. Apart from the cast members and helpers, the only person she knew was Matyunin, and his alibi was watertight. He was in the front row with George Coppin, receiving the plaudits of the crowd, and Effie had already advised Harry that she had not seen him move from his seat during the performance.

'Thank you, Mr Borodin, that's all I need to know from you,' Harry concluded. 'You've been very helpful.'

Borodin downed the vodka shot with one gulp. 'I take it you have no need to detain us further, Inspector?' he inquired. 'We are due to perform in Melbourne in a few days. I would like to leave this damned place as soon as possible. After all, the show must go on, as they say.'

Harry considered the request. There was really no basis to detain the troupe, he was quite certain none of them were involved in the murder. In any event, Coppin had advised that the troupe would perform in Melbourne for a number of weeks, so they were readily contactable if any connection should arise.

'No, you are free to leave,' he said. 'And I understand that you'll be in Melbourne for a while. I am hopeful we can resolve this business in that time and advise you that we have brought Miss Kuzmina's murderer to justice. That may be of some comfort to you and your people.'

With that he stepped forward and shook Borodin's hand, the latter bowing stiffly to him and making a rapid exit. Harry sat back in his chair, rubbing his tired eyes.

'You look a bit done in, boss,' Willie ventured.

'It's hard work, mate,' Harry replied. 'And not much to go on, really. In all the murders. What do you make of it?'

Willie thought for a few moments, then spoke carefully. 'I agree, but I reckon we can make some conclusions.'

'Go on.'

'Well, point number one, we know that all the victims were Russian, and they knew each other. Well, at least Sergei knew both Dave and Natalya. So, it's a fair bet that their murders are all connected as well. Which kind of points to the same person murdering them all.'

'Agreed,' Harry said. 'The same person, or persons.'

'Yes, right, or persons,' Willie conceded. 'Point number two, I reckon the two blokes, at least, were up to no good. They seem to have been lying real low somewhere. Maybe out at that empty shack. No-one seems to have come across them much at all, and in my experience, that means they didn't want anyone to know what they were up to.'

Harry nodded. 'Another reasonable conclusion, mate.'

'The only person we can connect with one of them at least, is the bloke out at the lime kiln,' Willie noted. 'You know, the manager, Wilkes.'

'Yes, of course. That's true. Thanks for reminding me.'

Willie's brow furrowed. 'There's one other thing. I've been thinking about that murder last night.'

'What's about it?' Harry eyed his colleague intently.

'Well, how did the killer know the girl was in the dressing room? So that he could get through the window and attack her. She was meant to be on stage.'

'A very good question, mate,' Harry observed. 'It had occurred to me as well.'

Willie rubbed his chin. 'So, he must have been in the audience and noticed she had gone missing. Just like Effie noticed. Then he must have slipped out and down the side to the back, saw her through the window, and we know the rest.'

Harry sat back and nodded slowly. 'Yes,' he agreed, 'and there was a hell of a crowd at the back of the theatre. Would've been dead easy to duck out without us noticing.'

'Not sure where that leaves us though,' Willie observed, rather gloomily. 'Not with any suspects, that's for sure. Except perhaps for that bloke, Wilkes. Though he's not really a suspect, I suppose.'

'Oh well,' Harry sighed. 'Push on, mate, push on. Let's investigate all the leads we've got, even if they don't seem very promising.'

Willie's expression suddenly brightened. 'On that score, what about that bloke up in the sand hills? The foreign one at the camp that Effie mentioned. Petrenko, that's his name. Remember, she told us they found out he's off to Melbourne tomorrow. Bit of a coincidence, don't you reckon? A Russian girl gets murdered and a dodgy Russian painter heads back to Melbourne straight after. Should we bring him in for questioning?'

Harry tapped the table with his fingers. 'Not sure we've got any basis to bring him in,' he replied eventually. 'Can't see that there's any connection, apart from his nationality. And we're not even sure he is Russian. But I agree, he does seem a bit odd, and I trust Effie's instincts on that score. So, we need to keep a close eye on him.'

'Should we put someone on his tail then?'

'Not someone, mate. You. I want you to tail him to Melbourne and let me know where he goes. Probably nothing in it, but still worth our while. Anyway, weren't you going back to see the Ferret again about those missing jewels? Not that I'm expecting a result there either. They could be anywhere by now.'

'Yeh, I was due to check the Ferret. That'll work out okay then. I'll get on the boat in the morning and see how we go.'

'Make sure you know who you're tracking,' Harry added. 'Better take Effie down to the pier with you, she knows what he looks like. She'll love being part of the case.' And he allowed himself a brief smile.

Willie smiled too. 'I'm sure she will.'

Harry pulled out his old notebook and examined his to-do list. 'One other thing, mate. Did you get a chance to follow up with Chester about that whiskey? You know, the bottles we found at the deserted shack.'

Willie looked blank for a moment, then recalled. 'Yes, I did, actually. No luck there, he doesn't stock that brand. Too pricey, he reckons. His customers prefer their whiskey cheaper. And rougher too, no doubt.'

Harry whistled softly. 'I don't know about 'no luck', mate. I find that fact very interesting. If those Russian blokes were there, what were they doing drinking posh grog? And where did they get it, eh?'

Willie shrugged and eyed his boss with a surprised look, 'Dunno. One of the other pubs, perhaps? Anyway, not sure that it matters much.'

'And I'm not sure you're right about that,' Harry responded. His detective instincts told him to store that little fact away carefully. 'You never know, it might matter. It might matter a lot.'

❧

Hearing that Winston Marks had returned from Melbourne to re-establish himself at the Continental Hotel was far from welcome news to Harry. The missive that Harry received, demanding his presence at the Continental for an urgent meeting was even less welcome.

Harry's expectation was that Marks had heard about the third murder and had hastened down to Sorrento in order to give Harry a severe bollocking about this latest killing.

So, it was somewhat of a surprise when Harry entered the private lounge to find his boss ensconced there in the company of Commander Jackson of the Victorian Military Forces. Furthermore, the Chief Inspector was not in an extreme state of apoplexy, as Harry had expected. On the contrary, he looked up as Harry entered, placed his generous glass of whiskey on the table and fixed Harry with a conspiratorial and somewhat triumphant look.

'I've returned to Sorrento as a matter of priority,' Marks began portentously. 'It's become critical that I deal with this development personally.'

Harry sought to get on the front foot immediately. 'I agree, sir, the Russian girl's murder is a most unwelcome development. But we have a witness to the attack, one of our policemen here in Sorrento, and I'm confident that ...'

Marks cut him short with a contemptuous wave of the hand. 'That's not what I'm talking about, man. It's no great matter to me if these Russian insurgents go round bumping each other off. No, what I'm talking about is a development far more important than that. It goes to the security of our state. That's why I've asked Commander Jackson to attend.'

'I'm afraid you've got me there, sir. I'm not aware of any other developments,' Harry said, in some bewilderment.

Marks eyed him sharply. 'I've said all along, Holloway, that these murders are related to the Russian Government plotting against our state. We now have evidence that confirms such a plot.'

'Really?' Harry stared at his boss in disbelief.

'Yes, really. It concerns that fellow, Matyunin. The Russian Government chap. Always thought he was a bit dodgy. Slippery looking character.'

Harry was stuck for words. What was Marks on about? How could Matyunin possibly be implicated in Natalya's murder?

'I don't think Mr Matyunin is a suspect in this latest murder, sir. He has a watertight alibi.'

Marks snorted impatiently. 'For god's sake, Holloway, forget about the Russian sheila. I'm not talking about that.'

'Sorry, sir,' Harry replied, resolving to make no more assumptions about what Marks was talking about.

'Earlier today,' Marks continued solemnly, 'I am told Mr Matyunin requested a private room in this hotel, to meet with a certain person.'

'Which person was that?' Harry inquired politely.

'An unknown person. A stranger. And by all accounts, a suspicious-looking individual.'

Harry resisted the urge to ask in whose opinion the man was suspicious. Instead, he sat quietly, waiting for Marks to finish sipping on his whiskey.

'In any event, following this meeting, Matyunin was seen to send off a telegram. Because of the suspicious nature of the meeting, and given recent events, it was decided to obtain a copy of that telegram and provide it to me.'

Harry was starting to see 'international incident' written all over this latest development, but he held his tongue. He simply asked, 'I take it this wasn't one of our people providing you with the copy of the telegram, sir. May I ask who it was?'

Marks stared at him briefly, perhaps sensing a hint of insubordination in Harry's question. 'It doesn't really matter who it was, Holloway,' he replied eventually. 'But if you must know, it was Oliver Ridgeway. And I'm glad he had the gumption to give me the information, because that telegram is damning.'

'Really?' Harry, despite his incredulity, was becoming intrigued. 'What did it say?'

'Well, it was in Russian actually. But Oliver found someone on his staff with a Russian background who was able to translate. It was addressed to some fellow in the Imperial Ministry of Foreign Affairs, and the telegram read as follows.' Marks picked up a sheet of paper from the desk and read aloud: '*All barriers to our engagement have been removed. Expect Russian ships in Port Phillip Bay very soon.*'

It certainly was an interesting telegram, but Harry wasn't yet jumping to any conclusions. He could think of quite a few questions he needed to ask Ridgeway before concluding a Russian attack on Melbourne was in the offing. But clearly, Marks had no such reservations.

'We have to move urgently on this, Holloway. Captain Jackson here has already initiated a number of military preparations.' And Marks nodded at Jackson, indicating for him to outline the said preparations.

Jackson leaned forward and spoke earnestly. 'Inspector Holloway, I have immediately alerted the premier, Sir George Turner, to this development, and I understand other relevant ministers have also been informed. And I have immediately reinforced our artillery garrison at Fort Nepean, under Lieutenant Windsor, as well as our other batteries, with additional troops. Obviously, they are all on high alert for an immediate foreign incursion.'

Harry breathed an inward sigh of relief that the captain had put his trust in Windsor, and that no loose cannon had been brought in, to start shooting at any unknown boat entering the bay. He hoped he could count on the lieutenant's good sense.

'What would you like me to do, sir?' he inquired of Marks.

'I'm not sure that you need to be involved, Holloway,' Marks replied peremptorily. 'We have this in hand. You can keep chasing down your murderers, if you like.'

But Harry very much wanted to get involved. He had a fair suspicion that all might not be as it seemed, or at least not how his superiors seemed to view it.

'I think it might be useful if I interviewed Mr Ridgeway,' he offered. 'He may be able to give us some leads on who the stranger was that Mr Matyunin met. It'll be important for the government to apprehend that person, if he's a spy in our midst.'

To Harry's relief, Marks nodded enthusiastically at this suggestion. 'Damn it, you're right, Holloway, that would be useful. Get onto it as a matter of priority.'

'I will, sir, I will.'

'Excellent, Holloway. See that you do. That'll be all for now,' he added, waving Harry away to indicate the meeting was over. 'And by the way, on your way out, send someone in to refresh our drinks.'

13

MONDAY 19 JANUARY 1898

AS HARRY HAD SUGGESTED, Effie took to her role as assistant spy to Willie with great enthusiasm. Here she was, standing alertly by Willie's side near the *Ozone* gangplank, suitably disguised under a very large hat as the throng of passengers boarded the Melbourne-bound ship.

In due course, Willie felt a sharp tug on his sleeve and heard a whispered, 'There he is!' as a red-haired fellow strode past them onto the gangplank. He was wearing an open-necked white, flowing linen shirt and a jaunty boater, set at an angle. Shouldn't be too hard to follow, Willie thought, as he gave a surreptitious farewell wave to Effie, before following Petrenko at a safe distance up the gangplank.

Willie had purchased a first-class ticket to ensure that he had access to all three of the *Ozone*'s decks, if necessary. But as it turned out, he could have saved the department the extra cost, because Petrenko headed straight for the second-class bottom deck. There he joined the crowd of middle-class holiday-makers returning home from their dream weekends in the boarding-houses of fabulous Sorrento.

The *Ozone* crossed the bay via the South Channel in good time, heading to the Sandridge Dock at Port Melbourne. Having found a suitably shaded seat with a clear view of his target, Willie occupied himself with pleasant musing on the turn his life had taken in recent months.

His promotion to sergeant jostled with the ever-present image of Rachel for primacy in his thoughts. These days, he considered himself the luckiest man alive, to be doing the job he loved under a boss like Harry, and to be married to the most beautiful and sweetest girl he could imagine existing on this Earth.

Absorbed in this reverie, Willie suddenly realised that they were entering the port and would soon dock at the Sandridge Pier. Petrenko was still sitting in his seat some half dozen rows away, so Willie quietly stood and moved to the side of the deck near the gangplank gate. He wanted to make sure that Petrenko would not be lost to him in the crush of disembarking passengers.

The second-class passengers naturally had to give way to the first-class deck and lounge, who sauntered past them without so much as a disdainful glance. Among them, Willie noticed with interest the Russian consul, Matyunin, in the company of a tall, ruddy-faced, sandy-haired fellow. Both appeared to be in a jovial mood, chatting animatedly together as they walked past.

Hullo, Willie thought, maybe that's the suspicious stranger Harry was talking about. Doesn't look much like a spy. Actually, looks more like a grazier from the Western District.

Given the importance that Marks had obviously placed on this latest development with the consul, Willie briefly flirted with the idea of abandoning his current assignment, and instead following the Russian and his companion. But he decided against that plan; Harry had tasked him with this job and he would follow it through.

In due course, it was the turn of the second-class passengers to disembark, and Willie readied himself to follow his man. Petrenko now seemed in something of a hurry, pushing to near the front of the queue, and Willie had to do a bit of judicious shoving to maintain visual contact. But he did so and was able to follow Petrenko onto the train at Station Pier, finding a seat directly behind the Russian and some five rows back. Over the Sandridge Bridge they rattled and very soon into Flinders Street Station.

Here, Willie's task became significantly harder, as the train occupants alighted and merged into the crowded hurly-burly of the station. Willie was forced to trail somewhat closer to Petrenko, who pushed impatiently through the crowded station, soon emerging onto Flinders Street itself, from whence he turned left and bustled along in the direction of William Street, walking at a lively pace.

Again, Willie had to maintain uncomfortably close contact if he was not to lose his man in the crowded street. Then, as they neared William Street on their right, Petrenko suddenly veered sharp right and as he did so, glanced over his shoulder in Willie's direction. Willie, momentarily distracted by Petrenko's abrupt change of direction, had stopped dead in his tracks and was standing there, looking directly at Petrenko. The two men made brief eye contact.

Cursing himself for his mistake, Willie resumed walking, as casually as he could, straight past Petrenko, who stood there watching Willie pass by. Willie was reluctant to stop and turn back again too soon, for fear of completely giving the game away.

Some twenty paces on, he felt emboldened to look back, only to see the bobbing boater and red hair heading away from him at a rapid pace, towards the Customs House and an equally crowded Market Street. In a matter of seconds, he was gone from view, and despite Willie shoving roughly through the crowd and hurrying down Market Street for a considerable distance, there was no trace of him.

Damn it, Willie thought, I've messed this up good and proper, and he cursed himself for his momentary lapse of concentration. Oh well, he sighed to himself, nothing to be done about it now, and besides, Petrenko might have no connection to the murders. Still, he couldn't help but feel a pang of disappointment at having failed in his mission.

Willie pulled his watch from his fob and examined it: half past ten. Allowing himself a half hour or more to catch a cable tram across to North Melbourne, he stood a good chance of catching up with the Ferret at the Caledonian, then a quick trip to Russell Street, before getting back to the Sandridge Pier in plenty of time to catch the *Ozone* back to Sorrento. He didn't hold out much hope of garnering any useful information about the stolen jewels from the Ferret, but you could never tell with him. Somehow or other, he seemed to have accurate information on most rackets and misdemeanours that were afoot in the town. In addition to those in which he was directly involved, of course.

Willie began the walk back to the North Melbourne line terminus further down Flinders Street, feeling in his pocket as he strode for the clean handkerchief that Rachel had given him that morning. He glanced up at an increasingly burning sun as he wiped his brow. It was going to be a hot one, and he was suddenly glad that he could justify an ice-cold ale with the Ferret as being necessary in the line of duty.

But in due course, his enjoyment of the refreshing brew at the Callie was tempered by the disappointment of the information provided to him by the Ferret. Which in essence amounted to nothing, despite the Ferret's efforts to embellish things in order to justify full payment.

'I was talkin' to a bloke who reckons some good gear's comin' on the market real soon. Could be the stuff you're lookin' for.'

'Did he say what it was? And where it came from?'

'Nah, not really. But this bloke's usually got the good oil.'

'Could be anything, Ferret. That info's no good to me at all.'

The Ferret's narrow features puckered into a scowl, as he realised his commission was at risk. Willie slipped him a quid for his trouble, and off the Ferret went, melding sulkily back into the crowded bar.

Willie finished off his beer, picked up his hat, and headed back out into the heat of the day. A sweaty walk to Russell Street resulted in an equally fruitless meeting with his colleagues in the CIB. No-one had heard anything on the street about exotic jewels being fenced anywhere. And there was general consensus that it would be damned difficult to turn over jewellery pieces of the kind described to them by Willie.

So it was a frustrated Sergeant Milton who headed to Flinders Street for the journey back to Sorrento. A wasted day, that was for sure. Willie just hoped that Harry was having more success in pursuit of Natalya's killer.

Harry stood on the Sorrento pier among a gaggle of holiday-makers, and watched the *Ozone* churning its way across the water towards them. He was there to catch up with his returning sergeant, but he was not yet focusing on what information Willie might have. His mind was still tracing the events of the past forty-eight hours, trying to make sense of it all.

Harry agreed with yesterday's assessment by Willie of where they were up to. That is, that the three murder victims were known to each other, or at least that Natalya and Dave were known to Sergei Karpov. And that their murders were all connected, probably as part of some illegal or surreptitious activity.

So far, so good. Now all they had to do was find out what Sergei and Dave were up to, and who they were associated with in that illegal activity. And that was going to be a very difficult task.

The most extreme possibility, of course, was the one that Marks clearly favoured, that it was some sort of conspiracy to mount a Russian invasion, or at least a raid, on the port of Melbourne. This was the scenario that various alarmists, in politics and the press, had been promulgating for decades, ever since the Crimean War. That Russia, or at least rogue Russian interests, had their sights set firmly on the goldfield riches that had catapulted Melbourne to be one of the wealthiest and fastest growing cities in the world.

It was an extreme possibility, but one that was still consistent with the conclusions he and Willie had reached so far. So Harry had to take it seriously, particularly given Marks' obsession with the subject. But there were elements of the murders that didn't fit with such a scenario.

Firstly, if Karpov and Dave were part of a Russian plot, perhaps being directed by Matyunin, why had they been bumped off? Perhaps they were going to spill the beans to the Australian authorities, and that was behind their murders. But there was absolutely no evidence of that, as far as Harry could tell.

And more critically in Harry's mind, if the two Russians were spies, why in heaven's name would Karpov reveal that to Natalya? Everything he had seen of her had convinced Harry that she was exactly what she seemed, a naive young woman who was suddenly terrified by the murder of her sweetheart. And distinctly terrified, in Harry's judgement, rather than just grief-stricken.

He was convinced she knew something about Karpov's activities, something that could put her in danger as well. He just couldn't believe that those activities were part of a Russian plot and that Natalya was part of some Russian spy ring.

Harry's reveries were broken by the blast of the *Ozone's* horn as it eased into its berth at the pier. Ropes were cast over mooring bollards, the gangplank was lowered, and excited holiday-makers began pouring off the foredeck. Harry leaned against a lamp post, patiently waiting for the crowd to pass. He spotted Willie trudging wearily down the gangplank, among the tail end of the passengers.

'You look a bit done in, mate,' Harry remarked as Willie joined him on the pier. 'Been a hard day?'

'A lot of walking for no result,' Willie responded, and proceeded to confess, somewhat shamefacedly, to losing Petrenko in the crowd. 'And neither the boys at Russell Street nor the Ferret had anything to offer,' Willie added gloomily. 'Not that I really expected much from him. From what the Kozminsky brothers said, those jewels are something of a specialist collector's item. Not something that a mate of Ferret's would be flogging on some street corner.'

'My thoughts exactly,' Harry concurred, as they turned and set off down the pier. 'Don't think the Ferret moves in the kinds of circles that'd be interested in those jewels. And don't worry about losing Petrenko. Not sure he was going to lead us to anything worthwhile anyway. He seems an odd fish, but there's nothing at all to connect him to the murders. Where did you lose him exactly?'

Willie squirmed with embarrassment. 'Just out of the station, actually. Down Flinders Street a bit. Near the Customs House.'

Harry nodded slowly. 'You reckon he saw you? Then made himself scarce?'

'Sure seemed that way.'

'Well, that's interesting for a start, mate. Shows he's up to something he wants to keep under his hat. Let's see if he returns to Sorrento. I'll rely on Effie and her gang to keep us informed on that front.'

'I did see one thing though,' Willie remembered. 'That Russian bloke, Matyunin, and another fella. I reckon he was the mystery man Ridgeway was talking about. You know, the one they reckon's a spy.'

'Really?' Harry exclaimed, turning towards his sergeant as they walked. 'Where was that? On the boat? How did they look?'

Willie shrugged. 'Yeh, it was on the boat. I gotta say they looked pretty pleased with themselves, actually. Chatting away without a care in the world.'

'And what about our mystery man? Did he seem foreign?'

'Not really,' Willie replied without hesitation. 'Well, not Russian, anyway. Looked more like he could have been from the old country. Or a Scot. Youngish bloke, red face and fair hair.'

Harry nodded. 'Good stuff, mate, that's useful information.'

Willie was starting to feel a bit better about life. 'Goodo, boss. What now, back to Mrs M's for a spot of tucker?'

Harry grinned. 'Great idea, mate, but since we're walking past the front door of the Sailors Arms, what say we wet the whistle on the way?' And he pointed up the Esplanade to the hotel, from which emanated the sound of numerous whistles being wet.

Willie needed no further persuasion and so they sidetracked into the pub, joining the thirsty horde, and were soon ensconced in a relatively quiet corner, beers in hand. Harry began to run through their mutual conclusions on the case, and Harry's reservations that it could be part of a Russian conspiracy.

'I reckon you're right,' Willie agreed. 'It seems far-fetched to me too.'

'Anything else you can think of, mate?' Harry asked. 'Any other thoughts on where we should be looking?'

'A couple of things come to mind.' Willie took a swig and continued. 'I reckon that bloke Madigan could have something to do with it. If the local boys are right, he's a bit of a villain.'

Harry nodded. 'Agreed. He's on my list of dodgy characters who might have been involved with the Russians in some sort of criminal enterprise. Not sure what though. Anyway, I've got him on the list of suspects that we should talk to real soon. Let's see if he's got an alibi for Saturday night. Now, what else has got you thinking?'

Willie rubbed his chin. 'Well, it's about Natalya's murder. I know we reckon it was probably some bloke in the audience who noticed her go off the stage, then ducked out the back and got lucky. But gee, he'd have been taking a chance, wouldn't he? Like, how would he know she was heading for the dressing room?'

Harry contemplated his beer reflectively for a moment or two. 'Yeh, I thought about that too, but maybe that was it. Our murderer just got lucky. And I'm not sure he'd be taking a hell of a risk, actually. He probably scouted out the back of the place before the event, so he would've known there was good cover and plenty of different ways to make himself scarce after doing the deed. Through the backyard next door, or straight across the vacant block at the back and away.

'Though, on the other hand, we had our two constables patrolling the outside of the theatre, so he was certainly lucky that they missed spotting him.'

'Hang on, boss,' Willie interrupted, looking over Harry's shoulder. 'That good-looking sort behind the bar's waving at you. You know, your mate, Gloria.'

Harry turned, following Willie's gaze, and saw Gloria waving cheerily at him. He waved back amiably and turned back to Willie. 'Now, where were we?'

Willie grinned and pointed in Gloria's direction. 'I know you're used to women being friendly to you, mate, but I think she wants us to go over there.'

Harry turned again, and this time Gloria's gesturing was clear. She was summoning them across the room.

Gloria flashed Harry a welcoming smile as they fronted the bar. 'G'day, Harry love, sorry to break up your chat, but I've got something that might interest you. Remember you told me to keep an eye out.'

'Absolutely, Gloria,' Harry responded, expectations rising. 'Anything would be most welcome.'

'Well, you told me to watch out for anything unusual,' Gloria began, leaning across the bar and lowering her voice confidentially.

'Anything unusual, we'd be keen to hear,' Harry encouraged her.

'Well, the last couple of nights we've had a couple of young blokes in here. Getting a skinful and by the end of the night they were both pretty tight.'

'Nothing unusual in that, I'd reckon,' Harry suggested.

'And then, later in the night, after things quietened down a bit, they started to get, well, sort of friendly with me.'

'Doesn't surprise me at all,' Harry smiled. 'Not at all unusual.'

Gloria smiled back and winked at Harry. 'Don't you be cheeky, Harry. I'll tell your wife, if you're not careful. No, it's what they told me in their cups that I thought you'd find interesting.'

'What was that?' Harry asked, serious now.

'Well, apparently they cleared out from the Quarantine Station a few days back. You know, from the ship that was bailed up there.'

'Aha!' Willie exclaimed. 'Our missing Russian sailors.'

Gloria shook her head. 'Don't know about Russian, Sergeant. They were definitely foreign, but they sounded more like Krauts, if you ask me. We get a few in here from time to time.'

Harry whistled softly. 'Interesting. The ship's captain said they were Russian, didn't he, Willie?'

'He sure did,' Willie replied. 'Confirmed by the purser too.'

'That's what I thought,' Harry mused. 'Bit of a turn-up. I thought they'd be halfway to the goldfields by now.'

Gloria gave a low chuckle. 'They let on that's where they were headed, Harry. But they didn't get very far before they realised it's quite a long way to walk. They got to Sorrento and decided they'd give that plan away.'

'Well, what did they plan to do?' Harry asked. 'They should've realised they'd probably get caught if they hung around here.'

Gloria laughed again. 'They're young and wet behind the ears, but even they realised that. Apparently, they snuck back to the Quarantine Station with the idea of giving themselves up and rejoining the crew. But before they could do that, a couple of their mates told them the coppers were after them for nicking some jewels. They said they didn't do it, but they were scared then to hand themselves in.'

'Right,' Harry said, sipping on his beer. 'So they came back here?'

'Yeh, apparently they've been living rough. Out in one of the empty fishing shacks, I think. And spending what little money they've got in here, while they try to work out what to do.'

'Quite a story,' Willie observed. 'I'm surprised they unloaded all that on you though, Gloria. Bit of a risk, I would've thought.'

'You'd be very surprised at some of the things I've been told in this bar, love,' Gloria replied. 'Nothing like a friendly barmaid to unburden your troubles onto. Especially when you've had a few.'

'For sure,' Harry agreed, grinning. 'I bet you've got a lot of stories that would interest us, eh? We should have you on the payroll.'

'You couldn't pay me enough, Harry,' Gloria quipped.

'Probably not,' Harry agreed. Then he got serious again. 'Any chance those two lads are still around the place?'

Gloria nodded. 'Haven't seen them yet today, but they were in last night. So there's a good chance they might turn up again later tonight.'

'Great,' Harry replied. 'Tell you what, we might come back after dinner, say eightish, and try our luck. Could you point them out to us if they're here?'

Gloria's usual smile evaporated, replaced by a slightly worried frown. 'Sure, Harry, but I hope they don't get into too much trouble. They're only just kids really, and I don't think they've done anything wrong. I don't blame them for deserting their ship. From what they told me, it was a pretty awful set-up there.'

Harry reached across the bar and patted Gloria's hand reassuringly. 'Don't worry, my dear, us picking them up will be the best thing for them. I agree with you about them being innocent of theft, so they've probably got nothing to fear.'

'So you'll take them back to their boat? And smooth things out with their captain?'

'Not just yet, I don't think,' Harry replied thoughtfully. 'Think we'll stick them in the clink here for a couple of days first. They won't mind that, decent food and lodgings for a day or two. And it'll give them a chance to dry out. Meanwhile, we might head back to the Quarantine Station and sort out a couple of things with the captain. I've got a feeling that might be helpful for those two lads as well.'

Gloria looked slightly puzzled, but smiled at him nevertheless. 'Good on you, Harry, you're a good bloke. Tell you what, why don't I fill up your glasses, eh? One for the road. And it's on the house.'

Willie exchanged a glance with Harry. 'Are you sure that's okay with Mr Chester?' he asked Gloria. 'We don't want any special favours.'

Gloria chuckled again. 'I'm sure it's okay. The boss likes to keep in sweet with the local boys in blue. We're told to offer them the odd free one. As long as it doesn't get out of hand, eh? Anyway, from what I've seen, you two blokes have done more to earn a beer or two than Newgate and his crew ever did.'

Harry made no objection and was happy to raise his refreshed glass to Gloria's good health.

'Good on you, Gloria, just this once, eh? Here's to all your useful information. And hopefully, here's to catching up with those two sailor boys later tonight.'

The extended Holloway family, plus Willie and Rachel, were seated around the largest table in the Back Beach Palace dining room, tucking into yet another of Mrs Meriwether's gargantuan meals. Mrs M refused to be restricted in her culinary program by the dictates of the hot weather, and so the fare was a fine roast of beef with all the trimmings, followed by plum duff and custard.

Not that the Holloways were deterred in any way by this offering. They all attacked their plates with enthusiasm. Harry hadn't seen his parents with such an appetite for years.

'Must be the sea air, son,' Clem suggested, in response to Harry's surprised comment. 'We've put in a decent day looking after the little ones. Young Alfie here takes a bit of keeping up with, I can tell you.'

Harry glanced down at his son, who was refuelling at a rate of knots, and smiled quietly to himself. Glancing in turn at Effie, he felt grateful that her independent spirit wouldn't allow her holiday to be spoilt by his absence.

'What's on the program tomorrow then, Eff?' Harry inquired. 'Lunch with George Coppin again? What has Lydia got planned?'

'No, no,' Effie replied with a laugh. 'Rachel and I are doing the organising tomorrow, aren't we, dear? We're planning a family beach morning, then in the afternoon, because cooler weather is expected, Rachel has suggested we go on another expedition to the back beach.'

'Sounds great,' Harry responded. 'You enjoyed the back beach, Rachel?'

'It was lovely,' Rachel enthused. 'So wild and romantic. And so beautiful, with the sea and the rocks and the rugged cliffs.'

'Wish we could join you, don't we, Willie?' Harry said. 'But we're making a bit of progress, so we need to stick at it.'

'It's a pity you lost track of that Petrenko chap,' Effie observed. 'Find out what he's up to and I reckon you're a long way to solving these murders, Harry. Mark my words.'

'Maybe, darling, maybe,' Harry conceded. 'Don't quite know what he's up to, but I think I share your assessment he's certainly not an artist.'

With the plum duff disposed of, the family retired to their upstairs balcony. While Effie settled Daisy in her cot, Harry took an increasingly weary Alfie onto his lap for a bedtime story. Willie and Rachel sat a little way off, Willie's arm around her shoulders as they gazed at the panoramic view over the back beach.

It was only a matter of minutes before Alfie's attention waned and he fell asleep in Harry's arms.

'He's well and truly out to it,' Harry murmured to Effie, as she came back in, her mission accomplished.

'I'm not surprised,' Effie responded, reaching down to lightly brush Alfie's hair from his eyes. 'He's had a huge day.'

'To tell the truth, I wouldn't mind having a kip myself. Wish I didn't have to go back to the Sailors Arms tonight.'

'Do you have to?' Effie asked. 'Can't it wait till the morning? Or can't those local policemen do it instead?'

Harry gave a contemptuous snort. 'Leave it to those blokes? You've got to be joking. No, I'm afraid it's up to Willie and me, and it's got to be done tonight, I'm afraid. I'd kick myself if we let them slip away.'

'So you think they've got something to do with the murders?'

'No, I don't,' Harry replied. 'But the jewellery theft is something they might shed some light on.'

Effie glanced across at Willie and Rachel, snuggled together in the dimming light of the encroaching evening.

'And you can't let Willie stay here? And give him some time with Rachel?'

Harry sighed. 'Fraid not, Eff. Hopefully, those two sailor boys will come quietly. But we don't want a fuss, and if they do play up a bit, I'll need Willie there. With a bit of luck we won't be long. And we'll all be tucked up in bed by half past nine.'

'That would be nice,' Effie smiled. 'Not just for them. I'd like my husband to myself for a change.'

Harry smiled back. 'I'm all yours at half past nine then. Agreed?' And he returned her kiss as she leaned in towards him.

By half past eight, the Sailors Arms had quietened down a little. But only a little. The bar was still pretty much fully lined with drinkers, and the tables were mostly occupied.

Harry looked for their two absconding seamen as they entered, but there was no obvious sign of them. So he and Willie found an opening at the bar, and within seconds were joined on the other side by Gloria, tea towel and glass in hand.

'Back corner, the two with sailors' hats on,' she muttered as she walked past, with a toss of her head indicating the corner in question. Harry glanced across and spotted two young blokes, each with the distinctive peaked caps common to merchant sailors. They were hunched morosely over their beers and looked to have been living rough. Both were unshaven and their blue serge jackets were crumpled and dirty.

'That's our boys I reckon,' Harry murmured. 'Let's have a chat.'

They wandered casually up to the two sailors and plonked themselves down on the spare chairs at the table.

'G'day, boys,' Harry began amicably. 'You look a bit the worse for wear. Been doing it tough, by the look of it.'

The two men sat bolt upright, staring at Harry and Willie in obvious alarm. They said nothing.

'We're the law,' Harry explained, and when that elicited no response he added, 'Police. You need to come with us.'

Now the penny dropped and one of the men abruptly pushed back his chair and went to rise. But his attempt to flee got no further; Harry's large hand gripped his arm like a vice and held him in his seat. A quick glance at Harry's towering frame obviously convinced him that flight was futile, because he slumped back in his chair, defeated.

His compatriot didn't even attempt to escape. He just sat there, looking forlorn and wretched.

'We did not take jewels,' the fellow in Harry's now relaxed grip asserted. 'We are not thieves.'

'Don't worry,' Harry responded. 'I believe you. All I want to do is have a chat and find out a bit about you both. Let's start with names, eh?'

Harry's words appeared to have a soothing effect, because the sailor calmed noticeably.

'*Gut*!' he replied. 'I am Willem, he is Gunther.'

'I'd guess you boys are German, right?' Harry said. '*Deutsche*?'

'*Ja, Deutsche*,' Willem responded readily. 'From Hamburg.'

'Now then,' Harry continued. 'You may not have stolen the jewels, but you are in breach of the law, you know. We need to take you in.'

'*Nein, nein*!' Willem exclaimed, alarmed again. 'We do nothing wrong. *Nichts*. Nothing.'

'Well now,' Harry replied affably. 'That's not strictly true, you know. You have deserted your ship.'

'We go back to ship,' Willem proposed. Clearly, he preferred his captain's wrath to the uncertainties of Australian justice. 'We not go to prison. You cannot take us to prison.'

'Again, not true,' Harry countered. 'We have every right to detain you. Under the *Seamen's Act 1890* for deserting your ship.'

'Not to mention public drunkenness,' Willie added. 'That's in there too.'

'That's right, Harry concurred. 'So it is. But don't worry, boys, you'll get back to your ship. Just not quite yet though. We'll keep you at Her Majesty's pleasure for a day or two, until we sort out a few things. So, come quietly, eh?'

And with that, Harry took Willem's arm and eased him to his feet, with Willie applying similar support for Gunther. There was no resistance. Whether it was Harry's calming words, or the inescapable grips on their arms, both sailors meekly obeyed. The party of four walked from the room, Harry only pausing to give Gloria a grateful wave with his free hand.

14

HARRY HAD SENT Wally Morris around to the Continental to request Mr Ridgeway meet with him at the police station urgently. That very hour, if at all possible. Ridgeway was also advised that Inspector Holloway considered the information that Mr Ridgeway had provided to Chief Inspector Marks to be of vital importance, and to be immediately investigated.

None of this was strictly true. Harry was far from sure whether Ridgeway's second-hand story had much validity, but he wanted Ridgeway to think that it was being taken very seriously indeed, just to dissuade him from any embellishments that might occur to him. And Harry also wanted to get Ridgeway off his home patch at the Continental and into the more confronting environment of the interview room in the Sorrento Police Station.

When Ridgeway appeared at the station, in company with Morris, Harry was gratified to observe that his strategy seemed to have worked. Ridgeway was more subdued than Harry had previously seen him, and there might even have been a slightly worried crease to his brow.

'G'day, Mr Ridgeway,' Harry began. 'Good of you to take time off for this meeting. Glad you appreciate the seriousness of what you've claimed.'

Ridgeway looked taken aback, recoiling slightly in his chair. 'I'm not sure there's any 'claim' about it, Inspector. I saw the telegram with my own eyes, and related it verbatim to your chief inspector. Damning evidence there in black and white, I would have thought.'

'Perhaps, perhaps not. Though it's not quite as cut and dried as you claim, Mr Ridgeway. From what was related to me, I believe the telegram may be open to other interpretations. And of course, we'll also need to sight the actual telegram in question.'

'Certainly, Inspector. That can be arranged.'

'I'll get Constable Morris here to pop over and pick it up. Now, I do have a couple of questions about the telegram. And the meeting you witnessed that aroused your suspicion.'

Ridgeway shifted slightly in his chair and adjusted his collar. 'Certainly, I'll endeavour to answer them.'

Harry pressed on. 'From what was relayed to me, I understand you became suspicious when Mr Matyunin requested a private meeting with his guest. What was suspicious about that? The gentleman that Mr Matyunin was meeting with? Or the fact that he requested a private room?'

Ridgeway looked startled and shuffled more noticeably in his chair. 'Well, both I suppose.' He seemed to be having trouble looking Harry in the eye.

'Fair enough,' Harry commented. 'Well, let's first deal with Matyunin's guest, shall we? Tell me, what was so suspicious about him?'

Ridgeway cast his eyes around the room, as if looking for the right answer. 'Well, I don't know really. It's just an impression I got. The fact that he was meeting with a Russian, I suppose. And he certainly wasn't dressed for a beach holiday, that's for certain. So, what with all the suspicion about the Russians at the moment, I thought that was rather odd.'

Harry nodded slowly. 'I see. But on the other hand, the meeting could have been for business purposes. I understand that it's a significant part of Mr Matyunin's role, to promote trade between the state of Victoria and his countrymen. So, given he is currently in Sorrento on other matters, as we know, it's not inconceivable that he could have arranged a business meeting at your establishment. Wouldn't you agree?'

Ridgeway's expression changed from confused to defiant. 'Well, I suppose that is one interpretation you could put on it. If you wanted to. But I still think my reaction was fully justified.'

Harry didn't debate the point, instead replying calmly, 'Okay, let's turn now to the request for a private room. Wouldn't be unusual if the meeting was for business purposes, would it? Perhaps confidential business purposes?'

Ridgeway shrugged. 'I suppose. But clearly, it wasn't, was it? As you can see from the content of the telegram.'

'Ah yes, the telegram.' Harry leaned back in his chair. 'It was in Russian, I understand?'

'It was,' Ridgeway declared triumphantly. 'Now, don't tell me that wasn't suspicious.'

'Not particularly suspicious, I wouldn't have thought, given it was sent to someone in the Russian Government. But anyway, I understand you found someone on your staff who was able to translate for you?'

Ridgeway began to look uncomfortable again. 'Yes, I think that's correct,' he muttered vaguely.

'Can I ask who that was?' Harry inquired evenly, fixing Ridgeway with a very direct look. 'I'd think it unusual to have a Russian speaker on your staff.'

'I'm not sure I can remember,' Ridgeway replied, studiously avoiding Harry's eye.

'Really? Because we would consider it important to know who that person was. And as I said, I'd also like to see the original Russian telegram, in order to check the accuracy of the translation.'

Ridgeway sat sullenly, staring out the window. He appeared to come to a decision. 'Perhaps it wasn't a staff member,' he said. 'I may have mis-remembered. Yes, thinking about it now, it was an acquaintance rather than a staff member.'

'A name?' Harry inquired pleasantly.

Ridgeway began to sweat slightly. 'I'd rather not, actually. It was a lady acquaintance, you see. One whose name I would rather not reveal.'

Harry smiled. 'Fair enough. To protect your reputation? Or hers, perhaps?' Harry wondered if the lady acquaintance was one of the Cossack dance troupe, supplementing her income with a casual liaison. Or perhaps one of the many other very friendly ladies prevalent in Sorrento at this height of the season. No matter, no need to push him further, Harry could easily get the telegram accurately translated.

'Don't worry, Mr Ridgeway, I don't intend to probe your private life. I'm sure we can make do with the original telegram in Russian. If you could provide us with that, as promised.'

'Yes, absolutely, certainly.' Ridgeway relaxed visibly in his chair. 'Will that be all, Inspector?'

'Not quite,' Harry replied 'There's one other piece of information you might be able to help me with.'

'If I can, Inspector, certainly.'

'I'm just wondering whether you stock Irish whiskey? Powers Gold Label, to be precise.'

Ridgeway stared at him blankly. 'That's an odd question, Inspector,' he replied eventually. 'I'm not sure, to be honest. I'd need to check with my bar manager.'

'That would be appreciated,' Harry responded. 'Again, I'll send Constable Morris here around to the hotel to get an answer on that. From you or your bar manager. And while you're at it, could you inform the constable who your liquor supplier in Melbourne is? That would be useful to us too.'

'I can't really see how,' Ridgeway replied, in an irritated tone. 'Don't know what that's got to do with that Matyunin character and his suspicious goings-on.'

'Nor do I, mate, nor do I,' Harry replied. 'But Mr Matyunin is not the only thing we're investigating, as I'm sure you can appreciate. So your cooperation on that other request is greatly appreciated. Now, I'll let you go. I'm sure you're a very busy man. Good day to you.'

And Harry shook Ridgeway's hand, leaving that gentleman to beat a hasty retreat.

Harry turned to Constable Morris. 'Got your head around those little jobs, Wally? If you could chase down that telegram and those other answers, as soon as you can.'

Morris leapt to attention. 'Certainly, sir, I wrote it all down. I'll get onto it immediately.' Then, in a slightly puzzled tone, 'Though I'm not too sure what all that whiskey business is about.'

'Perhaps nothing, Wally,' Harry replied thoughtfully. 'Just tidying up a couple of loose ends. Because, mate, if I can offer you a bit of free advice that might be useful in your future career, loose ends can sometimes turn into important links. You just never know.'

Harry and Willie sat in the bow of the police launch as it steamed across the bay toward the small group of trading ketches anchored some several hundred yards offshore. They were heading in particular to the ketch closest to shore, the *Argus*, identified by Jim Cleaver to belong to Tosh Madigan. 'You'll need to catch him by five,' Cleaver had advised. 'After that, you'd need to drag him out of the Sailors Arms.'

Harry had contemplated pulling in Madigan to the station for an interview, just to remind him of the gravity of their investigation. But that night-time vision of the ketch sailing towards Melbourne had piqued his interest. And Madigan seemed to be on top of the list of local rogues likely to be involved in a bit of smuggling. So a good look around his boat might well be a useful exercise.

The *Argus* looked to be about a fifty-footer, square-rigged and broad-beamed in the usual ketch configuration. A dinghy tied up to its side signalled that the man in question was still aboard. This was confirmed when a figure materialised on the starboard rail, in response to the sound of their approach.

'That's Mr Madigan, I assume,' Harry muttered to Willie, as they eyed their target. 'Let's see what he's got to say for himself.'

As they came up alongside, they could see that Madigan was a man of about Jim Cleaver's vintage, grey and grizzled, with red, pockmarked features that reflected a lifetime exposed to the elements. Or perhaps more likely, a long-held fondness for the interior of the Sailors Arms. He sported a dirty cap and tattered coat, despite the warm morning, and his scowl indicated they were not about to be greeted with open arms.

'What the hell do you blokes want?' he shouted down at them, as their pilot, Constable Jones, eased the launch alongside and tied up to the side ladder.

'Afternoon, Mr Madigan,' Harry shouted back cheerily. 'I'm Harry Holloway, Criminal Investigation Branch in Melbourne. Mind if we come aboard and ask you a few questions?'

A look of alarm now supplanted Madigan's irritated glare, and Harry could see that his touch of name-dropping had done the trick.

'Nothing to be alarmed about,' he added in the same friendly tone. 'Shouldn't take too long.'

'Orright,' Madigan conceded grumpily. 'Up you come then. But make sure you don't damage my boat.'

Harry and Willie clambered up the ladder, leaving Jones on the launch below. Harry looked around the deck before shaking hands with Madigan. This initial cursory inspection already answered his first question: the encrustations of white lime around the deck, plus the strong prevailing fishy stench, told him that Madigan carted both fish and lime to Melbourne.

So he started on a different tack. 'Not sure whether you know, but we're investigating a recent murder in the town. Fellow by the name of Sam, real name Sergei. A Russian, we understand. And two other murders too, one a local bloke called Dave, probably a mate of Sergei's, and then last Saturday, a young Russian lass by the name of Natalya.'

Madigan peered back at Harry, squinting in the bright sunlight. His only response was, 'Yeh, I heard about all that.'

'The thing is,' Harry continued, 'We're trying to find out what this fellow, Sergei, was doing in Sorrento. We reckon he was working in the fishing trade somewhere, but no-one seems to know where. Which is odd, in a small town like this. You seem to have your finger on the pulse of what's going on around the town, Mr Madigan, so we thought we'd ask you. Whether you'd ever come across this foreign bloke, called himself Sam?'

Madigan continued to squint, and Harry fancied there was a hint of defiance in the thrust of his jaw. 'Never heard of him. I already told your blokes that.'

But there was something in his manner, and in his slightly nervous shuffle, that alerted Harry's detective antennae. He decided to press the issue. 'You know, Mr Madigan, if he did work for you, we'll find out. Eventually. Someone's bound to have seen him with you somewhere. And we won't be happy if we find you've kept it from us. So best to tell us now if he did.' And he looked hard at Madigan, inviting a response.

Madigan continued to stare from beneath beetling brows, and a further bout of contemplative shuffling ensued.

'He might have worked for me a couple of times,' he conceded eventually. 'What's wrong with that?'

'Okay,' Harry replied. 'In what capacity, might I ask?'

Madigan looked at him blankly. 'What d'you mean?'

'What did he work on? The boat? The dock? Loading? Unloading?'

'I dunno. Bit of this, bit of that. On the boat, mainly.'

Harry eyed him quizzically. 'Weren't you concerned when he went missing? And when you heard a bloke had been drowned off the pier?'

Madigan shrugged. 'Nah, not really. He only worked for me now and then. I just thought he'd cleared out. Off to the goldfields or something. Happens all the time. Bloody hard to keep deckhands these days.'

Harry nodded sympathetically, then changed tack again. 'Not too many of these ketches about, are there? We noticed one sailing towards Melbourne the other night. Wouldn't have been yours, would it? Doing a bit of moonlighting? I've heard you're up for that from time to time.'

Madigan stared hard at Harry, seemingly at a loss for words. Harry smiled back at him.

Madigan's demeanour now changed, from defensive to belligerent. 'If you're accusing me of anything, copper, you're on the wrong tram. You've got a bloody nerve, accusing a respectable sailor of that sort of thing.'

Harry stuck his hands in his pockets and glanced at Willie, whose raised eyebrows reinforced Harry's suspicion that Madigan could indeed be their night-time sailor. But what was he up to? What was the cargo he was delivering to Melbourne under the cover of darkness?

'Tell you what,' Harry suggested, 'why don't we have a quick look around your boat? Just to satisfy ourselves that everything's aboveboard and shipshape, if you'll excuse my pun.'

'Go your hardest,' Madigan replied. 'I got nothing to hide.'

Madigan walked over to the cargo hatch, threw it open, and pointed to the stairs leading into the hold. The two policemen made their way down into the hold, a surprisingly large space in the flat-bottomed ketch. A dim light pervaded the area from a small number of portholes on either side. They could see that the hold was empty, though again, grey-white residue everywhere indicated that lime must be regular cargo.

'Nothing to see here, mate,' Harry muttered. 'No sign of anything other than lime.'

They remounted the stairs back into the sunlight, where Madigan stood waiting for them. 'Told you, coppers,' he sneered. 'You've wasted my time. And yours.'

'Not at all,' Harry responded. 'All part of the job. Now you can relax, you're in the clear, eh?'

Madigan simply snorted, turned on his heel and strode off to the wheelhouse without another word.

'Oh well,' Harry grinned. 'Suppose we'd better see ourselves off.'

'Suppose so,' Willie agreed and they clambered back down the ladder into the launch. Constable Jones started the engine, cast off, and they were on their way.

'What do you reckon, Jonesy?' Harry inquired. 'Is our friend Madigan up to no good?'

Jones shrugged. 'Dunno, Inspector. But I do know something else.'

'What's that, mate?' Willie asked.

'I reckon that bloke's taking a fair risk carting lime in that tub.'

'Why so,' Harry asked, intrigued.

'I had a bit of a look at the hull while you were on board,' Jones replied. 'A good few of the timbers look in pretty poor shape. I wouldn't be surprised if she sprang a leak sometime in the not-too-distant future.'

'So what?' Willie responded. 'A minor leak or two surely wouldn't be enough to sink her.'

'That's not what I mean,' Jones explained. 'Lime and water don't mix too well, Sarge. Generates a lot of heat pretty quickly. In a confined space like that, with a full load of lime, a significant leak could be real dangerous, I can tell you. Put it this way, I wouldn't like to be on board when it happened!'

15

'I DON'T KNOW WHY THE HELL we're bothering with those couple of runaways when we've got three murders to deal with.'

Thus spoke Sergeant Clive Newgate, leaning back in his chair and sipping on a cup of tea, supplied courtesy of Constable Wally Morris. At his side, his other constable, Arthur Staples, nodded in silent agreement.

Harry resisted an urge to rise from his chair and throttle the pair of them, instead responding calmly, 'You're right, Sergeant, those boys aren't involved in the murders, but I'd remind you we've got a jewellery theft to investigate as well. And I reckon these two might help us shed some light on that.'

'Can't see how,' Newgate muttered. 'Those two are so wet behind the ears, they wouldn't have the nous to pull off a jewellery job.'

'My point exactly,' Harry replied. 'Which is why Willie and I are heading over to the Quarantine Station today to find out who really nicked those jewels. Would be good to clear up at least one inquiry.'

'Please yourself,' Newgate replied offhandedly, and went back to sipping his tea.

Harry ignored the disrespect and said, 'Anyway, enough of our guests out the back. How have you blokes gone looking for witnesses to the Kuzmina murder? Any breakthroughs?'

Newgate looked up from his tea and shook his head. "'Fraid not, boss. Arthur and I have conducted extensive inquiries, as you requested, but no luck. No-one saw anyone heading around the back before the murder. They were all inside, y'see, watching the show.'

'And after the murder? No-one saw anything suspicious? No-one at the Coffee Palace next door saw anything?'

Newgate nodded towards Staples, who replied, 'No, sir, I spoke to the manager there. He said no-one was out the back around that time, so he couldn't help me. Actually, he said it was dead quiet in the Coffee Palace that night, on account of everyone being at the Cossack show next door. Seems like the whole of Sorrento was in the hall that night.'

'Well, one person wasn't in the hall,' Harry observed grimly. 'At least for that one part of the night when the murder took place. That much we know.'

Newgate simply shrugged. 'I suppose so. Though I still reckon it could've been someone waiting back there the whole time.'

Harry glanced at Newgate. 'I doubt it. But anyway, it's clear then, no leads there. Though I do have one bit of news to convey. May or may not be useful. Got a message back from Molly yesterday.'

There were blank looks from all except Willie, who enquired, 'What's that about, boss? The fingerprints on the sash lifts?'

'Spot on, Willie. Molly tells me he managed to obtain an excellent set of fingerprints off the lifts. And very interestingly, just one set. So, in my mind, that means they could be the prints of our murderer. As he raised the window to get out.'

Willie looked puzzled. 'Hang on. It still could be someone else associated with the theatre. I mean, our bloke opened the window from the outside, so he might not have needed to touch the lifts to get back out.'

'Agreed,' Harry replied. 'That's a real possibility. Which is why I want you, Wally, to organise fingerprints for anyone who might have touched those window lifts in the last week. Cleaners or any other theatre staff. That way we'll know for sure if they came from our murderer.'

'Yes, sir, I'll get onto it right away.' Morris looked pleased to have been given this important responsibility.

Harry eyed him quizzically. 'And you're familiar with the process for taking fingerprints, Wally?'

'Absolutely, sir. Part of our basic training. We have the kit right here in the station,' he added proudly.

Wonders will never cease, Harry marvelled. The force is actually keeping up with the times.

'Good man, Wally,' he said. 'Good to see you're on the ball.' He pulled his watch from his fob. 'Well, that's it for today, boys. It's time Willie and I took to the water and made another trip to the Quarantine Station.'

As the men rose and began filing out of the room, Harry tapped Morris on the shoulder. 'Wally, would you mind staying behind for a minute or two?'

'Certainly, sir,' a slightly puzzled Morris replied, returning to take the seat indicated by Harry. He sat there, looking rather nervous.

'Nothing to worry about, mate,' Harry reassured him. 'I just wondered whether you had any luck tracking down Ridgeway and his whiskey supplies?'

'Yes, sir,' a relieved Morris replied instantly. 'That is, I did have luck, sir. Well some luck, anyway.'

'Let's hear it, mate,' Harry encouraged him. 'Tell us what you found.'

'Well, sir, I was directed to Mr Ridgeway in the first instance. He indicated that he thought the hotel didn't stock that particular brand of whiskey.'

'He was sure of that?' Harry asked.

'He seemed to be. He's the one who orders the spirits, so I thought he should know.'

'So that was it?' Harry asked. 'Not much joy in that, I wouldn't have thought.'

'But that's wasn't the end of it, sir,' Morris replied brightly. 'Because, as I was leaving the hotel, I bumped into Jock Stemple.'

Harry was puzzled. 'Who's he when he's at home?'

'He's my mate, sir. We played football together for the Sorrento Seagulls last season.'

'And that's important why?'

'Sorry,' Morris said, momentarily flustered. 'Turns out he's the bar manager at the Continental as well. You see, I didn't know that before.'

'Go on, Wally,' Harry directed. 'What did Jock have to say?'

'Well, Jock told me he thought the hotel did stock that brand, Powers Gold Label. So he went to find some, but it was all gone. He thought they must have run out, which is why Mr Ridgeway said they didn't have it. Jock said it was a pretty popular brand at the Continental. Kind of exclusive.'

'Right,' Harry said. 'That's very interesting, Wally, well done. And you found out where they get their supplies?'

'Oh yes, I've got it here somewhere.' Morris opened his notebook and thumbed through it. 'Here it is, McSweeney and Sons, in Melbourne.'

'Well done again. Very commendable.'

Morris looked as pleased as punch. 'Thank you, sir.'

'And another thing, Wally. Can you keep an eye out on the harbour for any signs of a night-time run by Madigan? You don't have to shadow him full-time, but look for any signs of activity at his boat. You know, goings-on out there at the end of the day that might indicate he's getting set for a night-time sail.'

'Absolutely,' Morris replied promptly, again chuffed at being chosen for another important task. 'By the way, sir,' he added, 'I've got that telegram you were after too. The Russian one.' And he handed the telegram to Harry.

'Oh, right,' Harry replied, stuffing the telegram into his pocket without examining it. 'I'll get around to looking at that later. Right then, Constable, better get to it,' he added. 'If you want to stay in my good books.' And he smiled quietly to himself as Morris sprang to his feet, saluted and hurried out the door.

The usual afternoon cooling southerly breeze was wafting in from the ocean, and Effie, Rachel and Lydia were thoroughly enjoying their walk along the back beach.

As in their previous foray, once they had left the sheltering curve of the natural amphitheatre, they were on their own, with only the wheeling seabirds above to keep them company.

Today, the swell was up, driven by the southerly breeze. The waves rolled in, crashing onto the many rocky outcrops that dotted the beach at regular intervals.

A mile or so into their walk they encountered the same strip of tall rock that had barred their way previously, running from the cliffs to the sea.

'Oh well, I suppose we'll need to turn back,' Effie conceded, disappointed, for she was enjoying the wildness of the landscape.

'Why don't we explore over there against the cliff, there may be a way through,' Lydia proposed.

So they made their way along the line of jagged rocks to where it met the cliff face. At this point the ridge curved away from them, parallel to the cliff face, forming a narrow passageway. It was only when they had entered this passageway that they noticed a small natural archway through the ridge, formed no doubt by millennia of storm surges crashing against the rocks.

'Well, I'll be darned,' Lydia exclaimed. 'A way through! Are we up for it, girls?'

'Absolutely,' Effie replied. 'Are you game, Rachel?'

'Of course,' Rachel agreed. 'It looks easy enough.'

And it was. With their sturdy plimsolls, they easily scaled the few flat rocks that led up to the archway, and in a trice they were through and on the other side. Here the view was even more spectacular, the cliffs towering above them on one side, the ocean rolling in inexorably on the other. There was now nothing to stop their progress further down the beach, with only the occasional small rocky outcrop that could easily be circumvented.

They strolled down this beautiful white beach for a good two miles, stopping occasionally to take in the panoramic view on all sides. Then, ahead of them, they noticed a tall rocky outcrop, standing out in the water. As they neared it, Effie could see that the rocks formed a natural bridge, with an archway underneath, through which the seawater surged with each breaking wave.

'My goodness, what a spectacular sight!' she exclaimed. 'That's a natural wonder, if ever I saw one.'

'That, my dear, is the famous London Bridge,' Lydia announced. 'Wondrous indeed, except if you happened to be aboard the *Sierra Nevada*, when it crashed into those rocks on a stormy night last year. Then, I imagine, it would have been a terrifying sight.'

'How awful!' Rachel exclaimed, and they all stared at the huge rock formation out in the water, imagining the sheer terror the sailors must have felt on that dreadful night.

'Anyway, I think this is the end of our walk,' Lydia announced, pointing some fifty yards past the Bridge, to where the beach narrowed and the water came up right against the cliff face.

'It must be high tide,' she added. 'We could probably sneak through there at low tide, but not today.'

They walked up to the water's edge and looked around the curve of the cliff where it formed a natural small inlet.

'Look,' Rachel exclaimed, pointing to the cliff face at the end of the inlet. 'I think there might be some sort of cave in there.'

'I think you're right, dear,' Lydia agreed. 'I didn't know that was there. It's well-concealed, and you'd only get in at low tide. How exciting! I suppose there must be a number of caves like that along this rugged coastline.'

'I suppose so,' Effie agreed. 'All part of the romantic charm of this stretch of beach. Anyway, I suppose we'd better be getting back. They'll be wondering where we've got to.'

They turned to retrace their way, but as they walked back past the bridge, Effie noticed something glinting in one of the many adjacent rock pools.

'Hang on a second,' she said. 'I think there's a bottle in that pool over there. Perhaps it's a message in a bottle, from some faraway place. Maybe it's a call for help from some sailor stranded on a desert island.'

She walked over to the shallow pool and lifted the bottle from the water. But it was no message, it was just a bottle, filled with a clear brown liquid. She examined it. The label was missing but she could clearly make out the glass imprint on the bottle, Power and Sons.

'My goodness!' Lydia exclaimed. 'Do you know what that is? It's a bottle of whiskey from the *Sierra Nevada*. They say they still wash up here occasionally.'

'Really?' Effie was intrigued. 'Do you think the whiskey's still drink-able?'

'Not sure,' Lydia replied. 'Can't see why not. The cork keeps the whiskey in. I suppose it should keep the seawater out too.'

'Anyway, I think I'll take it home to Harry,' Effie declared. 'He likes a nice whiskey. Hopefully, it's not spoiled. It's not wrong, is it, for a policeman to have a bottle of whiskey, if it's washed up on the beach?'

'Don't be silly, darling,' Lydia chortled. 'Surely not this long after the wreck. Bounty of the sea, I'd say. Though, mind you, apparently there was a lot of pilfering immediately after the shipwreck. When the merchants were trying to recover some of their cargo. That was rather ghoulish, I thought. Not that there was much whiskey left eventually, by all accounts.'

'That's dreadful behaviour. Particularly when all those sailors were lost.' And again Effie stared back at the London Bridge, looming out of the water, as she imagined the terrible scenes on that fateful night.

The three women turned and began their walk back along the beach. As they set off, Effie noticed that there was a break in the cliffs to their left, and for a stretch of a hundred yards or so the sandhills ran gently down to the beach. There was also a well-worn track winding up the gentle slope, through this gap in the cliffs and into the dunes.

'Look!' she exclaimed to the others. 'I wonder who uses that.'

'Fisherman, I would expect,' Lydia speculated. 'It probably leads over the dunes to some shacks on the other side. I imagine the fishing's quite good off these rocks, when the tide's right.'

'I think I'll mention it to Michael,' Effie mused aloud. 'James should come down here and paint the London Bridge. It would make a wonderfully dramatic subject.'

'It would indeed. A splendid idea, darling. Come on now, let's hurry along. We might just be in time for afternoon tea at the kiosk.'

❧

The redoubtable Mrs Couper Johnston again took charge of matters when Harry and Willie arrived at the Quarantine Station.

This time Harry had telegraphed their visit in advance and Constable Andrews was waiting for them at the pier. He led them immediately up the hill and into the administration rooms at the villa. They were soon joined by Mrs Johnston, looking her imperial best in what seemed to be some sort of glorified nursing garb, consisting of a stiffly starched long white tunic and a nurse's flossie cap on her head.

'Good afternoon, Inspector,' she began briskly. 'I believe you're interested in speaking with Captain Romanov again?'

'That's right, Mrs Johnston,' Harry replied, half wondering whether he should have addressed her as 'matron'. 'I was hoping I would be able to speak with him. And his purser as well. Mr Schwartz, I think it was. Are they available?'

'That can be arranged,' Mrs Johnston replied. 'But in the first instance, I need to remind you that the entire personnel of *The Queen of Hamburg* remain under quarantine, and, while they may be past the infectious stage, it is recommended you keep your distance from those two gentlemen when they enter the room. Just to be on the safe side. I can assure you contracting smallpox is no minor matter.'

'I'll do my best,' Harry assured her, while privately wondering how that might be achieved, if things developed in a certain direction.

Mrs Johnston gave him a stern glance, before turning to whisper an instruction to a young nurse standing behind her. The lass dashed off and soon returned with Captain Romanov, accompanied by a thin, balding nervous-looking younger man, who was introduced to Harry as Daniel Schwartz, the ship's purser.

'Thank you, gentlemen, for meeting with us,' Harry began. 'We're continuing our investigation into the theft of valuable jewels from your ship, as reported to us by Mr Kozminsky.'

Romanov returned Harry's gaze impassively. 'Yes, Inspector, I understand.'

'The thing is,' Harry continued, 'in order to focus our investigation and eliminate certain possibilities, we have a few questions for you.'

'Of course,' Romanov replied. 'Though it is obvious what has happened. Those two absconding sailors have stolen them. That is where you should be directing your inquiries.'

'Ah yes,' Harry replied. 'The two Russian sailors.'

'Yes, the Russian sailors,' Romanov confirmed, with a sideways glance at his purser. 'Though I would think they're well and truly disappeared by now. Gone to Melbourne. And beyond, probably. I think it will be an insurance claim by Mr Kozminsky in the end.'

Harry nodded. 'Perhaps you're right. But just to tie up loose ends, I've a couple of questions. Firstly, there are no other sailors, or passengers for that matter, gone missing from your vessel?'

Romanov shook his head. 'No, they are the only ones missing from my crew. I can't speak for the passengers. The good lady here may be able to advise on the passenger side of things.'

'As I advised you previously, we have a regular count of passengers,' Mrs Johnston affirmed. 'Every second day. And as of yesterday, there were none missing. We take our duties seriously.'

'Right, that's clear then,' Harry noted. 'Two Russian sailors are the only ones missing. And by the way, you can confirm that the missing men are Russian? Just so we know who we're looking for. I believe that's what you told Sergeant Milton here.'

Romanov glanced at Schwartz again, before replying. 'That is what Mr Schwartz informed me, yes.'

Harry looked directly at Schwartz and said firmly, 'And you can attest to that, Mr Schwartz? You are certain of it?'

Schwartz looked at the ground and cleared his throat, before glancing nervously up at Harry. 'I believe that to be the case, Inspector. I mean, I think so.'

'Are they Russian? Yes or no?'

'Well ... yes.'

Harry smiled. 'Well, I have to tell you, gentlemen, we've found your missing sailors. And they're definitely not Russian. They're German to the back teeth. So, either you have a very poor knowledge of your crew, Mr Schwartz, or you're telling porky-pies. And I think I'd back the porky-pies.'

Schwartz stared at Harry, ashen-faced and sweating. He said nothing. Harry glanced at Romanov, who was staring hard at his purser.

'Here's the thing, Mr Schwartz,' Harry continued calmly. 'I think this robbery's an inside job, and I'm pretty sure you've got nothing to do with it. I think you've been put up to say the missing sailors are Russian, because your captain here thought it would suit our other investigation and get us off his back. That somehow, we'd think they were murderers as well as jewel thieves. So, here's what I'm offering you. Tell us the truth about those sailors, and we'll let you off the hook. Because lying to the police is a criminal offence, if it makes you an accessory to theft.'

Schwartz continued to stand there, transfixed, alternating his gaze between Harry and Romanov. Sweat ran freely down his face.

Harry felt a little reassurance might do the trick. 'If you're worried the captain here might make things hard for you if you tell the truth, my advice is, don't worry. If we find the jewels where I think they are, the captain will not be troubling you, I can assure you.'

Schwartz now turned his full attention to Harry, avoiding his captain's now angry stare.

'It's true,' he admitted. 'I was told to say the sailors were Russian, and to alter the crew list accordingly. He told me he had made a mistake when he spoke to you about them, and he didn't want to be thought incompetent.'

'And 'he' is Captain Romanov?' Harry asked.

Schwartz simply nodded.

'This is nonsense,' Romanov snarled. 'This man is lying to protect his own skin. What evidence do you have against me? Tell me that. It could just as easily be him who took the jewels. He has full access to that room. Or it could easily have been any of the crew on guard at the time.'

'That's true,' Harry replied. 'Mr Schwartz does have a key to the safe, along with you. But your other premise I find very hard to accept. I doubt very much whether any of your crew would have the skill, or the nerve for that matter, to pick their way into both the purser's storeroom and the lock to the safe, and make off with the jewels. For a start, where would they hide them? And even more importantly, what would they do with them, here in a strange country and with no knowledge of criminal networks?'

'The same questions apply to me,' Romanov sneered. 'What would I do with them here also?'

Harry smiled. 'I don't think you'd do anything with them here, Captain. Unlike your crew members, and your purser for that matter, you're well acquainted with the value of the jewels, and know that they would fetch far more in your home country than in a backwater like Australia. I'm betting you've got some very good criminal contacts in Hamburg who would readily be able to fence the jewels for you. So all you have to do is take the jewels, conceal them, then make it look like a break-in.

'And the disappearance of your two crewmen was the motivation to put your plan into action. You thought they'd be far away, probably on the goldfields somewhere, by the time we started looking for them. Sadly for you, they didn't get any further than Sorrento.

'And you stupidly embellished your plan by trying to link them to our other investigation. A spur-of-the-moment decision, but one that has backfired very badly on you.'

Romanov stared at Harry scornfully. 'A fanciful tale, Inspector, one that would do credit to the Brothers Grimm. But you do not have a skerrick of evidence to support this fantasy. So I demand you withdraw your scandalous allegation.'

Again Harry smiled agreeably. 'There's something in what you say, Captain. We don't have the evidence we need. But on the other hand, if we find the jewels hidden on board the ship, that might begin to supply the evidence we currently lack. Particularly if we find them hidden in your private quarters. Which is where I strongly suspect they are secreted. That's clearly the safest and most secure place for you to hide them. So, Constable Andrews and his colleagues here at the station are going to search your private quarters, very thoroughly, and see what they can turn up.'

Romanov's scowl deepened. 'You can't do that! I am a foreign citizen! You have no right!'

'Not so,' Harry replied. 'The laws of this state apply to all vessels, foreign or otherwise, berthed within three miles of the shore. Which your ship undoubtedly is. And I have a lawful warrant to search your ship.'

And Harry produced a slip of paper from his coat pocket and handed it to the captain.

Romanov stared at the document, then wheeled around to Mrs Johnston. 'I must insist you prevent this search, madam!' he demanded. 'It is unlawful, this vessel is in quarantine.'

Mrs Johnston eyed him up and down scornfully. 'Nonsense, man,' she declared. 'A load of poppycock. The ship has now been thoroughly cleaned and disinfected to my and my husband's satisfaction. From our perspective, the inspector is free to search to his heart's content.'

Romanov scowled again and retreated into sullen silence.

Harry turned to Mrs Johnston. 'Thank you, Mrs Johnston. We're sorry to intrude on you and your good work like this, but hopefully we'll clear this up quick smart and we'll be on our way. And we'll be able to take the good captain here off your hands too.'

'Only too happy to assist the law, Inspector,' Mrs Johnston replied, bestowing Harry with the ghost of a smile. 'And you can take this fellow any time you like. He's been most unhelpful. I'm sure his first mate can take control of the ship, if necessary. Now, if you'll excuse me, I've work to do. Feel free to wait here until your men have completed their search.'

So wait they did, but not for long. After a mere quarter of an hour, Constable Andrews returned with his sergeant, who was carrying a wooden box.

'Sergeant McEvoy reporting, sir,' the Sergeant said. 'I can attest that we discovered this box, hidden under loose planks on the floor of the captain's quarters. It contains a quantity of jewellery pieces. I believe you have your evidence.'

Harry nodded, solemn now. 'Captain Romanov, I'm arresting you on suspicion of the theft of a number of jewellery pieces, being the property of Mr Simon Kozminsky and Mr Isadore Kozminsky. I must ask you to accompany us to Sorrento where you will be held in custody, and from there to Melbourne, to be tried in the Melbourne Criminal Court.'

Effie put down her knife and fork and looked across the dining table at her husband. 'You two are looking a bit more pleased with yourselves tonight,' she observed. 'First time I've seen you really smiling since we got here.'

'I suppose we are a bit satisfied with today's result,' Harry replied, his smile broadening further. 'One issue sorted at least, eh, Willie?'

'Yeh,' Willie responded. 'Though precious little thanks you got from the chief, I must say.'

'Oh well,' Harry sighed, 'I didn't expect too much from him. The murders are what he's mainly focused on. And he still thinks it's all part of some Russian Government plot.'

'And clearly you don't, darling,' Effie suggested.

'No, not really. It seems unlikely, and that fellow Ridgeway's evidence didn't do any more to convince me either. But I'm keeping an open mind.'

'Your boss needs to listen to you more,' Clem exclaimed stoutly. 'You're twice the policeman that he is.'

'Shh, Clem,' Millie chided her husband. 'Don't say things like that. You'll get Harry into trouble.'

Harry laughed. 'Don't worry, Mum. I don't think anyone around this table will dob Dad in. And Mrs M knows how to be discrete, I'm sure.' He reached over and patted his mother's arm.

Effie looked at him quizzically. 'Seriously darling, if it isn't the Russian Government committing all these murders, who is? Are you close to solving it?'

'Come on, Eff,' Harry responded, a little apologetically. 'You know I can't reveal the details of what we're up to. All I'll say is there are a number of leads and a number of issues that are buzzing around in my head, but I haven't really made proper sense of them yet. Can't quite see how they all fit together.'

'Well, that doesn't tell us much, I must say. But we understand, darling, you need to be discrete. I'm sure you'll resolve it all soon.'

'I hope so.' Harry's smile evaporated as he began to puzzle again over the various elements of the case.

'Well, if you can't tell us what you're up to, we can at least tell you about our day. Because we had a lovely time, didn't we, Rachel?'

Rachel smiled her agreement. 'It was very special.'

'You went to the back beach again, didn't you?' Willie enquired.

'That's right,' Effie replied. 'But this time we found a way through the rocks and walked all the way down to London Bridge. It was so spectacular.'

'I've heard it's impressive,' Harry observed.

'And we found a cave. Just a little bit further on from London Bridge.'

Harry looked at her with some surprise. 'Really? I hadn't heard about that. But I suppose there must be quite a few caves along the cliffs on the seaward side. Worn out by the action of the sea over the years.'

'Oh! And there's something else,' Effie exclaimed, remembering. 'I got you a present.' And she jumped up from the table and went to her bag, lying in a corner of the room.

'What is it?' Harry wondered. 'Seashells? A couple of nice whiting?'

'Much better than that,' Effie replied, producing the whiskey bottle from the depths of her bag. 'Here you are. I hope it's still alright.' And she handed it to Harry.

But Harry's reaction to the gift was completely unexpected. He grasped the bottle and examined it closely and intently, staring at the inscription stamped on the glass. 'Where did you get this?' he asked.

'In a rock pool, near London Bridge. Lydia said it must have been washed up after the *Sierra Nevada* shipwreck. Do you think it's still drinkable?'

'What? Oh, I dunno, maybe. But that doesn't matter.' And he lapsed into silence, thinking hard.

Suddenly Harry gave the table a thump with his fist. 'Damn it! I think I'm onto it! I think I know what's been going on.'

Effie stared at him. 'What are you talking about, Harry? You're not making sense.'

Harry pushed his chair back, stood up from the table and began to pace around the room. His expression was grim. 'Actually, Eff, it's making perfect sense. The damn penny's dropped. Bloody hell, I've been an idiot!'

Effie was getting an inkling of what Harry was on about. 'You mean, the murders? Do you think you've solved the murders?'

'I might well have. But I'll need to confirm a few things. I need to go to Melbourne, first thing tomorrow. Willie, can you get me on the *Ozone* in the morning? And on the trip back to Sorrento in the arvo. And I need you to set up a few meetings for me in town.'

'Sure thing, boss.' Willie's expression showed he was just as puzzled by this turn of events as Effie. 'Do you want me to come with you?'

'No, just see to the meetings. And there's a couple of important things here I need you to watch. I've asked young Morris to keep a close eye on Tosh Madigan and his boat. So keep in touch with him about that. Plus, there's a couple of other people I need you to watch. But let's finish dinner, then I'll fill you in on all the details.' And with those words, Harry resumed his seat at the table. 'Now, how about some pudding? Shall I ring the bell for Mrs M?'

16

THURSDAY DAWNED BRIGHT and sunny in Sorrento, the morning enhanced by a gentle breeze off the bay. A pleasant trip to Melbourne lay ahead for the passengers on the *Ozone*, with the sea relatively calm and the sun, at this early hour, still only mildly warming.

The crowd on board consisted of the usual melange of returning holiday-makers, chatting animatedly among themselves about their recent experience in Sorrento's seaside paradise. And prominent on the second-class deck, among the mothers and their sunburnt offspring, was the imposing figure of Inspector Harry Holloway, clad in suit and tie in deference to his upcoming list of Melbourne appointments, and gazing calmly out to sea as the *Ozone's* paddlewheels churned their way up the South Channel.

An interested observer of this tall figure would likely conclude that here was a man in a perfectly relaxed mood, at peace with the world, and with not a worry to trouble his serene contemplation of the sea around him.

But that assessment of Inspector Holloway would change once the *Ozone* docked at the Sandridge pier. He was the first ashore, the first into a carriage at the Station Pier, and once the train arrived at Flinders Street, he could be seen setting off at a lively pace towards William Street, a now intent expression on his face.

Before the William Street intersection, the inspector turned right and made his way resolutely through the grand entrance of the Melbourne Customs House, and once inside, to the office of one, Mr John Christie, whose door was adorned with the brass nameplate, Inspector of Liquor and Excise.

Roll forward half an hour and Inspector Holloway could be observed exiting the Customs House, a satisfied expression on his face, then turning right up William Street to the Flinders Lane corner where he strode purposefully into the premises of the Melbourne Harbour Trust. Another half hour on, and the inspector emerged again, set off up Flinders Lane, then along Market Street and down Collins Street to a rather unprepossessing three-storey building, whose list of tenants included the Consulate of Russia.

A short time later he left the building, this time accompanied by an earnest young moustachioed fellow, who pressed the inspector's hand fervently and bowed an elegant farewell. Inspector Holloway doffed his hat in somewhat embarrassed acknowledgement of this display of diplomatic manners, before heading off again, this time north up Queen's Street, then along Bourke Street to number 471, a grand building with the title 'Dalgety House' stuccoed above its entrance.

Another sojourn here, and then Inspector Holloway headed off to make one final call, this time retracing his steps back to Flinders Lane, where he entered a large warehouse, its occupant emblazoned in large letters above the huge front swing doors: J McSweeney and Sons, Licensed Victuallers.

The final meeting concluded, Inspector Holloway's stride was perhaps not quite so vigorous as he headed back to Flinders Street Station, though the satisfied expression remained. Pausing only to consume a pie and a pint at the Prince's Bridge Hotel, the inspector was soon on the train, back to the pier and aboard the *Ozone* for the afternoon voyage back to Sorrento.

The inspector did not hasten ashore once the *Ozone* berthed at Sorrento, instead waiting patiently for the excited throng to surge onto the pier, before disembarking at a leisurely stroll, with a cheerful wave to one, Sergeant Willie Milton, waiting expectantly for him.

※

Harry Holloway and Willie Milton sat in Mrs Meriwether's private parlour, enjoying a cup of tea provided by that good lady. Harry had just finished an exhaustive account of his day's encounters and was now eying his sergeant to assess his response.

Willie stared back at Harry, wide-eyed with surprise. 'Crikey, mate,' he exclaimed, momentarily forgoing his usual mode of address to his boss. 'I reckon that trip to town has nailed the case for us. What a turn-up!'

'I hope it has,' Harry reflected. 'Though there's still a couple of loose ends to tie up. Mainly around the extent of the scheme, and the full list of participants. But I think the plan I've outlined should settle all that.'

Willie rubbed his chin in contemplation. 'I imagine we'll need to be pretty careful in how we go about it,' he suggested. 'Don't want to give the game away.'

'We don't,' Harry agreed. 'And we'll need to move quickly, I reckon. I've dealt with McSweeney, so he should stay mum, but you never know.'

'And Ridgeway? What about him?'

'In due course,' Harry replied. 'But not yet.'

At that moment, their ruminations were interrupted by a knock on the door, and the appearance of Mrs Meriwether in the doorway.

'I'm terribly sorry to interrupt your meeting, Inspector,' she exclaimed, somewhat breathlessly. 'But one of your officers has requested to see you. He says it's rather urgent.'

Harry sat upright. 'Which of the officers is it?'

'Constable Morris, Inspector. The nice young fellow.'

'Show him in,' Harry replied immediately.

Hearing Harry's words and needing no further invitation, Wally Morris appeared in the doorway behind Mrs Meriwether.

'Sorry to intrude, Inspector, but you told me to keep an eye on that Madigan bloke and his boat, and to advise you of any suspicious behaviour.'

'Right,' said Harry, leaping to his feet. 'What's going on?'

'He's just gone aboard, and I reckon he's preparing to set sail.'

'Damn it!' Harry exclaimed. 'We'll miss him. We don't have time to organise the police launch.'

'Don't worry, sir, that's all in hand. Constable Jones has the launch ready to go. It's tied up at the pier.'

'Come on then!' Harry exclaimed, dashing from the room, Willie and Morris hot on his heels.

Outside, darkness had set in though the moon was up and casting a pale light.

'Well done, Wally,' Harry called back over his shoulder, as the three men sprinted down Ocean Beach Road to the foreshore. 'Keep this up and you'll be promoted in no time!'

By the time the three men joined Constable Jones aboard the police steam launch, Madigan's boat had already disappeared.

'About five minutes ago,' Jones reported, in response to Harry's query. He pointed to the water immediately to their north. In the dull light of the waning moon, there was no sign of any boat.

'He was moored over there,' Jones added. 'And as far as I could make out he's headed to the north-east. Up the South Channel, I reckon.'

'Can you catch him?' Harry asked. 'He's got a good head start.'

'Don't worry, Inspector,' Jones reassured him as he wound furiously on the capstan to haul in the mooring rope. 'This girl will outpace any vessel in the bay, no problem at all.' And he retreated to the wheelhouse, from where he began to manoeuvre the launch out into the bay.

With the help of his stoker, Jones soon had the launch skimming along at a lively pace, but the light was poor and Harry had doubts as to whether Jones would even find the South Channel, let alone catch up and apprehend Madigan's ketch. He and Willie stood at the bow, peering into the gloom, but no sign of any ship.

Then, ahead of them, Harry spotted something, a faint pale smudge in the distance. As they steamed on, the smudge gradually solidified into the outline of a mainsail, and then a triangular topsail above it.

'There he is!' Jones exclaimed triumphantly. 'Got you now, mate!' And he throttled up the steam engine to even greater speed.

'What d'you want to do?' he shouted to Harry, leaning out the cabin window. 'Board her?'

'You bet,' Harry replied. 'I need to see what he's got on board.'

Jones nodded and, reaching down at his feet, produced a loud hailer which he offered to Harry. 'You'll do the honours, sir?'

Harry nodded his agreement. Grasping the loud hailer in one hand, he moved back to the bow and continued to peer into the gloom. The vessel in the distance grew gradually more distinct, until they were only some fifty yards astern.

'Heave to!' Harry shouted into the loud hailer. 'This is the Water Police, heave to, so we can board!'

'I don't think he's going to cooperate!' Jones shouted. 'He's taking on more sail!'

And indeed Madigan was. Harry could see a further foresail being raised, as the vessel ploughed through the waves ahead of them. And, as the increased sail began to take effect, the boat, already low in the water, was beginning to list alarmingly to one side under the force of the fresh southerly breeze.

'The man's mad!' Jones shouted. 'He's overloaded, he'll capsize if he keeps up that speed!'

'Heave to!' Harry shouted again through the loud hailer. 'Don't be a fool, man!'

There was no response and the boat ahead continued its reckless course. Harry briefly contemplated calling off the pursuit, but then settled on another plan.

'Can we get ahead of him?' he shouted to Jones. 'And make him see he can't outrun us? We don't want him to capsize.'

'Course we can,' Jones shouted back, and began to steer a course around their quarry. 'But capsizing's not the main problem,' he added over his shoulder. 'If that tub's full of lime, he's liable to set the whole lot alight. He's taking on a fair bit of water!'

Harry remembered Jones' previous warning and stared at the ketch as they loomed up on its starboard side. Jones was right. The swell was not heavy, but the boat was so low in the water that the sea was running over the bow as it crested each wave.

'Bloody hell!' Harry exclaimed. And then into the loudhailer. 'Heave to now! You'll set the boat on fire!'

But the damage was already done. As they watched, they could see smoke beginning to billow from the centre of the boat, and then two figures appeared at the stern and began frantically waving at them, before leaping headlong into the sea behind the ship.

'That's enough, Jones, stop and pick up those men!' Harry shouted. But Jones had already swung into action, shutting down steam and bringing his boat about to return to the stricken men in the water.

'I reckon Madigan's still on board!' Morris shouted, pointing to the ketch now heading away from them, smoke billowing copiously from its hold. As they watched, there was a sudden flash and a column of flame shot into the air, illuminating the water around the ship, which abruptly keeled over on its side, its forward momentum halted.

Against the rapidly growing inferno, they could clearly see the outline of a man leaping into the water and beginning to swim away from the conflagration.

'He's overboard!' Harry exclaimed. 'I hope the bugger can swim, we can't get much closer, it's too damn hot!'

Jones expertly manoeuvred the launch back to where the first two sailors had bailed out, and Harry and Morris soon had them on board, with the help of two rope lines provided by Jones. Cold and bedraggled, the men huddled in the bow of the launch, one of them muttering something to Harry in a foreign tongue.

Harry took it as an expression of thanks and turned his attention back to Madigan and his ship. The ketch was now fully ablaze, flames shooting into the air amid the columns of smoke and throwing an eerie light across the water.

In the orange glow, Harry could see Madigan in the water, some forty yards from them, thrashing desperately in their direction away from the burning ship.

'There he is!' he shouted, pointing, but Jones was already onto it, edging the launch towards Madigan. As they got closer, Harry cast a line in his direction. But just as he did so, the flaming ketch sank deeper into the water. The roar of burning lime was replaced by a loud hiss as the boat disappeared into the sea, steam rising to mingle with the smoke, before the fire was extinguished and all was plunged back into darkness again.

In the sudden darkness, Harry could no longer discern Madigan in the water, but a tug on the rope he had thrown told him that the captain had taken the offered lifeline. Harry heaved away and before long Madigan's grizzled features materialised in the water beside the launch. Harry reached down and, with Morris's help, hauled the sodden figure from the water, dumping him unceremoniously on a bench in the bow of the boat.

'We meet again, Mr Madigan,' Harry said. 'This time I think you might have a bit of explaining to do.'

Madigan stared at him silently, wet to the skin and presenting an entirely forlorn picture.

'Oh well,' Harry observed. 'Perhaps now isn't the right time for a chat. Let's get you out of that wet gear, and perhaps a tot of brandy into you to warm you up. Our little chat can wait till the morning.'

Again Madigan said nothing, but his forlorn look was now replaced by an angry glare, a glare that didn't intimidate Harry one whit. On the contrary, it encouraged him, because that seemed like the look of a man caught undertaking an act that he knew would not be looked upon kindly by the law.

17

MADIGAN WAS STILL IN A SURLY, defiant mood when Harry sat down opposite him in the station's interview room the next morning.

'Morning, Mr Madigan,' Harry began brightly. 'You still seem a bit down in the dumps. A good night's sleep and Mrs Newgate's hearty breakfast haven't improved your spirits?'

'Very funny,' Madigan spat back. 'How do you think I should feel, my boat and my livelihood gone? All because of you bloody coppers.'

'I beg to differ,' Harry replied calmly. 'It seems to me that we had every right to stop you and find out what you were up to, loaded to the gills with lime, heading off to Melbourne in the middle of the night. Don't you think?'

'I know what I think,' Madigan growled. 'Bloody coppers harassing a man going about his lawful business. Bloody disgrace, that's what I think.'

Harry leaned back and chuckled. 'Lawful business, my foot. Mate, we've already checked with the harbourmaster in Melbourne, and you had no lawful business running lime to Melbourne in the middle of the night. In fact, the lime docks are closed at night, as confirmed by the harbourmaster. No, my friend, my contention is that you were transporting stolen lime to a contact in Melbourne, who was prepared to take it at a good price, no questions asked.'

'That's a load of codswallop,' Madigan sneered. 'You're making it up. Who am I meant to have nicked this lime from?'

'From Mr George Coppin, actually.'

'What? Rubbish! If you reckon I nicked it, prove it.'

'Don't need to,' Harry replied. 'You see, we've arrested your colleague, Mr Wilkes, the mine manager, this morning, and it turns out he's nowhere near as practised a liar as you seem to be. He's sung like a little bird, told us everything. In fact, he reckons it was all your idea, says you're the one that put him up to it. Claims you said Mr Coppin wouldn't notice if a bit of lime went missing now and again. And that it was you who suggested one last run, before the smuggling operation was closed down. Apparently Mr Wilkes wanted out. He was getting a bit nervous after we started investigating the human remains at the kiln.'

'That's all a lie!' Madigan exclaimed, his features twisted in fury. 'It was all his idea! I was just carting the lime for him. I didn't even know it was hot.'

'Well, you certainly knew it was hot out there last night,' Harry observed, leaning back and allowing himself a brief smile at his own witticism. 'But frankly, I don't much care whose idea it was. You're both in the frame for theft and smuggling anyway. Actually, what I'm more interested in is what connection you, and Mr Wilkes for that matter, have with the disappearance and murder of the Russian they called Dave. The bloke who used to work out at Coppin's kiln.'

Madigan's demeanour transformed instantly from fury to alarm. 'No, no, I had nothing to do with no murder!' he protested. 'Nothing! And that's God's truth.'

'That's something that's still a strong possibility, as far as we're concerned,' Harry replied. 'After all, we know Dave worked for Wilkes and you said yourself Sergei Karpov worked for you. And I've got no doubt Dave worked for you on occasion as well. Now they're both dead, murdered. Bit of a coincidence, I would have thought.

'What if you got into a dispute with those two blokes about your activities, and they were going to make trouble for you? I know you've got an alibi for the murder of the young Russian woman, but we're going to have a good look at what you were up to the night Karpov was chucked in the harbour.'

Madigan's weather-beaten features paled as he protested, 'No way! I was in the pub that night! Ask anyone. They'll tell you I was there. I'm there every night.'

'Exactly,' Harry replied. 'And I don't need to remind you that Karpov was killed not far from the pub that night. Maybe you slipped out for five minutes to settle a score with him. Or maybe you bumped him off after closing time. You would've had plenty of opportunity, I reckon.'

Madigan stared at Harry, open-mouthed. 'It wasn't me,' he managed to say eventually, but the fight seemed to have gone out of him. 'I don't know how to prove it, mate, but it wasn't me.'

Harry nodded slowly. He got up from the table and wandered to the window, gazing pensively out, before turning slowly back to face Madigan. 'You know, I'd be more inclined to believe you if you were able to provide us with some useful information. For example, information that would connect Sergei to somebody else who might also have had a decent motive to do him in.'

Madigan looked puzzled. 'How could I do that? I mean, I didn't know nothing about the bloke. What do you expect me to tell you?'

'Well,' Harry replied, 'I recall you said that Sergei only worked for you part-time. Did you have any indication from him as to who else he worked for? Or associated with, for that matter?'

Madigan sat for a few moments in thought, then shrugged. 'Not really. He kept to himself pretty much. Didn't give too much away.'

'Think about it,' Harry persevered. 'Anything. Anything that might help us work out where and when he might have worked elsewhere.'

Madigan sat silently, staring at the desk in front of him. Then he looked back up at Harry. 'Well, I dunno if this will help, but sometimes he said he couldn't crew my boat at night because he had something else on. Bloody annoying, I can tell you, because I had to get someone else at short notice. One of the blokes you picked up last night, actually.'

'That would have been annoying,' Harry agreed. 'And you couldn't get him to change his mind? I imagine you were slipping him a decent quid for his trouble.'

'I couldn't. It was sort of like he couldn't get out of it. Couple of times, in fact, I offered him an extra bob or two, but he wouldn't change his mind.'

Harry returned to the desk and resumed his seat opposite Madigan. 'There you go, mate, you can help if you try hard enough. That might actually be useful information.'

Madigan looked at Harry hopefully. 'Does that mean I'm off the hook? For the murder, I mean.'

Harry smiled. 'Not necessarily, my friend, not necessarily. You're still our person of most interest, as far as the murders go. But I'll tell you what. If you didn't do him in, you'd better hope your bit of cooperation helps lead us to whoever did. A charge of smuggling stolen goods is far better than murder, any day of the week.'

For Harry, the end was in sight and almost all the ducks were lined up. But before he could put the final pieces in place, he needed to report back to Winston Marks to settle his concern about an impending Russian invasion. Usually a briefing with Marks was a rather unpleasant affair, but he was looking forward to this one with a certain amount of relish.

Marks seemed to have established a temporary office at the Continental Hotel, and it was here that Harry was required to present himself. Ushered into one of the hotel's private meeting rooms, Harry found his boss settled on a leather sofa, whiskey in hand. At the other end of the sofa was Commander Jackson, similarly armed with distilled fortification.

'Ah, Holloway, you've deigned to grace us with your presence,' Marks intoned, with heavy irony. 'Four days after we provided you with critical information, which we asked you to act on urgently, if I recall correctly.'

Harry resisted the temptation to bite back, instead conceding mildly, 'Sorry, sir, but we've been pretty busy tracking down the issue you raised, as well as a number of other leads pertaining to the case.'

Marks snorted. 'Dead ends most of them, I'll warrant. They better not have distracted you from the real issue, finding out what those damn Russians are up to.'

'Not at all, sir. I've been able to ascertain who Mr Matyunin was meeting with, and for what purpose.'

'Really?' Marks exclaimed, leaning forward in his chair, his interest now well and truly piqued. 'What the hell was he up to?'

'Actually,' Harry responded, savouring the moment, 'he was in the process of finalising a trade deal.'

'A trade deal?' Marks looked momentarily confused. 'A trade deal with who?'

'With Dalgety and Company. For the shipment of Australian wool to Europe. Very lucrative, I'm given to understand.'

'Who told you this?' Jackson interjected, eying Harry suspiciously. 'Who or what is the source of your information?'

'The Russian consulate in Melbourne,' Harry replied calmly. 'They're very pleased with the outcome, I can tell you.'

'You'd take their word for it?' Marks blurted out. 'Why the hell would you trust them to tell you what's really going on?'

Harry allowed himself a small smile. 'Well, they seemed quite open and above board about the matter. And very pleased to tell me all about it too. But of course, I took the opportunity to check with the other party.

Dalgetys were equally open about the deal, now that it's finalised. And equally pleased, I might add. A very good price, they informed me.'

Marks sat, silenced by this revelation.

Jackson spoke instead. 'So, the fellow with Matyunin ... here in the hotel ... not a Russian?'

'No, it was Dalgety's chief negotiator. David McCaffrey is his name. A Scotsman, I'd say, judging by his accent.'

'And the Russian ships coming to Port Phillip Bay?'

'Freighters, to cart our wool to Russian and other European ports.'

Jackson too lapsed into silence, reflectively swirling his whiskey in its glass. A slightly uncomfortable pause ensued.

'Would you like to hear about our progress on the murder investigation?' Harry offered brightly.

Marks lifted his eyes. 'I suppose so,' he responded grumpily. 'But it better be good news. Your inquiry has gone on too long.'

'I'm very hopeful of winding things up in the next day or so,' Harry replied. 'I had cause to arrest a local fisherman last night on suspicion of operating a smuggling racket.'

'And he's your man?' Marks asked. 'Your murderer, I mean.'

'We're not sure about that. Actually, I doubt it. But it's certainly opened my eyes to other illegal activity, of a broadly similar nature, being carried on in the Sorrento region. And that's what we're targeting at the moment.'

Marks stared at Harry. 'It doesn't sound to me like you're close to solving the case,' he observed testily. 'So, just who do you reckon is behind it all? And what is this illegal activity you're talking about?'

Harry swallowed and politely replied, 'I'm sorry, sir, but I'm unable to divulge any further information in front of Commander Jackson here. I'm sure the commander appreciates police protocols.'

Marks' scowl deepened, but Jackson nodded wisely. 'Of course, I understand entirely. Would you like me to leave the room?'

'Not necessary, Commander,' Harry responded politely. 'Our inquiry isn't yet at the point where I can brief the Chief Inspector with any degree of certainty.'

To Marks he added, 'But rest assured, sir, the moment I've resolved all the loose ends and made an arrest, you'll be the first to know.'

Marks gave Harry an irritated glance and seemed on the point of taking issue with him. But then he appeared to change his mind, sitting back in his chair, raising his glass to his lips and dismissing Harry with a wave of his hand.

❦

It was three o'clock by the clock on the wall when Newgate and Staples sauntered into the briefing room at the Sorrento Police Station to join Harry, Willie and Wally Morris. Harry had called the meeting for two-thirty, but it seemed some of the local constabulary operated on a different schedule.

Despite his annoyance, Harry resisted the urge to lose his temper. 'Welcome, lads,' he greeted them instead. 'Sorry to drag you away from what must have been important police business.'

'That's okay,' Newgate replied, oblivious to the heavy sarcasm in Harry's welcome. 'We were just chasing down a couple of leads.'

'Anything to report?' Harry asked.

'Nah, nothing really,' Newgate replied. 'We've been asking around the town again. Just in case we might have overlooked somebody. Just trying to be thorough. But it seems like no-one knows anything, or had anything to do with them Russians.'

'Well, we know one who did have something to do with them,' Harry suggested, pointing in the direction of the cell block in the backyard. 'Tosh Madigan out there. And he's keeping us company while we work out the full extent of the charges we're going to hit him with.'

'Right, of course, we heard about what happened last night,' Newgate said. 'Young Morris couldn't stop talking about it. Hell of a show. You reckon Madigan's the one behind those murders?'

'Not sure,' Harry responded. 'We know he was up to no good, smuggling lime to Melbourne, and we know the bloke they called Dave was working for him. So that's not a bad basis for making him our main suspect at this stage.'

'I'll say,' Newgate responded enthusiastically. 'Clear as daylight, I'd say. You gonna charge him, boss?'

'With murder? Not quite sure we're ready for that yet.'

'You gotta be joking,' Newgate protested. 'Why the hell not?'

Harry smiled. 'Steady on, Sarge, let's not get too hasty. There's a couple of other important rabbits we need to chase down first.'

Newgate looked puzzled. 'I don't get it.'

Harry smiled. 'You will, Sarge, you will. Actually, it's why I've called this meeting today. To explain where we're up to, and to organise our next move.'

Newgate shrugged. 'Okay. Then in that case, we're all ears.'

Harry rose from his chair and strolled over to the window, staring out, deep in thought. He turned to address his men again. 'Here's the thing, lads. We now know that Madigan, with the help of Dave, Sam and others, was involved in an ongoing racket of stealing and smuggling lime to the Melbourne black market. But I'm not convinced that's the full extent of smuggling going on around here. I reckon Madigan, and probably other local criminals, were involved in a much wider smuggling ring.'

'You reckon?' Newgate responded doubtfully. 'I mean, there's always been a bit of that sort of thing going on around here, but nothing big. Nothing worth worrying about, I wouldn't reckon.'

'That's not the information I've had,' Harry said firmly. 'We've had word of something very much worth worrying about, in fact.'

Newgate looked at Harry doubtfully. 'Really? That's news to me. What do you reckon's being smuggled? And where from?'

Harry shrugged. 'That's what I'm not sure about. But I don't reckon it's being brought in from the bay side of the peninsula. From my discussions with Lieutenant Windsor up at the fort, I don't reckon any boats would get through the Heads without them noticing. They keep a twenty-four hour watch. So that leaves the ocean side, from the back beach up to the Heads. There's plenty of spots there where a small boat could beach in calm weather. And bring in any amount of goods, of one kind or another.'

'I suppose so,' Newgate conceded, but he still sounded doubtful. 'Though it's one thing to drop off gear on the beach, but how the hell are they going to get it to Melbourne without being noticed.'

'Not too hard, I wouldn't have thought,' Harry replied. 'There's plenty of spots in the sand hills where they could store gear without much chance of being noticed. Or even along the beach, for that matter. There's plenty of nooks and crannies where stuff could be stashed. It's all fairly isolated, and there'd be plenty of opportunity to transport it over to the other side and onto a fishing boat at their convenience. I reckon that's where Madigan has come into it. But I'm sure it's bigger than him.'

'Right,' Staples said slowly, the full implication of what Harry was saying apparently dawning on him. 'And you reckon the murders might have something do with Madigan and this smuggling gang?'

'I do,' Harry affirmed. 'More than likely, I'd say.'

'But maybe it was just Madigan who done the murders,' Staples responded. 'He's a nasty piece of work, after all.'

'Maybe,' Harry conceded. 'And maybe not. That's what we need to find out. And besides, we need to take this opportunity to crack down on a major smuggling ring, if it's operating from these parts. I've been in touch with the Customs boys in Melbourne, and they're dead keen to break the ring too.'

'Fair enough,' Newgate said. 'What's our next move then?'

Harry put his hands in his pockets and stood facing his men. 'We need to find what they're bringing in, and where they're storing it. That'll give us a much better idea of who and what we're dealing with. As I said, I'm reasonably confident that there's a hiding place, in the sand hills or along the beach somewhere, where the contraband is being temporarily stored before it's moved on. Our first task is to find that hiding place. So I've organised Customs to send some blokes over here tomorrow morning. Between us and them we'll be able to do a thorough search in the sand hills and along the beach. Let's see what we can find.'

'How many blokes are Customs sending?' Newgate asked. 'We'll need a few, that's a pretty big area to cover.'

'They said they could spare about twenty,' Harry replied. 'Plus us five, that should be enough to cover the area pretty well. And they said if we don't finish the search tomorrow, they'll send them back again on Sunday.'

Newgate whistled softly. 'Geez, they're keen! Must be big fish they're looking to land.'

'Must be,' Harry agreed. 'And hopefully it'll lead us to our murderer, or murderers, if he's not already sitting in the cells out there already. Now, we've got a big day tomorrow. The Customs blokes'll be over on the first boat, so make sure you all get a good rest tonight and be ready to go in the morning. That means not too late in the pub, okay?' And he gave a stern look in Newgate and Staples' direction.

'Right, boss, will do,' Newgate promised, but his slight smirk indicated that he, and probably Staples for that matter, had no intention of abstaining completely from the pleasures of the Sailors Arms.

Harry wrapped his coat a little more tightly around him. The evening had begun mildly enough, but as midnight came and went, the ocean breeze had cooled considerably and now had a distinct chill to it.

From his strategic vantage point, hidden amongst ti-tree scrub in the sand dunes directly above the beach, Harry continued his surveillance of the scene below. The stretch of sand stood pale in the faint moonlight and, looming behind it, Harry could discern the hulking shape of the jagged rocks that formed London Bridge.

By his side, as they had agreed, Willie kept watch over the sandy path that snaked from the beach up into the hills on their left. The waning moon was low in the sky, but still threw sufficient dull light to identify any movements across the scope of their watch.

Three hours they had been sitting here, with the occasional eerie call of a beach stone curlew the only sound to breach the night air. A faint glimmer of doubt had begun to infiltrate Harry's confidence, and he kept telling himself to be patient. All his detective's instincts pointed to his plan succeeding.

Harry shifted slightly on the little ledge of sandstone that served as his chair, seeking to relieve the gathering ache in his lower back. As he did so, he received a sharp jab in his left side and, glancing at Willie, he saw he had a finger raised to his lips. Willie silently pointed back up the track, and again signalled for silence.

Then Harry heard it too. The faint jingle of harness gear, then the creak of wagon wheels approaching. Taking extra cover behind the ti-tree shrubbery, the two men peered down at the winding track below their dune lookout. Within seconds it came into view, a small dray, with one horse in harness, and two figures perched in the seat up front. Both men were well-concealed in large coats and caps drawn down over their faces. In the dull night light, Harry had no hope of identifying them.

The horse trotted steadily past, down towards the beach, sure-footed on the sandy track.

'I guarantee that nag's done this trip a few times,' Harry whispered after it was well gone.

Both men shifted their gaze towards the beach below, and in the gloom could make out the shape of the horse and dray heading right, past London

Bridge, the jingle of the harness faintly audible on the still night air. Then as the two strangers continued on their way, they disappeared behind the cliff edge jutting out over the beach.

All went quiet and Harry settled in to wait. Beside him, Harry felt Willie shuffling impatiently.

'How much time should we give them?' Willie whispered.

Harry smiled to himself. 'As long as it takes to get the evidence,' he whispered back. 'Don't worry, if it's who I think it is, we'll hear them soon enough.'

And he was right. After a few more minutes they heard the muffled grunts of men at work, interspersed with an occasional stifled curse and the clink of something being loaded onto the dray.

This went on for what seemed an eternity, though it was less than an hour according to Harry's fob watch. Then all went quiet again, except for the soft jingle of the horse resuming its gait.

'They're done,' Willie whispered. 'Shall we intercept them now?'

'Patience, mate,' Harry advised. 'Wait till we see them coming back up the path.'

'What if they take another way back?' Willie speculated.

'They won't,' Harry responded. 'There's no other way back. Anyway, we've got all the options covered.'

Harry was right. The soft jingling grew louder, and soon enough the dray appeared around the bend in the path, its two occupants still perched on the front ledge. The horse was no longer trotting, instead walking slowly, straining at its harness under the weight of the dray, fully loaded with a large number of boxes.

'Let's go,' Harry muttered, leaping to his feet, and plunging down the small dune in a few giant strides, Willie hot on his heels.

They came to a halt on the path directly in front of the horse, which snorted and threw back its head in alarm at this unexpected arrival.

'Stop!' Harry exclaimed. 'Stop in the name of the law!'

'Bugger me!' came the shocked response of the horse's driver, as he jerked back on the reins.

'Get out of here!' his companion shouted, sliding out of his seat, stumbling to the ground, then getting to his feet and heading back down the path at a laboured sprint. The driver wasted no time in following suit, flinging the reins aside and making his escape too.

'Quick!' Willie shouted. 'After them!'

Harry's only response was to reach into his pocket and raise his police whistle to his lips. The shrill blast rang out into the still night. Immediately the sound of voices could be heard shouting instructions, as well as the sound of feet running along the beach.

Harry grabbed the reins and steadied the horse. 'Here mate,' he said, handing the reins to Willie. 'You look after this. It's evidence. And valuable cargo.'

And leaving Willie with the horse and dray, Harry raced off down the path, in pursuit of his quarry.

He caught up with one of the men less than fifty yards down the track. Panic had not lent the fellow the necessary wings to flee. He was labouring along, gasping loudly as he went, clearly completely out of breath. Harry seized him by the collar and hoisted him up as he began to sag to the ground.

Harry whipped the cap from the man's head to reveal Sergeant Clive Newgate staring back at him, still gasping for air, and too exhausted to be defiant.

'Evening, Sarge,' Harry offered jovially. 'I thought I told you blokes to get a good night's sleep. And here you are, out gallivanting in the middle of the night.'

Newgate said nothing, merely raising a scowl at Harry's witticism. Ahead of them down the track, a posse of men were approaching, led by a tall, red-haired fellow, who had a similar firm grip on a surly Constable Arthur Staples.

'Well done, Ted,' Harry exclaimed. 'Looks like we've nabbed a villain each.'

'Sure looks like it,' the red-haired fellow agreed. 'Why don't we see what these gents were so keen to pick up in the middle of the night.'

'Good idea,' Harry said, and between the two of them they led Newgate and Staples back up the track to where Willie was still minding the cart. Behind them trailed about a dozen men, all clad in plain clothes and including in their midst Constable Wally Morris, looking at his fellow officers with a shocked expression.

'Right then,' Harry began, 'let's see what we've got here.' And he lifted the lid on one of the thirty or so boxes piled onto the dray. He reached in and extracted a bottle.

'Powers finest Irish whiskey, if I'm not mistaken,' he announced, holding it aloft. 'And plenty of it too, I'd say.'

'Jolly good,' the red-haired bloke commented. 'I'm sure the Inspector of Customs and Excise will be very interested in what these two policemen are doing with this haul.'

'I'm sure he will,' Harry agreed. 'Looks like you've got them for smuggling stolen goods, Ted. And I reckon I've got them for murder.'

'What the hell are you talking about, Holloway?' Newgate snarled, his breath and defiance returning in equal measure. 'You can't pin that on us.'

'I think I can, Sarge,' Harry retorted immediately. 'In fact, Sergeant Clive Newgate, I'm arresting you for the murder of Miss Natalya Kuzmina on Saturday the seventeenth of January 1898. And Constable Arthur Staples, I'm arresting you as an accessory to the murder of Miss Kuzmina. Rest assured, gentlemen, other charges will flow in due course, both in relation to this little smuggling racket you've got going here, and in relation to the deaths of Mr Sergei Karpov, otherwise known as Sam, and Mr Dimitri Seminov, otherwise known as Dave. Now it's time we headed back and found you some comfortable accommodation at the Sorrento Police Station.'

18

⁂

SATURDAY 24 JANUARY 1898

A NIGHT IN THE CELLS had done nothing to improve the mood of either Clive Newgate or Arthur Staples. And it had also seemed to have steeled their resolve to deny Harry's murder charges against them.

Both now stared defiantly across the table at Harry, in the small interview room at the station. Behind them stood a still slightly shocked Constable Morris, standing beside Constable Andrews, co-opted at short notice from the Quarantine Station garrison.

Harry leaned back in his chair and studied Newgate and Staples carefully. 'I must admit I made a mistake about you blokes,' he said reflectively. 'I first thought you were both just lazy: lazy and incompetent. It took me a long time to come to the realisation you were also both corrupt. Corrupt and murderous, as it turns out.'

Newgate snorted contemptuously. 'There you go again, Inspector, trying to pin us for murder. You got nothing on us, like I said last night. There's nothing to connect us with those murders.'

'I think there is,' Harry retorted. 'As I'm happy to demonstrate.'

'All right,' Staples cut in, 'if you think we murdered those blokes, tell us why the hell we would want to. We didn't even know them.'

'Oh, but you did,' Harry replied. 'Why don't I tell you how and why you were involved with them, and you can let me know where I go wrong.'

Neither man replied, both just scowled darkly in Harry's direction.

'Okay,' Harry continued. 'Here's the story then. We have established, from the harbourmaster's records, that both Sergei Karpov and Dimitri Seminov were among the five survivors of the tragic sinking of the *Sierra Nevada*, near London Bridge last year.

'My understanding is that the other survivors were happy to be returned to their home countries. But not our two Russian friends, apparently. They had set their sights on the riches Australia had to offer. I imagine the lure of the goldfields was firmly in their minds.

'But they had a problem. They were both illegally in Australia and were under the watch of the Sorrento police. So they had you fellows to deal with, if they wanted to avoid being sent back.

'Meanwhile, you blokes were also looking for an opportunity to get rich, from a very different source. The *Sierra Nevada* had gone down with very valuable cargo on board. And the most valuable part of that cargo was six hundred cases of finest Irish whiskey, cases that floated in seawater, and a fair number of which were washed up on shore near London Bridge.

'Of course, the townsfolk, as soon as they heard about this booty, flocked to that part of the beach to loot and pillage, as good, upright folk tend to do. So you blokes were sent to stand guard over the booze and arrest any looters, while the owners worked out how the hell they were going to salvage the whiskey from that remote part of the coast.

'Clearly, that sort of planning took time, and in the meantime, you blokes were standing around looking at all this valuable booze and dreaming about making a bob or two from it.

'Anyway, poking about at the site of the wreck, you came across a cave back in the cliff face, a cave that had very narrow access for the first ten yards or so, but eventually opened into a large chamber. A chamber large enough to store plenty of cases of booze without it being found. And that would give you plenty of time too, to carry the stuff back to one of the old deserted fishing shacks on the other side, and then off to the black market in Melbourne. In Arthur's boat, we suspect. A boat that's being impounded by the Customs people as we speak, and thoroughly examined for evidence.'

Harry paused and glanced at his two prisoners. 'How am I going? Not boring you, I hope.'

'You're bloody dreaming,' Newgate snarled. 'Making it all up.'

'We'll see,' Harry replied with a smile. 'Anyway, perhaps I should continue. Here were you two blokes, guarding this potential gold mine on the shore. The locals had given up trying to pilfer the grog, so you now had the opportunity and you'd come up with a good plan. But you also had a problem. There were a lot of cases lying about, far more than you could manage between you, and then there was the ongoing problem of moving it about. Bottom line, you needed help.

'Then one of you, or perhaps both of you, had a great idea. The two Russian sailors had already expressed their desire to stay in Australia, and you suspected they'd be happy to help out with a bit of shady activity if you helped them do that. So you put the proposal to them, and they jumped at the chance. Particularly when you added a little financial incentive.

'It was dead easy for you to keep them here under assumed names, while signing off that they were on the boat back to their home port. Don't worry, I've managed to track down the paperwork at the harbourmaster's, with your signature on it, Sarge. I reckon that's rather incriminating, for a start.'

Newgate scowled again, but Harry could see his bravado was waning in the face of the gathering evidence.

Harry continued. 'So you got to work in a hurry with your new mates. They carted as much of the whiskey as possible back into that cave, while you blokes stood guard to prevent anyone seeing what was going on. When that was all done, you simply reported that most of the whiskey was lost at sea, but that the owners were welcome to what was recovered. And that wasn't much.

'The owners were mightily pleased when you offered to organise to have what was left shipped back to Melbourne. In fact, the local constabulary was praised in the *Argus* for its vigilance in guarding the booze, and its assistance in getting what remained back to Melbourne.

'The next step was to organise to have the stolen whiskey sold on the Melbourne black market. That wasn't too hard either. You had the good fortune to remember that Oliver Ridgeway at the Continental was a former acquaintance from your earlier police days in Melbourne. In fact, he had a police record for fraud that didn't sit at all well with now managing a posh joint like the Continental.

'So it wasn't too hard to persuade him to organise an arrangement with one of his dodgy contacts in Melbourne, in return for your silence on his shady past. Again, with a little financial sweetener to make it worth his while.'

'What a load of rubbish,' Newgate sneered. 'I've never had anything to do with that bloke.'

Harry sat back. 'I wonder if Mr Ridgeway agrees with that? My colleague, Sergeant Milton, is over at the Continental as we speak, interviewing him. I expect he'll be prepared to tell the truth to avoid being implicated in a murder charge. And I expect his statement will entirely corroborate the information given to me by McSweeney in Melbourne, which is that Ridgeway set him up with a supplier of cheap whiskey, no questions asked.'

Again, Newgate responded with a resigned scowl, while Harry fancied that Staples was beginning to look more than a little worried.

Harry continued. 'All was going real well for six months or so, wasn't it? You and Arthur here were making a small fortune shipping cases of whiskey to McSweeney, with the help of your Russian pals. But a week or so ago, things got a bit tricky with the Russians. Whether it's because they got greedy, or more likely because you were paying them a pittance. Anyway, I reckon they came to you demanding a bigger cut for their trouble. A much bigger cut. Or else they would spill the beans on your little enterprise. I guess they reckoned they had stronger leverage over you than you did over them, and they were probably right.

'So what could you do? The obvious answer was to bump them both off and carry out the rest of the job by yourselves. After all, who was going to notice the disappearance of two illegal sailors, with no family or friends in the country to miss them?

'But a couple of things went wrong. Before you could carry out your plan, Karpov began to get belligerent. Belligerent and indiscreet. I reckon he bailed you and Arthur up in the pub that Tuesday night, Sarge, and began demanding more money. Or else he would rat on you. Probably under the influence of a reasonable skinful, as Doctor Mollison identified. I expect you panicked and reckoned you'd better act straight away and get rid of him. So you lured him outside, took him down to the pier to discuss a new deal, then donged him on the head and tossed him into the harbour. You thought you could easily pass it off as an accidental drowning.

'I expect it was you who delivered the fatal blow, Arthur, while the Sarge here was sweet-talking him.'

'Wait a minute,' Staples exclaimed, paling noticeably. 'You got no proof it was me. It could just as easily been Clive.'

'Shut up, you fool!' Newgate hissed, glaring balefully at his constable.

Harry smiled. 'Thanks for that, Arthur, I'll take that as a confession that you were at least there.'

'Anyway,' Harry continued. 'In for a penny, in for a pound. As luck would have it, Dave, Seminov as we now know him, wasn't in the pub that night. Madigan's confirmed he was loading up for a night run of lime that night. So you were able to wait till Wednesday morning, sneak out to the lime pit, and between you, overpower him and chuck him into the pit.

That's why you two weren't about when we found Karpov's body in the drink that morning.'

Newgate folded his arms and sat erect, his nerve now apparently recovered.

'That's one hell of a story, Holloway, but like I said before, where's your evidence? You got nothing to connect us with the death of those two Russians. So book us for the whiskey job and leave it at that.'

'Fair enough, Clive, you make a reasonable point. Though Doctor Mollison was able to find a couple of prints on the shovel that we impounded from the lime kiln site. One partial set of which we have identified as not belonging to the other worker there, young Sam Georgenson. It will be very interesting to see how it compares with the prints I intend to have taken from you two blokes.'

This revelation elicited a further scowl from Newgate, and Harry was encouraged to see a look of sheer alarm suffusing Staples' features.

'Anyway,' Harry continued, 'let me get to the next problem that came up. You see, unfortunately for both of you, someone turned up in town who was very well known to Karpov, and who was very keen to be with him. Natalya Kuzmina joined the Cossack group with the express purpose of joining her sweetheart in Australia. I expect they intended to disappear together once she got here. No doubt, he'd promised her a wonderful life here, compared with what was on offer back in Russia, and she must have known that opportunity would not be forthcoming through legal means.

'Of course, her joy at being reunited with her boyfriend disappeared, once she discovered he'd been murdered. And that enabled us to identify the link between them. Now you had a real problem, Clive. How much had Karpov told her about your relationship with him? Was her obvious fear and distress driven by suspicion that you'd murdered him? And was she about to spill the beans to me about all of it?

'While you were worrying about all this, fate presented you with an unexpected opportunity. You were put on security watch in the theatre while the Cossack show was taking place, and lo and behold, while you were wandering up and down the corridor, Natalya herself dashed past in tears, making for the dressing room.

'You were seized with inspiration, made sure she was on her own, then quickly followed her into the empty dressing room, strangled her, threw up the window, raised the alarm and when we turned up, came up with the cock-and-bull story about a mystery intruder.'

'Geez, Holloway, you've got a bloody good imagination,' Newgate growled. 'Again, where's the proof?'

'I don't have it yet,' Harry conceded. 'But I expect I will soon.' In response to Newgate's puzzled stare, he added, 'You see, while you've been enjoying your well-funded lifestyle down here in Sorrento, things have been developing back at headquarters in Melbourne. Things like fingerprinting, for example.

'As you may recall, Doctor Mollison was able to extract a clean set of prints from the window lift in the dressing room, prints that would belong to the murderer if he lifted the window to escape. Or to the murderer, if he lifted the window to make it look like someone escaped.'

Harry watched Newgate's supercilious confidence evaporating as the import of these revelations sunk in. He was now staring sullenly at the table before him. Staples just looked totally defeated.

'Importantly,' Harry added, 'There was only one set of prints discovered on those lifts, and we know from Constable Morris' evidence that the window was definitely shut before the performance, even if perhaps not locked. So, Clive, once we've taken your fingerprints, and if they match those taken by Doctor Mollison, we can definitely conclude that it was you who lifted the window that night. Which directly contradicts your version of events and puts you squarely in the frame for Natalya Kuzmina's murder.'

Arthur Staples raised his hand. 'I'd like to make a statement, sir,' he suggested, the meekness of his tone in direct contrast to his former belligerence.

'What is it, Constable?' Harry replied.

'I'd like to say, sir, that I knew what Sergeant Newgate was up to. You know, murdering those Russians. But I had nothing to do with any of that. I swear to it.'

Harry eyed Staples steadily. 'Constable, thanks for admitting that your sergeant murdered those two blokes. Of course, I don't believe for a moment that you had nothing to do with it. For example, it's clear to me that the two of you must have been required to overpower Simenov and chuck him into that lime kiln. But you never know, your willingness to acknowledge his guilt is helpful and may be in your favour when it comes to sentencing. Now, Constables Morris and Andrews, could you kindly escort these two fellows to their new quarters out the back?'

The entire Holloway clan were relaxing on the beach, on a beautiful Saturday afternoon in Sorrento. But the crowded sands of the front beach were not for them. Instead, at Effie's insistence, they had walked down to the back beach and set up their deckchairs on the sands below the rotunda and kiosk.

In front of them, the Southern Ocean was sending gentle waves to the shoreline, and on either side the cliffs and dunes stretched majestically into the distance. Clem, Millie and Effie reclined on their chairs, enjoying the sun's warmth. Effie held little Daisy on her lap, well-protected in an outsized bonnet and smock. Harry sat on the sand, sporting bare feet and rolled-up trousers, contentedly helping Alfie put the finishing touches to a prodigious sandcastle.

'Isn't it terrible?' Millie sighed, addressing no-one in particular.

'What do you mean?' Harry asked, glancing up, bucket in hand.

'Those policemen, that's what I mean. Murdering those people. And involving themselves in all those criminal goings-on.'

Clem nodded. 'You're right, dear. It's a scandal, I reckon. Paints the whole force in a bad light, that's what it does.'

Harry shrugged. 'Oh well, there's bad apples in every barrel, I suppose. Important thing is, we weeded them out.'

Effie leaned down and affectionately rubbed her husband's shoulder. 'You weeded them out, darling, no-one else. Certainly not that idiot boss of yours.'

Harry smiled and leaned over to tickle Daisy under the chin. She gurgled with delight and reached out for him.

'Don't worry, Marks is taking full credit for solving the case now,' Harry replied, smiling in spite of the glimmer of irritation he felt. 'At any rate, things have been smoothed over with the Russian Government. All that paranoia about a Russian invasion seems to have been put to bed. For the moment, at least.'

'How did you do it, son?' Clem asked. 'How did you work out those two were up to no good?'

Harry gazed out at the gently rolling ocean, thinking about the hectic last two weeks. 'Well, I have to own up, I was stumped for a fair while. I mean, I never really thought it had anything to do with spies, and I came to doubt that theory pretty quickly. I knew the murders had something to do with some sort of criminal enterprise, but I couldn't think what.'

'What was the breakthrough?' Effie said. 'What made you suspect Sergeant Newgate?'

Harry thought for a few moments. 'Well, I had my doubts about Newgate from the start. And Staples, for that matter. I thought for a start, they were just slack. Slack and incompetent. For example, they claimed they didn't recognise Karpov, even though we knew they were both regulars in the pub that Karpov and Simenov also both frequented. But I gave them the benefit of the doubt on that one. You know, busy pub, not very observant, and so on.

'And it was apparent to me that Newgate and Staples had both been in Sorrento far too long. They'd gotten lazy and work-shy, and not particularly interested in enforcing the law.'

'Yes, but when did you suspect they were actually *breaking* the law,' Effie persisted.

'It was Natalya's murder,' Harry reflected thoughtfully. 'The more I thought about it, the more I couldn't really see how Newgate's story about a mystery intruder made a lot of sense. It seemed too much of a coincidence that a would-be assailant would be at the back of the building when she unexpectedly left the stage and fled back to the dressing room.

'And it seemed odd to me that Staples hadn't noticed anything back there. Even allowing for his slackness.

'Plus, I couldn't quite understand why the murderer's prints would be on the window lift. If he had lifted the window from the outside, got in, killed her and then fled through the open window, he probably wouldn't have to touch the lifts on the inside. So I thought at first those prints must belong to a cleaner or someone involved with running the Athenaeum. But we couldn't actually find anyone who had touched those lifts in recent days.

'But all that wasn't the main reason I began to wonder about Newgate.'

'Go on, smarty-pants, don't keep us in suspense,' Effie cajoled him.

'It was motive,' Harry explained. 'I was convinced that Natalya was murdered because of her relationship with Karpov. But no-one really knew about that relationship, except Matyunin and us. By 'us', I mean me, Willie and the local police.

'Once I was satisfied that Matyunin was in the clear, I began to think about Newgate and that doubtful story he spun about the intruder. The more I thought about it, the more I suspected he and Staples were up to something. It's been a problem in the force before, cops stationed in an out-of-the-way place too long, getting lazy and then corrupt, with not enough oversight from above.

'I was wondering about smuggling, but smuggling what? It was only when you presented me with that bottle, Effie, that the penny finally dropped. Once I had been to town and chased down a few leads, it became clear to me there was a very large amount of whiskey that had gone missing from the wreck of the *Sierra Nevada*, whiskey that was put under the guard of Newgate and Staples, and that was reported lost to the ocean. But that was now being sold on the Melbourne black market in large quantities.

'So we had a fair bit of evidence to support our case against Newgate and Staples, but I thought it would be the final nail in the coffin if we could catch them in the act. So we set up our little trap.'

'Very cunning,' Effie observed. 'But what made you think they'd fall for it? And try to collect one last load of whiskey?'

Harry looked at his wife. 'I was relying on their greed, Eff. And their arrogance, that we couldn't possibly suspect them. As it turned out, I was right on both counts. I mean, we might have had enough evidence anyway, with the fingerprints and so on, but catching them in the act was the icing on the cake. It made the case against them conclusive.'

'Oh well,' Effie grinned. 'I'm glad I was of some help to you, darling, even though I wasn't aware of it.'

Harry smiled back. 'You were very helpful in another way too, dear. And if I'm not mistaken, here he comes now.' And Harry stood and pointed back towards the rotunda, where a tall, suited man was strolling down the path towards them, his shock of red hair glinting in the morning light. Effie saw that the straggly beard had disappeared, but he was still instantly recognisable.

'My goodness!' she cried. 'It's Mr Petrenko! What's he doing here?'

'G'day, Harry,' the red-haired one exclaimed cheerily, as he reached them. And he leant over and shook Harry's hand vigorously.

'G'day, mate,' Harry responded, equally amicably. 'Effie, Clem, Millie let me introduce Mr Ted McCulloch. I met Ted when I went to town the other day.'

Effie gazed at him in some perplexity. 'Hello, Mr McCulloch,' she said eventually. 'You're obviously not Russian. And I would suspect you're not actually an artist either.'

'Spot on, dear,' Harry confirmed. 'Ted is Chief Fraud Investigator for the Customs Department. He's been operating undercover at the artists' camp, looking for any evidence of precisely what we found. The department has suspected there's been significant smuggling from the wreck of the *Sierra Nevada*, and Ted's been secretly searching the sand hills and environs looking for evidence of that.

'They didn't want to let the local police, or anyone else down here, know of their presence. They're naturally suspicious types, and they weren't sure who might be involved. And their secrecy was well justified, as it turned out.'

McCulloch reached down and shook Effie's offered hand. 'Good to meet you, Effie. As my real self, this time.' His awkward foreign accent had completely disappeared, replaced by a broad Australian drawl.

Effie smiled back at him. 'Delighted to meet you too,' she replied gaily. 'Well done on your success. You and Harry obviously make a good team.'

'Thank you,' McCulloch responded. 'And I must congratulate you on your choice of husband. Harry's a damned good detective. Our department's greatly indebted to him.'

'I'm sure they are,' Effie said proudly. 'And I'm also sure you're good at your job too. In fact, I'd confidently reckon you're a better investigator than you are an artist.'

'I wouldn't argue with that,' McCulloch laughed. 'It seems your friend James didn't have any trouble identifying my artistic weaknesses.'

Effie smiled at him. 'And I'd hazard a fair guess that the rather impressive work we saw exhibited at the Institute was not actually done by your fair hand?'

McCulloch laughed again. 'Absolutely not. Jane knocked that up for me. We had to keep up my disguise, you know. Anyway, I'd best be off. I just wanted to say goodbye and thank you to Harry.' And again he reached out to shake Harry's hand.

'Not so fast, Ted,' Effie exclaimed, getting to her feet and bundling Daisy into Millie's arms. 'How about afternoon tea at the kiosk before you go? We can resume our discussion about the Russian masters. After all, I understand you're an expert on that subject.'

McCulloch chuckled again and examined his fob watch. 'Why not indeed? Delighted to accept your invitation before I head back to town.'

With that, deck chairs and other paraphernalia were packed up, Alfie's sandcastle was abandoned in favour of the promise of chocolate ice cream and the little group set off, up the steps to the back beach kiosk. Their perfect family seaside holiday was finally underway.

Effie put her arm through Harry's as they strolled and, leaning over, whispered, 'Now darling, remember, if you see any more dead bodies, just look the other way.'

AUTHOR'S NOTE

Fresh Air and Foul Play is a work of fiction. All incidents and dialogue, and all characters, with the exception of some well-known historical figures, are products of the author's imagination, and are not to be construed as real.

Where real-life historical characters appear, the situations, incidents and dialogues concerning those persons are entirely fictional, and are not intended to depict actual events or to change the entirely fictional nature of the work. In all other respects, any resemblance to actual persons, living or dead, is entirely coincidental.

ACKNOWLEDGEMENTS

As always, I would like to extend my grateful thanks to my editor, Irma Gold, for her incisive editing and positive support, and to my designer, Sandy Cull, for her brilliantly creative cover design and layout.

My thanks also to the Nepean Historical Society for their support in providing a wealth of historical materials.